CW00376329

ALVESDON

www.penguin.co.uk

Also by James Holland

Non-fiction

FORTRESS MALTA
TOGETHER WE STAND
HEROES
ITALY'S SORROW
THE BATTLE OF BRITAIN
DAM BUSTERS
AN ENGLISHMAN AT WAR
BURMA '44
BIG WEEK
RAF 100: THE OFFICIAL STORY
NORMANDY '44
SICILY '43
BROTHERS IN ARMS
THE SAVAGE STORM
THE SECOND WORLD WAR: AN ILLUSTRATED HISTORY
THE WAR IN THE WEST Volume I: Germany Ascendant 1939–1941
THE WAR IN THE WEST Volume II: The Allies Fight Back 1941–1943

Ladybird Experts

THE BATTLE OF BRITAIN
BLITZKRIEG
THE BATTLE OF THE ATLANTIC
THE DESERT WAR
THE EASTERN FRONT 1941–1943
THE PACIFIC WAR 1941–1943
THE BOMBER WAR
THE WAR IN ITALY
THE BATTLE FOR NORMANDY 1944
THE WAR IN BURMA 1943–1944
VICTORY IN EUROPE 1944–1945
VICTORY AGAINST JAPAN 1944–1945

Fiction

THE BURNING BLUE
A PAIR OF SILVER WINGS
THE ODIN MISSION
DARKEST HOUR
BLOOD OF HONOUR
HELLFIRE
THE DEVIL'S PACT
DUTY CALLS: DUNKIRK
DUTY CALLS: BATTLE OF BRITAIN

For more information on James Holland and his books,
see his website at www.griffonmerlin.com

ALVESDON

James Holland

bantam

TRANSWORLD PUBLISHERS
Penguin Random House, One Embassy Gardens,
8 Viaduct Gardens, London SW11 7BW
www.penguin.co.uk

Transworld is part of the Penguin Random House group of companies
whose addresses can be found at global.penguinrandomhouse.com

Penguin
Random House
UK

First published in Great Britain in 2024 by Bantam
an imprint of Transworld Publishers

Copyright © Griffon Merlin Limited 2024
Map © Tony @ Global Creative Learning

James Holland has asserted his right under the Copyright,
Designs and Patents Act 1988 to be identified as the author of this work.

This book is a work of fiction and, except in the case of historical fact,
any resemblance to actual persons, living or dead, is purely coincidental.

Every effort has been made to obtain the necessary permissions with
reference to copyright material, both illustrative and quoted. We apologize
for any omissions in this respect and will be pleased to make the
appropriate acknowledgements in any future edition.

A CIP catalogue record for this book
is available from the British Library.

ISBN 9781787636705

Typeset in 11/14.5pt Sabon LT Pro by Jouve (UK), Milton Keynes
Printed and bound in Great Britain by Clays Ltd, Elcograf S.p.A.

The authorized representative in the EEA is Penguin Random House Ireland,
Morrison Chambers, 32 Nassau Street, Dublin D02 YH68.

Penguin Random House is committed to a sustainable future
for our business, our readers and our planet. This book is made
from Forest Stewardship Council® certified paper.

For my beloved eldest niece, Katy Holland

Dramatis Personae

CASTELL FAMILY
Alwyn Castell (b.1864)
Maud 'Maimes' Castell (b.1866)

   Denholm Castell (b.1890)
   m. 1918 Grace (d.1919)
   m. 1937 Lucie Frenais (b.1906)
      Constance 'Coco' (b.1919)

   Walter 'Stork' Castell (b.1893)
   m. 1915 Deborah 'Debbo' Kingsford (b.1894)
     Edward (b.1916)
     Tess (b.1918)
     Wilfred 'Wilf' (b.1920)

   John Castell (b.1895)
   m. 1920 Carin Wolff (b.1899)
     Elsa (b.1921)
     Robert 'Robbie' (b.1923)
     Maria (b.1925)

VARNEY FAMILY
   Richard 'Dick' Varney (b.1893)
   Eleanor Varney (b.1893)
     Agnes (b.1917)
     Oliver (b.1920)

ALVESDON ESTATE
Claude Timbrell (b.1884) – foreman
Tom Timbrell (b.1914) – gamekeeper
Maurice 'Smudger' Smith (b.1895) – mechanic
Gilbert Rose (b.1888) – head shepherd
Donald Smallpiece (b.1894) – head dairyman
Susan Smallpiece (b.1895)
Billy Smallpiece (b.1919) – ploughman
Alf Ellerby (b.1895) – head carter
Mary Ellerby (b.1894)
Frank Ellerby (b.1918) – shepherd
Sid Collis (b.1903) – ploughman
Percy Merriman (b.1906) – ploughman
Cecil Merriman (b.1909) – carter

Land Girls
Jill Goodland (b.1920)
Susan 'Susie' Stephenson (b.1921)
Hattie Williams (b.1918)

ALVESDON VILLAGE
Dr Philip Gready – doctor (b.1889)
Maggie Gready – billeting officer (b.1890)
PC Jack Allbrook – local police constable (b.1901)

Shop
Donald Pierson (b. 1902) – ARP warden
Margaret Pierson (b.1901)

Blacksmith
Reg Mundy (b.1905)
Mikey Mundy (b.1927)

Carter/Garage
Bill Sawcombe (b.1898)
Jack Sawcombe (b.1927)

School

    Edith 'Edie' Blythe (b.1913)

ALVESDON MANOR

    Jean Gulliver (b.1892) – cook

    Hannah Ellerby (b.1920) – housemaid

    George Burroughs (b.1883) – handyman, chauffeur

    Cyril Penny (b.1877) – gardener/groom

FARROWCOMBE

    Betty Collis (b.1889) – cook/housemaid

LONDON

    Diana Woodman (b.1917)

    Alex Woodman (b.1915)

    Brenda Portman (b.1916)

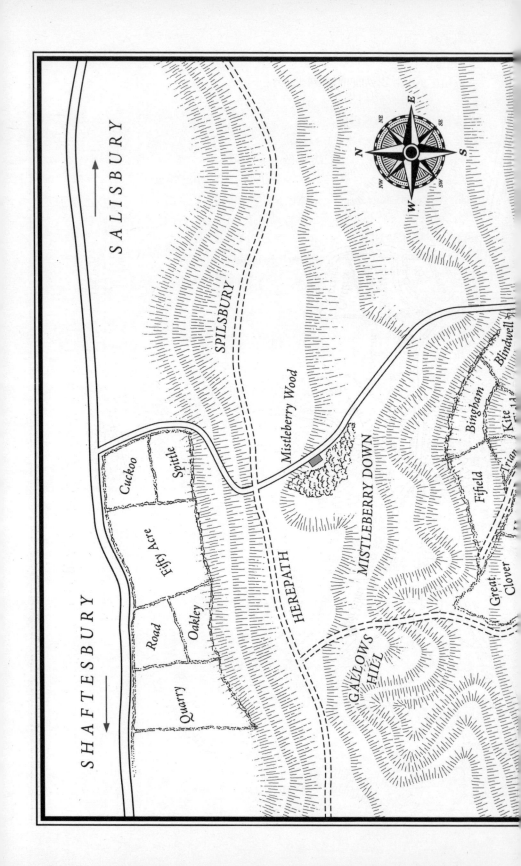

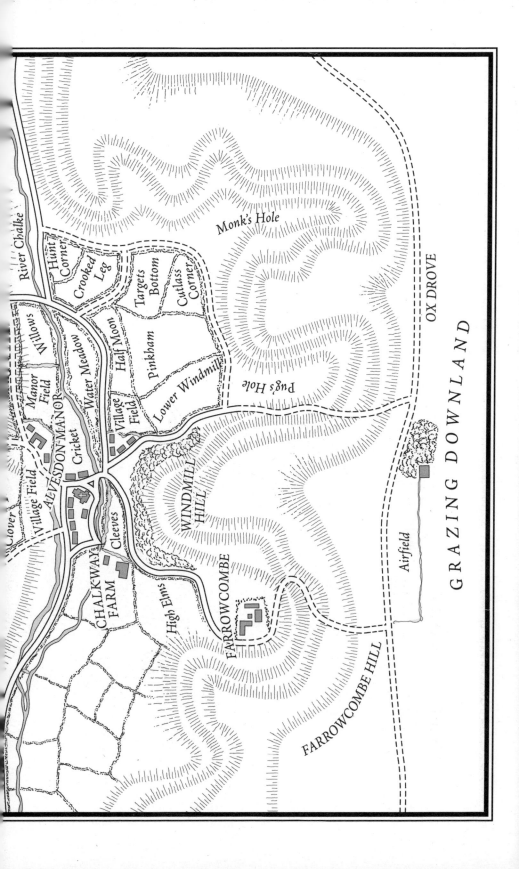

1

Morning Flight

Friday, 18 August 1939, 6.30 a.m.

AS THE AIRCRAFT LIFTED FROM THE GROUND, STORK CASTELL FELT the familiar jolt of the wheels over the rough grass cease and a wave of relief swept over him. Behind him, the sun was rising over the long stretch of chalk downs. Glancing out over the edge of the cockpit, he saw the shadow of his plane separate and stretch away. In moments he was climbing high over Farrowcombe and able to turn his gaze southwards across the Chase, all the way to the Purbeck Hills and beyond to the sea. Despite his scarf he felt the chill wind find and envelop his body beneath his jacket as though he were ducking under the waves at the start of a dip in the sea. He shivered, but after the hot, sticky night and the exertion of pushing the plane clear of its hangar, the cold was deliciously fresh and invigorating. Breathing in deeply he smelt the sweet morning freshness crisp in his nostrils but also the musty mixture of oil, wood and leather that was unique to the DH.4's cockpit.

The Rolls-Royce Eagle growled gutturally with the strain of the climb, but at three hundred feet above the ridge, he eased back the throttle, set the trim to adjust the pitch of the propeller and banked away to the south in a wide arc until he could see the spire of Salisbury Cathedral some ten miles to the east. Straightening, he set his course towards the familiar marker, with the long line of chalk to his left.

It really was a fine morning – a sky clear and cerulean already, the

1

rolling country below finely contoured by shadows from the rising sun. Not for the first time in his life, Stork thanked God both that he had never lost his love of flying and that he'd had the foresight to buy his DH.4 once the war was over. While many of the RAF's aircraft had been retained for post-war service, the DH.4 had been withdrawn, and with more than they had known what to do with and no obvious buyers overseas, the Air Ministry had sold them off. Stork had bought his complete with a spare Eagle engine and a box of spares, and renamed it 'Dorothy'; it seemed like a good way of putting a bit of distance between it and its original martial function. And all for twenty-five pounds – a lot of money back in 1919, which he'd been able neither to afford nor justify, yet he'd not once regretted his rash purchase. Of course, having the farm made all the difference. His family had land and farm buildings, and that meant somewhere to store the machine and the space to operate it. He felt the occasional pang of guilt that he'd seen out that last summer of the war at Larkhill, but then would remind himself he had spent much of the previous three years flying over the front lines: three years of being shot at, of witnessing friends and fellows burning alive, being riddled to pieces and colliding. He'd flown over the hellish gash of no man's land, tangled in heart-stopping fights across the sky, had been forced to kill his fellow man, and taken part in much of the heaviest air fighting of the entire war. Somehow, he'd suffered barely a scratch; it had always seemed a miracle that this should have been so, yet by May 1918, just as his darling Tess had been born, he had realized his tank of courage had been spent and that if he was kept at the front any longer he might well break entirely.

And then, as he had wondered how he could solve this predicament without killing himself, he had been posted. Perhaps it had been the new medical officer. Or just pure and simple luck. At any rate, he'd been sent home and given a job instructing at Larkhill, only fifteen miles or so from Alvesdon. It had been an August morning in 1918, not so very different from this one today, that he'd flown across the plain south-west to the valley and over Alvesdon Farm. He'd whooped for joy to be alive then: to see the home he loved so deeply, the farm, the folds of the chalk downs and their combes, the village nestling in the heart of the valley; to know that he had a wife he adored, a son and daughter to whom he would return.

He flew back towards Alvesdon, the fourth village along the valley, lined on either side by the chalk downs. There was the church, its tower poking up from amid the trees, and the River Chalke, snaking its way through the water meadows, silvery in the morning light. The dairy herd stood in the meadow and in a group between some willows by the water's edge, while at the foot of the steeper line of chalk to the north, the fields were filled with stooks, the harvest almost complete – and before the end of the third week in August too. They'd not managed that on the farm for a dozen years or more.

It all looked so peaceful, so placid, so stunningly beautiful, and his heart ached to think this Eden was threatened once more. He could hardly bear to contemplate what another war would mean for his children. Edward was already in the Territorial Army and soon, inevitably, would be called up, his time studying art at the Slade cut short and with it, he supposed, any career as an artist. Wilf was already in the RAF and would be among the first to face the firing line should it come to war. Tess was in London, working for the War Office, and would not be immune if bombers targeted the capital. Many of the farm boys would go as well, torn from their families. His anger rose. He just felt so damned impotent.

Then he cringed as he remembered how pleased with himself he'd been when he'd told his parents he'd joined up back in 1914. His mother had not been able to hide her horror or her tears, the colour draining from her face and her lip trembling as she'd tried to speak. But he'd made it through – all three brothers had: John and even Denholm. A miracle, when so many families had suffered such terrible losses. But was it one that could be repeated? He swallowed hard and tried to push such thoughts from his mind.

Right now there was much besides to trouble him. Decisions about the farm. Glancing over he could see the gyro-tiller on the top of the southern ridge of chalk, evidence of its toil all around: stretches of exposed soil and chalk where decades-old furze had been dramatically ripped up; next year, it would be covered with crops.

Change was coming and with it a lot of wastage, and the overthrowing of the truly mixed farm he'd nurtured so carefully over the past decade since he'd taken over. He was forty-six and, he had accepted some years earlier, well into his middle age. There was a touch of grey in his dark brown hair, a few lines on his brow and at the sides of his pale blue eyes. He was a man who no longer craved change, or adventure. What excited him now was the certitude of his life, of improving the farm, of knowing his family was safe and happy and supported. He loved his younger brother, John, his sister-in-law, Carin, and their children almost as much as his own. The family brewery had grown hand in hand with his development of the farm and now that future, that constant in his life, seemed uncertain. He worried for them all but he especially worried for the children. If anything happened to them it would break his heart. *Don't think about it*, he told himself. *Put it out of your mind. It hasn't happened yet.* War had not broken out. Perhaps good sense would prevail, and peace be preserved. Perhaps.

And then there was his father. For much of the summer they had been rubbing along quite well for once, but trouble was brewing. It always did eventually. The threat to their uneasy peace this time was his father's conviction that he was going to be asked to join the Wiltshire War Agricultural Executive Committee: he had spoken to Richard Stratton, the chairman-in-waiting for Wiltshire, who had – apparently – told him as much.

'Really?' Stork had said.

'Don't sound so surprised,' his father had replied. 'I was a district committee member in the last show, so I know the form, and I've the knowledge, experience and, more to the point, time.'

But Stork knew this couldn't be true because he had a letter from Richard Stratton sitting on his desk at Farrowcombe, asking him to join the county War Ag if and when Britain should find itself at war. It was inconceivable that two men from the same family should be asked; his deafness notwithstanding, his father tended to hear what he wanted to hear.

Stork had not told his father about his own invitation because he'd not decided whether it was something he should or wanted to do; the amount of time the job would take him away from the farm, the compromises he might have to make, and the responsibility – it was not a decision to be taken lightly. It had not occurred to him, however, that his father would believe he'd been asked or, even worse, that the old man would be so obviously pleased about it.

'Of course, the Ministry of Ag isn't going to make the same

4

mistake as last time,' he'd told Stork. 'It's one thing ploughing up fallow land and adding phosphates and lime to poor soil, but it was a mistake to put so much emphasis on arable. They want to make farms more productive, not make them uniform. Not the same thing at all.'

Stork had tentatively suggested that, while his father had a point, the government would almost certainly insist on ploughing the land because cereals were bulkier to ship than meat and offered considerably more food per acre than livestock.

'It was a disaster last time,' his father told him. 'They won't make the same mistake again.'

'It wasn't, Pa,' Stork had replied. 'It was a huge success.'

'When half the country's farmers were brought to their knees in the aftermath?'

Stork had let it go. It had not been worth getting into an argument in the face of his father's infuriating certainty with which he made such pronouncements. Worse, though, was knowing that his father wasn't going to be on the War Ag Committee, and that they would most likely have to sell all the beef cattle – his father's pet project and the only part of the day-to-day running of the farm in which he still played a direct part. And he knew who would be blamed and ranted at for his father's humiliation and disappointment.

Stork flew on towards Shaftesbury, then banked and turned towards Win Green, the highest point in the county with its clump of beech trees marking the spot. It was a perfect storm in the making.

Nor was that all. The following day, his father was turning seventy-five and all the family were gathering. His older brother, Denholm, was arriving from southern France later today, on the London train, with his daughter, Coco. The prodigal son, to be fussed over, pandered and feted. It never ceased to amaze Stork that his parents could put Denholm on such a pedestal. Such a feckless, egocentric, morally bankrupt individual deserved no special treatment; he deserved to be cut off and ignored, more like. Stork felt hot with anger just thinking about his older brother: the easy charm, the smarmy praise of their parents, the patronizing digs and the endless showing off about life on the Riviera. The eldest son. The heir. The one who could do no wrong. The one who had buggered off, eschewing any responsibility to the family, who had sat out the last

5

war sailing a desk in the Navy, and who contributed nothing to the future of the farm and the family, other than accept the regular handouts of cash Stork had recently discovered his father still wired to him.

Stork glanced southwards towards the sea. Far away, perhaps thirty miles or so, he saw the Isle of Wight and even the Needles. Ships were out at sea – colliers and freighters – the distant smoke from their stacks faintly visible as they slowly steamed along the coastal trade routes. Beyond that, far away, too far to see, was France, the continent of Europe and eventually Germany, no longer ruled by the Kaiser but instead by a ridiculous-looking fanatic with a ludicrous moustache. What were the Germans thinking? He thought of Carin, a German, but as normal and peace-loving, as kind, gentle and caring as any person one might wish to meet. What did she have in common with the Nazis? Nothing at all, yet her brother had become a rabid National Socialist. It all seemed so impossible, so implausible, that once again, war with Germany was looming.

The early-morning flight had been supposed to provide solace, and a chance for him to get his thoughts in order. Instead, he felt more troubled than before. A thought entered his brain: to push down the stick and hurtle into the ground. It would be a quick, painless end to all of these worries and the heavy dull weight that hung over him, like a leaden shroud.

Ahead, the rising sun shone in his direction as he continued east-wards towards the landing strip on the downs above Farrowcombe. Its rays warmed his face and he marvelled at how breathtakingly beautiful his small corner of England was. Down below he saw his home, the lawn and the outhouses, the barns on their staddle-stones and the cob-walled kitchen garden, nestling at the foot of the combe, surrounded by a sylvan carpet of ash, beech, elm and hazel. He flew on, banking as he turned to come back into land, the brief thought of death quickly erased from his mind.

Landing smoothly, he taxied back to the hangar, a Dutch barn with a corrugated iron roof that stood sheltered beside a copse of ash. Smudger Smith was there, waiting to guide him into the barn. 'How was she?' he asked, as Stork clambered down and took off his flying helmet.

'Good as gold, as always,' Stork told him.

'More than can be said for the Fordson.'

'What's wrong with it?' They both moved to Dorothy's tail and began to move it around so that it once more faced outwards.

'Bugger's a bastard to start, guv'nor. Temperamental. The lads don't like it and Claude began binding on at me about it.'

'That's ridiculous. It should be perfectly straightforward to start. I'll talk to them.' He glanced at his watch. 'We need to get our skates on, Smudge, or we'll be late.'

Chocks under the wheels, tarpaulin slung over the cockpit and they were done and walking towards the pick-up.

'The thing is, they know you're a bloody miracle worker,' Stork continued, as they clambered into the Ford. Smudger lit a cigarette, pushed his cap back off his brow and looked out as they trundled towards the track that led back down into the valley. Stork glanced at him. 'Whenever there's anything mechanical to solve, they all think you're the answer.'

Smudger nodded – *That'd be right* – and drew on his cigarette. He was a small man, and although a couple of years younger than Stork, his face was more lined, his skin almost stretched back from his jaw with a pronounced Adam's apple, and his stubble was going grey. The combination made him look older. He hadn't shaved for several days – something about which Stork was punctilious no matter what hour he rose. His jacket looked worn while his flannel shirt was frayed around the collar. It wasn't that he couldn't afford new clothes but rather that he wasn't interested. His fingers were stained with oil and nicotine. Stork could barely remember ever having seen him eat. As far as he was aware, Smudger survived on a diet of sweet tea and cigarettes.

Smudger Smith had been Stork's fitter in France – his personal mechanic. When Stork had been posted back to England, they'd lost touch until a year or so after the end of the war when a letter had arrived out of the blue. Smudger had been released from the RAF and was struggling to find work. He wasn't expecting any favours, but if Major Castell knew of anyone needing a mechanic, he would be most grateful if he would be willing to let him know and put in a good word. *Hoping this finds you in good health and heart,* he had signed off, *Yours sincerely, Maurice Smith.*

For a few minutes Stork had struggled to think who the letter was from. Then the penny dropped; he'd never known his Christian name. The letter had arrived serendipitously, however, because Stork had recently bought his DH.4 and had realized belatedly that he would need a mechanic. He had also recognized that mechanization was the future for farming, and while at the time that was a battle still to be won with his father, he could think of no one better, or whom he would trust more, to take care of such matters than Smudger Smith. He had offered him a job and with it a small house, part of a thatched terrace, at the edge of the village. Smudger had been with him ever since and, although he was a Londoner, had adjusted to rural life well enough. He'd never married but had seemed content, tinkering, stripping engines, instinctively working out how the mechanics of new machinery operated, and supported with a burgeoning workshop at Farrowcombe. Stork didn't know how he would have survived without him. The trust he'd had in him in France had never once been tested.

'Is there anything you can do to improve matters?' Stork now asked, as they rumbled down the holloway towards the combe below.

Smudger glanced at him.

'Tinker with it to make it start better?' continued Stork. 'No such issues with the Allis-Chalmers, are there?'

Smudger took a final drag of his cigarette, flicked the butt out of the cab, then muttered, 'Maybe. I'll take a look.'

They drove on past Farrowcombe towards the village, the road winding its way through the hedgerows and around Windmill Hill, jutting out from the ridge of chalk to look down upon the village.

'Ready for the party?' said Smudger at length.

'I'm looking forward to having the children back.' As they crossed the bridge by the village church of St John the Baptist and reached the junction, Stork looked left and right then pulled out. 'It's hard feeling much in the mood for a party at the moment, though. God knows what's going to happen to us all.'

Smudger said nothing more and they continued in silence as they made their way along Duck Street, turned down the drive towards Alvesdon Manor, and continued around the back to the outbuildings, barns and the yard. Most of the workers were already there, punctually, just as they always were, including Edward, his eldest boy, and Elsa and Robbie, his younger brother John's children. Other, younger children of the farm workers were there too; everyone was expected to pitch in at harvest time. Rain or shine, summer and winter, seven in the morning was the start of the working day, six days a week for all except the dairyman and his team, who worked even on Sundays and kept their own strange hours. It was five minutes to seven.

Stork climbed out and walked over to Claude Timbrell, the foreman, then looked at his watch and around the assembled labourers, more than forty in all, as well as some twenty children to add extra hands.

'Mornin', guv'nor,' said Claude. On his head sat his battered trilby, while his ample moustache, now flecked with grey, twitched. Next to him stood his son, Tom, absent-mindedly picking at a nail. Stork remembered when Tom had been young; the lad had always been a crack shot but so small until suddenly, one summer, he'd grown at an astonishing rate, as rapid as a sunflower, Betty Collis had said. Now Tom was broad, tall and strong, twenty-five years old and a fine, instinctive gamekeeper. Once, Stork had hoped he might take over from his father as foreman, and eventually maybe even be given a tenancy. Now, though, he wasn't so sure. Everything that had seemed certain was much less so.

Christ, thought Stork. The men and women before him chatted quietly, some already holding tools or bridles loosely. Everyone here was dependent on the farm: for their work, their wages, their dwellings. Most had barely left the valley in their lives let alone the county, except for annual church outings to the Dorset coast. Seventeen families worked on the farm; fathers, sons and daughters, even grandfathers. The cycle and rhythm of life in the valley was so regular, so constant. Until now.

'Right,' said Claude. 'It's another beautiful day and God's blessed us with a dry 'un an' all. Let's get this harvest finished and start on gathering the stooks. Anything you want to add, guv'nor?'

2

Home

Friday, 18 August 1939

BY LUNCHTIME, WHILE THE FARM WORKERS OF ALVESDON PAUSED
for their al-fresco dinner in the August sun, Tess Castell was walking along the River Thames in the direction of Westminster, thinking
about the farm she knew so well. She could picture the scene that
would be playing out that day and thought happily that tomorrow
she would be waking up at home in Farrowcombe, although this
time with Alex Woodman in a room just down the corridor. She
smiled to herself, thoughts of home replaced by the memory of the
past few heavenly days.

It had been Alex's suggestion to go to Aldeburgh. A friend of his
in the battalion had the place, no one was using it, and it was a
shame to let it go to waste, especially since the weather was so particularly lovely. At first, Tess had baulked at the idea, horrified by
the illicit nature of what he was proposing. It would mean lying to
her parents, and she had never done that. And she was apprehensive, too. It was one thing kissing Alex, cuddling him, but staying
with him, on their own, in a house by the sea meant they would
inevitably make love and that worried her. She had never been
naked with a man, let alone had sex. When he'd first mentioned
going away, she'd felt herself reddening and her immediate thought
had been of her inexperience and inadequacy, even shame for the
sexual innocence that would be laid bare.

10

'I've got two weeks' leave,' Alex had told her. 'I've got to go and see my people, but I thought I'd tell them I've only been given a week off. With everything that's going on, they'll believe me all right. It means you and I can have a whole week together.'

They had been at dinner in a restaurant in Shepherd Market, just around the corner from his club, and he'd been leaning forward, his hands holding hers. At that moment she'd thought how wonderfully long his fingers were – really quite delicate – not at all what one might expect of an officer in the King's Own Royal Guards. In that moment, her desire to be with him was stronger than her fears.

She had bitten her lip, looked down, and felt her eyes start to glisten, which annoyed her, but she knew she would be crossing her very own Rubicon if she accepted, and that a part of her would be left behind for evermore.

'Tess? Darling?'

She had looked up then. Alex was very handsome, she thought, a lean face, fair wavy hair, pale eyes that seemed to twinkle at her. Still rather boyish in many ways, even though he was three years older than her.

'It would mean lying to my parents,' she said.

'Not lying, exactly. More fibbing.'

She had smiled at this.

'I'll look after you, you know,' he said. 'Think of it: swimming in the sea, walks along the beach, fish and chips, and absolutely no one to tell us what to do. I'll have no company or battalion commander bossing me about, you'll have no general to answer to—'

'But I like my general. He's a darling, really.'

'I know,' said Alex, and Tess detected just the faintest touch of impatience, 'but that's not the point. We won't be lackeys to anyone. And, you know, we'll have ourselves to ourselves.'

Yes, and she wanted that, but it was terrifying too. But, no, perhaps it wasn't. It would be lovely. Everyone must feel the same the first time.

'It does sound heavenly.' She was unable to stop herself smiling and aware that her heart was beating considerably faster.

He stroked her hands. 'God knows what's going to happen in the next few weeks, and I don't at all want to make you do something you might regret, but I've fallen for you in a very big way, Tess.'

11

'Have you?' Her heart hammered even harder.

'Yes, and I would hate to go off to war knowing we'd been offered this wonderful holiday together and I'd not dared to tell you about it for fear of offending you. I honestly cannot think of anything I would rather do than spend a week alone with you.'

She had paused a moment. Then, with resolve and new excitement coursing through her, she said, 'All right. Let's.' And they had laughed happily. When he'd kissed her goodnight outside the Pimlico house she shared with his sister Diana, she had felt dizzily in love.

Her parents had swallowed the 'fib'. General Ismay was in Scotland, she had told her mother, but had wired saying that because of the escalating situation, he really did need her and Louise, the other secretary, to remain in Whitehall.

'Well, I'm very sad, darling, of course,' said her mother, 'but it's harvest and everyone's busy so I'm not sure how much you'd have seen of them. You will be able to get down for Grandpa's birthday, though, won't you?'

Tess had promised she would.

And they had been six most glorious days – more wonderful than she had dared hope. Alex had been as good as his word: he had looked after her, and although she had felt acutely embarrassed as they'd headed to bed the first night, he had discreetly turned off the lights so that only a faint milky glow from the moon had shone through, which had somehow made it better. The moment they had finally been naked together, she had felt such an overwhelming sense of relief that she forgot her inhibitions and allowed herself to give herself to him completely. It had hurt quite a bit and that first night she couldn't help feeling disappointed. But in the nights that followed the pain had dissipated and been replaced with the most unexpected and unimaginably pleasurable sensation she had ever experienced.

As she walked past the Tate Gallery and on towards the Houses of Parliament, she felt quite a different person, as though a skin had been shed. Life seemed to have accelerated this past year. Childhood had continued for what at the time had seemed for ever, so much so that she'd taken it all for granted. Then suddenly she was eighteen and heading to a new life in London with her best friend, Diana Woodman. Tess's older brother, Edward, who had been at Cambridge at the time, had urged her to try for university too, but she'd felt impatient to go to London. Not least because Diana was going to secretarial college there, had a spare room in her parents' London house and because the lure of independence and living with her oldest friend had sounded an intoxicating prospect. Her time at the college had flown by, and before she knew it, she had a job working for Major General Hastings Ismay, newly appointed Secretary to the Committee of Imperial Defence who had been looking for a new secretary.

The Houses of Parliament loomed up ahead, in all their Gothic splendour. She found herself thinking about Cambridge. Had Edward been right? Should she have gone? Possibly, but she didn't regret her decision. Certainly, there had been plenty of opportunity to use her wits working for General Ismay and it had been thrilling, too, to be so close to great events taking place, to see and hear the country's leaders at first hand. As she entered Parliament Square, she glanced down Whitehall. She had liked Ismay from the moment she'd walked into his office, a room of panelled wood, leather and cigar smoke; he had a kindly face and warm smile and she had felt herself relax almost at once, despite the imposing nature of the room and the vast desk that stood between them. Mostly he'd asked her about herself, explaining that it was important to him to have people working for him he could trust and like. He also needed to know she would be good under pressure. The hours would be long, his demands many, but accurate work would be of vital importance. He would, he told her, need her to use her initiative from time to time and to keep abreast of events.

'And what do you think we should do about Hitler?' he'd asked her.

'Make firm alliances with every country that is worried about him,' she had told him. 'All the democracies of Europe should unite in a joint alliance. Hitler might not threaten Czechoslovakia if he knew that by doing so he would be risking war with half a dozen countries, including Britain and France.'

'And what about those who say it was such alliances that caused the last war?'

'From what I've read, sir, it was rather different. Hitler has an alliance with Austria but that hardly compares with the Central Powers of 1914.'

Hastings had smiled. 'All right, Miss Castell, thank you.' And then he had stood up, the interview over. She remembered how she had cringed as she'd left, convinced she'd blown her chances – been too outspoken, too full of herself. But a few days later a letter had arrived offering her a job. A miracle at the time, and no sooner had she started working for the general than the Munich crisis had happened and she'd had privileged access to what was going on. But no grand alliance had materialized, and when in March the Germans had rolled up the rest of Czechoslovakia, Ismay had stopped by her desk one evening and said, 'You may have been right, you know, what you said in your interview. He's picking off countries one by one.'

Having crossed Westminster Bridge and walked up onto the concourse of Waterloo Station, she was relieved to see Alex waiting for her under the large four-faced clock that hung from the ceiling, just as they'd planned.

'Darling,' he said, as he leaned down to kiss her lips. 'I've missed you.'

'But I only saw you two hours ago.' She laughed, then said, 'Thank you again for the most wonderful week, Alex.'

'It's been marvellous, hasn't it?' He grinned and picked up her case. 'You look beautiful, Tess.'

She threaded her arm into his. 'You look jolly handsome yourself,' she replied, but still felt herself pinking with pleasure. 'We need to find our platform.'

'It's number eleven,' said Alex. 'What about your uncle and cousin? Shouldn't we be meeting them?'

Tess looked around. As ever, the station was teeming with people. A guard's whistle at the nearest platform, gushes of steam belching from the train's boiler, then a slight jolt as it began inching away. A hawker was selling nuts, another newspapers. People dashing past. A porter with a trolley loaded with cases and an elegant young lady with a wide-brimmed hat walking tall ahead of him. Servicemen – Tess noticed more men in uniform than was usual for August.

'Mama rang earlier to say we should look out for them and that they'd be on the same train, but wasn't more specific than that.' She looked around. 'Can't see them.'

They bought their tickets, then boarded the waiting train, finding an empty compartment in second class and sitting opposite one another. Alex leaned forward and took her hands in his. 'Do I need to be feeling a little nervous?' he asked.

'No, of course not. You know Edward and Wilf already, and my parents are perfect poppets. So, too, Uncle John and Aunt Carin. I'm sure you'll love the cousins. Grandpa can be a bit gruff sometimes but Gran's a darling. And you'll meet the Varneys too. They're practically family and you'll adore them, I know. Dick was at school with Dad and Uncle John and is Dad's best friend. They farmed in Devon but lost everything in the crash. Fortunately, it was the year Dad took over the farm from Grandpa, the tenants of the farmhouse moved away and the Varneys took it on instead.'

'That was jolly good of him.'

'I suppose it was. It just all worked out. So, serendipity too. My cousin Elsa is in love with Oliver, Dick and Eleanor's son. They've loved each other since they were quite young.'

'Rather romantic.'

'Isn't it? I honestly think they'll get married when they're a bit older. Everyone does.'

Alex smiled. 'I suppose if you know, you know.' He looked at her and held her hands a little more tightly. Tess glanced down, then out at the people still moving past on the platform, a wave of wistfulness sweeping over her. Everything seemed so uncertain. She had been so happy all week, but as she thought of Ollie and Elsa she was reminded that at any moment they might be at war, and both of an age when they would inevitably be drawn into it. Ollie was nineteen and she knew Elsa was worried he would soon be called up.

And then there was Alex. Her general still hoped war might be avoided, but she knew he thought it unlikely. That she had just found such happiness with Alex but would soon lose him made her want to cry.

'Let's not think about it,' he said. 'That there might be a war.' He smiled weakly. 'You suddenly seemed rather wistful.'

'I feel it.' She looked up at him and smiled in turn, hoping she would not cry.

'We don't know what will happen,' added Alex, 'but we do know we've had a wonderful week and have the weekend to come. I want to cherish every moment, not waste the next couple of days feeling sad about what follows.' He looked at her intensely. 'Gosh, you're beautiful.'

Tess's heart quickened. His hands, surprisingly soft, held hers firmly.

'I've not said this before, Tess, but I—'

The compartment door opened before he could finish. Standing there were a tall man and an elegant young woman, a sultry expression on her face, painted lips, blonde bobbed hair.

'Well, look who we've found, Coco!'

'Uncle Denholm!' exclaimed Tess, getting to her feet, Alex following suit. She embraced her cousin, Coco, then her uncle, and introduced Alex.

Denholm grinned, pulled out a cigarette, lit it and collapsed into the seat next to Alex. 'Ah!' he said. 'Final furlong.'

'This journey's been endless,' muttered Coco.

Tess hadn't seen her in nearly two years. She'd always been rather in awe of Coco's sophistication, but now she felt even more conspicuously lacking in elegance. 'Oh, poor you,' she said.

'It's been ghastly.'

'Oh, rubbish! Stop making such a bloody fuss,' said Denholm, then breathed a large exhalation of smoke towards the still-open compartment door. Tess was a bit shocked to hear her uncle swear so openly.

'We went via Paris, had a very acceptable dinner with chums, and have basically sat on our arses the rest of the time, reading, staring at the scenery and quivering with anticipation at the thought of our return to the homestead. I'd hardly call that ghastly. Rather civilized, more like.' He grinned and coughed wheezily.

'C'est un long chemin à parcourir pour une fête,' muttered Coco.

'Oh, honestly, Coco!' said Denholm. 'Don't listen to her, you two. She's just being spoiled. Everything's a bore for Coco at the moment. Too bloody spoiled by half.' He laughed, as Coco scowled at him. 'And she's had to leave her dashing French beau behind.' He leaned forward, patted his daughter's knee. 'And that makes two of us because I'm without Lucie.'

'I thought she was coming?' said Tess.

'Hmm,' said Denholm, drawing on his cigarette, 'I thought so too. But she's worried if she comes over, the bloody war will start

16

and she'll get stuck. You can take the girl out of France but you can't take France out of the girl. Or so it seems.'

He winked at Alex. 'Words were said, but, er, I chose to make a tactical retreat on that one. Lose the odd battle to win the war, if you get my drift. In any case, it's not like Ma and Pa know Lucie much anyway, and I'm afraid she's a girl who likes the bright lights. Not a country lass, really.' He leaned back and grinned at Coco. 'Not flesh and blood, like you, eh, darling?'

Tess glanced at her uncle. There was a clear resemblance to her father, but Denholm was taller, bigger, fleshier and, unlike her clean-shaven father, he had a thin, trim moustache. Handsome enough and those pale eyes she, too, had inherited, and the distinct Castell shape of the eyebrows. Crow's feet stretched from the corners of his eyes – her uncle had always been quick to laugh. She knew there was bad blood between Denholm, her father and Uncle John so they saw little of him – or Coco. She could remember the wedding, though. Denholm's first wife, Grace, had died giving birth to Coco. No one ever talked about her much, but Tess knew that she had had money, that Denholm had been living in his wife's inherited villa in the hills above Cannes ever since and that he'd spent all of the money. There had been other women since then, but out of the blue, he'd announced he was getting married – to a Frenchwoman twenty years his junior.

'He's only doing it for the moolah,' she'd heard her father say. But they had all headed over to France, travelling *en masse* by train, boat and train again. For Tess, her brothers and cousins, the Côte d'Azur had seemed impossibly glamorous; none had been abroad before. Everything about France had felt so far removed from home, the valley and the farm. She had liked Lucie – beautiful and petite, speaking English with an exaggerated French accent. At the time, Tess had fallen madly in love with Lucie's brother, Étienne, three years his sister's elder; he had been her first crush. That had been two years ago. A lifetime, she thought now.

'So,' said Denholm, flicking a bit of ash from the sleeve of his ivory flannel suit, 'how is all the family? How's farming? Your father still modernizing?'

'Everyone's well,' Tess told him, 'although I've not been down much recently.'

'Ah, yes, you've got your frightfully hush-hush job, haven't you? Enjoying London life?'

'Very much.'

'Even more so now you've got this dashing young fellow to keep you warm at night, I'll bet.'

'Oh, Papa, honestly,' said Coco.

Tess blushed and glanced up at Alex, who was clearly every bit as mortified.

'I'm only teasing,' Denholm said. 'Take no note of it.' He turned to Alex. 'Has Tess told you that I'm something of the black sheep?'

'Er, no, sir,' said Alex.

'Tess's father and I, well, he doesn't exactly approve of me.'

'Really, Uncle Denholm, I'm sure that's not true,' said Tess.

'I'm embarrassing you and I apologize,' Denholm continued. 'Making mischief unnecessarily.'

'You're embarrassing *me*,' said Coco.

'Isn't that what fathers are supposed to do?'

Coco glared at him.

'Well,' he continued, 'I'm looking forward to seeing everyone, even your father, Tess. And the old place. Who knows what's round the corner, eh? Need to make the most of it. That's what I told Coco, isn't it, darling? Enjoy the place while we've got the chance. Enjoy the journey while we've the chance. It might all come crashing down.' He lit another cigarette. 'That bloody little German twerp has a lot to answer for, don't you think? Bloody popinjay.'

Edward was waiting for them at Salisbury, standing on the platform, dressed in scruffy slacks and a blue checked shirt. Tess hurried towards him and, having kissed his cheek, hugged him tightly.

'And I've missed you too,' he laughed, then added, 'but can I say hello to everyone else?'

The two looked startlingly alike: the same pale blue eyes, dark, almost black hair, same eyebrows and full lips. Edward's hair was dishevelled, as it always seemed to be, and Tess wondered how he ever managed to smarten up for his Yeomanry.

'It'll be a bit of a squeeze, I'm afraid,' he said, heading to the boot and loading Coco and Denholm's cases. 'Uncle Denholm, you sit up

18

front with me, and Tess, you'll have to have your case on your lap, I'm afraid.'

'The lovebirds won't mind snuggling up together,' said Denholm, lighting up another cigarette, 'and Coco's a slip of a thing.' He inhaled deeply and glanced around him. 'Jolly good to be back. Such a reassuring presence, the old cathedral, don't you think? Christ, just look at that bloody spire. How the hell they ever did it will never cease to be a cause for wonder.'

Tess saw Edward grin at her and raise an eyebrow.

'Ignore him,' said Coco, catching the look. 'He does it for effect,' she continued as Denholm eased himself into the front with a sigh. 'Just showing off.' Tess couldn't help imagining what would happen to her if she spoke to her own father in such a way.

'My darling princess,' said Denholm, turning to Coco, 'there's really no need to be so po-faced. It's nothing more than good-humoured and affectionate chit-chat.' He turned to Tess and smiled. 'But she's right – take no notice and I apologize, dearest Tess, if I spoke out of turn.'

'No, no, you didn't,' said Tess. But she felt flustered and sensed Alex's discomfort too.

'Well,' said Edward, as he pulled away from the station, 'it's splendid to see you. How are things in France?'

'Life in general or the current state of the country?'

'Both, I suppose.'

'Country's a bloody shambles. Daladier's not a prime minister but a damned dictator, the military have their heads stuck up their arses with ghastly complacency, and the population as a whole is demoralized and lacerated by social strife. Everyone's scared. On the other hand, I'm out at sea most days, the food is excellent as ever and the wine not bad. So, can't complain.' He laughed.

'That last bit's heartening to hear,' said Edward. 'So, do most French people think it'll be war?'

'Yes, and they're having nightmares about it.'

'We're not going to talk about war, Edward,' said Tess. 'I'm forbidding it for the whole weekend.'

'Quite right, sis,' Edward agreed. 'No more war talk.'

'*Verboten*,' said Denholm.

'I want this weekend to be perfect – not just for Grandpa but for all of us,' said Tess. 'The sun's going to be shining and we're all going to have fun.'

'And that's an order,' said Denholm, then, turning to Edward, added, 'Tess tells me you've been on camp with your Yeomanry.'

'Yes, got back on Sunday. Did a lot of horse-riding and drank a lot in the camp mess, but wouldn't say we're quite the finished article for taking on the Nazi hordes.'

'Edward!' said Tess.

'All right, all right. I did manage to do a bit of painting and sketching, and this week I've finished the mural at the manor.'

'Really?' said Tess. 'I can't wait. Is everyone pleased with it?'

'Well, I'm not sure. I hope so.'

'A bit late if not, isn't it?' said Denholm.

'It is rather, yes.'

'Is it much further?' said Coco, her eyes closed and her hand rubbing her forehead.

'Are you all right, Coco?' asked Tess.

'I feel sick.'

'You always say that,' said Denholm, 'but you never are.'

Coco opened her eyes and scowled at her father.

'It's not too much further,' said Tess.

'Beastly, feeling car sick,' muttered Alex.

'Quarter of an hour, tops,' added Edward.

'Look, there's the valley!' exclaimed Tess, a moment later, as they crested the brow past the Salisbury racecourse. She saw the friendly tower of the church of Stoke Combe, nestling among the ash, elm and willows that lined the River Chalke that gave the valley its name. She looked west and there was Lower Chalke, comforting rooflines amid the verdant valley floor. *Ah, home.*

Edward pulled a cigarette packet from his pocket, then passed it to Denholm. 'Would you?'

'Here,' said Denholm, tapping one out, gingerly placing it between Edward's lips, then taking out his American lighter. As Edward briefly looked at the flame, he swerved, then straightened. Coco groaned.

'Edward!' exclaimed Tess. 'Concentrate!'

'Sorry about that,' he said.

Tess now saw that her uncle was rather more pensive, his hand gently stroking his chin. She wondered why he'd left. He was the eldest so the farm should have been his. He still had a stake – all three brothers did, as well as her grandparents – but she knew he had never really come back from the war. Her father had been a pilot, Uncle John had survived the trenches, and Uncle Denholm had been in the Navy, although she wasn't sure in what capacity; but while her father and John had returned to the valley, Denholm had made a life in France. She realized she'd never talked to her uncle about it or really her parents.

'Uncle Denholm?' she said now.

'Hmm?'

'Do you mind me asking why you never took on the farm? As the oldest?'

He laughed. 'Can you imagine me as a farmer? Ha, ha, ha! Christ, my cheek against the flank of some bloody cow!'

'Did it never cross your mind?' asked Edward.

'Gracious, no.' He chuckled again, then scratched his temple. 'No, well, to be perfectly honest, I've always had itchy feet even as a kid. You know, we were all packed off to boarding-school, so one got used to being away from pretty early on. Then, in the war, I travelled around a fair bit.'

'In the Navy?' asked Edward.

'Hmm? Yes, yes, exactly. Anyway . . . Ah, Middle Chalke, almost there. Maybe we should call on John and his tribe first?'

'No, please, can we just get to Gran and Grandpa's?' groaned Coco.

'Yes, we'd better,' said Tess, then, turning back to Denholm, persevered: 'So did that give you wanderlust, Uncle Denholm?'

'Yes, I suppose so. In a way. Married Grace by then. Her parents had this place in France and very decently gave us the villa for our wedding present. Quite something, really. When she, er . . . Well, I liked it there, you see? Anyway,' he added, brightening, 'much better all round, eh? Old Stork got the farm and he's been absolutely the right man for that, and John has done wonders with the brewery, so it's all worked out for the best. But, you never know, I might come back one day. Claim my right of primogeniture.' He laughed again, but then was silent, as they trundled along the valley

21

road. Presently, they reached the water meadows, where the dairy herd stood half in the water, under the shade of some willows, aimlessly munching grass still rich and green even in mid-August.

Up ahead was the church, on its perched rise, and then, beyond the meadows, the cricket ground and Alvesdon Manor.

'Well, well,' said Denholm. 'There she is.'

'This is Alvesdon,' said Tess, taking Alex's hand, feeling excitement and apprehension all at once, hoping the weekend would be a success, that her parents, especially, would like Alex and that all would go smoothly.

'Hold on,' said Edward, as he slowed to drive over the Chalke. On, across the ford, past the forge and the Three Horseshoes on the corner, past the small triangle of the village green, and the turning to Farrowcombe on the left. It never ceased to amaze – and relieve – Tess how unchanging Alvesdon was. Great events happened – kings abdicated, dictators crossed borders, factories made tanks and guns and aircraft – yet here, in this tiny corner of south-west Wiltshire, time seemed to stand still. She saw Mrs Carter cycle past, Edward overtook Eleanor Varney on her horse, and then they were turning right, into the drive.

And there it was: the manor, a house of silvery Chilmark stone, cut from the same quarry that had made the cathedral, but now mottled with age and lichen, old russet tiles on the roof, high brick chimneys and, a little to one side, the round stone-and-flint dovecote. A large white marquee stood on the lawn that ran down to the stream, ready for the party tomorrow evening. Beyond, behind the main house, were the barns, the dairy and outbuildings, while away to the right, the grounds extended towards the stream and the walled kitchen garden.

'Here we are,' said Edward, cheerfully.

'Thank God,' muttered Coco.

As the wheels crunched on the gravel, the door opened to reveal her grandfather, bow-legged, silvery-haired, moustache covering his top lip, waving happily, while her grandmother was just behind him, dark streaks still in her hair, which was, as always, clasped in a neat bun. She was, thought Tess, fondly, still a very elegant lady, even at seventy-three.

'Hello, Pa!' grinned Denholm, as he got out of the car.

'Aha! There you are, my boy!' beamed Alwyn Castell, taking his son's hand and clasping his shoulder. 'It's good to see you – and looking damned well too! Ah, and there's Coco, as pretty as ever! How are you, my dear?'

Welcomes, smiles, embraces – a happy occasion, thought Tess, as her grandmother kissed her and she felt the silk-soft skin against her cheek. Then she realized Alex was standing behind her, looking, just for a brief moment, a little awkward.

'This is Captain Alex Woodman, Maimes,' said Tess.

She held out a hand, which Alex graciously kissed.

'A great pleasure to meet you,' he said, then straightened quickly.

'You are most welcome,' she said. 'Welcome to Alvesdon.'

A moment later, Edward said quietly beside her, 'Come on, let's leave them to it and get to Farrowcombe.'

Back in the car, Edward said, 'Gosh, Coco's a bit of a madam, isn't she? Very pretty, but I hope she makes a bit of an effort.'

'She doesn't say much, that's for sure,' agreed Alex.

'Unlike Uncle Denholm. Chalk and cheese, those two.'

'Do they really not get on?' asked Alex. 'Your father and Denholm? I couldn't tell whether he was acting up or not.'

'No, they really don't,' said Tess. 'They're very different. I just hope he behaves himself this weekend.'

'Who?'

'Uncle Denholm.'

'And Stork,' said Edward. 'Mum's told him he's to try to keep away from Uncle Denholm and Grandpa as much as possible.'

'Well, that's a forlorn hope,' said Tess. 'How is it possible? Dinner tonight, cricket tomorrow, then the party.'

Edward grinned. 'There're fireworks tomorrow night, you know. Let's hope those are the only ones. Wouldn't bet on it, though.'

Although Tess was very fond of Alvesdon Manor, it did not compare with the deep and profound love she felt for Farrowcombe. Growing up, she had, of course, completely taken it for granted, but since leaving home and moving up to London she realized how very fortunate she had been to be brought up in such an Eden.

Now, as Edward drove up the track that wound its way around the base of Windmill Hill, she felt overcome by a sense of yearning, wistfulness and even regret. Such freedom they had had as children! The house was more than a mile from the rest of the village, nestled at the foot of Farrowcombe Hill, which rose steeply at the nape of its curve. She glanced up at the corduroy lines of soil creep and animal tracks, sharpened by the evening shadows and pimpled by soft, mossy mounds of anthills. As children, they had climbed and rolled down the ancient chalk, and had endlessly played in the woods that stood at the bottom on the western flank of Windmill Hill. There had been dens, rope swings, tree climbing. She'd been such a tomboy, she thought, smiling to herself, but it was to be expected with an older and a younger brother.

Farrowcombe had been derelict when her parents had moved there after the war – part of the Alvesdon estate but largely abandoned except for one wing, which had been lived in by the gamekeeper, while the stables and other outbuildings had become a dumping ground for all the detritus of a farm that had once had three separate dairies and an array of mixed livestock. During the last war it had been forced to turn over almost entirely to arable.

Tess had always enjoyed hearing her parents' tales of renovating Farrowcombe. Her mother was an artist – a portrait painter of some renown – and had brought her natural artistic flair to the project. The outbuildings had been cleared out, along with Tom Hayward, then the keeper, who'd been moved to one of the cottages in the village. Repairs had been made, mains water and electricity installed, and Farrowcombe had magically transformed, a Sleeping Beauty awoken from a long slumber. Stork and Debbo had even taken a motoring tour of Europe to buy furniture and art for their new paradise, which had been shipped back and arrived, some time after their return, in a procession of lorries. The way her mother told the story, this had caused no small amount of chatter among the farm workers and villagers.

Tess remembered almost none of this. There was a vague memory of men moving in the large tallboy that still stood in her bedroom, but in her mind, Farrowcombe was timeless: as immutable and beautiful as the downs behind, with its double-pitched tiled roof, myriad chimneys, its rose brick and flint walls, and the paintings,

24

the chairs, the tables, the flagstones, the chests and wardrobes all as they had always been.

Despite its situation at the foot of Farrowcombe, the house faced south-west and was light and airy in summer, warm and secluded in winter. The stables had been long ago returned to their former use, there was a workshop for Smudger, while the larger tower that cornered the stables and outbuildings had been, for as long as Tess could remember, a studio for her mother.

'Gosh, what a place!' said Alex, as it revealed itself around the curve of Windmill Hill.

'Isn't it beautiful?' Tess was happy that his first glimpse had prompted such a naturally enthusiastic response. Then another stab of wistfulness caught her. This might well be it – the last weekend here in peacetime. She had seen and knew too much – that the diplomatic mission to Moscow was little more than a token and bound to fail, that neither the Prime Minister nor the Committee of the Imperial General Staff really believed Hitler could be tamed. She knew that General Ismay still held out a small hope for peace but that short of Hitler being assassinated, war was unlikely to be averted. It was too awful, too upsetting to contemplate, and no matter how hard she tried to banish such thoughts, they were there, in the background, seeping into her consciousness.

Tess had taken Alex to the top of the downs, shown him the DH.4 and then they climbed back down in time to see Wilf arrive on his motorcycle. Her younger brother had ridden from Tangmere, in Sussex, where his squadron was based. Wilf was still only nineteen and had passed out of the RAF college at Cranwell that May. He was now flying the new Spitfire. Tess and Edward had not seen him since he'd finished his operational training course and been posted.

'I can't believe you're being let loose in a Spitfire,' said Edward. They had dressed early for dinner down at the manor but it was still warm so were sitting at the table by the walnut tree in the garden. 'Look at you – you look about sixteen, Wilf. Have you even started shaving yet?'

'It's not about age or growing a moustache,' retorted Wilf. 'It's about whether a fellow can fly or not.'

Edward put up his hands in surrender. 'Well, you've got me there, little brother.'

Wilf grinned. 'Actually, it's quite easy once you get the hang of it. Good fun, too. Imagine being up in Dorothy, then times that by fifty.'

Tess gazed at Wilf, standing beneath the walnut tree. He did look young, she thought. He took more after their mother, with lighter brown hair and hazel eyes, smooth-skinned and light-framed but suddenly more muscular. A pilot, training to shoot down enemy aircraft. It made her sad to think of it. Wilf was a quiet doer, without the easy charm of her older brother. Edward made friends wherever he went, was clever, funny and effortlessly charismatic, but Wilf was sweet, kind and thoughtful, independently minded, and she was not at all surprised he'd done so well at Cranwell. 'He's an instinctive pilot,' Stork had said. 'He's got a feel for an aircraft that comes quite naturally.'

He was, she thought, mature beyond his years, despite that boyish face of his; he was methodical, deliberate. *Imperturbable.* She hoped that would stand him in good stead. Her father had said it was a fine attribute for a pilot.

'So, how was the ride over?' asked Stork.

'Had a bit of trouble with the carburettor but it was easy enough to fix,' Wilf told him. 'After that she was very well behaved.'

'You'll have to show her to Smudger.'

Wilf nodded. 'I will. Actually,' he added, 'I was hoping I might be able to take up Dorothy in the morning. That is, if you don't mind and there's time?'

'Of course you can. Why don't you take Alex with you? Show him the place from the air.'

Alex brightened. 'Really? That would be marvellous. I've never been in an aeroplane.'

'That's settled, then,' said Wilf.

'Thank you. I say, what a thrill!'

Debbo looped an arm through Wilf's, then turned to Edward and Tess. 'And how were Denholm and Coco?'

'Coco looked as though she'd rather be anywhere but here,' said Edward, 'but Uncle Denholm was rather amusing, actually. Says the French are in a bit of a lather about the prospect of war.'

'I've told you, Edward,' said Tess, 'we're not going to talk about war this weekend.' She looked around at the others. 'Please, let's not. It's too much. Let's just try to enjoy the next couple of days.'

'Quite right,' said Edward. 'No point getting blue.'

Stork looked at his watch. 'We should get going shortly. I've just got something to sort out. Excuse me.' Then he turned and went back towards the house.

'Is Daddy all right?' Tess asked her mother.

Debbo smiled. 'He's worried, as we all are. But he's been asked to join the War Ag and doesn't know what to do about it.'

'Utterly thankless task,' said Edward. 'If I was him, I wouldn't touch it with a bargepole.'

'But he'll be brilliant,' said Wilf. 'He's one of the most successful farmers around and he's still young. Better him than some of the other old sticks.'

'The trouble is,' Debbo continued, 'Grandpa thinks he's been asked to join the War Ag, not your father.'

'Crikey,' said Edward. 'And he hasn't?'

'He can't have,' said Debbo. 'Stork's had a letter formally inviting him. Somehow Alwyn must have got the wrong end of the stick.'

'Oh dear,' said Tess.

'I know. He's terribly worried about it. The last thing any of us needs is another row. I've told Stork to put it to one side until next week but, of course, T. K. Jeans and Richard Stratton will be coming tomorrow evening. The worry is that Alwyn says something to them.'

'Lawks,' said Edward. 'At his birthday party.'

'Stork's tied himself up in knots as to whether he should say something first, tonight. They've actually been getting on a bit better recently too, which is what makes it even more awful.' She turned to Alex. 'Do your family cause you such anxieties, Alex?'

'Most definitely,' Alex replied. 'All the time.'

Soon after, once Stork had reappeared, they set off, this time in the trap, which Ambrose Milburn, the gardener-groom and former ploughman on the farm, brought around from the yard. Tess looked at her father and gave him what she hoped was a reassuring smile, then glanced at her brothers and at Alex. *Stop it*, she thought. *Don't think about it.* The light of the setting sun cast a deep golden glow across the valley so that clouds of gnats and other evening insects could be seen caught in the day's last rays as the horses trotted rhythmically down the track towards the village. The air smelt fresh and sweet: the scent of harvest time. *How lovely, how peaceful*, Tess thought. She prayed it might last but could not shake off the pervasive shroud of dread that hung around her.

3

The Dinner Party

MAUD SAT AT HER DRESSING-TABLE FITTING THE PEARL-DROP earrings Alwyn had given her following the birth of Denholm back in June 1890. Nearly fifty years ago. Half a century! And yet she could remember it vividly. She'd had their first-born suckling at her breast, Alwyn watching from the wing-back chair in the corner. It had been a gorgeous sunny day, and the light was streaming through the sash window, lighting up half of her husband's face, which wore an expression of intense pride and happiness. *I have a son, an heir, and my wife is well. All is well!* She'd always been able to read Alwyn's mind, because he wore his emotions so visibly. Then the nurse had come in and taken the fat little bundle away. Alwyn had felt in his pocket and produced the little box, moving over to sit beside her on the bed.

'I, er, thought you might like these, Maud,' he'd said, handing over the small leather box. 'You really are an absolute marvel. You've made me terribly happy.'

Now, with the pearls in place, she paused briefly to look at the three photographs of her sons on the table – each taken when they'd been around four years old. Denholm and Stork had her own pale blue eyes and dark hair, although facially Denholm was a neat blend of them both, with Alwyn's fuller face. John, though, was unmistakably Alwyn's son, with his dark auburn hair and dark eyes, just as Stork was a male version of herself. Even on their infant faces, she could see it clearly.

'Wonderful having Denholm back, isn't it, darling?' said Alwyn, sitting on the edge of the bed, tying his black tie. 'I'm so glad he could make it. And Coco. Pretty little thing she's become.'

'It is, although she seems a little troubled to me. I don't think she's a very happy young woman at the moment.'

'Bit moody perhaps. Tiring journey. But Denholm seems on marvellous form.' He sighed. 'I do wish he didn't have to go and live in the South of France. Particularly with all this war talk. I hate the thought of him stuck down there.'

Now it was Maud's turn to sigh. Alwyn had been muttering about Denholm's emigration to France ever since 1920 and at least once a day during the past week. 'I know, Alwyn, but it's where he's made his life. Cannes is as much his home as Alvesdon is ours. In any case, what would he do here? Stork and John have the farm and the brewery, and you know perfectly well that Denholm's not the slightest interested in either.'

'But he'd be safe. He's the eldest. The manor is still his home. It'll be rightfully his when we fall off our perches. He could come back and live with us.'

Maud got up and walked over to him, running her hand through his still thick but now snow-white hair. 'He doesn't want to live here, my darling. You have two sons right by us, which is more than any father could hope for. Can't you be thankful for that?'

She felt his shoulders drop.

'I miss him, damn it. And I'm worried about what's round the corner. A second war with Germany. What if that happens?' He looked up and smiled sadly. 'Do you remember him calling you Maimes? Couldn't say Mummy or Mother, could he?'

She smiled. 'No. And now he's nearly fifty. It makes me feel awfully old. And you'll be seventy-five tomorrow. To think of it. But don't regret what can't be, Alwyn. Think how lucky we were to get all three sons back from the last war. If Hitler's to have his way, it's not Denholm we need to worry about, but darling Edward and Wilf. And Robbie will soon be of age too. It's too ghastly even to think about.'

'Even so,' said Alwyn, 'I'm going to talk to him.'

He was, she thought, not for the first time in fifty years of marriage, a stubborn and pig-headed man. 'Come on, my darling,' she said. 'Let's go down. They will all be here soon.'

Over dinner at the round table, Maud wondered how many times the family had sat around it over the years. It had been bought new back in 1819 by Alwyn's grandfather as a wedding gift for his wife. 'I'm like King Arthur and his knights in our dining room,' Alwyn was fond of saying. 'We're all equals at this table.' That invariably prompted smirks and raised eyebrows. Maud had always joined in with the knowing looks, for although Alwyn really did like to be the king of his castle, she had long ago learned how win her own battles and to manipulate her husband gently when necessary. In any case, she had always loved the table and the room. All the rooms on the ground floor were of a reasonable height, but the dining room was perfectly square in a corner of the house, with large windows on two sides that looked out onto the lawn and towards the village cricket ground, with the southern ridge of chalk downs beyond. It was a fine view, although the light was rapidly fading now. The back wall had also been transformed by Edward's wonderful mural, with which both Maud and Alwyn were thrilled. What had been before a wall of pale yellow with uninspiring still lifes had been transformed into a large Arcadian landscape of hills, mountains, a lake, distant ruined temples and a hunting scene. 'It's inspired by those marvellous eighteenth-century French landscapes, Maimes,' Edward had told her. '*Après* Boucher and Fragonard.'

Alwyn and Maud always ate in the dining room, whether breakfast, lunch or dinner, on their own or with guests. On special occasions such as tonight, radial leaves could be added to the table, which allowed fourteen to be seated comfortably, and fifteen at only the gentlest of squeezes, and it was fifteen who sat around the table now. The entire family, Maud thought, with satisfaction: three sons, two daughters-in-law, of whom she really was very fond, and seven grandchildren, completed by the presence of Tess's beau, who seemed, she thought, most charming. Even little Maria had been allowed to join them, John and Carin's youngest, and still only fourteen but growing up fast.

Only Lucie was missing, but, then again, Denholm's new wife

wasn't really part of the family *proper*. She was French, after all, and had only been to Alvesdon once, and briefly. While it was true that Carin was German by birth, John's wife was really quite Anglicized, having lived here – *Gosh*, Maud thought, *twenty years already*. Carin might still speak with a faint German accent, but she had made her life with John, had embraced the village, made friends, raised three wonderful children and been such a support to dear John. Carin was her daughter-in-law but she considered her a friend and a confidante too. She glanced across at her, between Edward and Stork, caught her eye, and Carin looked back with that lovely warm smile of hers. Alwyn might wish Denholm would return but would Lucie settle here? Maud somehow doubted it.

Alwyn tapped a glass with his knife, then stood as the conversation around the table died.

'It's wonderful to have the entire family here – er, Lucie excepted, of course – and I thank you all for coming. But it's particularly wonderful to see Denholm back among us and beautiful Coco. Who knows what lies ahead? Before we eat, though, let's raise a glass. To the Castell family. May we grow and prosper.'

They all raised their glasses and repeated the words. Then Denholm said, 'Well, happy birthday, Pa! Wouldn't have missed it for the world.' And Alwyn, now seated, raised his glass again and beamed at his eldest son.

'And,' Denholm added, 'I'd also like to commend Edward on his marvellous mural. It's marvellous, isn't it?'

'Absolutely first class!' agreed Alwyn.

Edward smiled raffishly. 'Well, I'm jolly glad you like it, Grandpa. It was enormous fun to do.'

'Like it? We absolutely adore it, don't we, Maud?'

'Reckon you could make a killing on the Côte d'Azur,' cut in Denholm. 'French aristocrats, American and British expats, they'd all love to have their villas and mansions decorated with this kind of thing.'

'Really?' said Edward.

'Absolutely. Tell you what, you could come over, stay with us – long as you like – and make a name for yourself. You'd become quite the fellow. Wouldn't he, Coco?'

'I'm sure,' Coco agreed.

'Be careful what you say, Uncle Denholm, because I might just do that,' said Edward. 'But thank you, although I've got another year to complete at the Slade. That is, of course, assuming I'm able to.'

'You're at the cut and thrust, Tess,' said Alwyn. 'Will it be war?'

Tess cleared her throat. 'I'm afraid I can't talk about it, Grandpa, but let's not think about it in any case. Let's just enjoy being together and having a wonderful weekend.'

Alwyn wiped his moustache with his napkin. 'Yes, yes, quite right, m'dear,' then muttered, 'Damned Germans. Why have they got to be warmongering again?'

'Alwyn!' exclaimed Maud.

'And it's not Germans, Pa,' added John. 'It's the Nazis.' Everyone looked at Carin, who reddened.

'It's all right,' she said, and, regaining her composure, smiled at Alwyn. 'It's all right, Alwyn. And for what it is worth, I agree with the sentiment.'

For much of the evening, Stork reflected later, it had been a surprisingly convivial dinner. He'd not allowed himself to become riled by his father's blatant favouritism of Denholm and instead had been happy to see the family together and, especially, to have Edward, Tess and Wilf at home once more, looking so well. He had felt inordinately proud of them and immensely fortunate.

It was only once the ladies had moved to the drawing room and the men had been left to their cigars and port that Denholm had dropped the bombshell. Alwyn had been talking again about how livestock would triumph over arable in the years to come, then mentioned how he was looking forward to playing his part on the Wiltshire War Ag.

'But Stork's been invited onto the War Ag, Pa,' said Denholm. 'Surely there can't be two Castells on the same committee? People would talk.'

The colour had immediately drained from Alwyn's face. 'What?' he said, turning to Stork.

'Yes,' said Denholm. 'Stork's had a formal letter, haven't you, Stork?'

'How the devil d'you know that?' said Stork.

'I heard Debbo and Carin talking about it. Sorry – didn't realize it was a secret. Have I said something wrong?'

'You just cannot resist stirring the pot, can you, Denholm?' Stork put a hand to his eyes, partly in exasperation and in part so he couldn't see the amused smirk on Denholm's face or the expression of horror and rage on his father's.

'My dear fellow, I can assure you—' Denholm began, but his father cut in.

'He can't have,' spluttered Alwyn. 'We can't both be . . . Stork, is this true?'

'Let's forget it about it now, Pa, please,' he said. 'The family's here. Alex is our guest, and this is your birthday weekend.'

Alwyn clenched his fist and brought it down silently on the table. 'A word, Stork,' he said, pushing back his chair. 'In private.'

'Oh, Pa, really, not now. Forget about it.'

Through clenched teeth, Alwyn said, 'Now, Stork.'

Stork sighed and turned to Alex. 'Forgive me, Alex. Children.' He got up and followed his father, conscious the rest of the table were all watching. It was as though he were up before the headmaster.

His father led him in silence to his study, then shut the door.

'Oh, for goodness' sake, Pa!' said Stork. 'A bit theatrical, don't you think?'

'Well?' spluttered his father. 'Well? What have you to say for yourself? Is it true?'

'Yes, it is, but I haven't accepted.'

Alwyn erupted. 'Then why the hell didn't you tell me?'

'For precisely the reason that you're shouting at me now. I haven't the faintest idea what's going on, Pa, but I have had a letter from Richard Stratton. Of course we can't both be on the War Ag, so some kind of ghastly mistake has happened. I intended to have a quiet word with Richard tomorrow, because I knew you'd be upset and I didn't want this to ruin your birthday.'

There was a knock at the door and John opened it. 'Come on, Pa,' he said.

'Leave us, please, John,' said Alwyn.

'No, Pa, I will not. This affects me too.'

Stork could have hugged his brother.

'This is your fault, Stork,' said Alwyn. 'You belittle me. Make me look foolish in front of my friends and neighbours.'

'Steady on,' said John. 'You can hardly blame Stork for this.'

'Can't I? He undermines me at every turn. No matter what I say or do, you can be certain Stork will say the opposite.'

'That's simply not true,' said Stork.

'Stork has turned this farm around and you know it,' said John. 'He's brought progress and modernity and made it a huge success. You should be thanking him, not putting him down.'

Stork could feel his hands starting to tremble with rage. *Keep calm, keep calm,* he told himself.

'It's a damnable outrage!' said Alwyn, fuming still.

'Pa, please,' said Stork. 'It was a surprise to me. I don't want to be part of the War Ag, and had no idea I was even being considered. What did Richard Stratton say to you to make you think you'd been asked yourself?'

Alwyn rubbed his brow. 'He said, um, he said, "We need a Castell on the War Ag."'

'And you thought he meant you, not me?' said Stork, desperately trying to keep his tone measured. 'So you humiliate me in front my children and in front of our guest because of your own damn pride!'

'I think you owe Stork an apology, Pa,' said John, quietly.

'Apology be damned!' growled Alwyn. He was quiet for a moment. They all were.

Christ, thought Stork. His father might have suffered injured pride, but he himself had never felt more humiliated in his life. 'I think,' he said, 'it's time we left.'

'Yes,' agreed Alwyn, placing his hands carefully on the edge of his desk. 'I think I might turn in.'

As he turned to leave, Stork paused. 'Come on, Pa. Let's not make a mountain of a molehill. It's your birthday tomorrow. Let's not spoil things.'

Alwyn remained standing there, hands on the table.

'Well,' said Stork, as he walked to the door, 'good night.'

4

Intrusion

HANNAH ELLERBY HAD BEEN DREADING THE WEEKEND. NORMALLY, being housemaid to just Mr and Mrs Castell was something she could manage quite well, but with Mr Denholm and Miss Coco arriving and dinner for fifteen followed by a party for more than a hundred people the following day she knew she would be run off her feet. There was so much to remember, and although old Mrs Castell, especially, was always kind to her, she didn't like mistakes. According to Jean Gulliver, the cook, there had been eight full-time servants before the last war. Now there were just two, and she was one of them. 'But, of course,' Jean had told her, 'back in them days, there were three boys livin' 'ere too and more entertaining, and anyway, life was different then, weren' it?'

Hannah had been up at the manor since six thirty that morning and now it was past eleven; she wouldn't be home until after mid-night, she knew, and then expected to be up again with the lark the following morning. She was nineteen, of medium height, shapely, and had a pretty, neat face with pale, freckled skin, green eyes and auburn hair. All her family worked for the Castells. Her father was the carter, her brother, Frank, one of the shepherds under Mr Rose, and her mother also helped with the dairy. They lived in a tied cottage at the beginning of Farrowcombe Lane. She'd been at the manor since she was fourteen and knew she'd been fortunate to walk into a job straight from school. She assumed she'd remain there until she married.

And she hoped she might marry Tom Timbrell, son of the fore-man on the farm and the gamekeeper at Alvesdon, not that Tom knew anything about this. Hannah had loved Tom ever since she could remember. His good looks helped, of course, but she also knew him to be kind, decent and gentle. Her father said he was the best shot he'd ever seen and had a way with the land that he'd clearly been born with.

'Reckon one day he'll be foreman here,' he'd said. To begin with, her love for Tom had been merely a childhood passion for an older and clearly untouchable man. Now, though, she was a woman and the six-year difference in age meant nothing at all. Plenty of girls got married at her age and to older men too. She also knew she wasn't alone in thinking Tom the finest catch in the village yet, as she could only admit to herself and to no one else, she was the best-shaped, prettiest girl in Alvesdon and prayed that her looks, if nothing else, might draw him to her. How to make him see her, to realize what they might have together, was something for which she had no answer. Her shyness, her reluctance to risk making a fool of herself, and her inexperience in any kind of courtship meant she felt crip-pled into muteness if he even so much as looked at her.

From the manor that morning she had seen him in the yard, and later walking past leading a horse pulling a wheat cart, but even she had been too busy to give him much thought that day. After the dinner party had broken up, it had taken a while to clear the dining and drawing rooms, she and Susan Smallpiece, brought in for the occasion, shuffling back and forth with trays from the kitchen, a large room at the back of the house with a range, a copper water-heater and adjoining pantry, larder and separate cold store.

'There was summat going on tonight, make no mistake,' said Susan, as Jean finished tidying away what little food had not been eaten.

'I know,' said Hannah, pouring a large vat of hot water into the sinks. 'It all broke up so sudden. Mr Stork looked as angry as I've ever seen him, and Mr John none too pleased neither.'

'Ah, it's always the same when Mr Denholm appears on the scene,' said Jean. ''E's the prodigal son. Mr Castell's favourite, allus 'as been.'

As Hannah began washing the crockery, Susan stood beside her with a tea-towel. 'Well, I don't 'old with 'avin' favourites. It's not right. I love my lot equally. They're each of 'em different – and don' get me wrong, they drive me doolally at times but I couldn't pick out one above another.'

''Tis a shame, though,' added Jean. Hannah glanced across at the cook as she began preparing more food at the table, her long, dexterous fingers expertly mixing flour and margarine in a large bowl. What a kind soul Jean was, she thought. She couldn't remember ever having heard her raise her voice at anyone – it wasn't her way – yet Hannah knew she'd suffered more than her fair share of tragedy and hardship. 'Mr Castell's birthday tomorrow an' all the family here,' Jean went on. 'But you're right, Susan, that Mr Denholm always stirs things up. Mr Stork don't see eye to eye with him at all. Never has in all the time I've been here at the manor an' I 'spect never will.'

'I don't blame 'im,' said Susan. 'Mr Stork, that is. Transformed this farm, 'e 'as.'

'It's men,' said Jean. 'They're proud. It's 'cos Mr Stork 'as done so well that's caused the problems. Mr Castell don't like bein' showed up by his son. An' 'e's old-fashioned, bain't 'e? In 'is way o' things, Mr Denholm should be runnin' the farm. 'E's the oldest, an' the oldest is the heir. That's how things are.'

''Cept they ain't,' said Susan.

'An' Mr Castell don' like it. So 'e takes it out on Mr Stork.' She looked up, thoughtful for a moment. ''E's a lovely man, is Mr Stork. I'll never forget what 'e did for me, payin' for me to go out and visit my Reg's grave. God knows I mightn't 'ave visited him yet if it weren't for 'is kindness.'

'Both 'e and Mr John are good men,' agreed Susan. 'They must be worrying now about their young 'uns with all this talk of war.'

They were silent for a moment. Then Hannah said, 'D'you think Tom Timbrell and the other men will have to join up? They'll still need farmers to work the land, won't they?'

Jean smiled at her kindly. 'Oh, Hannah, my love. Who knows what's around the corner? We got to hope them politicians come to their senses and sort it all out so we don't 'ave to go through what we suffered last time.'

It was nearly midnight by the time they had finished. All three were preparing to leave for home when the kitchen door opened and Denholm stood before them.

'Goodness,' he said, 'you're still here.'

'We're just off home, Mr Denholm,' said Jean. 'All done now, unless there's anything I can get you?'

He nodded. 'I was feeling a little peckish, but don't worry yourselves.' He looked at Hannah, then said, 'Tell you what, I could do with a little air. Allow me to walk you ladies home.'

'Oh, no, sir, there's no need,' said Susan, quickly.

'No, no, I shall brook no dissent,' Denholm said, smiling amiably.

Exchanging glances among themselves, Jean then said, 'Very well, thank you, Mr Denholm. Susan and I are just off the end of the driveway, and Hannah here lives at the foot of Farrowcombe Lane. By the church and opposite the Three Horseshoes.'

They went out of the back door, into the yard. The night was still – fresh, but not at all cold. The moon was up, casting the valley in a monochrome glow. Their shadows could be seen on the track leading into the village.

Denholm breathed in deeply. 'That does smell good, doesn't it? Earthy and sweet.'

'D'you miss the place, sir?' asked Hannah.

'Sometimes. I have a good life in the South of France, though. England on a fine summer's day is close to Heaven, but I don't miss the rain, mud and cold of winter, I can assure you.'

They paused at the end of the driveway and Susan said, 'Jean an' I will be fine from here, thank you very much, Mr Denholm.'

Denholm bowed. 'Goodnight, and thank you for all your hard work this evening. Dinner was delicious. You are a marvel, Mrs Gulliver.'

'I'll be all right from here, too, sir,' said Hannah.

'Can't have pretty young girls walking about the village on their own at night,' said Denholm. 'I said I'd walk you home and so I shall. Really, it's no trouble.'

Hannah looked at Jean and Susan. Jean nodded to her. 'See you in the morning, Hannah.'

They walked on, down the empty road. No other sound could be heard. Denholm took out and lit another cigarette, the brief light of the match casting an orange glow on his face. Hannah hugged her arms around herself and edged away from him as he exhaled upwards, a great swirl of smoke caught in the moonlight.

'Absolutely impossible to think there could be war just around the corner on a night like this,' said Denholm. 'Don't you think? It's so still. So peaceful.'

'Let's hope there isn't, sir,' said Hannah. 'I'm tryin' not to think on't.'

They reached the village green, then the pub, and crossed the road. Hannah wasn't sure why but her heart was quickening. The church loomed, dark against the sky on its slight rise. Farrowcombe Lane and the terraced thatched houses lay ahead.

'This is home, sir,' she said. 'Jus' there.' She looked at him. 'Thank you, sir. I'll say goodnight, then.'

'Goodnight, Hannah,' he said, then added, 'You're a very attractive girl, you know. If you, er, ever wanted to make a little more on the side – a few extra shillings . . .'

'A few extra shillings?' Her heart was racing now. 'What do you mean, sir?'

'I mean, we can be very discreet. I'd not tell a soul and nor would you. It could be our little secret, Hannah.'

For a moment, she stood before him, frozen to the spot, her mind racing. She was unsure whether to run or what to say. Then Denholm leaned down towards her, kissed her cheek and placed his hand on her behind.

'You run along, but I'm here for a few days. The offer stands until then. All right?'

Hannah turned and walked to the front door of her family home with all the calmness and dignity she could muster, although the smell of cigarettes and alcohol and the scratch of his chin stayed with her long after she was inside.

Half a mile further down the lane at Farrowcombe, Stork was equally wide awake.

'At least you didn't say anything you'd regret,' said Debbo, as she got into bed beside him. They had returned to Farrowcombe a couple of hours earlier, and although Stork had wanted to go straight up, his wife had coaxed him into having a nightcap with their children and Alex.

She turned off the bedside light. The window was open, as were the curtains, and moonlight poured through so that as Stork lay there, head propped up by a pillow, he could see the looming bulk of Farrowcombe Hill silhouetted against the sky.

'It was ghastly. So humiliating and in front of everyone. God knows what they must think, seeing us squabble like infants. I wouldn't be surprised if Alex were to run a mile.'

'I know it upsets you, darling, but you must try not to let it. Alwyn's a proud and stubborn old fool. He only loves Denholm so much because he doesn't see him. He idealizes him, but if your brother was here all the time, he'd soon test your parents' patience.'

Stork, still seething with his own hurt and humiliation, said nothing. Debbo moved towards him, kissed his bare chest and rested her head there, her arm across his.

'I love you, my darling,' she said, 'very much indeed.'

'Thank you,' he said, kissing her.

'And it's lovely to have the children here. I rather like Alex, don't you?'

'Seems very nice,' agreed Stork.

'And he's smitten with Tess.'

'So he should be. She's wonderful. Clever, pretty, good company.' He sighed. 'Ah, it's such a worry, though, Debbo. Really, Pa's the least of my concerns. What's around the corner? I just can't bear the thought of them all caught up in another war with Germany.'

She kissed him again. 'Stork?'

'Hmm?'

'Let's do as Tess suggested, shall we? Try to put it out of our minds just for this weekend.' She sat up and pulled off her silk nightdress.

Stork smiled despite himself, gazing at his wife's naked body, still slender and shapely. Still desirable. 'You really are very lovely, you know.'

'Even after all these years?'

She leaned over and he felt her mouth meet his. 'Yes,' he said at length, 'you are.'

5

Moonlight

Sunday, 20 August 1939

THE NORMAL WORKING WEEK WAS SIX DAYS LONG WITH SUNDAY the day of rest. The only exception was at harvest time, when everyone was expected to work whatever day of the week was fair and dry. As it was today.

Tom Timbrell and his father, Claude, had been at the yard meeting at seven o'clock, as always, although Tom had been up since five, checking on the pheasants at Mistleberry Wood. Poachers, human and animal, were a menace that never went away, while feeders needed to be checked too. Tom didn't mind getting up early, though. The farm was very often at its best then, when no one else was about. It gave him the feeling that it was all his. He liked the freshness too – the dew on the ground, the stillness, the wildlife that could be seen. Just that morning, he'd spotted a weasel and a stoat, as well as smelt the distinct musk of a dog-fox at the edge of the wood.

There were only four more fields of barley to harvest, but it would still take the best part of a week, weather depending. Since this Saturday was another clear and sunny day, Tom knew his father was cursing Mr Castell's birthday and the cricket match that would take away the key men of his workforce.

'Have a party by all means,' he'd growled the previous evening, 'but why he chooses to have a cricket match that takes up time, I'm jiggered if I know.'

'It's only a half-day, Father,' Tom had said, 'and 'is seventy-fifth birthday. I'm lookin' forward to it, I don't mind admittin'. Anyhow, weather looks set fair next week too.'

Tom had had half a mind to add that it barely mattered, what with a possible war around the corner. But his father, he knew, took his responsibilities very seriously. As foreman, much rested on his shoulders. He was Mr Stork's right-hand man on the farm, a fount of knowledge and a sounding board, and he took the success or fail- ure of each harvest personally, as he did all the peaks and troughs of the farm. It didn't matter that Mr Stork would never blame him for such variables as weather or the whim of holding a cricket match in the middle of harvest. None the less, a half-day lost, on such a fine day for harvesting, was, Tom knew, sacrilege to his father.

'It's a precarious business, farming,' his father was fond of saying. 'Take nothing for granted and leave nothing to chance if you can help it.' In fairness, it was probably sound advice, but Tom reckoned life was for living, whereas for his father it was all about grinding out an existence. Rare was it that his father would enjoy a pint in the pub or allow himself much in the way of entertainment. He had invested in a wireless set some years ago and he subscribed to and read *Farmers Weekly,* but otherwise most of his waking hours were devoted to the farm. Tom's mother, Phyllis, had died of flu in 1919 and he often wondered whether that had had a lasting effect on his father. She was rarely mentioned, but he supposed it must have been hard trying to do an efficient job for the Castells and raise a son at the same time. Maybe it had stamped out a spark in him. It was not, though, the kind of question he would ever ask his father. They got on well enough and he did not feel starved of affection, but his father had never been one to talk about himself or his feelings.

Tom was thinking about his father as he led Joshua, one of the horses, up the track to Great Clover shortly after the break for lunch. His father had told him only snatches about their former life. Originally they were from Suffolk; his father had been recruited by the Castells for his knowledge of arable farming during the last war. With a reserved occupation, and especially with his expertise in cereals, Claude Timbrell had avoided being sent away to war. They had arrived at Alvesdon in 1915 with Tom just a year old. He found it odd to think of himself as Suffolk-born when he felt so wedded to the chalk, but he recognized that no matter how a man might feel he had a certain landscape in his veins, it was really what went into the mind that shaped a person. With the absence of his mother from when he was five, and his father's need to work, Tom had had to grow up fast and learn to use his wits from an early age.

The farm had seemed an endlessly fascinating place, and the older men and women had taken him under their wings, perhaps, he realized later, because so many had lost sons in the war. Old Isaac Hudson, the gamekeeper before him, had lost his boy on the Somme and Tom had been a willing stand-in. It had nearly broken his heart when he'd found Isaac dead in Tippett's Wood four years back. A heart attack, the doctor had said. Tom had been more upset about Isaac dying like that than he had when his mother had gone; he remembered very little of her. Yet it was strange, because Isaac's going had given him the chance to become gamekeeper far earlier than he might otherwise have expected. He'd been dumbfounded when Mr Stork had offered him the job.

Tom was considering such matters when he saw a beautiful woman walking down the lane towards him. Only after a moment or two did he realize it was Coco, Mr Denholm's daughter. Quite transformed, she was, since he'd last seen her, maybe three years before. Back then, she'd developed a womanly shape but was still a girl. Now, she was something altogether more striking.

As he neared, he doffed his cap. 'Miss Coco, isn't it?' he said. 'Nice to see you back here, miss.'

Coco stopped and smiled. 'And you're Tom Timbrell, aren't you?'

'Tha's right.'

He pulled up Joshua and the horse came to a halt, the corn wagon creaking behind. By God, Tom thought, she was a fine-looking woman. He grinned at her, looking her directly in the eye.

'I saw you this morning,' she said, 'out in the yard.'

'Not spying on me, were you, miss?'

'I was a bit, actually. I couldn't sleep. In any case, you were all making such a noise that I peeped out of my window and there you all were. You stood out.'

'As do you, if you don't mind me saying. You've grown up a lot since last I saw you.'

'None of us stays the same.'

'Not even here, on the farm.'

She smiled. 'You could have fooled me.'

Just then a growing roar could be heard and the DH.4 thundered low over the valley.

'Could have sworn that's Mr Stork's plane,' said Tom, putting a shielding hand to his brow, 'but I happen to know he's on the binder in Great Clover.'

'It's Wilf,' said Coco. 'He's taking Tess's man for a flight.'

Tom nodded, absently stroking Joshua's neck, as he watched the plane disappear down the valley. Then he put his cap back on his head. 'Well, I must be gettin' along. I hope you have a good party later.'

'Will you be at the cricket?'

'Yep,' he said. 'Reckon I will.'

'Good,' she replied, then turned and walked on. Tom glanced back, admiring the sway of her narrow hips as she headed towards the manor. He wondered what she'd meant by that little conversation. She'd seemed quite flirtatious. But why on earth would she be giving him the time of day? It made no sense at all. She was beautiful, make no mistake, but her type was not for the likes of him. He walked on.

One day, he supposed, he'd get married and settle down, but he was certainly not going to do so until he met the right person. Several of the girls in the village had made a few moves towards him and he'd had a fumble with some. He had once even spent a night with Rosemary Laing, twenty years his senior and a war widow, but he'd regretted it afterwards.

The only girl in Alvesdon he'd ever really liked the look of was Hannah Ellerby. She was pretty – quite lovely, really – and there was something about her gentle demeanour that made him sometimes think it would be nice to make a home with her one day. But he knew she wasn't much interested in him, and there was something about her that made him reluctant to try his hand. Fear of refusal, he supposed. Alvesdon was such a close community. People talked and everyone knew everyone else's business. It was one of the many reasons he loved his job so much: he could be himself, do his own thing, without anyone knowing where he was. He looked back one more time and saw Coco turn in towards the manor, then shook his head in wonder.

Barely a cloud had crossed the sky all day, and at the cricket match it had been commented on more than once that God must be shining on Alwyn and the Castell family.

'I know,' Maud said to Helen Liddell, whose husband, David, farmed the neighbouring land at the eastern end of Alvesdon. 'It's such a blessing. One arranges a cricket match and a summer party praying the sun will shine but, really, one never knows in August.'

'Oh, it's utterly glorious, Maimes,' Helen had said, between bites of an egg and cress sandwich. 'If only it weren't for Hitler threatening us all, although I suppose it's best to try not to think about it.'

'It's always at the back of one's mind, somehow,' agreed Maud. 'But at least Alwyn seems happy.'

'You've given him a wonderful birthday – and to think there's more to follow.'

Maud sighed a little at the thought, then smiled to see Alwyn, umpiring in a long white coat and Panama hat, signal four more runs with a flourish. Most of the evening guests had now arrived and were politely watching the denouement of the game. The rickety old wooden and thatched pavilion sat across the church end of the ground, facing Alvesdon Manor, its normal silvery stone now a pinkish gold in the glow of the evening sun. Trestle tables had been laid in front and to either side of the pavilion, and while the tea had long ago been cleared away, waiters – boys from the village under the supervision of Mr Burroughs, Alwyn's driver-cum-gardener-cum-handyman – were now offering trays of lemonade, beer and champagne.

Dick and Eleanor Varney wandered over. Eleanor, thought Maud, looked a little strained. 'I think your village team is going to win, Dick,' she said.

Dick chuckled. 'I rather suspect that any side with Tom Timbrell on song is likely to end up victorious, don't you?'

Maud craned her neck around the edge of her deckchair towards the telegraph. 'Twenty to win. What has young Tom got now?'

'Ninety-odd. Yes, I'm afraid he's rather shown up the Varney family's effort.'

'Oh, but Ollie played awfully well,' said Maud.

'He looked good for a bit, but youthful impatience got the better of him.'

She turned to Eleanor. 'You must be so proud of him. He's turned into such a charming young man.'

'Thank you, Maud,' said Eleanor. 'Yes, we are.' She looked at Dick, then out towards the water meadows beyond. Maud wondered whether Eleanor might be about to cry, so decided to spare her blushes and change the subject. She was about to speak when the church clock struck seven.

'Goodness! Seven already.'

'I'm impressed with Tess's feller,' said Dick. 'He's bowled quite beautifully.'

Maud couldn't help thinking about the last war, watching her three boys each join up and disappear over such an unknown and horribly perilous horizon. She kept telling herself to banish such thoughts, but it wasn't so simple, was it? Everyone seemed a little on edge. Of course, they were all making an effort not to show it, but one saw it, none the less.

A cry came up from the field, followed by gentle clapping, and Claude Timbrell, a thunderous look on his face, was stalking back to the pavilion.

'I say, that's five wickets for Alex,' said Dick. 'But only nine runs needed.'

'And how many have you left still to bat?' asked Maud, glad of the distraction.

'This is our last man.' He chuckled. 'It's actually rather tense. Down to the wire.'

Out in the middle, Tom Timbrell saw Alf Ellerby walk out to join him, then noticed, first, Hannah Ellerby, with a tray of drinks from the manor, pause and look not at her father but at him, then Coco walking around the boundary towards her. Tom hoped Alf would survive the next ball from Captain Woodman, then determined to win the match himself in the following over. A few blows, that was all. Mr Stork was not a bad bowler at all, but Tom reckoned it was time to chance his arm.

'No!' he shouted firmly at Alf, after his new partner nicked an edge of the last ball. *Good*, he thought. Coco was now standing by Hannah, taking a drink from her tray. Both were watching him. He glanced around and saw Mr Denholm also looking in the direction of the two girls, then turned to face Mr Stork, as he came in to bowl.

In truth, Tom had already decided what he was going to do before Mr Stork had let go of the ball. Now he danced nimbly along the wicket, felt his bat swing downwards and connect on the full. The ball soared high into the air towards Mr Denholm, who was fielding by the boundary in front of the pavilion. Denholm, though, had not been watching until too late so that instead of catching the ball he knocked it up, above his head and over the boundary for six runs.

A polite cheer went up from the pavilion followed by a ripple of applause.

'Well batted, Tom! That's your hundred!' he heard Dick call.

Tom grinned and glanced again towards Hannah and Coco. He was pleased to see Hannah had remained still, watching.

'Very well batted, Tom,' said Mr Stork, advancing towards him, his hand outstretched.

'Thank you,' said Tom, 'but I've still got to win this match.'

He did so two balls later, cutting a short ball to the boundary for four, but by that time, Hannah had moved on, and was now hidden by a small crowd of people near the pavilion.

A little while afterwards, drinking what he felt was a well-earned beer, he saw Alex Woodman walk towards him.

'Very well batted,' said Alex.

'Thank you. And well played yourself.'

'I hear you're quite a marksman too.'

Tom shrugged. 'Practice,' he said. 'Been with a rifle and shotgun all my life, pretty much.'

'And, if you don't mind me asking,' continued Alex, 'what will you do if there's war?'

'Well, farmin's a reserved occupation, so I might bide by here.'

Alex nodded thoughtfully. 'It is, but is gamekeeping? I rather imagine that shooting for pleasure might have to take a back seat. I may be wrong, of course . . .' He let the sentence trail.

'I s'pose you might be right.'

'The thing is, Tom, the Army could make very good use of someone like you – a man who can read the land, who knows how to stalk and track and what-have-you. And who can shoot.'

'Are you trying to recruit me, sir?'

Alex smiled. 'I didn't come down here looking to find recruits, if that's what you mean, but I could certainly get you into my outfit. I'd be damned glad of you, and for what it's worth, the King's Own Royal Guards are a fine regiment. You'd be joining one of the best.'

Tom rubbed his chin. 'I'm flattered,' he said. 'To be honest, I'd not really given it much thought.'

'Not expecting an answer now, Tom. And who knows what'll happen? Perhaps there won't be a war after all. But you live in a marvellous part of the world, and if it does come to it, this will need defending. And very worth it, wouldn't you say?'

Tom nodded. 'Yes.'

'Here,' said Alex, handing him a card. 'Have a think.'

'All right,' said Tom. 'I will. Have a think about it, that is.'

Alex looked him straight in the eye and held out a hand, which Tom took. A firm, tight handshake. 'Good man,' said Alex. 'And, again, well batted. That was a first-class knock.'

Stork took the Wolseley back to Farrowcombe with Edward, Wilf and Alex so they might have a quick wash and change before returning to the manor for the party.

'Well done, Dad,' said Edward, as they turned into the village. 'You kept admirably calm, I thought.'

'I was given a stern talking-to by your mother,' he said, smiling.

'It was never out,' said Wilf. 'I could hear the noise of the ball hitting the bat and I was standing right behind Grandpa.'

'He's seventy-five,' said Stork, 'and getting hard of hearing. Really, it doesn't matter. Infuriating to miss out on a fifty by one run, but it was a good game and that's all that matters.'

Even so, he was painfully aware that his father had not directly spoken to him since the previous evening. Giving him out was the only eye contact they had had. In the car they were all silent, until Edward said, 'But what are you going to do, Dad?'

'About what?'

'About Grandpa and the War Ag.'

Stork sighed and ran a hand through his hair. 'I don't know. It all depends on what happens. Whether there will be—' He stopped and swallowed hard. He turned, a forced smile on his face. 'Let's worry about what's going on in the world when the party's over.'

He glanced up into the rear-view mirror and saw Wilf gazing pensively out of the window. *Oh, God,* thought Stork, *please let them be all right.*

Flares marked a path from the cricket field across the stream and into the garden of the manor. Within the open-sided marquee, round tables had been set out, posies of flowers on each, while at the far side the buffet had been laid on trestles alongside a bar. Boys and girls, earlier helping with the harvest, had washed, tidied, and put on their best clothes, earning a few extra pennies as waiters and waitresses, although Maud had insisted guests should help themselves to food.

'I don't want a standing buffet, Mrs Gulliver,' she had said, a fortnight earlier. 'That might have been the way when I was young, but we're older now and I, for one, prefer to sit.'

'Very sensible, ma'am,' Jean had answered.

Now, as the guests started arriving, Susan Smallpiece and Hannah stood either side of the flare path by the entrance to the marquee, each with a tray of champagne.

'Well, I must say it all looks very pretty, don't it?' said Susan.

Hannah was not listening. So far, she had avoided being alone with Mr Denholm. Then she thought of Tom and the way he'd been looking at Miss Coco when he'd been batting.

'Hannah?' said Susan, sharply.

Hannah looked up.

'I said, it looks pretty, don't it?'

Hannah nodded. 'Yes, I s'pose it does.'

Susan tutted. 'I don't know what's got into you, Hannah. Had a long face all day. Try and cheer up for the guests, will you?'

The guests started arriving and her tray was soon empty, along with the spare bottle of champagne.

'I've an empty tray,' she said to Susan.

'Best you go an' get some more then, from the cold store.'

Hannah sighed and headed towards the house. Turning the corner, she saw Mr Denholm emerge from the house, changed from his cricket whites.

'Ah, Hannah, good evening,' he said.

Hannah walked past him but he caught her shoulder.

'Now, now,' he said. 'No need to be like that. It was a friendly offer, that's all. No one need know.'

She shrugged herself free and hurried on into the house, her heart thumping. In the cold store she picked up several more bottles of champagne, then put them down again. She could feel the flood rise within her, uncontrollably, and putting her hands to her face she sobbed in a way she hadn't since she was a child.

'Hannah?' she heard Jean Gulliver call. 'You all right there, child?'

But Hannah couldn't stop. It was like nothing she had ever felt before, a terrible cocktail of hurt, anger, humiliation, regret and fear. She felt an arm on her shoulders and smelt the comforting aroma of flour, butter and rose water.

'Hannah, my lovely, whatever's the matter?'

Hannah felt herself being turned around, even though her hands were still at her face and her chest heaving.

'Come here,' said Jean, gently, clasping her to her. For a minute or two they remained where they were until at last Hannah felt her tears subside.

'I'm sorry,' she mumbled. 'It's nothing.'

'Don't seem like nothin'.'

'I'm sorry,' said Hannah, again. 'I don't know what come over me.'

'I'll not pry,' said Jean, 'but I know you, Hannah Ellerby, and I know it's not the extra work this week. Here.' She handed Hannah a tea-towel. 'Wipe your eyes and then you'd best be gettin' back to the guests.'

Hannah nodded. 'Does it look like I been weepin'?'

Jean smiled and clasped her shoulders. 'Barely, my love. Dab some water over your face and none'll be the wiser.'

Hannah did as she was told, feeling the water cool her face. She mustn't, she told herself, get caught alone with him ever again, then wished Tom might look after her. The sooner Mr Denholm and that po-faced girl of his went back to France, the better.

Coco was aware she was behaving badly, but in truth she didn't want to be there. She was fond of her grandfather, who always made such an extraordinary fuss of her and her father, and Maimes was a darling, but she didn't really know her cousins or her uncles and aunts. In any case, she was aware there was some rather long-standing antipathy towards her father on the part of her uncles, and although she didn't especially care about that, it made them seem a little more remote. It seemed ridiculous to her that one had to feel a bond with family members just because one shared the same blood.

She felt like a fish out of water. The valley was very pretty, but this world of English village and farming life was alien. She'd been brought up in the sophisticated city environment of Cannes overlooking the Mediterranean, and although she'd been packed off to boarding-school in Kent, every holiday she had caught the boat train back to the Côte d'Azur. England for her meant dormitories, awful food, shrew-like teachers, horrible team sports and endless cold and damp. When she had finally left school at sixteen she had promised herself she would never live in England. Coco felt wedded to the sun, heat, sea and sophistication of the South of France. That was what she felt was really coursing through her veins, not the farming Castells of Wiltshire.

Yet none of this was the main reason why she was sick at heart. She'd never experienced anything like it. Just a week earlier she'd been so happy, so carefree. People were talking about a possible war with Germany but she hadn't given a fig. She was in love and that was all that mattered. Then had come the bombshell. Étienne had arrived at the house – her father was out – and she had hurried to meet him, smiling. She had flung her arms around him only for him to turn his mouth from hers and push her away. That heart-stopping moment: shock, panic, hurt. He had to stop seeing her, he said. It wasn't fair on his wife, or his two children.

'But you love me,' she had said. How she cringed now, thinking of it. No, he'd said, he didn't. It had been fun, they'd had a great time, but it had to end. It was too difficult, too complicated.

'You're the daughter of my younger sister's husband!' he'd said.

'And he's my business partner! It's ridiculous, absurd! I was carried away by a kind of madness. You're a beautiful young woman, Coco, but there is no future for us. I'm sorry, but there it is.' And then he'd got back into his car and driven off. Gone, out of her life, the fun, the laughter, the languid afternoons and nights making love, finished. *Fin.* Except that it wasn't entirely over because he was also family – albeit by marriage – and because he still worked with her father.

She'd not seen him since that awful day but on her return she would and it would be terrible. Every time she thought of it she felt a new wave of despair.

'You'll get over him,' her father had told her. 'Damned foolish of you to get involved in the first place, if you ask me.'

'But I thought he loved me,' she'd said, and immediately regretted how pathetic it sounded. They'd been on the swing sofa on the terrace, looking out over the Mediterranean, Cannes nestling below a little way to the east. It was such a beautiful sight.

'Oh, my little darling,' he'd said. 'Everyone has their heart broken at some point. It's a rite of passage. I'm awfully fond of Étienne, but the fellow's an appalling boulevardier. I hate to be blunt, but you're not the first and you won't be the last. Men like him don't change their spots. He's a good-looking chap, debonair as a Dervish, charm oozing from every pore, but don't give your heart to him. If I'd known about your grand passion, I'd have warned you off.'

She had been unable to prevent her tears and he had held her, rocking her gently. 'Come on, now,' he'd said. 'My advice is find someone else as quickly as possible and you'll soon forget about him. We've got our trip to Alvesdon coming up, so that'll get you away for a bit. Best foot forward, eh, old girl?'

She had since learned that her father had found out and warned Étienne to keep away. It was one of the reasons why the journey to England had been so particularly painful – she'd barely been able to look at her father, let alone speak to him. Eventually, while heading to the Gare du Nord, he'd said, 'For goodness' sake, Coco, what I said the other day holds true. He's a philandering cad and the sooner you escaped his clutches the better. You think you're so wonderfully grown-up and sophisticated but you know nothing of life. If I can't keep a look-out for you, who the hell will?'

'But it wasn't up to you! It's my life!'

'It's my job to protect you, you bloody fool. And I should know a cad when I see one because I'm every bit as much of a bounder myself!'

'We were in love and you ruined it!' she screamed.

'Oh, Coco, really!' he said, exasperated. 'If he'd been madly in love, do you think he'd have broken it off? D'you really think he'd have listened to me? It pains me to tell you this, it really does, but he was using you, my darling. You were a happy diversion for him, nothing more, and I was damned if I was going to let him treat you that way. It was abominable of him. In any case, if it was all so wonderful, why keep it a bloody secret?'

Because Étienne had insisted . . . Over the course of that long journey she had re-run in her mind conversations she'd had with him and realized that her father had been right. Love had blinded her to Étienne's imperfections, to his lies, and he had never once said he loved her. She had taken it as a given. What a fool she'd been! Yet she'd remained furious with her father the entire journey for making her feel such a fool and because he was there and because she needed someone on whom to vent her heartbreak, hurt and humiliation. She'd begun to thaw by the time they'd finally reached Alvesdon but hadn't been quite sure how to come off her high perch. She'd tried to avoid people as much as possible, wishing she could be in Cannes and turn back the clock to those brief happy weeks when all had been laughter, light and love with Étienne.

And then she had seen Tom Timbrell and she had remembered her father's advice about finding someone else. Next week they'd be heading back to Cannes and inevitably she would see Étienne. She didn't want to feel weak at the knees and close to tears every time their paths crossed, and it occurred to her, in a flash of inspiration, that maybe she should seduce the Adonis walking towards her. Soon she would be a thousand miles away. And if he could take her mind off Étienne, what possible harm could it do? On the contrary, a fling with a farmhand might be just the tonic she needed.

So, she had paused to talk to him, had flirted with him and had noticed that he really was a rather beautiful man. The thought of making love to him excited her, although as she'd walked back towards the house she had realized what a ridiculous notion it had been. Just where would she seduce him, after all? In any case, he probably already had a girl – a good-looking man like him in a small village was bound to. None the less, for several hours afterwards she thought not of Étienne but of Tom, and there he was later that afternoon, playing the hero in the otherwise utterly tiresome cricket match. And she had felt her spirits rise a little.

But then there had been the party and endless tedious small-talk. All the same questions, while her cousins, the only ones her age, did their best to avoid her. She didn't blame them: she'd been truculent and hardly very forthcoming. And no sign of Tom anywhere. But of course there wasn't. Grandpa wouldn't be inviting his sort to his birthday party. Her mood had sagged again until finally, with the buffet dinner over and some of the guests beginning to slip away, she had done the same, wandering down the same lane she had walked earlier that day. It had been a relief to escape all those people and to feel the crisp night air on her face. Above her, a canopy of stars, while the moon continued to shine down, providing more than enough light to guide her. In the distance, she could hear the faint hum of the party, but otherwise the only sound was that of her steps on the chalky track. Otherwise, all was still.

Until she heard a second set of footsteps, which made her turn quite suddenly and she gasped, startled. A figure was walking towards her, a gun slung over his shoulder. Her heart quickened but she stayed where she was, by the side of the track, until there he was, right before her. Tom Timbrell.

'This is gettin' to be a habit, Miss Coco,' he said, in a low voice. 'Isn't it?'

He scratched his chin, glanced back in the direction of the house, then said, ''Ad enough of the party, then?'

'I fancied a bit of fresh air.'

'I see. An' where are you headin'?'

'I don't know, I hadn't really thought. But . . .', she swallowed, felt her heart beating faster, '. . . I had hoped I might bump into you, actually.'

'Me?'

'Yes. You see, I hoped you might be able to help me.'

Tom chuckled. 'Well, you've got me there, I don' mind sayin'. An' how can I help?'

She felt an impetuous madness sweep over her then. Taking his hand, she stretched up and kissed him on the lips, then again, more urgently. To her relief he didn't pull back or recoil in horror, but instead placed his hands around her, so that she could feel them reaching up her back.

He stopped kissing her and looked back again towards the manor. 'Not here,' he said quietly. 'Come with me.' He held her hand and led her on down the track. She could feel goosebumps on her arms. What on earth did she think she was doing? She wondered whether she should let go of his hand, turn and run, before it was too late. But she didn't really want to run. She wanted to be with this man. Everyone seemed to think there would soon be a war and that soon German bombers would arrive and flatten half of France. God, who knew? She might be dead in a month. What was the point of holding back now?

'I've a hut,' he said.

They were among the trees now, and although she could still see the moon in brief gaps among the foliage, it was far darker here and her eyes strained to see much at all.

'Don't worry,' said Tom. 'I know every inch of these woods.'

'And you don't ever get scared here, all on your own?'

Tom laughed. 'No! You only get scared of what you don't know. Anyhow, I'm not alone, am I? There's the birds, the badgers, foxes, stoats, deer and other creatures.'

She felt hardly comforted. Her mind turned briefly to her home in the hills above Cannes and she couldn't help laughing.

'What is it?' he asked.

'When I left Cannes on Wednesday, I never thought I'd be wandering in a wood at night with a man I barely know.'

'Quite an adventure you're having then, eh?' And he laughed. His accent made her think of a Thomas Hardy novel she'd read at school, but his laugh was attractive and light. Reassuring. They reached a grassy clearing and there, dark in the moonlight, was his wooden hut, resting on wheels so it could be moved about, and with steps up to the door at the front.

'Here,' he said. He unlocked the padlock, opened the door and held her hand as she stepped up, then took a lantern from inside the door and lit it, dimly illuminating the single room. There was a cot on one side, a chair, a small table, and a ewer of water. At the far end stood a shelf on which were a couple of books and another lantern.

He said nothing as she looked around. It smelt slightly musty but was clean enough. Her heart was quickening again and now she turned as he followed her inside and kissed him again. And he was kissing her back, hungrily, and pushing off his jacket.

'You, Miss Coco,' he said, 'are a wondrous, beautiful thing. I can' make you out at all.'

'You don't need to,' she said, as she pushed off his braces and began to unbutton his shirt.

Moments later, her dress in a heap on the floor and Tom lowering her gently onto the cot, she briefly thought of Étienne – his scented cheeks, his neat, smooth chin and delicate fingers – then dismissed him, reached up and pulled Tom down to her, her inhibitions and any reservations now gone.

6

Fading Hope

IT WAS JUST AFTER THEY HAD RETURNED FROM CHURCH THAT Sunday, 20 August, that the telephone at Farrowcombe rang for Tess. It was Wing Commander Bill Elliott on the phone, the general's right-hand man and assistant secretary to the Committee of Imperial Defence.

'The general's been recalled to London, I'm afraid,' he told her, 'and I need you too. I'm sorry, Tess. We've work to do on the War Book and Ismay will be back first thing in the morning. He's catching the night train from Aberdeen.'

'Of course. I'll come straight away, sir.'

'Can you be here by, say, five p.m.?'

'Yes, of course, sir,' said Tess.

'Good. I'll brief you then. I'm very sorry to cut short your family weekend, Tess.'

'It's all right, sir.'

'See you later, then. Goodbye.'

'Goodbye.'

She put the phone down and saw her mother standing in the hall looking worried.

'Everything all right, darling?' she said.

'I've been summoned to London.'

'Oh, goodness,' she said, bringing her hands to her mouth.

Tess and Alex packed quickly and her father drove them to the station.

'I'm sorry about lunch, Dad,' she said, as they motored down the lane towards the valley road.

'I am too, darling,' he said. 'But it can't be helped. I'm extremely proud of you, though. You're doing your bit in these worrying times. As are you, Alex.'

Tess knew her father was desperate to know what was going on. She was too, but suspected it had something to do with the Anglo-French diplomatic mission to Moscow. The general had not held out much hope for its success.

They drove on in silence; it pained Tess to see the pinched expression on Stork's brow. He was also grimacing with a lop-sided smile – something he always did when he was worried.

'We have to stand up to him,' she said. 'Hitler, I mean.'

Her father nodded. 'I know.'

'A couple of weeks ago I took the minutes of a meeting with Herr von Selzem, one of the secretaries at the German Embassy and the professor of a technical school in Danzig. General Ismay and von Selzem knew each other in India, you see, so they're old friends. He's actually rather nice and has an American wife, who is lovely. The professor talked on about Danzig and why it should be, by rights, part of Germany, then said, "Surely England would not fight for Danzig."'

'What did General Ismay say to that?' asked Alex.

'He said that Britain did not regard Danzig as a place so much as a principle. The professor looked at him with the most utter contempt and said, "But what could you do to save Poland?" It was ghastly. I wished he could have been sent packing there and then, but the general was wonderful. He warned him that the Kaiser had disregarded Britain's warning in 1914 and Germany had paid a terrible price. He hoped Herr Hitler wouldn't make the same mistake again. General Ismay never loses his temper but he did a bit then. "Let there be no mistake about it, Professor," he told him. "If you force us to go to war, we will get you in the end, as we got you last time." I must say, I felt like cheering and rushing over to give him a big hug.'

'He's quite right,' said Alex.

'Oh, I know he is,' said Stork, 'and of course we'll win. But twenty years ago we fought a hellish war to ensure no future generation had to go through it again. And yet here we are, on the brink, once more, facing a sabre-rattling Germany.'

Stork bade them farewell and drove back, taking the Shaftesbury road, then turned up and past the neat rows of stooks drying in the sun of the Fifty Acre field and climbed on up to the ridge. The stooks were a reassuring sight but so much else was uncertain. Next week, the week after, who could say? Might they be at war? Would hordes of bombers really be pulverizing British cities? It seemed unlikely to him from what he knew of aerial warfare, but modern all-metal monoplane aircraft were very different beasts from Dorothy or the machines he had flown in the Great War. Back then getting into bed at night and finding himself still alive had been a blessing; it had been impossible to think of any kind of future.

He remembered one particular night in April 1918, after a day in which three more of his men had been killed: he had vowed to himself that if he survived, he would settle down, back in the valley, surrounded by the chalk, and remain there for ever, farming the land.

He had done just that and, in the ten years since taking over the running of the farm from his father, he had given it a viable future too – at a time when farming had stagnated throughout much of the country. He'd modernized, been progressive, and damn well succeeded: his dairy herd was one of very few that produced the highest-quality milk, while they also ran more than four hundred sheep and grew arable crops as well. He'd invested in machinery, kept abreast of the latest developments and turned what had been a failing enterprise into one that was among the more successful in the south-west.

Now it seemed to him that the future he had so carefully built was no longer certain. His world seemed threatened in a way that was beyond his control. How had it come to this? How could they be on the brink of war again? He sighed and looked out. At least in the stooks there was a visible image of a more regular rhythm of life.

At the crossroads with the Herepath, he turned and parked. He could see Gilbert Rose repairing hurdles by his shepherd's hut and wanted to check the progress of the gyro-tiller a little further on.

'Afternoon, Gilbert,' he said, walking over.

Gilbert tipped his old felt hat. 'All the partying done, then?'

Stork nodded. 'Yes, thank goodness.'

Gilbert smiled ruefully. He was a big man – well over six feet tall, and although he was now over fifty, he remained fit and strong. Stork knew Gilbert had had barely any education, but had always reckoned him one of the wisest and most well-read men he'd ever met. 'He's an old soul,' Debbo had once remarked, and Stork had always thought that had been a very good way to describe him.

'So now you can finish off the harvest,' said Gilbert. 'Claude was none too happy about the cricket match yesterday.'

'Weather's set fair, though, isn't it?'

'For the next few days, certainly.'

Stork looked at the sheep spread out over the top of the downs. In the morning they were folded – collected together – then put into hurdles and fed cake and beets – but after dinner were driven up onto the downs. Stork never tired of watching Gilbert and his dogs at work, but then, looking out over the sheep peacefully munching the grass, he began to worry again about the changes that were sure to come. Ploughing meant less space for sheep.

'A penny for your thoughts, guv'nor,' said Gilbert.

Stork sighed. 'We've got to prepare for war,' he said. 'God willing, it might not happen, but we've got to be ready for it and that'll mean changes in how we do things. We've simply got to produce more of our own food. Free up shipping space.'

'Well, that's no bad thing. What farmers are s'posed to do. Anyway, there's always change,' said Gilbert, pausing to fill a pipe. 'Nothing stands still and it don' pay to feel soft about the past.' He gestured at the piles of uprooted furze, blackthorn and hawthorn, and the hill of flints that had been turned up by the gyro-tiller. 'It's a good job we're tidying up the downs, if you ask me. It weren't good to let all that scrub take hold up here.'

'It's awfully thin soil, though.'

'Mebbe,' agreed Gilbert, 'but the top of the downs was always ploughed when I was lad.'

'Not while I've been alive.'

'Mebbe not but it always used to be. An' my father used to fold his sheep up on the top of the downs. Thin it might have been, but with the sheep on it working in their dung it used to be good enough for arable. Yields weren't what they were down below on the better soil, but worthwhile until corn started coming in from America. That's what stopped it, but I reckon 'twould have been better to keep the downs clear and just had clover up here. That would have deepened the soil in time and that cursed furze wouldn't have taken root. It's an awful bind for the sheep. They goes wanderin' off and get caught up in it and it's a devil for adders.'

Stork smiled. 'I've seen Hector kill one.'

Gilbert smiled. 'Ah, he's a good 'un for catching adders, a'right, but I'm glad you're tidyin' up the downs. An' now they'll be wanting our grain again, won't they?'

Stork nodded.

'So, it's good to plough it up. Get it back to how it was.'

'Yes, I suppose so.' Stork smiled. 'But it may mean we have to cut back the flock, you know.'

Gilbert lit his pipe and shrugged. 'I wouldn't mind betting the two lads I've working for me'll join up. But with a smaller flock I'll manage, a'right. Your challenge won't be changin' ways, it'll be labour. When there's war there's allus young lads who wants to go off an' fight.'

'I'm not sure there's quite the same enthusiasm this time as there was in 1914, Gilbert.'

Gilbert sucked on his pipe. 'Mebbe not, but don't 'e be surprised when you start losing men.'

They walked over to piles of furze and thorn. 'We'll be clearing these as soon as harvest's done,' said Stork. 'And the RAF wants the flints.'

'Oh, aye?' said Gilbert.

'They're going to crush them down and use them for building ammunition bunkers over at Chilmark.'

'They payin' you for 'em?'

'Yes, and taking them away.'

'An' harvest almost in. Not all bad tidings, then.' Gilbert grinned. He let out another swirl of sweet pipe smoke and looked down the leeward side towards the village, with its folds and combes, all the way to the next ridge beyond. 'It's an ancient landscape, bain't it?

But folk come an' go. Things change, but the land allus needs farmin' one way or t'other.'

Stork left him, his mood a little improved. He had spent enough time away from the harvest this weekend, so headed straight to the yard to help build the ricks. He'd had a Dutch barn put up a couple of years earlier but that was already full to bursting with barley. For the remainder of the wheat and oats, storage would be the traditional way until it was time for threshing: building them up on the wooden base, next to a row of hayricks that had been put up back in May and again after a second cut just before harvest had begun.

Stork loved the smell of the hayricks, and their shape, rather like grass houses, always struck him as pleasing. There was a great skill to building such a thing. Claude Timbrell was the master rick-builder, but the Merriman brothers, Percy and Cecil, were also skilled and especially so at thatching them.

The hayricks were built from the ground up, but the cereal ricks had to be raised to keep the rats away. The rodents were the bane of any farmyard so a wooden base built upon staddle stones was the starting point. As Stork and Percy were laying down the start of an oat rick, Edward and Wilf arrived with a cart of sheaves and, having led the horses to the large stone trough by the stables, they began unloading, using the pitchfork to pick off the stacked bundles on the cart.

'Reckon you've finally got the knack of that, Wilf,' said Claude from the top of the neighbouring rick. 'How many harvests you done now?'

'He learned from the master, Claude, you know that.' Edward grinned.

'That 'e did,' said Percy. 'Me an' all!'

'Fork, swing, drop, fork, swing, drop,' said Wilf. 'I remember.'

'A'though,' added Percy, 'I reckon if 'e can master a Spitfire, 'e can master building a rick.'

Wilf laughed. 'An entirely different skill altogether, I can assure you. Flying a Spit is more like taming a stallion. They can be terribly frisky if you're not careful.'

All the men were glistening with sweat as the August sun bore down. Chickens clucked nearby, pecking at loose corn, and oats dropped from the bundles.

'You thought of building another Dutch barn, Dad?' asked Edward.

'I'm thinking of building two. Claude and I were talking of it just the other day. Chances are we'll have to grow more arable next year if . . .' Again, he stopped, then grimaced and sighed.

'It's all right, Dad,' said Edward, kindly.

'That bloody little man,' Stork muttered.

'Did you hear the story about Hitler and Göring at the top of a new radio tower in Berlin, Dad?' Edward said.

Stork, momentarily confused, said, 'No, what of it?'

'Well, apparently Hitler turned to the fat man and told him he wanted to put a smile on Berliners' faces so Göring said, "Why don't you jump?"'

The others laughed but Stork just muttered, 'I wish he would.'

Hannah Ellerby had spent much of that Sunday hoping she wouldn't get caught alone by Mr Denholm. Both he and Miss Coco had been down late to breakfast, but as she'd come in to clear some of the plates, he had winked at her and she had seen that Miss Coco had noticed it. Her stomach had churned and her cheeks burned with a mixture of embarrassment and anger.

For the next couple of hours, she and Susan had been clearing the marquee in the garden but then Mr Denholm had wandered out.

'Well done,' he said, as he ambled over to the tent. 'You're both doing sterling work.'

'Thank you, sir,' said Susan, who, having filled a basket, turned back to the house.

Seeing this, Hannah hurried to keep up, stumbled and tripped, the box of tablecloths falling onto the grass and the linen tumbling out.

Susan paused, but Mr Denholm said, 'Here, don't worry, I can help with this.'

'So,' he said, as he crouched down beside her, 'have you thought any more about my offer? I'll pay you very handsomely.'

Hannah felt tears pricking her eyes once more. Standing up, she said, 'I'm not that sort of girl, sir. I thank you for your offer but will have to decline and will thank you not to mention it again.'

Mr Denholm smiled. 'Good for you. A woman of principle. Well, you're a lovely-looking girl and I wish you health and happiness. But if you change your mind – well, I'm here until Tuesday.'

Hannah dared not look at him but instead strode towards the house, dabbing a sleeve to both eyes when she hoped no one was looking. She unloaded the dirty tablecloths in the laundry room, but with her hands shaking, and feeling light-headed, she stepped outside and went to the water pump. Here the water, drawn from the depths of the chalk below, was always wondrously cool. Pulling the lever, she waited for the first gush to tumble into the sarsen trough, then splashed her face. That felt better. She paused, hands on hips, trying to regain her composure when Tom Timbrell reached the yard with another corn cart.

'Hot work, eh, Hannah?' he said, grinning.

She nodded. 'How's the harvest going?'

'Nearly cleared Fifield. The binder's almost finished Great Clover.'

She forced a smile. 'That's good.'

Tom said to the horses, 'G'on then, have a quick drink now,' and led them to the giant trough. 'Hot work for us all.' He turned to Hannah. 'You all right, Hannah?'

'Yes, I'm fine,' she said, but she was about to burst into tears again. That couldn't happen – not here, not in front of Tom of all people. She tightened her hand on her apron but Tom saw this and said, 'What is it? You look all het up, Hannah.'

And at that she brought her hands to her face, unable to stop the flow of convulsive sobs.

'Hey, hey,' he said, and now she felt his arm on her shoulders. 'Whassa matter?'

For a moment she couldn't speak and kept her hands covering her face. 'It's nothing, I'm just bein' foolish,' she said at last. 'Please don't say anythin', Tom.'

She now looked around in panic that anyone else might have seen her. 'I mus' go,' she said.

'I don't like to see you upset,' said Tom. 'Here.' He handed her a patterned handkerchief from his pocket. 'Clean from the drawer this morning. Keep it.'

She took it and wiped her eyes. 'Thank you, Tom. I'm sorry you had to see me like this. Please don't say a word.'

'I promise. But if you need anything, you jus' tell me, all right?'

She nodded, did her best to smile, then turned and hurried back to the house.

Coco had accosted her father later that afternoon when she joined him in the rose garden. Most of the roses had long since peaked in June but there were some repeat-flowering varieties, and along the borders that lined the garden there was a shock of colour from dahlias, dianthus and zinnias. The pink brick reflected the sun's heat and trapped it, adding an almost Mediterranean warmth.

Denholm was reclining on a wicker lounger beneath a parasol, reading a book.

'Ah, Coco,' he said, looking up. 'Where are Pa and Maimes?'

'Grandpa has gone for a walk to look at his bees and Maimes is having a rest up in her room.'

'Come and join me. It's lovely out here.'

Coco perched on the edge of another lounger.

'And, tell me, am I still in the doghouse? I've barely seen you properly all weekend.'

'Why did you wink at the housemaid this morning?'

'Hm? Oh, she's a sweet girl. Just being friendly.'

'She looked awfully flustered.'

'I don't suppose she's used to being noticed. Pretty little thing, though. No doubt soon to be defrocked by some lusty farmhand from the village.' He smiled amicably.

'Later she was in tears.'

'Good gracious. Poor thing.'

'I saw her out in the yard by the pump. Something had upset her.'

Denholm put down his book. 'What are you driving at, Coco, darling? You're being terribly pointed, you know.'

'You were the one who said you were a boulevardier.'

'I didn't. I said Étienne was.'

'You said he was a bounder and you should know because you were one yourself.'

'So now you think I'm having my wicked way with the housemaid? Honestly, Coco, it's like some ghastly penny dreadful. "Keep your harnds orf me, maister!"' he said, feigning a bad West Country accent.

Coco could not help smiling. 'Make sure you behave, Papa. Otherwise, I'll have to tell Lucie.'

'Snitch on your own father? Good Lord, darling, what's the world coming to?'

Coco hadn't really believed him. Later, it occurred to her there was so much deceit between them. Many parts of his life were unknown to her: the evenings and even entire nights away, the sudden trips for days. If she ever grilled him, he always brushed aside her questions with smiles, charm and obfuscation. Then again, she had lied to him too – she always had. Small things for the most part, but later she had kept Étienne from him. It was almost as though there were an unwritten code between them: *I won't be entirely honest with you but I won't ask you too many questions either.*

The truth was, though, she had now begun to thaw. Already, her feelings for Étienne were changing from deep love to dislike; one night with Tom had seen to that. She had already begun to wonder whether she'd ever really been in love with Étienne at all. Perhaps she, too, had been in lust – in a kind of heady brain-addled state in which she'd not been thinking straight at all. Suddenly, though, that cloud had lifted and she could see more clearly again. Her father had been right, she thought, and she felt a kind of grudging gratitude towards him. She was also looking forward to her second tryst with her Paris in the old hut in the woods. She smiled. Really, the contrast between Étienne and Tom could not have been more marked.

'Did I say something amusing?' asked her father.

She didn't answer him but instead leaned over him, kissed his forehead and headed back towards the house.

Maud had been anxious to let Jean and Hannah get off home early after their efforts the previous two days and, after an early dinner that evening, announced that she was exhausted. Everyone turned in early, even Denholm. Fortunately for Coco, their rooms were at opposite ends of the house so while she had no doubt her father would be awake for some time yet, she was able to creep out without being seen or heard. She met Tom, as arranged, at the edge of Tippett's Wood at midnight.

'So, you came, then,' he said.

'Did you think I wouldn't?'

He shrugged in the moonlight. 'I weren't sure, to be honest.'

'You're the most perfect distraction, Tom,' she said, putting her arms around his neck and kissing him. She was touched to discover he tasted of toothpaste.

Once in the hut, they wasted no time, and afterwards, he led her to the step, wrapped with her in a rug, to gaze out into the moonlit wood, smoking a shared cigarette.

'I meant to ask, Tom,' she said, 'why are you always carrying a gun at night?'

'I'm the gamekeeper here. I've got to make sure my pheasants are safe. Guard them against predators.'

'Foxes?'

'Humans too. Poachers.'

She sat up. 'You mean poachers might come here and find us?'

He laughed. 'No chance. They'd never come here. No, normally I'd go looking for them. Hide where I think I might catch 'em.'

'Goodness,' she said, shuddering. 'Don't you get exhausted from all this night-time activity?'

'No, not really.'

It was her turn to laugh. 'How extraordinary. I'll probably sleep in until the middle of the morning.'

'Wasting the best part of the day, then.'

'It's either that or miss out on you. I need my beauty sleep, Tom.'

'You're that all right,' he said. 'A beauty, that is. Don't want that goin' to your head, mind.'

She passed him back the cigarette. 'And you're quite the most beautiful man I've ever met. A bit rough around the edges, perhaps, but handsome for an Englishman. All the girls in the village must simply adore you. How come you haven't got a girl? Or have you?'

He shook his head. 'No. No, there's no one.' He took the cigarette, inhaled, then breathed out again, the cloud of smoke swirling in front of them.

'Not even the housemaid at the manor? Hannah?'

He turned a little too quickly.

'Ah! So, you do like her, then!'

'She's a sweet girl,' he said, 'but she don't like me, not in that way.'

'I saw you with her earlier. In the yard. She was upset.'

'She was. Dunno what that was about. She wouldn't say. She was real het up, mind.'

'Poor girl.'

'Couldn't jus' ignore her. Most we've said to each other in a long while.'

'Maybe you should try a little harder with her.'

He drew on the cigarette. 'Not while you're here.'

'Not for long. We go back to France in a couple of days. This was only ever going to be a brief romance, sadly.'

He nodded silently, and they were quiet for a moment.

'It all seems so uncertain, don't it?' he said eventually. 'All this talk of war.'

'What will you do?'

'That fellow of Miss Tess's – Captain Woodman – he wants me to join his guards' regiment.'

'And will you?'

'I'd rather stay here. But if there's a war, they'll need men like me. I'm a decent shot, and I know how to look after myself.'

'Won't you be needed here too? Everyone will want food.'

He flicked away the cigarette and ran a hand through his hair. 'Oh, I dunno. God knows what will 'appen. I'm sick of all the talk of it. What will be will be, eh?'

She leaned her head against his shoulder. Even now she could smell the dust and corn, a faint residue of horse and sweat. It wasn't at all unpleasant, she thought.

Later, Tom walked her to the manor and, in the yard at the back of the house, said, in a low whisper, 'I daren't go any further in case we're heard.'

'Off you go, then,' she said.

Tom glanced around furtively, gave her a somewhat chaste kiss on the cheek, then set off back towards the track. Coco smiled to herself and took out a cigarette. It still felt curiously warm – she realized she wasn't a bit cold. Lighting the cigarette, she watched him for perhaps a minute, as he walked silently towards the wood, until he disappeared from view. Rather like a ghost, she thought. There one moment, then vanished. Gone.

She walked round into the garden, the gate creaking painfully loudly. No one stirred, though, and no dog barked. She breathed in the late-summer air – so fresh and sharp. A mixture of grass and yew and dry soil. She sought a bench cut into an alcove of the yew hedge and looked up at the moon, high over the downs. She wondered whether she would ever see Tom again, and felt a pang that surprised her.

But it did not last long. Who knew what lay around the corner? In these times, it seemed to her, there was not much point in thinking too far ahead. Neatly extinguishing her cigarette, she exhaled the smoke into the moonlit night air and turned back towards the house.

7

Call-up

Monday, 21 August 1939

THE PREVIOUS DAY TESS HAD REACHED THE OFFICES AT WHITEHALL
by half past four to be met with a pile of memos that needed typing
followed by the latest revisions for the War Book. Not until she'd
handed it back to Bill Elliott some time after ten o'clock did she
learn what had been going on.

'Thank you, Tess,' said Elliott, as she'd stepped into his office and
handed over the document. Sitting on the other side of his desk were
two of the majors on Ismay's staff, Ian Jacob and Leslie Hollis. A
bottle of whisky stood on the table and each man had a tumbler.
Cigarette smoke hung heavily in the air despite the open window
that overlooked the Thames. 'Looks like the Moscow Mission failed,'
he muttered, 'and now it seems von Ribbentrop is in Moscow too.'

'What does that mean, sir?' she asked.

'We're not sure exactly, but it may well be they'll agree some kind
of pact over Poland.'

'I can't believe that,' said Hollis. 'It beggars belief. They're ideo-
logically opposed and the Nazis and the Bolsheviks loathe one
another.'

'Hmm,' muttered Elliott. 'I'm not so sure.'

Jacob picked up the War Book. 'We need to get the ball rolling,'
he said. '"Institute Precautionary Stage."'

'I agree we should urge Ismay to advise it,' agreed Elliott. He

71

looked up and saw Tess still standing at the edge of the desk. 'Thank you, Tess. You head home now, but we'll need you in early tomorrow. Ismay's on the night train and will be here by eight.'

Tess nodded, bade them goodnight and left, her mind reeling. She walked back to the house in Pimlico barely conscious of the buildings and streets around her. If Germany and the Soviet Union agreed a deal over Poland, it was ever more likely that Hitler would invade. And that meant war. As Ismay and his staff had repeatedly stressed, Britain was not bluffing: there could be no more standing back and watching from afar.

That night she went to bed and held Alex tightly, wondering how many more nights they might have together. To have found love and then, after such a brief idyll, to have it taken away. Closing her eyes, she prayed hard that war would, somehow, some way, be averted and that if it really should happen, that Alex, her brothers and all her family would be safe.

The next day confirmation arrived that the Anglo-French Mission's talks in Moscow had collapsed. 'I can't say I'm surprised we got nowhere,' Tess heard Ismay say. 'Our heart wasn't in it. I'm sure most of us in Britain find Communism almost as odious as Nazism.' The following day, however, Tuesday, the bombshell reached them, via the Joint Intelligence Committee, that the German and Soviet foreign ministers, von Ribbentrop and Molotov, had agreed a deal, which was publicly confirmed the following day, Wednesday, 23 August.

Ismay had called an immediate meeting, his whole team present. Tess was taking minutes. He sat at the head of the table, looking immaculate as he always did, medal ribbons of the last war and beyond above the right-hand pocket of his khaki tunic. He sighed deeply. 'Who could have imagined that two gangsters, having spent the past few years heaping the vilest abuse on one another, would kiss and make friends overnight?'

'But they are vile, sir,' said Elliott. 'I agree it demonstrates a new level of cynicism we've suspected but which has now been laid bare.'

Ismay nodded. 'Yes, indeed. But I'm afraid the Prime Minister is still reluctant to institute the precautionary stage.'

'Even now?' said Hollis.

'Even now. He's still not given up all hope of reaching some kind of an accommodation with Germany. Both he and the Cabinet are determined to avoid doing anything that might heat the temperature or make the rest of the world start feeling war is inevitable. Obviously, from a practical point of view, implementing the precautionary stage straight away would be extremely advisable, but as you are all very well aware, gentlemen, it's also true that in doing so innumerable measures of immense variety would be set in motion all around the world, from the armed forces to merchant shipping to the impact on our empire, and could hardly escape notice.'

'So we do nothing for the time being?' asked Bill Elliott.

'Not exactly. Let me spell out some changes. Chamberlain's setting up a small War Cabinet, rather as Lloyd George did in the last war, and the secretariats of the Cabinet and the Committee for Imperial Defence are merging into a single body. It will be headed up by Sir Edward Bridges. There'll be two wings – one civilian and one military. I'm going to be in charge of the latter.'

'That sounds like much the same,' said Elliott.

'Except that it brings military and civilian defence requirements under one overall umbrella that's ultimately answerable to the much smaller War Cabinet. Our task for the moment is to meet daily with the various heads of all government departments and work out the minimum precautionary measures that can be postponed no longer. I'm afraid that mobilization will be one of them – very probably as early as tomorrow.'

It was only with the very greatest of self-discipline that Tess was able to keep writing her shorthand of General Ismay's words. Alex, Wilf, probably Edward as well. She wanted to weep.

'Does that include Territorials?' asked Ian Jacob.

'Yes, but not all at once. We need to avoid a rush and undue strain on the railway network. As for everything else, from the evacuation of children from cities to the implementation of ARP measures, to shipping and any large-scale military movements, we'll take a view on each passing day.'

Later, when Tess handed Ismay the fully typed-up minutes, he thanked her. 'I don't think I've ever asked, Tess, but do you have any brothers or sisters of fighting age?'

She nodded. 'My older brother is in the Yeomanry and my younger brother a pilot in the RAF flying Spitfires.'

He nodded thoughtfully.

'We're not going to avoid war, are we, sir?'

Ismay sighed. 'I fear not. I don't mind admitting I'm furious. With the Nazis and with ourselves. Barely twenty years ago the Germans were prostrate at our feet but now here they are, at our throats. I can't believe we've been so craven and careless as to let this happen. And I'm sorry from the bottom of my heart that this time around it's young men like your brothers who'll be facing the enemy.'

Tess could not speak. The enormity of his words seemed to fill the room with an awfulness she could barely comprehend, as if Ismay's panelled office had palpably changed in the moments since he'd uttered them. She felt quite suffocated by it somehow. It seemed so mad, so fantastical, that Hitler and his Nazis could have been allowed to reach a point at which another war in Europe was about to erupt. She nodded at him, smiled, then turned and left.

Thursday, 24 August 1939

By eleven in the morning, Edward was helping Percy Merriman and others at the rick when his mother drove into the yard in the Wolseley in a cloud of dust. Screeching to a halt, she clambered out and, waving a piece of paper, called, 'Edward! Edward!'

Hurrying over he saw her ashen face. 'A telegram,' she said. 'I thought I'd better open it.'

'Of course,' he said. He almost dared not take it from her and could feel his heart starting to quicken. He knew what it was but forced himself to read the words. *So,* he thought, *mobilization.* He was to join the regiment immediately. Swallowing hard, he said, as brightly as he could muster, 'Goodness. Sounds a bit serious, doesn't it?'

Debbo nodded. 'Oh, darling. First Wilf off to rejoin his squadron and now you've got to go as well. It's too awful.'

'We're not at war yet,' he said, hoping he looked and sounded more cheerful than he felt. 'And it'll probably be over before Wilf and I are needed. I'm sure it's not going to be like the last war.'

She put a hand to his cheek. 'My darling boy.'

'We'll be all right, Mum.' He looked at his watch. 'Well,' he said, 'I suppose I ought to get back to the house and collect my things.

74

I'm afraid Percy might take a bit of a dim view of my bunking off like this, though.'

'Where's your father?' she asked.

'He's on the binder at Blindwell.'

'You can't go without saying goodbye to him.'

'I might well be back by the weekend, though,' he said doubtfully. He looked at his watch again. 'I can borrow Percy's bicycle and hurry on over.'

It was harder work on the bicycle than he'd expected and Edward was sweating and short of breath by the time he found his father. When he told him his news, he'd never seen his father look so upset. 'Try not to worry, Dad,' he said. 'I'm sure it'll blow over.'

'Let's hope so. Make sure you write – or call if you can.'

Edward held up three fingers. 'Scout's promise.' He looked around the field. 'Well, at least harvest's nearly in. It's been a marvellous couple of weeks, Dad. I've loved being at home and helping. Look after Mum, won't you?'

His father swallowed hard. 'Of course.' He held out his hand. 'Good luck.'

As Edward cycled away, towards the farm, he glanced back and saw his father still watching him. He was sorry to be leaving and felt rather as he had at the end of the long summer holidays when he'd had to go back to school. As it was, the regimental headquarters at Devizes were not so very far from Denleigh College, so much of the journey he was about to undertake was the same.

He wondered now, though, when he might next be back. Lurking in his mind was the terrible thought that he might never see his home again, although he swiftly pushed it away. Trying to think more rationally, it seemed to him unlikely the regiment would be seeing active service any time soon, for he was quite aware they were barely trained and far from ready to face any foe. Not on horseback, at any rate. That would be absurd! Surely those higher up the chain would recognize that.

Just over half an hour later, he was in his Yeomanry uniform of khaki tunic, Sam Browne and bandolier, riding breeches and cavalry boots, his kitbag and paint box, easel and brushes in his old Austin Ruby in the yard at Farrowcombe.

'You look just like the photograph of Uncle John when he went off to war,' said his mother, who had come out to bid him farewell.

Edward grinned ruefully. 'I do feel a bit ridiculous. It's been good fun with the Yeomanry but I'm not sure mounted cavalry is going to cut the mustard. The regular army all have tanks.'

'Perhaps they'll give you tanks too.'

'Perhaps, although I doubt any time soon. I suppose I'll find out a bit more about what's expected when I get to the regiment. Honestly, though, Mum, I don't think it'll be as it was in 1914. I shan't be on a steamship to France this time tomorrow or anything like that.'

She kissed him. 'I shall try to hold on to that thought, darling,' she said, as she brushed something from his shoulder. 'You look so different in your uniform. No longer my little boy.'

'I feel different in my uniform. And I am twenty-three, Mum.' He looked at his watch. 'Time to go,' he said, a leaden feeling consuming him. 'Send my love to Uncle John, Aunt Carin and the cousins. And to Grandpa and Maimes.' He was rather glad he'd not had to say goodbye to them all. It would have been too disheartening and Edward was determined not to feel disheartened, even though his stomach was churning with a dead weight of apprehension.

He got into his car. Lowering the window he blew his mother a kiss, put the Austin into gear and lurched off. *They haven't declared war yet*, he told himself. *It might not happen.* And if it didn't, he could return to the Slade and still become the artist he hoped to be. He gave a last wave, sighed and pulled out a cigarette. *I'll be fine*, he told himself again, but was aware of an unmistakable heavy feeling in the pit of his stomach.

8

Countdown

AT ROSE BOWER, THEIR HOME A COUPLE OF MILES FURTHER WEST from Alvesdon towards Shaftesbury, John and Carin Castell were still at the breakfast table, although all three children had cycled to the farm to help finish the harvest. Carin was reading the previous day's *Times*.

'Goodness,' she said. 'There's a letter here urging people not to be unkind to German dogs. If the writer's worried about dogs, what will it mean for German people here?' She put down the paper and glanced anxiously at her husband.

John smiled. 'I know it's a bit alarming, my darling, but no one will treat you differently here. I'm sure measures of some sort will be taken but not for people like yourself who have lived here for so many years.'

She smiled nervously. 'I hope you are right.'

John got up and moved towards her. Leaning over her, he brought his arms around her and kissed the top of her head.

'Remember what it was like when we first came here, already married? Everyone was horrified!' He laughed. 'We shocked a few people then, didn't we? But they soon saw what a wonderful person you are and accepted you as part of the family and the community. It didn't take long. There might be a little bit of anti-German senti-ment if there's war, but it won't last, and we mustn't take it

77

personally. You're different, my beloved Carin, but in all the right ways.' He kissed her again.

'And we have three perfectly English children,' she said. 'That must make the authorities look more kindly upon me, surely.'

'Of course it will. Really, darling, please try not to worry. Not about that at any rate.'

She turned her head and kissed him on the lips: her adored John, with his still-thick auburn hair and wide, gentle face. His words hardly allayed her worries, though. It was true that she did feel accepted but her accent was, she knew, still markedly German despite her very best efforts to iron it out. She was also aware that she looked much as many perceived Germans to look: lean-faced, still-blonde hair – she'd not yet found a single grey – and blue eyes. She stood out, she knew, among these English farming folk and this was not a time to feel conspicuous.

She finished her coffee. She hoped John was right, but last year, during the Munich crisis, she'd heard a few comments here and there, in the village stores and round about. In Salisbury someone had even shouted at her to 'go home'.

'I must go, darling,' said John. 'Poor Stork. He's a lot to think about at the moment. Dickie Varney too. I'm not sure now is the time to be a dairy farmer.'

'But people will still need milk, surely?'

'They will but they'll want grain even more.'

'I think the farm is the least of their worries if there's war,' said Carin. 'All those children going off to fight.' She sighed. 'I think Ollie will join up.'

'Ollie? Are you sure?'

She shrugged. 'It was something he said the other day. About volunteers having a choice about what they joined. Elsa wasn't here at the time. I thought it best not to say anything. She'll be heartbroken.'

'Well, it hasn't happened yet. We've been waiting for Hitler to invade Poland and he's done nothing these past few days so maybe he'll confound us and leave the Poles alone.'

After John left, Carin went out into the garden. The sky above was clear blue; it was going to be another hot day. Outside, the back of the house was lined by a brick path then a lawn extending down towards the River Chalke. There was a pair of ash trees, in which the remains of the children's tree house still stood, a reminder of the carefree days. Maria was still only fourteen but she was growing up fast and, with Robbie and Elsa older, desperate not to be left behind.

Carin walked slowly down the lawn, past rows of flowerbeds, towards the river. There was a bench overlooking it and reaching it she sat down and gazed into the crystal-clear water. A dragonfly, brilliantly turquoise, hovered above the surface then darted off. From one of the ashes a wood pigeon cooed rhythmically. So English, she thought, and glanced back towards the house. She smiled to herself. Really, she could not have married into a more English family or existence.

A remembered conversation with John. The first time she had taken him to her family's country house in the mountains, south of Munich at Walchensee: a traditional, chalet-style wooden house, overlooking the lake and with the mountains towering all around.

'But, Carin,' he had exclaimed, 'it's exactly how I'd imagined! The perfect German alpine house. Heidi and the Brothers Grimm rolled into one!'

And, really, the British were not so very different from the Germans. Traditional, conservative, northern Europeans. The links from the deep past were greater than that, though, as she'd realized when she'd first walked the Herepath, the ancient chalk track that ran the length of the northern ridge of chalk downs. *Here* was originally Anglo-Saxon, a word meaning 'army'. So, the Army Path – a military route of some kind. In German the word was still *Heer* – much the same. She had pointed this out to John, who had been astonished, and then, she recalled, rather delighted. 'Well, I'm an Anglo-Saxon, so German in origin,' he'd said, 'so really, when you think about it, I haven't married a foreigner at all but one of my own kind.'

There was a German word for this link between land, culture and family: *Heimat* – what Martin Luther had called 'the land of my kindred'. This place, she thought, this hidden valley of chalkland, was the Castells' *Heimat*, just as the Bavarian Alps at Walchensee had been hers. In her childhood memory it had been a paradise that was always beautiful, whether in summer, autumn, winter or spring, and good and pure, somehow. Superficially, perhaps, it remained unchanged – her childhood homes in Munich and Walchensee remained one and the same after all – but now the entire country was stained with flowing swastika banners, vivid red, white and black, while the entire nation, it seemed, had become bewitched by this awful malaise: a cancer that kept the nation in thrall to Hitler and his appalling ideology. How could it have happened? And how could her father and brother have been so hoodwinked? A terrible, jarring thought kept infecting her mind: that perhaps, had she remained in Bavaria and not been whisked away by her fairytale prince to England, she, too, would have been equally under his spell. Such thoughts were hard to dispel, hard to understand.

She'd last seen them the previous Christmas, when she and John and the children had all gone to Walchensee, snow on the ground and everything looking so very lovely and perfect. Yet it had been far from lovely and perfect: her brother, Otto, wearing a Party badge on the lapel of his suit, their boy, Julius – her nephew! – soon to complete his training as a pilot in the Luftwaffe and talking quite openly and proudly about how the new German air force was the standard-bearer for the new military might of the Reich.

Even her father had extolled the virtues of the Führer. She winced, remembering that Christmas Eve dinner. The dining room, with its open fire, wood panels, antlers on the walls and Alpine landscapes, had been the same as it had always been, yet it was transformed by the words spoken that night. She remembered John suggesting they all leave politics behind and everyone had agreed, until Carin had commented that Bavaria seemed reassuringly the same as always.

What a mistake that seemingly innocuous remark had been! Oh, but it wasn't, Otto had pronounced. Bavaria and all of Germany had embarked on a new golden age in which Germany would dominate Europe and become one of the greatest nations in the world. And they had Hitler to thank for this transformation. His vision, his charisma, his leadership. He'd brought jobs and prosperity, managed to regain German land lost in 1919 and without a shot being fired, and he was standing up to the Bolsheviks, the single greatest threat to European prosperity. Germany had had democracy, her father had chimed in, and looked what had happened. It had descended into a moral quagmire, the laughing stock of the world.

'But he's a despot,' Carin had replied, 'and a liar, and he's going to lead us all back into war.'

'Carin,' Otto had said, 'the British should keep their noses out. This is not their quarrel.'

'But you have secret police and the Gestapo and SS thugs. It's horrible. You're no longer free to think what you like and anyone who disagrees is put in some dreadful prison camp. And what about the poor Jews? His treatment of them is appalling. It's monstrous.'

'There are police forces to keep order in England just the same,' Otto retorted, 'and as for the Jews, I happen to think Hitler is quite right. They've brought nothing but disaster to this country. They're different from us. We have to make Germany pure again.'

'You simply can't believe that, Otto!' she had exclaimed.

'Can't I?'

'The Jews are a different people, Carin,' added her father. 'I have known some fine Jews but there has to be a general clear-out. It's not nice having to drive them out, I agree, but within a generation or so, they'll be gone, living elsewhere, and everyone, Jew and German alike, will be glad of it. You mark my words.'

'And the English should be grateful to the Führer for fighting Bolshevism,' continued Otto. 'One day, Germany may well have to fight the Soviet Union. To defend the West from the East, to protect Europe from the spread of Communism. Think of that, Carin, before you come over here and start preaching to us. You were not here in the days of the Weimar. You have no conception about how difficult it has been. But at last Germany is strong again – strong and increasingly prosperous. Business is good, thanks to Hitler and the National Socialists. It's because of Hitler that we can all sit here tonight, the family together again, eating and drinking and enjoying Christmas.'

She had been so shocked, so upset. Her parents had not been early enthusiasts of Hitler and neither had Otto, but that Christmas it had been as though they had all transformed into entirely different people; they looked the same, but their minds had been taken over. Recently, she had read Kafka's *Metamorphosis* and had felt like the protagonist – an outcast suddenly from her own family.

The relief she had felt on returning to the valley had been overwhelming. This, she had thought, was her home. This was where she belonged, yet now, with Britain and Germany on the very brink of war again, she felt a little like the outsider she had been when first she'd returned as John's wife nearly twenty years before. She was now glad she had offered to help her friend Maggie Gready, who was the billeting officer in Alvesdon, if and when the evacuation of children from the cities began. Maggie had been on standby since the announcement of the German–Soviet pact, and together they had lined up a number of people in the village to take in children. Most approached had agreed, accepting it as part of a civil obligation, although few were much thrilled at the prospect of welcoming strange children from cities into their home.

She looked back at her English house and English garden, and for all the uncertainty, for all the possible anguish to come, she offered a silent prayer of thanks to God: that she had met her John, to whom she had been happily married for twenty years, that she had been blessed with three wonderful children, that she had made her home here, in this little forgotten corner of England, and that she had not remained in Germany. She thought again of her family, so seduced by Hitler and the Nazis. She hoped they would be safe but she also vowed that, no matter what happened, she would fight to save her life here. This was her *Heimat*.

Stork had asked Dickie Varney and John to meet him in his office at Farrowcombe, the brick-and-flint tower at the corner of the three-sided yard of outbuildings and stables. Once a grain store, it had been Debbo, with her artist's eye, who had suggested the second storey could be his office. Rotting beams had been replaced and new floorboards put in, along with a small stove and chimney; windows had been enlarged providing views towards Farrowcombe Hill and the house. Since 1929, when he had taken over the day-to-day running of the farm, this had been the headquarters of his modernizing. In 1932, an electricity cable had been strung from the main network that led to the house. There was a large leather-topped desk, filing cabinets, shelves and two armchairs. It meant he could work there, in comfort, and leave Farrowcombe purely for living.

When he had arrived back in Alvesdon after the war, the farm had been in trouble. Farmers had been largely abandoned by the government in the early 1920s. They had been ordered to plough the land during the war, which particularly affected the mixed farms of Wiltshire, and had been given no price guarantees once the fighting was over. When cheaper grain had started flowing again across the Atlantic from North America, the bottom had fallen out of the market and British farmers had been left to fend for themselves. Many had faced ruin. Many had been ruined.

Alvesdon had survived. The family owned a number of properties, not just in Alvesdon but in Salisbury too, and the rent brought in a steady and welcome stream of income. They had also had enough financial reserves to keep going, and then there was the family-owned brewery in Shaftesbury, which had done well enough in the twenties. Even in the hardest times there was still a demand for beer. None the less, these assets were not enough to enable them to survive for ever, which was why Stork had worked so hard to turn the farm around. To modernize. To spread the natural risks of farming by becoming a truly mixed enterprise. And to invest in machinery and other, ancillary, means of bringing in income. Much of their arable crop, for example, was barley, which was used for malting and for the brewery, run by John but jointly owned by the family.

Stork was not sure how a war would affect the brewery. Beer would still be needed but they might now be forced to grow more wheat and oats. He thought it entirely possible they could do both. It would mean some changes. Then there was what to do to help Dickie, who ran an almost entirely dairy operation. Not only was Dickie an old friend, he was also their tenant. They had to face these challenges together.

John and Dickie arrived within minutes of each other, punctually at eight.

'What can Hitler be waiting for?' said Dickie, as they sat down.

'I haven't got anything out of Tess, I'm afraid,' said Stork. 'Official Secrets and all that. Last-minute diplomatic wrangling, perhaps? Hitler trying to work out whether Britain and France are bluffing? But God knows.'

'I saw Reg Mundy on my way here,' said Dickie. 'He told me with enormous confidence that the war's off.'

'Hmm. Wishful thinking, I fancy,' said Stork. 'Anyway, we've got to be ready if it does happen.'

'Have you made up your mind about the War Ag, Stork?' asked John.

'I'm going to see Richard Stratton this afternoon over at Codford.

I want to know a bit more about what's needed first, but I rather feel as though I ought to, don't you?'

'I think so,' agreed John. 'We're all going to have to do our bit.'

'But we also need to make sure to stick to the new guidelines, which will inevitably come in, and we still have to maintain profitable enterprises. That means we'll have to change how we do things and will hold true whether I'm part of the War Ag or not. Regardless of what Pa says, the government is going to want more arable. It's what delivers the most calories per acre.'

'Milk production will be a priority, though,' said Dickie.

'Yes, it'll be important and especially the quality you produce. My guess from what I've been reading and hearing is that those aligned to the standards of the Milk Marketing Board will be all right.'

They talked on. There would be more ploughing – not just of the downland but also pasture. That might affect Dickie's dairy herd. Then there was the question of more machinery to make up for the inevitable loss of farm workers. The government had a deal with Fordson for tractors but no one liked them much.

'I'm trying to work out whether we can afford a couple of Allis-Chalmers,' said Stork. 'Truth is, there's a hell of a lot to think about. But I'd like to pool resources, Dickie. It makes sense. You've worked damned hard to get Chalkway into decent shape. I appreciate there's not a lot of room for manoeuvre so we'll do what we can to help.'

'Well, I can't deny that's a great weight off my shoulders. As you know, I sank much of my capital into the Hosier milking machines. Thank you – both of you. Yet again, I seem to be in your debt.'

Stork waved a hand. 'Don't think of it like that, Dickie. You're also our tenant and it's in our interest to ensure your farm is profitable.'

'Stork's right,' agreed John, then said, 'And the brewery?'

'I'm hoping that by sowing the top of the downs and turning over more fields to the plough we can maintain the amount of barley and keep the brewery going as strongly as ever. Again, though, it all depends on what the government decides about the need for beer in wartime.'

'And the beef herd?'

Stork grimaced.

'I think I should come with you when you tell Pa,' said John.

'They'll have to go. They produce less food per acre than any other beast or crop. I can't help that. But I'm certainly not planning to do anything until we know for sure what's happening and what's expected.' He sighed again. 'I suppose we need to hold on to what certainties there are – and one thing is sure: if we go to war again, us farmers are going to have to produce a lot more food because they'll be wanting to keep shipping for other goods as much as possible.'

'That's not going to be without its challenges,' added Dickie.

Stork rubbed his forehead. 'I know.'

The following day it was announced that the evacuation of children would begin on Friday, 1 September, prompting Carin and Maggie to cycle hurriedly round to all those who earlier in the year had pledged to take in children. By two o'clock that afternoon Carin was waiting at the village hall with Maggie for the first busload to arrive from Southampton when Maggie's husband, Philip, the village doctor, arrived with the news that the Germans had invaded Poland earlier that day.

'It was on the lunchtime news,' he said. 'The government has given them until Sunday morning at eleven to pull back or we'll declare war.'

Carin felt a nauseous sensation deep in her stomach.

'I can hardly believe it,' said Maggie. 'I know we've all been expecting it, but it seems so incredible that we should be going through this all over again.'

'We will manage,' said Carin. She looked at her clipboard with its list of all those who were willing to take in children. 'We have a job to do and it will be much better to be busy.'

'Yes, yes, you're quite right,' said Maggie. 'Keep our minds off things.'

Soon after, Philip reappeared at the village hall carrying several cardboard boxes and was followed by another man similarly laden.

'This is Mr McKinnon,' he told Maggie and Carin. 'The medical officer for the rural district.'

'Hello,' he said cheerily, in a Scottish lilt from behind the boxes. 'I thought it might be quicker and easier to start distributing this stuff myself.'

'It's medical equipment for the head warden,' said Philip. 'In case we're bombed.'

'Goodness,' said Maggie.

'Not that some Dettol, bandages, lint and splints are going to do an awful lot of good,' added Mr McKinnon cheerfully. 'Let's hope you won't need it.'

'Yes, let's,' said Philip.

'Should I get Donald Pierson?' asked Maggie.

'No, don't worry,' said Philip. 'I'll nip round in a minute. You'd better wait here for your evacuees.'

The bus arrived soon after. There were just sixteen children in all, aged five to thirteen, and one young woman, who had accompanied them and who told them she was called Edith Blythe. 'But please call me Edie,' she added. She was of medium height, in her mid-twenties, Carin guessed, hair freshly curled, bright lipstick, and had an air of intelligent competence about her.

'I'm a teacher,' she added. 'These children are at the school where I work in Southampton.'

'Are we expecting any more?' asked Maggie.

'I'm not entirely sure,' said Edie, 'but I don't think so. We were part of an entire trainload but the billeting officer in Wilton divided us up. We were put on different buses and we've ended up here. But I do know all these children. It was thought best to try to keep them together. Some are brothers and sisters.'

'Well, let's keep them together here, if we can,' Maggie suggested and, with Edie's help, began taking a note of them all.

Carin headed into the village hall where two trestle tables had been set up. Earlier, she had prepared egg sandwiches and a number of *Windbeutel*, small traditional Bavarian pastries filled with cream, cherries and raspberries. Carefully, she took off the tea-towels laid over them to keep the flies away, then began pouring tumblers of lemon squash from a large jug. The task complete, she took a deep breath and looked around. On the wall hung a large, framed portrait of the King, George VI. Near the entrance was a noticeboard with ARP instructions pinned to it; Donald Pierson, the village ARP warden and also the shopkeeper, had held regular classes here for the village, first the previous autumn during the Munich affair, and then again over the past few weeks, with the help of a warden from

Wilton. Everyone knew the drill: how the blackout was to be strictly observed, how to cover windows efficiently, what to do if any incendiary bombs fell nearby, basic fire drill, and how to use a gas mask. Would Hitler really drop gas? Carin wondered.

With everything ready, she took another deep breath and went back outside onto the green. 'We're ready in the hall,' she told Maggie, who nodded, then clapped her hands. 'Children, I expect you must all be terribly hungry.'

'I had a sandwich on the train, miss,' said one of the older boys.

'He stole mine!' a girl said.

'All right. Well, there are some refreshments in the hall if you'd all follow me. Then we can get you to your respective hosts.'

Inside, the older children made a beeline for the tables. 'Do help yourselves,' said Carin. 'To a plate, then sandwiches and pastries.'

'You sound funny,' said another of the boys, a short, round-faced lad. 'Are you foreign? Not German, are you?'

'That's enough, Denis,' said Edie, sharply. 'You remember your manners, thank you very much.'

'Actually,' said Carin, 'I was born and brought up in Germany, yes, but I have been living here for twenty years.'

'Cor!' said the boy. 'A real German, here in this village!'

'I said that's enough!' said Edie.

'Really, it's all right,' said Carin. She poured more squash but overfilled the tumbler and it spilled onto the tablecloth. 'Too clumsy of me,' she said, and noticed a number of the children pointing at her and sniggering. *They're just children*, she told herself, then to Edie, added, 'My husband was born and brought up here. We have three children.'

'Well, it's a lovely tea you've laid on,' said Edie, smiling. 'Thank you ever so. I'm afraid they're all a bit excitable today. Most have never been to the countryside before so everything seems a bit new.'

Mr Roberts, the village schoolteacher, arrived soon after and introduced himself. 'Do call me Christopher,' he said to Edie.

'Very nice to meet you,' she said. 'I'm here to help with the teaching.'

'Ah, yes, thank you,' he said. 'We could certainly do with an extra pair of hands now we have all these new children joining us.'

Billeting the children took the rest of the afternoon. One family of two brothers and a sister was sent to Alvesdon Manor, with Edie Blythe, while Stork and Debbo took in two boys, both aged twelve, who were given one of the spare rooms. The Piersons agreed to have a young girl, while Reg and Eileen Mundy at the forge took a girl; the Greadys found rooms for two boys, and the Varneys for a nine-year-old girl. The Liddells took three, the vicar and his wife took in another two, and Carin agreed that a thirteen-year-old girl called Ruby should go with her to Rose Bower. By half past five the last child had been found a home.

While her mother had been helping with the evacuees, Carin's elder daughter, Elsa, had spent the afternoon with Oliver Varney. She had worked hard on the farm for much of the summer, but with the harvest now all cut, if not yet entirely gathered in, her uncle Stork had been only too happy to let her go for the afternoon. They had taken their bicycles and ridden further down the valley to a quiet patch on the river where there was the remains of an old sluice gate, long since abandoned, and beyond it was a deep pool where they could bathe. It was overlooked by ageing willows.

It was at this very spot that Ollie had first kissed Elsa the previous summer. They had been the best of friends in their early teens. They had just got out of the pool, feet muddy from the chalky clay at the edge of the bank, and were drying on the grass beneath one of the willows. Ollie had leaned over, looked at her with wonderment and, without a further word, closed his eyes and brought his mouth to hers. After that, Elsa had told him she loved him, had always loved him, and always would. And Ollie had said he felt the same. 'I think we're meant to be together for always,' he'd said, with a certainty she found both thrilling and reassuring.

To look at, Elsa was the image of her mother, slender, with very fair blonde hair and pale blue eyes. But her pragmatism came from her father. Long before Ollie had kissed her beneath the willow tree, she had been certain she wanted one day to marry him and live in the valley on the farm, and remain there for evermore. She quite accepted that others were not yet so certain of what they wanted from life, but for her, the path was clear. It was just how it was.

Of course she adored her parents, got on perfectly well with her younger brother, Robbie, and even Maria, despite the four-year age gap. She also loved her cousins very much and had always looked up to Tess, especially. However, for all her love of her family and for the friends she had made at school, there had been no one she would rather be with than Ollie. They loved the countryside, were interested in much the same things, and enjoyed long walks, rides on their bicycles and sailing. Sailing was in the Varney blood and their farm in Dorset had been on the coast; Dickie had been in the Royal Navy in the last war. Since moving to the valley, they had kept a small yacht at Poole and had introduced Elsa to its mysteries and pleasures when she had been just eleven years old.

Yet there was more between them than shared interests and time spent together. Ollie was funny and teased her gently whenever she became too dogmatic or bossy. She had always felt completely at ease in his company and she loved the freckles on his face and the way his dark brown hair grew upwards from his brow on the right-hand side of his head but not the left.

Over the past ten years, the only time she'd worried about her relationship with him was during the summer holidays before he'd kissed her. He had just left school and she still had a year to go, but it wasn't that: it was that they had grown up. His physical change had been gradual through his teenage years; he'd never had spots or suddenly spoken with a deep voice. Ollie's evolution had been as gentle as his character. She, too, had developed gradually and seamlessly but at seventeen she no longer thought of Ollie as a friend whom one day she would platonically marry, but as someone with whom she wanted a more intimate relationship. She wanted him to kiss her, wanted his hands on her body. She no longer loved him but was, she realized, in love with him. But what if he did not feel the same? And all that summer they'd done what they'd always done, walking, talking, spending as much time as possible in each other's company but without him giving even the slightest hint that he wanted anything more.

And then had come that day at the river, and her relief and explosion of happiness had been almost overwhelming. Now, on this hot, sultry afternoon, they emerged from the water once more and lay down on the rug they'd brought with them and positioned beneath the willow tree, him wearing old khaki shorts, his chest bare and hairless, she wearing a bathing costume she had put on earlier beneath a pale blue cotton dress, which now lay in a pile next to Ollie's shirt. She could see insects silhouetted in the sunlight against the willows on the far bank and could feel just the lightest of breezes on the air. She closed her eyes, the warm, orange glow of the sun strong on the lids, then felt Ollie move beside her and kiss her again, just as he had that last summer. A drop of river water fell from his hair onto her cheek.

'I love you, Elsa,' he said. 'When I think of you, it shall always be like this: smiling at me in the sunlight by the riverbank.'

She laughed. Then, having digested his words, she sat up and saw the sadness in his expression. 'You don't mean back to Cirencester, do you?'

His face fell and he looked down.

'Oh, no, Ollie, what have you done?'

He smiled. 'I love you and I want to be with you always.'

Elsa could feel her pulse quickening in panic. She took his hand. 'Ollie, tell me.'

'I've joined the Navy.' He swallowed. 'Well, the RNVSR. I applied back in March, but didn't tell you because it's quite hard to get accepted and I hadn't heard anything. Then, out of the blue, I got a letter. I had an interview last Monday and now I've had another letter. I've been accepted.'

Elsa looked at him, searching his face, and felt tears pricking her eyes.

'It's why I took the Yacht Master's Certificate last month.'

'But I thought that was just because you wanted to.'

'It was. But I also thought it might improve my chances of getting into the Navy. I didn't want to say anything because it was quite likely nothing would come of it.' He sighed and rolled onto his back, staring up at the sky and the willow branches above them. Dusty soil clung to his shoulders where he'd not dried himself properly. Elsa felt utterly crushed – as though the air had been knocked from her lungs. She had been so blind.

'I'm going to be called up,' he said. 'I don't want to be in the Army and I don't want to fly planes either. I don't really want to be in the Navy – I don't want to be in the military at all – but it's the least worst option.'

'But – but you're supposed to be going back to agricultural

college and farming is a reserved occupation.' She felt a tear run down her face.

Ollie shook his head. 'I'm not a farmer yet. My father is, but I can't be exempt. And even if I could, how could I stay here when everyone else is signing up and doing their bit? And we've got to stop Hitler. Your mother believes that and I believe it too. We have to protect this. I want our life here to be long and happy but I have to play my part to protect it, see? And if I'm to have any control at all of what becomes of me I've got to sign up now, while I still have the choice.'

She put her arms around him and buried her head in his neck.

'I wanted to tell you,' he said, 'but I thought you might try to talk me out of it. Part of me wanted you to, but I know it's something I have to do. I'm so sorry, Elsa. All I want is for us to be left alone, to lead our lives how we want to and to be together for ever. The thought of leaving you, of leaving the valley, it's – it's breaking my heart.'

Elsa lifted her head and looked at him, tears running down her cheeks. 'This can't be happening. Why does there have to be a stupid war? Promise me,' she said, 'promise you'll come back to me?'

He held her tightly but she was aware he hadn't answered. 'I want to be with you more than anything,' he said eventually. 'It's not fair. Not fair at all that we have to deal with the mistakes of others.'

When Elsa returned home that evening, Rose Bower seemed just the same. The same smell of floor polish and flowers – her mother always kept a vase of flowers from the garden in the hallway during the summer. There was the same table, the same pictures. Yet it was not the place she had left earlier because that morning she had been feeling carefree and happy and now she was heartbroken. She knew, deep within herself, that her life had changed, that from now on it would be different, less complete. Less contented. She walked through the hall and, hearing voices, wandered numbly into the drawing room. There she saw a strange girl playing Ludo with Maria.

Of course, she thought. *The evacuees.* Another sea change. Another upheaval.

'Hello,' she said, as brightly as she could manage.

'This is Ruby,' said Maria. 'Ruby, this is my older sister, Elsa.'

Ruby looked up sullenly. 'Hello.'

'It's very nice to meet you,' said Elsa, then turning to Maria said, 'Where's Mummy?'

'In the garden with Daddy.'

Elsa wavered. She felt she ought to be a little more welcoming to Ruby but she wanted so desperately to talk to her mother.

'Where have you come from, Ruby?' she asked.

'Southampton,' said Ruby. She looked utterly miserable, thought Elsa. Well, that made two of them.

Elsa went over and sat on the sofa next to her. 'I know it must seem very odd for you and I expect you're missing your family already, but you've come to a lovely part of the world and we'll try to make you feel as much at home as we can. Won't we, Maria?'

Maria nodded, then passed Ruby the die. 'Your turn.'

'Is it true your mother's German?' Ruby asked.

'Yes, which makes Maria and me and our brother, Robbie, half German, but you can rest assured we're not half Nazi. In this family we all want to see the end of Hitler as quickly as possible.' She stood up again and said to Maria, 'I need to speak to Mummy.' Maria glared at her but said nothing.

She found her parents on the bench overlooking the river. As she neared, they turned to her. In that moment she felt unable to hold back any longer. Standing there, she felt the tears welling and then she was sobbing, her face in her hands, shoulders rising and falling convulsively. Her mother rushed over and put an arm around her. 'Oh, my darling.'

'Ollie's joined the Navy,' she managed to say.

Her mother led her to the bench and sat her down between them. 'Darling Elsa,' said her father. 'It's hard, I know.'

'I'm going to miss him so much. And I'll worry about him all the time. What if he doesn't come back?'

Her father held her and kissed her head. 'Ssh, ssh,' he said. 'Ollie will be all right. We've the biggest and best Navy in the world, so I'm sure they'll look after him. During the last war, we in the infantry were always terribly envious of those in the Navy. Much safer. I rather wished I'd joined them myself.'

'Will there definitely be war?' she asked him.

He nodded. 'Yes, I'm afraid so. No point hiding things from you, old girl. Hitler's invaded Poland. It was on the wireless. The government has given him until Sunday morning to pull out, but that's not going to happen now.'

'It's a terrible thing,' said her mother. 'To think how a monster like that could ever take power, let alone lead us all into another war. It's too dreadful.'

'And poor you, Mummy,' said Elsa. 'You must be worried about the family back in Germany.'

'I'm worried about all of us. It's horrible not to know what will happen to us all and incredible to think that here we are, sitting in our lovely garden on a beautiful evening and about to be at war. I can hardly believe it. But we all have to be very brave.'

'Ollie says Hitler has to be stopped.'

'And Ollie's quite right, the darling boy,' said her mother.

'He'll need you to be brave, Elsa,' added her father. 'I can tell you he'll be worried about you. But we all have to buck ourselves up, get on with life and make sure that when he comes back we've got a home and life worthy of him and all those in the family who will be caught up in this. God willing, Hitler will come to his senses and it'll all be over soon. In the meantime, best foot forward, eh? You're a wonderful girl, my darling. You'll just need to be extra wonderful in the weeks to come. For us, for the whole family – and, of course, for Ollie.'

She nodded. She'd never felt more miserable or desolate in her entire life.

Two days later, eleven o'clock came and went, and Hitler's armies remained in Poland. Elsa was with her parents, brother and sister in the drawing room, listening to the wireless as the Prime Minister announced that Britain was now at war with Germany. No one spoke. She looked at her mother, who covered her mouth and turned her head away. Then her father laid a hand on her shoulder. Elsa felt a knot of dread in her stomach. There was no need to speak. The expressions on her parents' faces said it all.

9

At War

Sunday, 3 September 1939

IN THE OFFICES OF THE MILITARY WING OF THE WAR CABINET Secretariat on Richmond Terrace, the staff had listened sombrely to the Prime Minister's announcement on the wireless. Soon after, at 11.27 a.m., through the open windows, the wail of an air-raid siren filled the late-summer air. Tess could barely believe what she was hearing. It was as though the doomsayers had been right all along and that, at any moment, apocalyptic masses of German bombers would be flying over to flatten London. A brief but sharp stab of panic struck her. She stopped typing and found herself gripping the edge of her desk.

'My God!' exclaimed Martha Sillitoe, one of the other secretaries.

Moments later, Bill Elliott flung open the door. 'All right,' he said, 'lock all the papers into the safe, then let's get down to the shelter.'

Neither Tess nor the other girls said a word; Tess felt too shocked to speak. Like an automaton, she collected folders and box files, hurriedly placed them in the safe, then followed the rest as they trooped down to the shelter in the basement that had been prepared the previous year. She could still hear the mournful drone of the siren from beyond the building and an alarm now ringing shrilly inside.

It was crowded down there and stuffy, the air heavy with cigarette smoke and sweat. Tess found a seat and sat, still dumbfounded at the speed with which the siren had rung out. She wondered

94

whether these were her last moments, whether they were all about to die. Several of the girls were crying. General Ismay arrived, having come from a Chiefs of Staff meeting that had been in session when the eleven o'clock ultimatum had passed.

'Try not to worry,' he said, in a loud voice, as he stood at the centre of the shelter. 'It's bound to be a false alarm, and in any case, you'll be entirely safe down here.'

Tess knew that was not true – Ismay had admitted as much to her just a few days before that the shelter was inadequate. And then, minutes later, the all-clear sounded and Tess put a hand to her chest in relief. *Thank God.* The general had been right about the false alarm at any rate. Back upstairs they fetched the documents and files from the safe and returned to work. Tess wondered how many more false alarms there might be before Armageddon arrived. It was extraordinary, she thought, how quickly life could change so dramatically. Just a couple of weeks earlier she had been with Alex in Suffolk, then at Alvesdon. Even this morning, when she had walked to the office beneath a canopy of silvery barrage balloons floating overhead, and past ever-increasing walls of sandbags, the country had remained at peace, but with the single passing of a minute-hand, Britain was now at war. Ismay and others, Bill Elliott included, had all insisted they should pay no attention to the doomsayers. The last prime minister, Stanley Baldwin, might have warned that the bomber would always get through but that had been back in 1935. Now they were a bit better prepared, and yet, when the air-raid siren had sounded that morning, she had been briefly gripped by intense fear and knew she had not been alone.

With order and a certain degree of phlegmatic calm restored, Ismay called a meeting at which Tess was asked to take minutes. The situation in Poland was catastrophic, he told them. Polish armed forces were far less powerful than had been supposed and Poland's air force, especially, appeared to have been utterly crushed by the Luftwaffe. The Royal Navy was due to impose an economic blockade across the North Sea, trapping the Germans within Europe and barring them from the world's oceans. Efforts to crush Germany economically were a key part of the strategy. Ismay also reported that the Chiefs of Staff expected the French to follow suit and declare war that day too. Their army, already well over a million strong, and with reserves being mobilized, would soon be double that strength. The plan was for the French to invade Germany from the west, through the back door, while the Nazis had their hands full in Poland.

'It's worth reminding ourselves that we have the largest and most powerful navy in the world, gentlemen,' he said, 'and that the French have the potential to field the largest army. We go to war with heavy hearts but with confidence that we will soon bring Hitler and the Nazis to heel.'

Some fifty miles to the north, at Debden airfield, the station's fighter squadrons, part of 11 Group, RAF Fighter Command, had been on alert since first light in anticipation of war being declared. Built a few years earlier on Suffolk farmland near the town of Saffron Walden, Debden was now a substantial base, with three large C-type hangars, a standard RAF brick mess hall, and accompanying accommodation blocks. There were two Hurricane squadrons, 85 and 87, and a night-fighter squadron, number 29, of twin-engine Blenheims, and one of the new Spitfire squadrons, number 599.

When Wilf Castell had first joined 599 Squadron straight from the RAF college at Cranwell, they had still been flying Gloster Gladiator biplanes. So too had 87 and 85 Squadrons but then, much to the chagrin of 599's pilots, their neighbouring squadrons had been upgraded to Hurricanes. How enviously they had watched these new monoplane fighters! But then, in early July, news reached them that they would be converting to Spitfires, the latest and most modern of the RAF's fighter planes. And, unlike the Hurricane, this new wonder was not a development of earlier biplanes, but a brand-new, specially designed fighter, with superior speed to the Hurricane, both in level flight and especially in its rate of climb. It was a thing of beauty, too – all the 599 pilots were agreed upon that, not least Wilf, who was thrilled to be given such a wonderful thoroughbred of modernity to fly.

That morning, in their squadron hut at the far end of the field, they had turned on the radio at 11.15 a.m. to hear Neville Chamberlain make his sombre and weary announcement. Since then, there had been a mixed response. Some had been visibly excited: Bluey Thompson had made it clear that he couldn't wait to get stuck into

manipulate the undercarriage pump. Wheels safely retracted and a quick glance at the dials to check speed, altitude and oil pressure, he then looked to either side of him. There was Sim, away off his starboard wing, Tony a little up ahead and beyond him, slightly to port, A Flight in two vics of three, and behind them a further vic of Green Section. Twelve Spitfires, in model formation. They might now be at war, Wilf thought, but this was no different from countless flights they'd already flown. In fact, it was no different from the one he'd flown the previous day. Fixing his oxygen mask, Wilf breathed in deeply and was grateful he'd joined when he had, that he had some six hundred hours in his logbook and already more than forty on the Spitfire. He no longer had to think about flying – it was entirely second nature – which allowed him to focus on keeping in formation and looking all around him at all times. Those completing training now that war was upon them would not have the luxury of improving their skills in peacetime; he pitied them.

'Hello, Garter, Snapper Leader calling,' he heard the CO say through his headset. 'Now at angels fourteen heading one-one-zero.'

'Hello, Snapper Leader, Garter answering,' came the reply. 'Bandit reported heading two-nine-zero, seventy miles east of London.'

Bandit. Singular, thought Wilf. They flew on, towards the Thames estuary. The whole of south-east England could be seen: the curve of East Anglia, the arrowhead leg of Kent extending towards France. Faint lines from shipping were visible in the Channel, vessels plying their trade down the east coast of England and along the continental coastline. It looked peaceful enough – there was certainly no massed formation of enemy bombers anywhere to be seen.

They flew on, out over the estuary and towards the Channel still in formation. After a further twenty minutes, he heard the CO in his ears again.

'Hello, Garter, this is Snapper Leader. Can't see any bandit.'

There was a pause then a crackle of static, then Wilf heard the ground controller again.

'Hello, Snapper Leader, Garter answering. X-raid. Hostile identified as friendly. Return to base.'

Wilf wanted to laugh. So, it had been nothing after all. Still, he thought, as he glanced down over southern England, looking calm and resolute in the late-summer sun, there were worse ways of spending the first afternoon of war.

The day Britain, then France had declared war on Germany had passed peacefully in Alvesdon too, without any air-raid alerts. Early the following morning, Monday, 4 September, Hannah Ellerby and Jean Gulliver arrived at Alvesdon Manor with their gas-mask cases hanging over their shoulders, although they quickly put them to one side once they were in the house.

'Really,' said Jean, as she began preparing the breakfast, 'it's ridiculous having to wear these out here. You'm not goin' to get gassed in the countryside. But them politicians can only think it's one rule for all whether town or country folk.'

'I don't think I'll ever get used to carryin' mine about,' agreed Hannah. 'And the blackout's jus' as bad. Waste o' time, if you ask me. Took for ever to get our home done and that on top of fixing the blinds here.' She disappeared to lay up in the dining room, then came back to do the same in the kitchen for Edie Blythe and the three evacuees, only to find Edie already there.

'Here,' said Edie. 'Let me do that. I don't need waiting on.'

'How you settlin' in then, my love?' asked Jean.

'All right. I'm not used to such a big place. Back in Southampton I live in a two-up two-down terraced house. There's so much space here.'

'An' the bairnts?'

'They've barely spoken. It's all a bit overwhelming for them.'

'Course it is,' said Jean. 'D'you really think 'Itler will be sending his bombers over? I can't think straight on things. Alvesdon seems jus' the same, 'cept for the gas masks and blackout and whatnot. Don't seem possible, somehow.'

Edie shrugged. 'I don't know. But a U-boat sank the *Athenia* last night. It's a big liner that was crossing the Atlantic with evacuees.'

'It never did!' said Jean.

'I heard it on my wireless,' said Edie. 'So, it seems they mean business.'

'But what business is it to sink a liner?' asked Hannah. 'That's just wrong.'

'It is,' agreed Edie. 'It's terrible.'

Jean moved the porridge from the boil then began frying eggs.

'So, Edie, what do you make of Mr Roberts?'

Edie smiled. 'He's a little wary, I think. It must be strange for him suddenly having sixteen extra children at his school as well as another teacher.'

'He's a shy one, that's for sure,' said Jean. 'Did he teach you, Hannah?'

'No,' said Hannah, pouring porridge into a tureen. 'I think he came the year after I left. That were five years ago, now.'

'And you, er, got a feller, Edie? Back home?'

Edie shook her head. 'I was going steady with someone but – well, he wasn't for me.' She grinned. 'Maybe I'll find the man of my dreams here.'

Jean laughed. 'What – one of the farm boys?'

'Well, I was chatting to a very handsome fellow yesterday when I was out exploring with some of the children. He took us to a wood, showed them pheasants, animal tracks and his hut. You should have seen the faces of the kids! I don't think many of them have ever seen cows, or sheep or pheasants before. The only animals they know are cats and dogs.'

'That'll be Tom Timbrell,' said Jean.

'Yes, that was his name,' said Edie. 'Tom. Beautiful-looking man and charming too. Cheered me up no end! You'll tell me he's spoken for already now.'

Hannah glared at Jean, picked up the tureen and headed out of the kitchen to the dining room. It wasn't Mr Roberts who was shy, she thought. It was her. She had warmed to Edie until this last conversation but now saw that the newcomer threatened her entire future. She was fun, confident, and pretty too. Hannah cursed to herself, picturing Edie with Tom, laughing, flirting, making the eye.

As she walked back to the kitchen, she passed Edie in the corridor.

'I'm going to get the children down,' she told Hannah, then stopped and took her arm. 'Are you all right, Hannah?'

'Yes, perfectly, thank you,' said Hannah, more tartly than she'd intended. She was aware of Edie eyeing her carefully, uncertainly.

Edie smiled again. 'Thank you, Hannah, for being so welcoming. I do so hope we can be great friends.'

Hannah forced a smile. 'I'll get breakfast ready.'

At Farrowcombe, Stork had returned from the morning briefing and was just about to head out to his study when Debbo called to him from the kitchen.

'Stork, darling?'

He sighed, then turned and went to the doorway. His wife was sitting at the table eating toast and drinking tea.

'Won't you join me?'

He looked at his watch. 'Well, I ought to get on.'

'Come on,' she said. 'Sit down for a moment. Have some tea and something to eat.'

'Where's Betty?'

'She's taking the evacuees to the school. I'm surprised you didn't see them on the way.'

He sat down and ran a hand across his hair. 'I did, actually, now I come to think of it. Sorry – wasn't concentrating.'

'Maggie says no more evacuees are expected today so I think that might be it for the moment, at any rate. Our two seem rather sweet, don't you think? You should give them a tour of the farm – perhaps in the trap after school? Maybe you could take them up in Dorothy too.'

Stork sighed again. 'Yes, all right. If I've time. A lot to do, though.'

'You also need to find time to see your father, Stork.'

He nodded. 'I can't help feeling worried as hell about the children. Tess in London, Wilf with his squadron and even Edward. I expect he's all right, but what if the bombs do start falling?'

'There's no sign of them yet. Listen, my darling,' she said, taking his hands across the table, 'of course we're going to worry about them but we've got to knuckle down and get on with things. Now you know how I felt in the last war when you were over in France. At least there's no fighting yet and perhaps, who knows, there never will be. Perhaps it will all be over by Christmas as some are suggesting.'

'You're right, of course. And there's much to think about.

Manpower for starters, how much time the War Ag is going to take up, then telling Pa about the beef herd.'

'No one's joined up yet, have they?'

'No, but it's only a matter of time.'

'And what about Alwyn's beef cattle? Do you really need to cut them straight away? Can't you hold on a bit longer?'

'No, I don't think I can. If I'm on this damn committee I've got to lead by example and, in any case, we have to plan ahead. The sooner they go, the better. Pa is just going to have to face up to it.'

'As long as you're certain it's the right decision, darling.'

Stork grimaced. 'I am.' He stood up, went over to her and kissed her, then hurried across the yard to his study. Sitting down at his desk, he looked at the raft of government information that Richard Stratton had given to him the previous Friday. He had accepted a position on the Wiltshire War Ag, just as he'd known, deep down, he would. He'd driven over to Kingston Deverill, two valleys across to the north and on the edge of the Plain where Stratton farmed some 2,800 acres, making it one of the largest holdings in south Wiltshire.

Stork knew Richard Stratton of old, not as a friend as such but as a fellow farmer. One got to know one's farming neighbours from the county shows, markets and fairs, and from shooting days and other social gatherings. Stratton was in his early seventies and had been farming at Kingston Deverill for more than fifty years, although his son had taken over the day-to-day running, in the same way that Stork had taken over at Alvesdon. The difference was that Stratton was a highly progressive farmer whereas Alwyn was not; and while Stork's father had a deserved reputation for hot-headedness, his near contemporary was known for his hard-headed business acumen, albeit worn with a genial affability.

As he had been ushered into Stratton's wood-panelled drawing room, he had been offered tea, then Stratton said, 'And you know Mr William Price, I assume?'

A small, neat man in his forties, Price looked more like a bank manager, Stork thought, than the farming adviser he was as Wiltshire's county agricultural organizer.

'Yes, how are you, William?' said Stork, shaking his hand.

103

'As well as can be expected in the circumstances, thank you,' Price replied.

'Officially, the War Ags don't come into being until we're at war,' continued Stratton, 'but, as you know, an awful lot of planning is needed ahead of this rather depressing eventuality. William here is going to be the executive officer – perfect man for the job as he knows all the farms round about and has been advising farmers, landowners and farm workers here for more than fifteen years.'

'Makes sense,' agreed Stork.

'Some of the others on the War Ag you'll know. T. K. Jeans for one.'

'I'm very flattered to be asked, Richard,' said Stork, 'but why didn't you think of my father?'

Stratton chuckled. 'I'm terribly fond of Alwyn,' he said, 'and he's had a long life in farming, it's true. But I'm getting on a bit, some of the others we've got lined up for the War Ag aren't exactly in the first flush, and we all felt you'd be a good man to have on board. One of the younger generation, and you've done great things to turn the farm around – it's been most impressive. Now, I don't want to embarrass you but you're modernist in your approach. This coming war is going to be challenging. We've a lot of food to produce and a heck of a lot more than British farming has been producing over the last fifteen years or so. Mechanization and modern techniques are going to be vital because not only will we be expected to grow more and produce more, we'll be expected to do so with a smaller labour force. It'll be our job to help explain the government's needs and to guide our county's farming community. For some it'll be very tough indeed, which is why we need men of vision as well as experience and good judgement. You're a good fellow, Stork. You also did your bit in the last show, so you know what it's like to go off and fight, put your life on the line, unlike those of us a little longer in the tooth. We feel that experience might give you – and us – a bit of clout when talking to our farmers.'

'We're going to be enacting government policy but the Ministry has come up with a slogan, "No farming from Whitehall",' added Price. 'Dorman-Smith wants to give the County War Ags as much of a free hand as possible. He's a good sort and, of course, a farmer too.'

'Well, the ploughing campaign he announced early in the summer was a smart move,' said Stork. 'He's certainly proving the best minister we've had since I've been at Alvesdon.'

'Hear, hear,' agreed Stratton.

'It certainly seems we're going to be given a fair amount of local autonomy and discretion,' said Price. 'The Ministry is demanding a further million acres be ploughed up with various targets for milk and crops, but farmers will be allowed to use the knowledge of their farm and land to decide what they do and where, overseen, of course, by the War Ags.'

'But how will that work?' asked Stork. 'We can't possibly get ourselves to every single farm in Wiltshire. There must be hundreds.'

'There are indeed, which is why there are going to be district committees, each covering around six parishes or so. There's one being drawn up for the whole of the Chalke valley, for example. David Liddell is going to be your local district chairman, but we'd want you sitting on that committee too, as well as on the county executive committee.'

Stork nodded, thinking of the workload in addition to his own farm. Afternoon sunlight poured through the windows, highlighting the swirling dust motes. A grandfather clock ticked rhythmically, steadfastly. Beyond, outside, a parched lawn stretched away, lined by low, dark yew hedges.

'It's a mammoth undertaking,' said Stratton. 'Our industry of farming is to be transformed, Stork, into the country's fourth line of defence. No point in starving to death in an air-raid shelter. The more that can be produced here, at home, the fewer precious ships have to carry our food. It's as simple as that. Of course, it's going to be a devilishly tricky task for many of our farmers. You and I are all right. We've managed to ride out the past decade because of size, assets, and because we've already invested in machinery and because we've spread the risk. But many farmers simply don't have the mechanical equipment, let alone enough horses or the manpower to tackle the new levels of acreage expected of them. But it's got to be done. You were a pilot in the last war, weren't you? And I understand one of your boys is flying in the RAF too.'

'Yes.' Stork nodded. 'He's with 599 Squadron. Spitfires.'

'Well, good for him. But, you know, whenever I look up and see an aeroplane buzzing overhead, I'm reminded that our youth is once again taking the lion's share of risk. Middle-aged and elderly country folk need to toil in the fields below and play their part too, no matter the challenges and difficulties. We're all in this together and we farmers have a big point to prove.'

Stratton had been right and Stork rather moved by what the wily old farmer had said. He'd accepted the post on the spot.

Now, as he sat at his desk on that Monday, the second day of the war, it had become official. Richard Stratton had rung the previous evening: the War Ags were now formally activated, and that meant Stork was also a member of the County War Agricultural Executive Committee for Wiltshire and a part of the district committee too. He felt in part daunted, humbled and profoundly depressed but also, if he was honest with himself, invigorated by the prospect.

Clumping footsteps outside halted such ruminations. A knock at the door, and then Claude Timbrell was before him.

'Bad news, guv'nor,' said Claude. 'I'm afraid Perce and Cecil Merriman are joining up.'

'Curses,' muttered Stork. 'I thought they were looking a bit shifty earlier. Any others?'

'No, but there will be as sure as I'm standin' here now.'

'Tom?'

Claude shrugged. 'I know he's thinking on't.'

Stork pointed him to a chair in front of his desk. 'I've been looking at the accounts and I think we can manage the two new Allis-Chalmers and a crawler. I realize the government is doing deals with the Fordsons and giving over a large number to the War Ags to distribute, but as you know, they're fiendishly temperamental.'

'Well, if Smudger reckons they're the devil, that's saying summat,' agreed Claude. 'It's starting the buggers that's such a bind. An' it's one thing getting 'em goin' in summertime but come the winter . . .' He whistled. 'Give me an Allis any day.'

They talked on. The dairy herd was safe, Stork told him, although they would have to reduce the number of sheep. It also looked as though the government still wanted breweries to keep producing, which was good news too.

'And the beef herd?' asked Claude.

'I just don't see how we can justify it, Claude. Milk, cereals and root crops, such as sugar beet and potatoes, are the priority. We're going to be eating a lot less meat while this war continues.'

Claude sighed. 'It's going to create a God-awful stink, mind. An' I'll be sorry to see 'em go.'

'I know,' said Stork. 'But we can't afford to be sentimental. We're at war.'

Maud was feeling exhausted by the war already. Gas masks, ARP blackouts, evacuees and a teacher descending on them, and everyone looking rather pinched and brow-beaten. After breakfast she decided she needed some fresh air and walked into the village to the shop, then rather wished she hadn't. Susan Smallpiece was in there talking about German air raids.

'I 'eard there'd been a raid on Winchester,' she was telling Margaret Pierson. 'Thirty-five dead, twice as many injured, and two cinemas bombed.'

'They never did!' Margaret gasped.

'That's what I 'eard.'

'They're shutting down cinemas,' added Betty Collis, Stork and Debbo's cook and help. 'Was on the wireless. As a precaution. All public gatherings to be stopped. Don't affect us out 'ere none, but shows they're all a bit worried about bombin' an' that.'

'Well, my sister lives in Salisbury,' said Margaret, 'and she says the blackout is way more dangerous than any bomber. She said two people have been knocked down an' killed already.'

'An' that's now,' said Betty. 'Imagine what it'll be like when the nights start to really draw in.'

Mary Ellerby entered the shop at that moment and theatrically wiped her brow. 'Lor'!' she said. 'Them bairnts!'

'Your evacuees, Mary?' asked Betty.

'I dunno whether we've picked the short straw, but our two are a right 'andful, make no mistake. Glad to get 'em to school, I can tell you.' She leaned in towards Betty and Mary and spoke in a conspiratorial tone. 'D'you know, their manners is somethin' awful. And the way they go on! Always scrappin'. You'm think they'd 'alf tear each other to shreds. I 'ad a good mind to give 'em both a good hidin' this mornin'. Fair done in, I am, and it's only nine o'clock!'

All the talk of bombers, evacuees and upheaval left Maud

107

walking back feeling even more dispirited, but as she neared the manor she decided to give herself a talking-to. Hardship was part of life: wars, influenza pandemics, economic downturns, tragedy – it was what every generation had to face. People lived and died. The important thing was to appreciate what one had and to take each day as it came. To enjoy the seasons in all their variety. She had, she knew, been inordinately lucky with the hand she'd been dealt, and if she was entering a new and more challenging time, she must face it stoically. She breathed in deeply.

For a half-hour or so, her normal equanimity returned. The house was quiet now that Edie Blythe and the evacuees had gone to school. Alwyn was in his study reading the paper and she was able to write some letters in the drawing room in peaceful calm and, briefly, quite forget about the war.

She was interrupted by the arrival of Stork and immediately she could tell that trouble was brewing; his brow was furrowed and he was fingering the rim of his hat.

'Oh, do put that hat down, Stork, dear,' she said, in what she hoped was a kindly tone. 'It's putting me quite on edge.'

He looked puzzled, then said, 'Oh, sorry,' and tossed it onto one of the armchairs.

'What news of the children?'

'Haven't heard from Wilf, but he's back at Debden. Tess is busy in London and Edward's Yeomanry are about to be posted down to Cornwall of all places.'

'Goodness, why?'

'Apparently, the Plain is awash with the regular army and there's some connection to someone with an estate down near Truro. Someone's got to house all their horses.'

'Yes, I suppose so.'

'Anyway, Maimes, is Pa in?'

She sighed. 'Yes, he is, in his study. Why do I have a sinking feeling, Stork, darling?'

He kissed her lightly and hurried off without answering.

No more than a couple of minutes later she heard rapidly rising voices. Then Alwyn exclaimed, 'This is the absolute limit, Stork!'

Oh dear, she thought, and then, after a moment's pause, decided she should try to intervene.

'Really!' she said, as she opened the study door and walked in. 'Do you want the whole village to hear?'

Both men turned to look at her.

'Now he wants to get rid of the beef herd!' exclaimed Alwyn.

'As I've been trying to explain to Pa,' said Stork, 'we're now at war. What worked in peacetime will not work now. There are different priorities.'

'Have you been ordered to get rid of the beef herd by Whitehall?' demanded Alwyn.

'No, but we have to plan ahead. We need enough pasture for the dairy herd but the country needs to plough an additional million acres. Here at Alvesdon we have to play our part. Once the war is over, we can reintroduce them. It's not for ever, God willing.'

'I think you both need to calm down,' said Maud.

'We have to make tough decisions, Maimes,' said Stork. 'We have a duty to feed the country and – and to keep the farm in business. We can't be sentimental about some beef cattle.'

'First the War Ag and now the beef herd,' said Alwyn. 'It's a hell of a state of affairs to be constantly humiliated and undermined by one's son. Second son.'

'It's a hell of a state of affairs to be constantly humiliated by one's father, who so blatantly favours my older brother.'

'If Denholm had stayed we'd have farmed Alvesdon together,' said Alwyn. 'Harmoniously. Denholm doesn't constantly undermine me. I don't know what I've done to deserve such contempt, Stork.'

'Oh, honestly, Pa! That's ridiculous. It would have been catastrophic if Denholm had taken over the farm and you know it. And don't think I don't know about the handouts you've been giving him these past few years, because I do.'

'How dare you!'

'Money that Denholm is sinking into a lifestyle he cannot afford and which is being taken away from the farm.'

'Enough!'

'Alwyn, is this true?' asked Maud.

'Of course it is!' said Stork.

Alwyn fumed silently, then said, 'I'm not going to talk about this. Both of you, leave me. I'm not going to be lectured and – and hectored in my own study.' For a moment, neither moved, then Alwyn shouted, 'OUT!'

'For God's sake!' muttered Stork, turning and holding the door for his mother. Maud could not recall the last time she had seen her husband so angry. She felt lightheaded with the shock of it, but did as Alwyn had demanded, and left, flinching as Stork slammed the door behind them.

'I'm sorry, Maimes,' he said. 'He's impossible.' He stormed into the drawing room to pick up his hat then, in the hall, paused. 'Will you be all right? Can I get you something?'

'No, thank you.'

'Well, at least come and sit down for a moment,' he said, and she felt herself being led back to her favourite armchair with its views out across the garden to the water meadows and chalk downs beyond.

'It's true about the money, isn't it?' she said at last.

Stork nodded.

'Is it an awful lot?'

'I shouldn't have said anything. I'm sorry. I was just so riled.'

'How much?'

He looked away, avoiding her eye.

'I see,' she said.

'It's not the money, Maimes. It's . . .' He attempted a smile. 'I'm sorry. I wish I hadn't mentioned it, I really am.'

She sighed. 'I know the war against Germany has only just begun but, darling, the war between you and your father has got to stop.'

10

Autumn

Friday, 20 October 1939

TESS ARRIVED BACK AT THE HOUSE IN PIMLICO THAT EVENING TO discover Wilf there.

'Wilf!' she exclaimed, flinging her arms around him. 'What are you doing here?'

'I found him sitting outside the front door,' said Diana.

'I've got a forty-eight-hour pass. I was only released this afternoon so thought I'd come here first. You didn't get my message, then?'

'No, I'm so happy to see you!' She hugged him tightly.

He laughed. 'I'm happy to see you too, but I can barely breathe.'

'And I've the weekend free,' said Tess. 'We can go home together tomorrow morning.'

The three of them went out to see a new Bette Davis film since the cinemas had reopened. Tess was only half watching the newsreels. No upbeat commentary over footage of factories mass-producing shells could put a gloss on the turmoil she knew to exist at the heart of the War Office. Now, though, she glanced up as a sea of smiling British troops in France filled the screen.

'Look!' said Tess, a little too loudly. 'It's Alex!'

'So it is!' said Diana.

It was odd, Tess thought, to see him like that, in black-and-white, with his men. Far away, in another country, and with no knowing when he might be back. At the War Office no one knew how long the war would last but the planning was for at least three years. Three years! She couldn't think that far ahead. They'd all listened to Hitler's speech a couple of weeks earlier following the crushing of Poland. The country didn't exist any more. Rather, it had been carved into two between the Nazis and the Soviets. Untold millions had been left homeless. Reports she'd seen had been shocking. And then Hitler had returned to Berlin and asked for peace. Ismay had been seething. They all had. But the response from the Imperial General Staff and the War Cabinet had been emphatic: there would be no peace until Nazi Germany had been crushed. However long it took.

Tess had admired the determination and resolution but had felt entombed in disappointment. This state of war was now normality. Fear of mass bombing had already been replaced by dissatisfaction and weariness. She'd seen it at Grosvenor Place and she'd seen it in the faces of Londoners. The huge blimps hanging over London, the sandbags, the uniforms, the new identity cards they all had to carry, the long hot summer replaced by shortening days and autumnal rain. Wet feet, greyness. Uncertainty. The anger that the life she had planned and hoped for had been wrenched from her. As the news ended and *Dark Victory* began, she turned to Wilf and gripped his arm. He looked at her and smiled. At least she had Wilf with her and tomorrow they would be at Alvesdon.

The following day it was raining again. On the train west towards Salisbury, Tess and Wilf watched it slanting against the window of their carriage. While most of the trees were still in leaf, the country-side looked drab and grey, as though it had lost its zest for life, which was, Tess thought, rather how she felt too.

'There won't be much flying today,' said Wilf, brightly. 'I can't wait to be home. I'm going to take the dogs up onto the downs,' he added.

'In this weather?'

'It's only a bit of rain. It'll be refreshing.'

'Hmm,' she said. 'Maybe. It just feels like we've got a long winter ahead. I can't find much to feel very cheery about.'

'A weekend at Farrowcombe?'

She laughed. 'Yes, I suppose so.' She eyed her brother. 'Thank you.'

'What for?'

'Nothing.'

'What?'

'I can't explain.' She kissed his cheek. 'For being you.'

At Pug's Hole, a steep, sharp and narrow combe on the eastern side of Windmill Hill, Tom Timbrell was also feeling a little out of sorts. Normally, he wasn't the slightest bit bothered by rain; one got wet sometimes, but one could always get dry again, and he'd always liked petrichor, the damp, earthy scent of rain on soil, and raindrops on his cheeks. But it was always disappointing to have rain on a shoot day. Pug's Hole was one of the best drives on the whole farm, where the birds would hurtle overhead both fast and high. It was a drive for the better shots and Alwyn Castell was still certainly one of those. 'Separates the wheat from the chaff, eh, Tom?'

Today, though, the birds had barely got up at all. It was a disappointing start, mounted on top of a disappointing turnout for what, in normal times, would have been a much-looked-forward-to treat.

'I'm embarrassed to say, Tom,' Alwyn had said the previous evening, 'that we've only six guns tomorrow. All I can muster. This bloody war!'

That had dropped to five that morning when Stork had been called to see a farm further down the valley. Wilf was coming for the weekend, Stork told him, so he'd see whether he fancied joining in when he arrived, but Tom had sensed this was unlikely. And now the birds weren't flying either.

The damp squib of the shoot was not the only thing troubling him. Many conflicting thoughts kept swirling around his head. Matters of the heart. Matters of what to do. Something about Hannah Ellerby had got under his skin ever since he'd found her crying by the water pump. There was no girl he'd liked the look of more than her for some time but since then he'd found himself yearning for her. She was, he thought, just the kind of girl he could settle down with. He reckoned she'd be a wonderful homemaker and mother, and he did want a family some day. Yet, no matter how often he tried to catch her eye and contrive an excuse to speak to her, she seemed to elude him. It was confounding. He was good-looking enough, he knew, and his prospects were fair, too. He'd

113

been assured by Mr Stork that the position of foreman would be his one day. Yet none of this seemed to account for anything as far as Hannah was concerned. The trouble was, he had no one to talk to about her. The only person who seemed to guess his feelings for her had been Coco, yet she was far away in the South of France, and he'd not heard from her since the day she'd left. He couldn't mention it to any of the lads he worked with or saw in the pub because he'd be the butt of ribbing for evermore. It had crossed his mind maybe to talk to Susan Smallpiece or Jean Gulliver, but he'd quickly dismissed that idea too; Susan, especially, was a terrible gossip.

Then there was Edie Blythe. Somehow, he couldn't stop bumping into her. True, she was staying at the manor, but it was a rare day he didn't cross her path one way or another. Always very friendly and chatty she was too, and he liked her well enough. She was different from the girls in the village, more worldly, he supposed. She asked him a lot about the farm, about what he did, about life in the village. Edie was conspiratorial too: she'd ask him for his opinion on the local people. 'You're my number-one source of information,' she'd said once, smiling at him with that mischievous grin of hers.

Then on Thursday night she'd come into the pub, bought herself a drink, sat down on her own and begun reading a book. Tom had been having a pint with Smudger Smith, whom he liked and often drank with at the Three Horseshoes. Seeing Edie sitting there on his own, he couldn't help but smile to himself. She had confidence, that one, he'd give her that. There wasn't another girl in the village who would come in on her own, sit down and calmly start reading a book. And there was no mistaking her either; she might wear her hair straight these days, but her nails were still painted, her lips red. It wasn't the way of the country girls, that was for sure.

'Care to join us, miss?' Smudger had said, and Edie had looked up brightly, thanked him and, putting down her book, come over to their table.

'And how are you finding village life? Like it here?' Smudger had asked her.

'Very much. I've noticed the changing season – summer to autumn – more than I ever did before. You don't see it in quite the same way living in a city.'

Smudger had nodded. 'That's true enough. You and I are rather alike, as it happens, Miss Edie,' he said. 'I'm from a city too. Well, from London. Born an' bred.'

'I'd like to stay here,' said Edie, 'but I'm worried I may have to go home soon.' Many of the evacuees had already returned to Southampton. The school didn't really need two teachers, she explained, whereas in the cities there were now no longer enough, especially with so many male teachers joining up.

'What about Mr Roberts?' Smudger had asked.

'Well, I suppose he might join up too. That would certainly allow me to stay on. But I can't expect the poor fellow to go off to war on my account.'

'What about that lad that's allus hangin' round you, Smudge?' asked Tom.

Smudger smiled. 'Davey. He's a good lad. The other boy up at Farrowcombe went back – his mother turned up the weekend after the war began and took him home – but it seems Davey'll be staying put. For the time bein', at any rate.'

'Davey's not the slightest bit interested in his schoolwork,' said Edie.

'He don't need to be. Understands engines. Different type of brain needed for that. I 'ope he stays. I've got used to havin' 'im around and he's an extra pair of hands, to be honest.'

They had another drink, chatted some more, and left together. Outside it was pitch dark with no moon and Tom felt he ought to offer to escort Edie back to the manor.

'Oh, would you?' Edie had said. 'Thank you, Tom.'

'It's no trouble, an' the wrong direction for Smudger.'

They bade Smudger goodnight and began walking down the road, Edie folding an arm into his. They had chatted on, easily enough, in low voices, until they reached the yard behind the manor.

'Well,' said Tom, 'goodnight, then.'

'Thank you,' she said in reply, then leaned up and kissed him, not on the cheek but on the lips. Tom was so startled he didn't say anything and then she kissed him again. Suddenly her arms were around his neck and he was gripping her waist and pulling her tightly to him.

'I've wanted to do that, Tom Timbrell,' she said, 'ever since I first set eyes on you.'

'Really?' he said. He was thinking of Hannah and then Coco.

She leaned up and kissed him again, then whispered, 'Goodnight, Tom,' and disappeared into the house. He'd not seen her since but wondered whether there was now an understanding between the two of them. He liked Edie well enough and she was pretty and he enjoyed her company. But she wasn't Hannah. On the other hand, Hannah didn't seem the slightest bit interested in him, so what did it matter? He reckoned it didn't pay to think too far ahead at present.

The shoot day did not improve. Wilf and Stork joined the party for the final drive but none of the guns seemed to be enjoying it much.

Later, after the last drive and the party had gathered in the drawing room for tea and fruit cake, he was given his usual tips.

'Well done, Tom,' said Stork, slipping a ten-bob note into his hand. 'A tricky day with all the rain and I'm really sorry to have let you down.'

'Not to worry, guv'nor,' said Tom. 'I jus' feel a bit bad for everyone. And for Mr Castell.'

Stork patted him on the shoulder. 'You're a good fellow.'

Soon after, Tom said goodbye and left, but the master followed him out.

'Er, Tom,' he called.

Tom turned.

'Could I have a word?'

'Course, sir.'

He followed him into his study and Mr Castell closed the door. 'I'm not going to beat about the bush, Tom,' he said. 'I'm going to cancel the rest of the shoot days.'

'Cancel the whole season?'

The master was pacing. 'It's supposed to be fun, a chance to get friends together and have a bit of sport. But I had a devil of time getting any guns at all today. It's this damned war. People are busy and anxious, of course, and don't feel in the mood for gadding about shooting birds when young men are off at war. Seems wrong somehow.'

'Wrong?'

'Yes. You know full well how much I love it and it pains me to be saying this to you. Really pains me. But let's do some rough shooting and leave it at that. I know Stork needs you badly on the farm,

116

so you'll be more than busy enough. I'd appreciate you still keeping an eye on the birds, of course.'

'Of course, sir,' said Tom. He felt quite dumbfounded, but after shaking hands and taking his leave, he began to think. Perhaps the old man was right. And perhaps that fellow of Miss Tess's had been right. Perhaps he could be of greater use in the Army than he could ever be here, on the farm, especially now Mr Castell had cancelled the rest of the season. And perhaps if he joined up he could avoid any awkwardness with Edie Blythe, and Hannah might look at him afresh. He sighed heavily as he turned out of the drive and onto the village road towards the cottage he shared with his father. What was the name of that fellow? Alex. Alex Woodman. That was it. Of the King's Own Royal Guards. It was definitely something to think about.

Despite the rain, Tess had gone for a long walk with her mother that afternoon, and taken the dogs who had been deprived of a day's shooting as much as Stork. Up on the downs they had been past the DH.4's hangar, the old biplane safe and dry, the cockpit covered with a tarpaulin.

'Your father's put away Dorothy for the duration,' her mother told her.

'However long that will be,' added Tess. 'I suppose with petrol rationing he's got to.'

'It's partly that, although as a farmer and on the War Ag he's entitled to much more than most, but I think it's mainly because he doesn't feel it's right to be flying for fun now. He'll miss it, though.'

A patch of sky cleared far to the south and a shaft of sunlight shone down on the Purbeck Hills away in the distance.

'Gosh, I do hope there are some other rays of light soon,' said Debbo. 'I know you can't really talk about your work, darling, but everything seems to be so awfully hush-hush. We have no idea what on earth is going on or why we're not doing anything about that wretched little man and his Nazi hordes. Half the evacuees have gone home. Everything seems to be in the most ghastly limbo. The government don't tell anyone anything and neither does the BBC. Everyone wants to know why nothing is happening except black-outs and various other too-boring privations.'

Tess thought about this for a moment, trying to establish exactly what she could say and what she could not. 'The trouble is, Mummy, we're a little behind Germany in rearming,' she said. 'Fortunately, we can get pretty much everything we want from anywhere in the world and we've more and more factories being built. They're going up at a rate of knots. We need to get a bit stronger and then we'll strike alongside the French. That's the broad plan, at any rate.'

'What if the Germans attack first?'

'They very well might. But everyone's pretty confident we'll be strong enough to withstand anything they can throw at us. The belief now is that wars are won and lost over who can produce the most arms. The Luftwaffe might be stronger than the RAF right now, but it won't be for much longer.'

'Well, Tess darling, I do hope you're right. I just think that should be explained to everyone. Everything one hears on the wireless is so gloomy. The best thing I've listened to since this whole dreadful business began is Sir Seymour Hicks on the BBC talking about humour and the war. He said humour was vital to us in winning the war and that since we had plenty and the Nazis none it was bound to be all right.' They laughed.

'And what about Pa and Grandpa?'

'They're in the middle of a kind of truce. Grandpa hasn't forgiven your father for selling off the beef herd, but poor Stork has been so run off his feet they've not seen much of each other, which is probably just as well.'

'They've gone, though, the beef cattle?'

'Yes, the whole lot. Some sold at market, the rest taken straight to slaughter.'

Back at the house, Tess dried her hair and changed her clothes, then went down to the kitchen to make a pudding for dinner as she had promised her mother.

'That's kind of you, darling,' Debbo had said, when Tess had suggested it earlier. 'Betty's at home with flu. We've borrowed poor Hannah from your grandparents, but I'm sure she could do with a bit of help.'

She found Hannah frantically chopping vegetables at the kitchen table, potatoes already simmering on the range.

'I've come to lend a hand,' said Tess.

Hannah reddened. 'Oh, you don't need to do that, miss.'

'I'm very happy to. It's heroic of you to come to us but I'm sure you could use an extra pair. I thought I might make a pudding.'

Hannah wiped her brow. She looked flustered.

'Or do something else?' offered Tess. 'Honestly – I'm very happy to.' She smiled in a way that she hoped would be reassuring. 'I'd like to. I'd enjoy it.'

Hannah softened. 'Well, thank you. If you're sure.'

'Did you have anything in mind? I can do a pretty mean Queen of Puddings.'

She saw Hannah smirk.

'That's what I was planning to make, miss. Did you know?'

Tess laughed. 'Well, it's a Jean Gulliver special, isn't it? Who do you think taught it me?'

Hannah made to get up.

'Stay where you are,' said Tess, 'I know my way around.' She gathered the ingredients and implements she needed – eggs, sugar, bread, jam and milk, two bowls, weights, a wooden spoon and a whisk – then sat opposite. The kitchen was warm from the range, steam rising and condensing on the ceiling. A row of single-bulb lights hung over the kitchen table. Flagstones covered the floor, while a dresser stood along the wall opposite the range. The dogs had followed Tess into the kitchen and now lay next to the range, the smell of their damp fur blending with the savoury aroma that always pleasantly pervaded the room. Tess had spent many long hours there talking to Betty Collis over the years; on the other hand, she now realized that although Hannah had been working at the manor for a while she had barely ever spoken to her. She was one of those quiet people who said little. Or perhaps, Tess now thought, it was more that she had never made much effort to talk to the girl. She felt a pang of guilt. Time to make amends.

'I do love Queen of Puddings,' she said. 'And I suppose we should enjoy it while we can.' She added, 'I think rationing may be introduced before long, like in the last war.'

'Do you think so? Mrs Gulliver won't like that.'

'Nor will I.'

'You really think it'll happen?'

'Well, perhaps not everything will be rationed. But things like

119

sugar. It's not essential, is it? We'll be getting less from abroad and need to free up shipping. I'm sure living here, on a farm and in the countryside, though, we'll still have plenty to eat. Just perhaps not so many lovely puddings.'

'What do you think is going to happen in this war? Seems to me like not much 'as been goin' on so far.' Hannah put a hand to her mouth. 'Sorry, miss. I shouldn't have asked. Not with you workin' at the War Office an' all.'

Tess laughed. 'It is all pretty hush-hush but I'm still allowed an opinion just like the next person.'

Hannah's face relaxed.

'There's quite a lot going on at sea. And the balloon will go up in France at some point. That is, unless Hitler withdraws from Poland, but that's never going to happen. Hopefully, though, he won't do anything until our armies are ready to attack.'

'And if he does? I mean, if he attacks first?'

'The French Army is very big. Together we should have enough to stop him in his tracks.'

Hannah nodded thoughtfully. 'It all seems so far away when you're living here, in Alvesdon. I can't imagine there being fighting. Why can't Hitler be happy with what he's got?'

'I know. Sometimes it makes me so angry I want to scream. My . . .' she paused, suddenly feeling coy '. . . my friend, Alex Woodman, is in France already. It's all so worrying. And Wilf in the RAF and Edward off with his Yeomanry. All because of this one little man.'

'Father thinks more'll join. From the farm.'

'My father's worried about that too. The young ones like Tom Timbrell and, of course, in many ways, they're the most valuable.'

'Tom?' said Hannah, and Tess noticed her face reddening. 'You think he'll be off?'

Ah, thought Tess. Was there something between those two? She wouldn't blame either of them: Hannah was very pretty and half the womenfolk of the village swooned over Tom. It was quite the joke.

'Well, perhaps not Tom. Who knows?' She decided to change the subject. 'There – that's the yolks separated. Do you like cooking, Hannah?'

120

Hannah nodded. 'I do. Much better than changing beds and cleaning grates.'

'Yes, I'm sure. Well, we all think it's heroic of you to come up here and help.'

'Makes a nice change, to be honest.'

'And nice for me to have a chat with you, Hannah. I'm sorry we've not had much chance to talk before.'

Hannah smiled and looked down, bashfully. Then, raising her head, she said, 'Yes, it's very nice to chat, miss. And to someone more – well, someone closer to my age, if you get my meaning.'

Tess wanted to ask Hannah more – about her hopes and ambitions. Did she aspire to a different life? Or was a time in service, followed by marriage, children and keeping a home all she expected? All she wanted?

'Do you like living in London, miss?'

'Gosh, well, yes, I suppose so,' Tess replied. 'I have an interesting job and I share a house with a girlfriend and there's lots to see and do. But I do miss Alvesdon – perhaps all the more because there's this wretched war on. It makes it more precious, somehow. I always took it for granted but . . .' She didn't finish the sentence.

Hannah smiled. 'I always couldn't imagine living anywhere other than here. It's all I've ever known. Now, though, I'm not so sure. Hard to know what's around the corner, isn't it?'

Tess felt a dead weight in her stomach and a wave of dread swept over her. 'It's impossible to know,' she said at last. 'Everything has been tossed up into the air. I just hope it all comes back down again in the right order, don't you?'

Hannah had been asked to serve dinner at eight that evening and had duly delivered the watercress soup punctually as the grandfather clock in the hall chimed the hour. They'd all agreed not to dress up although Stork had announced that that was no reason to skimp on the wine.

'Delicious, Hannah,' said Stork, when she arrived to collect the bowls, prompting murmurings of agreement from the rest of the family. He was every bit as complimentary after tasting the stew and vegetables that followed.

'She's been a marvel,' said Debbo. 'You had a nice chat with her earlier, didn't you, Tess?'

'Yes. She's a bright girl,' she said. Tess had felt wistful all afternoon, although now they were sitting together for dinner the conversation flowed as it always did at family mealtimes; her mother and Wilf were never ones to let dark thoughts creep in for long. She also thought her father seemed more relaxed than she'd seen him in a while. She was watching him as he laughed at something Wilf had said when he caught her eye. He winked at her, something he'd often done when she'd been a child but not so much as she'd grown older. A brief moment of intimacy. Tess glanced around the room, unchanged since her first meals there as a young child. How old had she been when first allowed to eat with her parents? Six, perhaps? *Stop being so silly and sentimental*, she told herself.

'I wish Edward was here,' she said, articulating a thought she'd not really meant to share with them.

'Me too, but it sounds as though he's having a lovely time with his Yeomanry,' said Debbo.

'Just larking around on horses with his pals,' said Wilf. 'We shouldn't spare too many thoughts for Edward.'

'This is pretty much the last of the beef,' Stork now said, changing the subject. 'Roast for lunch tomorrow, then that'll be it. What's needed is some kind of domestic refrigerator like they have to freeze the meat coming from the Argentine. After all, if they can freeze meat on a ship, I see no reason why it can't be done on a smaller scale at home.'

'There's talk of food rationing,' said Tess.

'Bound to be eventually,' said Stork. 'There was in the last war. Hopefully our farming can answer the call, though.'

'And how is the farm?' asked Wilf.

'All right. We've ploughed up more than three hundred acres since last year and will do another two hundred in the spring. Labour's a worry. A number of the men have gone. Cecil, Percy and one of Gilbert's lads.'

'What about Tom?' asked Wilf.

'Not yet. Your grandfather's called a halt to any more shoot days this season, though.'

Wilf whistled. 'Grandpa's done that? Crikey.'

122

'But I need Tom to stay. We've got three land girls coming but it's not really unskilled labour we need. Wonderful help at harvest time, but through the winter and into the spring we need people who know what they're doing.'

'But you've those new tractors and the crawler,' said Tess.

'Well, yes. Of course mechanization dramatically reduces the amount of manpower needed, but it needs a terrific improvement in quality. And I'm not sure my land girls are going to be engineers *and* ploughmen, which is really what's needed these days.'

'Davey is proving a whizz, though,' said Debbo. 'There's not much he doesn't know about tractors.'

'So I hear,' said Tess. 'But he's only twelve.'

'And you've been awfully impressed with Elsa, Stork,' added Debbo.

Stork smiled. 'Yes, she's been brilliant. Has an uncanny knack of being able to start the Fordson. She's named him Thor and claimed him as her own. She says he's like a hammer to the ground the way he can draw a plough. Smudger scratches his head in wonder.'

They all laughed.

'So perhaps there's hope for your land girls after all,' suggested Wilf.

'There's got to be,' said Stork. 'Because they're coming and I need to make good use of them.'

The following day, after the roast lunch, Tess and Wilf left Alvesdon once more, Tess to return to her Pimlico house and her work in Whitehall, Wilf to Debden to rejoin his squadron. Debbo headed to her studio, while Stork decided to saddle up Jorrocks, a fifteen-year-old gelding, and ride around the farm; now that the harvest was long over, there was no work on a Sunday, not even in this time of national emergency. His men needed the rest, Stork reflected. They'd all been working long, hard days. The new tractors had helped but there was still ploughing to be done with horses and with a steam engine; thankfully, there was no shortage of coal just yet.

There were, of course, the younger lads still on the farm, but a huge amount had fallen on the shoulders of his middle-aged men: Don Smallpiece, his head dairyman; Alf Ellerby, the head carter; Arthur Morrow, his head ploughman. Even those working the machinery had to top and tail the day with maintenance, cleaning and checks. 'Grooming', Smudger called it, and in truth, that wasn't far off it. A tractor or crawler needed feeding and looking after just like a horse.

Now that the DH.4 had been laid up, Stork had taken to riding more. He'd never been a great one for hunting – unlike Edward or even John – but he did like to trot about the place. From the saddle he somehow saw more and, of course, he covered more ground than he could on foot. One noticed things: a gap in a fence, a gate latch out of alignment, a new mass of rabbit-burrowing. It also reminded him of the scale and scope of the farm. And it gave him time to think.

Some of those on the War Ags were starting to think a peace settlement might happen after all, and briefly Stork had clutched at such straws, even though, deep down, he'd suspected this was unlikely. Tess had confirmed there would be no climb-down, that Britain was preparing for a long, highly industrialized war. Three years, she'd told them, was the current estimate as to how long it would last.

Not for the first time, he prayed his children, his family and friends would be all right. As he reached the top of Farrowcombe and looked out over the Chase towards the English Channel, he marvelled at the beauty of the sight before him: the trees turning the autumnal colours of ochre, green and dun. The blue hills in the distance. He remembered a time when his father had brought him up here in the trap and had pointed out the Isle of Wight. 'That's thirty miles away,' he'd told the boy, to whom it seemed an impossibly long distance.

Stork grimaced. He'd barely spoken to his father in six weeks apart from brief conversations laced with *froideur*. Perhaps, he thought, it was time to try to build some bridges. His father was irascible but he was, Stork knew, a good man at heart. Their squabbles seemed so petty suddenly. So what if his father thought the sun shone from his older brother? As Debbo had pointed out, it was only because he was far away and they saw him so infrequently. Because Denholm was the eldest, the son and heir. 'Your father's outlook is Victorian,' Debbo had said to him. 'He believes in

124

primogeniture. Denholm waltzing off upset that. And when he comes back, flying in with all that confidence, he charms your father. You take it all so personally, my darling. But you really shouldn't.'

Perhaps there was something in that, Stork thought, his spirits rising at the thought of extending an olive branch to his father. And it would make his mother happy; he was aware she needed cheering. The war had thrown her completely. The old order unsettled. Yes, he thought, breaking into a gallop across the length of his old air strip. The following morning he would call on them and do his very best to clear the air.

The following Sunday, back at the manor once more, Hannah was helping Jean Gulliver to wash the pans and clear away Mr and Mrs Castell's lunch. The Sunday roast was a ritual that had never been missed in all the time Hannah had been working there and, by all accounts, was a tradition that had been part of the weekly routine every Sunday since before the dawn of the century.

Jean had been talking about knitting a new cardigan but Hannah had been only half listening. Instead she was thinking about her day at Farrowcombe, and how much she had relished the opportunity to be in charge in the kitchen, and around different people.

'So, what do you think I should go for?' Jean said, turning to Hannah.

'What do you mean?'

'Navy blue or dark green?'

Hannah had taken a moment to understand what was being asked – a hesitation not missed by the cook.

'I honestly don't think you've been listening to a word I've said. What's got into you today?'

'Nothing,' said Hannah, slightly more petulantly than she'd intended. 'Sorry, Jean – I was just thinking on something.'

Jean's face softened and she smiled. 'Well,' she said, 'as long as you're all right. If there's summat worryin' you, you can always tell me if you think it would help.'

'No, it's nothing. Honestly. But thank you.' *Ah, yes,* she thought, *the woolly.* 'And I think the blue would be better.'

Jean nodded. 'Yes. You're right. Navy blue it is.'

Hannah went back to drying the pans. She thought of Miss Tess and how much she'd enjoyed her company. She had been apprehensive when Miss Tess had appeared in the kitchen but had quickly found herself talking quite easily to her. Some younger company had been a welcome change and she'd been fascinated by her tales of life in London. And the family had all been so appreciative, each of them coming into the kitchen after dinner to thank Hannah personally. Much of the time she felt entirely anonymous at the manor. The most attention she'd ever attracted had been from Mr Denholm and that was not the kind she ever wanted to receive again.

She wondered whether she might ever go and work up at Farrowcombe. Betty Collis was, what, nearly sixty now? Perhaps she would retire soon. Perhaps she could take her place. Perhaps. Perhaps. Perhaps she should move away altogether. But then what of Tom?

'Can you take these out to the pigs, love?' Jean asked her, holding out a large two-handled pot full of vegetable shavings.

Hannah took it, and stepped out into the yard.

Only forty yards away, Tom Timbrell had been in the small workshop in the yard behind Alvesdon Manor, mending a wooden chair that he kept in his hut in Tippett's Wood. He enjoyed woodwork. The smell of the timber shavings was ancient and strangely intoxicating, while he also found creating something with his hands and just a few simple tools satisfying, a welcome distraction when unwanted thoughts strayed into his mind, as they had all too often recently. Of course, it being a Sunday, he was not expected to work, but what else was he going to do? In any case, he had never thought of his job as work exactly. Rather, it was something he did, a way of life as much as anything. The rhythms of the seasons, the routine of daily life, the inevitability of the way in which each year passed with its markers, change of light and temperature, its fluctuating activities – it was just how it was, and he had never really thought too deeply about it before now. Suddenly, though, his life had been thrown into a state of flux that jarred and discomforted him. Certitude had been replaced by uncertainty.

The chair mended, he swept away the shavings, tidied the tools and stepped out into the yard. Glancing down the lane, he saw Edie

Blythe walking towards him from the direction of the wood. She waved to him. 'I was hoping you might pitch up,' she said, smiling, as she neared him.

He couldn't help feeling awkward. 'Well, you found me,' he said. She walked right up to him and kissed him on the lips.

Startled, he immediately looked around and saw Hannah standing by the sties, staring straight at him.

Damn it, he thought, as Hannah turned and headed back towards the house.

Edie followed his gaze. 'It's all right,' she said, grinning, 'she's gone.'

Tom wiped his mouth.

'Going to the wood, are you?'

Tom nodded. 'I need to take this chair back to the hut.'

She looped her arm through his. 'Don't mind if I walk with you, do you?'

'No,' said Tom, Hannah's gaze still wrenching his heart.

'I do love this village,' Edie said, 'and the Castells have been so kind, but it is nice to have a bit of company occasionally.'

She talked on until they reached the hut when Tom made his excuses. 'I've got to set some traps,' he said, 'but nice to see you, Edie.'

She looked disappointed, but kissed him again, although this time on the cheek, and turned back towards the village.

In his hut, Tom put down the repaired chair and thought of Coco and how magical that had seemed in the warm late-summer nights. Perhaps he should have invited Edie inside. She was good fun, was Edie, but his heart wasn't for her, and he didn't need any more complications in his life. He thought of Hannah and remembered when he'd seen her so upset out in the yard back in the summer. He sighed. She was the girl he really wanted. Not Edie Blythe, not even Coco. Hannah.

He set the traps then headed north out of the woods and up onto the downs, compelled by an urge he barely understood to look down over the valley. It was a fine October afternoon, the rain gone, replaced by clear autumnal skies and the kind of visible sharpness that so often followed when the storm clouds had passed. He was striding up Mistleberry Down when he spotted Gilbert Rose, out checking his flock with his dogs.

On a whim, Tom walked over. 'The sheep look well,' he said.

'They need to be. Reckon it's goin'a be a cold win'er. Trying to fatten 'em up while I can.' He smiled and pulled out a pipe, scraping the bowl deliberately.

'I 'ear you've lost Ronnie.'

Gilbert filled his pipe. 'One thing's as sure as day. When there's a war on, young men'll allus head off an' fight.' He now lit the tobacco, the sweet smoke swirling around them. 'I'm sorry 'e's gone as 'e was a good lad.'

'I bin wondering what to do meself,' admitted Tom.

'You and others besides. One goes and you all start thinkin' you needs to go. Same as the last time.'

'I don't really want to,' said Tom. 'An' Mr Stork says 'e needs me here, but I dunno. Mr Castell has cancelled the shootin' an' I know I'm a good shot and would probably do all right in the Army. Mebbe I'd be better use fightin' than farming.'

'I'd be sorry to see you go,' said Gilbert, 'make no mistake. And I've no doubt what you say is right. I also reckon the farm will manage without 'e, mind. You got to do what you think is right.'

Tom gazed out over the valley with its patchwork of fields, its woods and combes, and at Alvesdon, the village he'd lived in all his life. There was the church, peeking up through the trees, the manor and the cricket ground. Yet he wondered whether he'd still be able to work this ground with a clear conscience if he didn't go. All the other lads would come back and he'd be the one who'd stayed behind, who'd shirked the firing line. Mr Stork had done his bit in the last war; he'd understand. Hopefully, his father's post of foreman would still be there, waiting for him, once he was back. Perhaps he'd see something of the world too. Some places he'd not see if he stayed here, at Alvesdon, for ever.

Tom sighed.

'Can almost see that brain o' yours doin' the rounds,' chuckled Gilbert. 'So you'm goin' to fight?'

Tom nodded. 'Yes, Gilbert. I reckon I am.'

Stork trotted back into the stable yard just before six o'clock that Sunday night and was just leading Jorrocks into his stable when an ashen-faced Debbo hurried from the house towards him.

'Oh, Stork, my darling, thank God you're back,' she said.

Stork felt a lead weight sink in his stomach and jar his entire body. 'What is it?' he said. 'What's happened?'

'It's your father. Philip Gready has just rung from the manor. He seems to think he's had a stroke.'

11

November

IT WAS AROUND MIDNIGHT AND EDWARD WAS DRIVING CAREFULLY around the narrow high-hedged lanes between Falmouth and the Helford River having just dropped Brenda Portman at her uncle's house in Port Navas. Somehow he now had to negotiate more of these ridiculously narrow lanes – narrower even than those around Alvesdon – and get himself back to his billet on the Roseland Peninsula, but he thought what a very small price it was to pay even though he was a bit tight and driving a vehicle with only narrow slits for headlights.

On another evening he might have cursed the government for imposing such ludicrous and, frankly, lethal restrictions on headlights when not a single enemy aircraft had once been seen over Cornwall, but not that night. In the darkness he wore a grin he simply couldn't wipe from his face. Really, it had been the most perfect day. He was determined to drive slowly and cautiously, and to hell with it if it took him an age. With Brenda's scent still lingering beside him and the thought of those last moments still wonderfully vivid, he felt in no particular rush to be back in his bed.

If Edward was perfectly honest with himself, the war had treated him very well indeed so far, almost as though he'd been at holiday camp for the past ten weeks. The regiment had been split up since moving to Cornwall in September, because of stabling. Four squadrons, each of three troops plus an HQ squadron, meant the best part of three hundred horses. No single landowner or institution had stabling for that many so, while HQ and A Squadron headed to Sir Richard Farriday's place just outside Truro, B and his own C Squadron had been sent elsewhere – in his case to a large house, or 'castle', as it was grandly titled, near Portholland on the Roseland Peninsula. While the horses had been stabled there quite comfortably, the men had been tented in the grounds and the four C Squadron officers had been billeted above the stables. Captain Monty Trethowan, the C Squadron commander, had been given his own room, but Edward and his fellow lieutenants, Mike Horsley and Peter Delafort, shared a gabled room. A further room acted as a four-man mess. Peter had been at Cambridge with Edward and had joined the Wiltshire Rangers on Edward's suggestion back in the summer. Edward had known Mike for years, albeit not well. He was also from farming stock; his people lived on the Plain, near Chitterne, and he was far more typical of the Wiltshire Rangers than Peter, or even Edward, for that matter. Squires, land agents, county solicitors, grooms, farmhands, country folk: these were the men who made up the Wiltshire Rangers Yeomanry, just as they always had, although there was now a smattering of real Army types too, posted to lick the amateurs into some kind of shape. Whether it was working, Edward was not sure.

Not that he was bothered. He was still prepared to bet very good money that no one would be sending them off to face down the panzers any time soon. This was a period of his life to be relished for as long as it lasted. And it was wonderful fun sharing digs with Peter and Mike. The three got on like a house on fire. It really had been most civilized.

By day they'd carried out drill, rifle practice, or performed reconnaissance patrols, training led by the real Army NCOs. Twice a month they'd carried out larger exercises as the entire regiment, while for the most part the weekends were their own, although the four men took turns to be duty officer. He'd had plenty of time to paint and had delighted their hosts by working on a mural in the main house, turning a small room on the ground floor into what

131

looked like a gloriously patterned tent, complete with views of the Tuscan hills through the flaps. There had been invitations to dinners from the local squirearchy, nights out in nearby pubs and rides along the coast.

They'd even gone sailing on the Helford a few times too. It was as though, once the initial alarm of being at war had died down, people were determined to enjoy themselves as much as possible while they had the chance. That was certainly Edward's avowed intention, at any rate.

And just the previous weekend they had been invited on yet another – admittedly windswept and decidedly chilly – sailing jaunt, which had been bracing, exhilarating and huge fun. This had then been followed by a truly wonderful dinner afterwards at the Farlowe-Scotts', a well-to-do local family, where Edward had met Brenda. She was Douglas Farlowe-Scott's niece, two years younger than Edward, and had finished reading modern languages at Newnham College the summer just gone; Edward had sat next to her and had shamelessly monopolized her all evening, despite a kick on the shins from Mike.

Edward laughed, thinking of his friend's scowls. But to the victor the spoils! He and Brenda had hit it off immediately through this Cambridge connection although their paths had never crossed; if Mike thought he was going to share the attentions of this goddess, he was much mistaken. And in any case, Edward had known immediately that she had warmed to him. She told him she had intended to move to London but, with her parents in Kenya, she had, at their bidding, come down to Cornwall to stay with her uncle and aunt to sit out the storm of war.

After that dinner, Edward had invited her dancing in Falmouth. All week he'd been looking forward to it with a mixture of excitement and nervous trepidation, yet it had been as magical as he had hoped. Dinner first, where they barely drew breath they talked so much. Then they had skipped around the dancehall, until at last he had offered to drive her home in the car he had borrowed from Monty Trethowan. At the top of the hill before the descent into the village, and feeling both intoxicated and emboldened, he had pulled over and kissed her. And, to his eternal relief, she had kissed him back, run a hand through his hair and said, 'You know, you're really rather lovely.' Yes, he thought now, as he wound his way around Cornwall. So far he was having the time of his life in this war.

Nearly two hundred miles away, his mother and father had spent the evening at Alvesdon Manor. They had driven home earlier than their eldest son but while Edward was negotiating the lanes around the Fal estuary, Stork was also still awake. Sitting in the drawing room with a tumbler in his hand, he was contemplating the changing relationship with his father. As a boy, he'd adored him. It was his father who'd encouraged him to ride a horse almost as soon as he could walk; it was his father who had played games of cricket with them all in the garden as soon as they could hold a bat, and who had eagerly taken Stork with him all around the farm at an early age. His father had also given him the nickname that had stuck: the young Walter, as he'd been then, had built a treehouse high in one of the horse-chestnuts beyond the yard, or rather, just a rough platform. 'You look like a ruddy stork up there, Walter!' his father had said, then had taken to referring to him as 'my young stork'. He'd been Stork ever since.

It was his father who had given him a 410 shotgun and who had instilled in him and John the confidence to go off and roam the land, make dens in the woods and develop their independence. He had also recognized that Denholm had always been somewhat aloof from Stork and John; they had got along well enough but while Stork and John had been inseparable at home, there was none of that intimacy with Denholm. As children they'd thought little of it, yet as he had grown older, Stork had become increasingly wedded to the farm and their life there as Denholm had spent more time away with friends.

Thinking back upon the glowing praise his father had always showered on their older brother now, it was as though the more Denholm distanced himself from life at Alvesdon, the more his father put his eldest son upon a pedestal. He was his heir; the farm should be his, yet he did not want it. Stork did. Perhaps he had been too obvious about it; maybe his father resented him for it.

Stork sipped his whisky. He'd thought about this so many times over the years, yet when they'd all survived the war, Denholm had abandoned them altogether and headed to France. 'Alwyn's hurt at

133

his eldest son's rejection,' Debbo had told him after one of the early rows with his father, 'is manifested in resentment towards you, my darling Stork.' Maybe she was right.

There had been times over the years when Stork had felt blind with rage at his father and had wondered whether it wouldn't be better for all if he were dead. He had not meant it, of course. And when word had reached him that his father had had a stroke Stork had been distraught. Panicked, even. He remembered the frantic rush through the front door, and the relief when he got to his parents' room and found his father alive. He had almost wept with relief. How funny, he thought now. Was it because he was thinking of the beloved father he had been when Stork had been young? No, of course it was not. It was because his father was still beloved. For all their disagreements and rows, for all his bloody-mindedness and for all the hurt his father had caused, Stork had known then how much he still loved him. The two were wedded to the place: to the farm, to Alvesdon. And, like it or not, that meant they were wedded together too.

It had been Hannah who had found him. She had heard him fall in his study, rushed to him and then, after shouting for help, had immediately called for Dr Gready. Her quick thinking, the doctor had told them, had very possibly saved Stork's father – or, at least, given him a far greater chance of a full recovery. She had also helped tend him until a proper nurse could be found. To think that just a few days before Stork had been wondering whether he could entice Hannah to Farrowcombe. That, of course, was out of the question now.

There was some paralysis down his father's right side and to begin with Alwyn struggled to speak. It was Debbo who had suggested to Stork that perhaps he should try reading to his father, just as his father had done to the three of them with such gusto when they'd been little. Whenever he could get away – and he tried to make sure it was every other day at least – Stork and Debbo would head down to the manor in the evening. At seven o'clock the nurse would spoon-feed Alwyn with soup and other easily swallowed food, while Stork would sit in an armchair near the bed and read. They'd already finished *Under the Greenwood Tree* and were now romping through an Agatha Christie. Then, at eight, he joined Debbo and Maimes

134

downstairs for dinner; as Debbo had pointed out, it was important to give his mother some support and company too.

That evening, though, as he'd closed the book and gently put it down on the bedside table, his father had turned to him and grabbed his hand. 'Thank you,' he said. 'I don't deserve your kindness.' The words were slurred, but Stork had not mistaken them.

'Don't be silly,' Stork had told him. 'I'm enjoying these evenings.' He'd leaned over and kissed his father's head. It was not something he had ever done before and he was surprised at himself.

Suffering a stroke could never be considered a blessing, but Stork wondered now whether perhaps some good had come of it. There were so many things he and his father had said to one another and so many others that neither could ever quite express. Perhaps, though, as his father made his gradual recovery, their own relationship would heal too.

12

Midwinter

EDWARD WOKE UP TO THE SOUND OF SEAGULLS MEWING AND croaking beyond the blackout curtain but managed to stagger as quietly as he could out of bed, pull down the blinds and look out over the pretty little harbour. It was nearly eight in the morning and only just beginning to get light. Soon the days would be growing lighter again, and that was a cause for cheer. He quickly got back into bed, where it was far warmer, and looked down at Brenda Portman, her dark hair spread out across the pillow and the pale skin of her shoulders even whiter in the monochrome of the mid-December morning. He thought about waking her and, while pondering this, gazed out of the window across the bay towards St Anthony Head. He remembered camping trips there as a boy – it had been quite a tradition for a few years. One of the landowners on the headland had been an old friend of his father so they'd come down for a week once the summer holidays had begun and before harvest had started. Milk and eggs from the farm, hiking on the cliffs, or scrambling down onto Porthbeor Beach where there was a cave, rock pools, sand and seclusion. In his memory, those had been golden summers of endless sunshine. Carefree and happy. He did remember quite distinctly his father saying once as they sat around the campfire that this was what they'd fought the last war for. Maybe it was what they were fighting for again.

Now, as he looked down at Brenda sleeping, he smiled to himself. What a whirlwind time of it they had had. From a kiss in the car to dancing a week later, then to dinners, to long walks, and then, now, daringly, a night in the St Mawes Hotel in St Mawes. It was one of the things he loved about Brenda: she was so game. Whenever he suggested some new activity, she invariably agreed. In fact, it was she who had first suggested the illicit night away. 'Do you think I'm too fast?' she had asked him, as he'd met her off the ferry from Falmouth.

'Not for me,' he had replied.

He wondered whether he would be waking up beside her were it not for the war. Time seemed more precious, somehow, this new-found love more urgent. Or was he being fanciful? He was so completely and totally smitten in a way he'd never experienced before or thought possible. And how absolutely marvellous it was that she seemed to feel exactly the same way about him as he did about her. He couldn't believe his good fortune.

He leaned over and began kissing her neck and shoulders. She stirred, turned, then, with her eyes still closed, smiled.

'Morning, Mr Pooter,' she said, sleepily.

They had booked themselves into the hotel as 'Mr and Mrs Pooter', a reference to a comic novel they both loved and thought hilarious.

'D'you know,' said Edward, 'I honestly cannot think of anything nicer than waking up beside your vision of loveliness every morning. You really are very beautiful, Brenda. Have I mentioned it before?'

She opened her eyes and laughed. 'But eventually I won't be so lovely. I'll get old and crinkly.'

'So will I but I can't imagine that right now, so I won't.'

'Who said you should stop kissing my neck?'

He leaned over again. 'I feel like a cat.'

'Miaow.'

He stopped and drew himself down beside her so that his face was just inches from hers.

'You're not so bad to look at either, you know,' she said. 'I could get used to it as well.'

'Are you propositioning me?'

'I don't know. Are you me?'

He grinned and ran a finger down her neck and across her breasts. 'Well, right now, I'd certainly like to be married to you. As I said, what could be better than waking up beside you each day?'

She kissed him. 'I've always thought of you as a romantic type, Edward, but to be perfectly honest, this is not the most romantic of proposals. If this is a proposal, that is?'

He kissed her, on the lips, then on her neck and her breasts, wishing he could hold this moment for ever. 'I'd love to marry you, Brenda, darling. I really would. But there's this bloody war, isn't there? They can't keep us larking about on horses in Cornwall for ever. We might get separated, and the last thing you'll want is to be married to me.'

'I might,' she said. 'I could play the role of the dutiful wife, writing you long letters and keeping the home fires burning et cetera.'

'At least we're married already in the eyes of this fine establishment.'

'That's true. I'm sure they've not been taken in for a single moment, though.'

He felt her arms pull him towards her and heard her sigh contentedly.

At Alvesdon, deep midwinter had descended on the valley. The start of the working day on the farm had been pushed back to eight a.m. following the changing of the clocks, but it was still far from fully light as Stork stood next to Claude Timbrell and the assembled workers – far fewer now. He gazed around them, thinking of all the missing faces from Tom Timbrell to Percy, Cecil and one of the Rose lads. Now there were four girls before him: Elsa, in her brown overalls, and the three land girls, Jill, Hattie and Susie. Hattie was making circular motions on the ground with a foot. He wondered whether she was listening to what Claude was saying.

The clearing of the furze had finished so the top of the downs was still being ploughed and it was this task that Stork and Claude were keen to finish while they could. October had been intermittently wet, November largely dry, while December had so far been mixed. There was an old adage that if there was no frost before Christmas, there would be plenty after and so far there had not been one. Now, then, was the time to plough and sow while the soil was still damp and soft enough to do so easily.

Elsa and Jill were to plough Airfield, a new field that it had pained Stork to see put under crop.

He glanced across at Elsa, who was biting a fingernail and wore an anxious expression. Today was her mother's tribunal, something to be faced by all Germans in the country, and although he had no doubt Carin would be fine, he appreciated his brother John's family were worried about her. Catching Elsa's eye, he gave her what he hoped was a reassuring smile.

Thankfully, for once, his diary was free of War Ag business. He would do some ploughing himself, then see to some paperwork so as to be on hand when John and Carin got back; they were due to come to dinner that night with Elsa, at Debbo's suggestion. She had thought the last thing Carin would need to do that day was prepare any kind of meal.

First, though, he would call on his parents. With the morning's briefing over, he went to Elsa. 'You'll not have any nails left, you know,' he said. 'It'll be fine.'

Elsa nodded. 'Ollie's also about to join his first ship.'

'And very proud of him we all are.'

'I can't stop worrying about him. There might be no fighting anywhere on land – other than Finland, of course – but the Royal Navy are still busy at sea. I can't bear to think about it.'

'It must all feel very worrying. But U-boats are after freighters, not warships, and by the sound of things our Navy's giving the Germans the run-around in the South Atlantic. I expect they might think twice before venturing out again.'

She smiled. 'I expect you're right. At least ploughing takes a lot of concentration. It keeps one's mind off things.'

Stork left her and went into the manor to see his parents. His father was still recovering, little by little, although Stork thought he appeared noticeably older, diminished somehow. He was also conscious that Denholm had sent one telegram and made one telephone call since the stroke but had otherwise not been in contact. By contrast, he and John had dropped in each day and he was still reading to their father more evenings than not. Once Alwyn had been well enough, Stork had even begun taking him out around the farm in a trap.

'Ah, Stork, there you are,' said Alwyn, as Stork entered the drawing room. His voice was still a little slurred – as though he had developed a bad lisp – but the words were increasingly distinct. His father was sitting in a tall-backed armchair, the wireless next to him on a sideboard. 'Sounds like the *Graf Spee*'s had it. Good riddance too.'

'Yes, it seems so.' Stork moved a footstool and squatted on it beside him.

'And Carin's big day.'

'She'll be all right.'

'Course she will! Any damn fool can see she's as English, these days, as you or I.'

'Would you and Maimes like to join us for dinner, Pa, for a change?' he asked. 'We've Carin, John and Elsa over. Would be lovely to have you both too. I could come and fetch you in the Wolseley, if you like. You've not been up to Farrowcombe since the stroke. Maybe the change would be good for you.'

Alwyn sighed. 'That's kind. And I'm sure your mother would love to. But I get so damnably tired in the evening. Gready says I've got to take it steady. Not push myself, if I'm to get back to full strength.'

'And I'm sure he's right. Well, it was just a thought.'

'And a kind one. Perhaps after we've finished the Wodehouse, eh?'

Stork smiled. 'All right, Pa.'

The tribunal was held at the County Law Courts in Salisbury. Carin and John drove into town and were so early they sat in the White Hart drinking coffee for more than half an hour until it was time for Carin to present herself.

'It'll be fine, darling,' John told her, for the umpteenth time, as they crossed Exeter Street. 'Do try not to worry.'

There were more than twenty others waiting. Who were these people? Carin wondered. Refugees, émigrés, workers come for a better life in Britain. Were some of them spies?

Carin was called by a police constable with a clipboard. John moved with her but was stopped.

'But I'm her husband,' he said.

'The gallery entrance is up the stairs,' the policeman replied. 'First door on the left. You're welcome to watch proceedings from there.'

He nodded. 'Break a leg, darling.'

Carin felt sick to her core as the constable opened the door for her and led her into the courtroom, then to the dock. Ahead was the county court judge, Mr Justice Atkinson. Clerks sat at the table beneath him.

She glanced around and saw John, looking down from the gallery. He was the only one there.

'Do sit down, Mrs Castell,' said Atkinson.

He looked through some notes, then said, 'Now, as I'm sure you're aware, the safety of the United Kingdom is of paramount importance. The aim of this tribunal and of others around the country is to satisfy ourselves that the more than seventy-three thousand German and Austrian nationals we have living here in Britain are accounted for and pose no possible threat to our national security. Is that clear?'

Carin nodded. 'Yes.'

'Good. The government has devised three categories. Anyone receiving an A classification will be detained at His Majesty's pleasure for an unspecified period. Those classified B are those whose loyalty is in some kind of doubt but who pose no immediate risk. They will be expected to remain within five miles of their homes, will be subject to police checks and will be unable to possess a variety of items such as firearms, maps and so on. Those given a C classification are those who pose no threat whatsoever and will be free to continue their lives here as normal.'

Carin glanced again at John. She already felt guilty somehow. The British rule of law, she knew, was to assume someone was innocent until proven otherwise. But sitting there, in the courtroom, with the dour, humourless judge staring down at her, she felt such principles had been turned on their head. She had been allowed no legal representation whatsoever.

Justice Atkinson began speed-reading through his notes, muttering aloud. 'So, you moved here in 1920 after you married your husband, John. Three children. Have lived in the village of Alvesdon ever since. That all seems fairly straightforward.'

Carin breathed a sigh of relief.

'What's concerning me a little, though, Mrs Castell, is that your father, Herr Wolff, is a member of the Nazi Party and your brother is not only a Party member but also now in the SS.'

'He is not,' she said. Her heart was now thudding in her chest.

'Not what it says here. He's a lawyer, has been given an SS rank and was involved in some legal work at the time of the annexation of Czechoslovakia back in March.'

'I – I don't know what to say. This is news to me, I can assure you.'

'I think we'd know if my brother-in-law was in the SS,' said John.

'Be quiet, Mr Castell.'

'But I abhor what the Nazis stand for,' stuttered Carin. 'I love this country deeply and it is where I have made my home. My children are as English as any other child.'

The judge looked down at his notes again. 'And yet you've been visiting regularly over the last few years. Previous visit last Christmas. Presumably you knew then your brother and father were Party members? And that your nephew has joined the Luftwaffe?'

'Yes. But we were shocked by how much they had fallen under the spell of Hitler. I still love my German family, but I do not, I cannot, agree at all with their politics.'

'Hmm,' said the judge, scratching his chin. 'And there's this letter you sent them on the eighteenth of September. "This is to let you know that we are well. I have been helping house the evacuees from the city and the children are all fine. Everyone here is being remarkably stoic. I hope you are all safe at this terrible time." How do you explain that?'

'This is outrageous!' called John. 'What's wrong with it?'

'Mr Castell, be quiet!' said the judge. 'I won't tell you again. Do I make myself clear?' He turned back to Carin. 'Well?'

Carin could feel the tears at the corner of her eyes. She paused a moment, desperately trying to compose herself. 'It was an innocent letter. Our two nations are at war. I was just letting them know I was all right. That the family was all right. I meant nothing more.'

The judge looked at her again, pursed his lips, then said, 'And you are still German. Not naturalized despite being married to an Englishman.'

'It simply never occurred to me.'

'Look here,' exclaimed John, 'I hardly think—'

'Mr Castell! Please – be quiet.' The judge turned back to Carin. 'I am inclined to believe you, Mrs Castell. But, as you say, our two nations are at war. I am sorry you find yourself in this invidious predicament but your German family's connections with the regime, your recent visits and the fact that you have been in contact since hostilities began, in addition to your stated nationality – despite long years here – mean I am compelled to classify you as category B.'

'What?' exclaimed John. 'How can this be? Is that it? Done and dusted in minutes. Is my wife not allowed to defend herself?'

'Now, now, sir,' said the constable, standing by the door to the gallery. 'You heard what His Lordship said.'

Justice Atkinson raised a hand. 'It's all right, Constable. I do appreciate this may be upsetting, but I have to put all personal feelings aside. Looking at the evidence of your situation, Mrs Castell, there is some cause for doubt, however small. The security of the nation dictates I make this judgement.'

For a moment, Carin stood there, unable to absorb what she had just heard, but a constable gently led her from the room. Outside, she found John waiting for her in the hall. Burying her head in his shoulder, she was unable to stop the flow of tears.

'It's utterly ridiculous,' John said, holding her tightly. 'We'll appeal. We'll get this monstrous injustice righted. You'll see.'

'I can't believe it,' sobbed Carin. 'Oh, John, what am I going to do?'

13

The Icy Furrow

Monday, 22 January 1940

A LOUD, SHRILL RINGING, AND ELSA WAS AWAKE, AN ANXIOUS dream about Ollie ended mid-flow by the alarm clock. She switched on the lamp beside her bed, blinking in the sudden light. Six forty-five and still dark outside. And another day of heavy frost too – she could see it on the windowpanes. She took a deep breath, pushed back the sheets and got out of her bed, shivering as she pulled off her night shirt and fumbled for her clothes. Another day. Of sniggers and glowers from the three land girls. Of freezing temperatures and temperamental tractors. Of exhausting toil.

Elsa was not used to feeling miserable. How sunny her life used to be! Only recently had she come to understand just what a charmed existence she had led before the war had begun – home, the farm, the valley, family who loved her, everything familiar and warm. And *safe*. And Ollie. She had never imagined the entire edifice could come crumbling down quite so quickly. Now she felt like an outsider in her own village. Even on the farm she was resented by the land girls and largely ignored by the men: she wasn't one of them because she was the boss's niece. Or did they give her a wide birth because they were wary of her? It had simply never occurred to her before that people might not like her so she had bounced confidently through life chatting to anyone. Now, though, she felt

144

self-conscious, aware she carried a different status. That she was, yes, an outsider.

She put on a thick pullover, made her bed and headed to the bathroom. If only Ollie was still at home. She missed him so much: his gentle, kind face, his understanding. His companionship. His touch. She worried about him and thought about him more than she had imagined she would. His life was so different, with people she did not know and could not visualize. Soon he'd be on a ship and that would be even worse. He would have to confront an enemy who wanted to attack him, sink his ship, kill him. It didn't bear thinking about, yet she couldn't help such thoughts entering her mind.

Elsa leaned on the washbasin, then ran the water, and cupped it onto her face. Goodness, but it was cold. She hated not knowing where he was or when she might see him again. Her ordered mind did not like this lack of information. Then she felt guilty – for feeling sorry for herself when her beloved mother was having a far worse time of things. *Poor Mummy*, she thought. She felt so resentful of and angry with those who had imposed a stupid, ridiculous letter upon her kind, loving and wonderful mother. How could they? How *could* they? It was a terrible wrong, a terrible injustice. She sluiced water over her face again, then smacked her hand against the side of the basin in frustration. *This war!*

By eight o'clock, Elsa was standing in the yard, swaying from foot to foot in a vague effort to keep warm. The old farmers' saying had proved correct. The new year had brought with it a sudden drop in temperatures as winds from Siberia swept across northern Europe, blocking warm air from the Atlantic and covering the country in a deep, bitterly cold frost. She'd not worked on the farm in January before as she'd always been at school, but now was rapidly learning what a tough and frequently dispiriting occupation it was in these short, dark days of biting cold.

Alvesdon, so beautiful and lush in high summer, had become skeletal, monochrome, almost desolate. Still beautiful in deep midwinter, she tried to reassure herself, but forbidding, too, as all around her were signs of the never-ending work that always needed doing, while the dim light and lifelessness of the countryside seemed to echo her own growing despair.

The three land girls were as disenchanted as she was, she knew, if not more so. There was no glamour in the task, little sense of satisfaction from doing their bit when all it meant was long days of back-breaking work. January was a time of heightened activity on the farm. The dairy cows were all in byres in the tithe barn and no longer living off pasture. That meant they needed feeding and mucking out every other day as well as the twice daily task of cleaning the dairy after milking. The yard, too, between the byres and the milking sheds, also needed cleaning. There was cake to prepare, mangolds to crush, manure to spread on the fields now that the frost had hardened the ground and made the going so much easier. Any moment now, lambing would begin, and although the plan was to reduce the flock, this would not happen until after the last newborn lamb, which meant she and the others were all expected to help get the lambing sheds ready and then were part of a rota to help Gilbert Rose. Why, she wondered, did ewes so often give birth at night?

She now knocked her boots together to try to keep her feet warm, her arms crossed and patting her sides. A little way from her, quite apart, were the three land girls and some twenty-five men and teenage boys. A number of the younger men had gone since the start of the war, although none of their departures had caused as big a stir as that of Tom Timbrell, the foreman's son. There was now a dearth of men in their twenties in the village. Even Mr Roberts, the schoolteacher, had left to join up. Edie Blythe was running the school on her own and living in the tied cottage that went with the job.

The farm and the village had changed more in the space of a few months than they had in all the time Elsa had been alive. She wondered if any of the labourers there that morning had been gossiping about her mother and her family. Growing up, Elsa had not been unaware of the sensitivities or unusualness of having a German mother, but she could not remember one single occasion when it had caused any kind of unpleasantness. Her parents had often talked about when they'd first returned to the village, newly married, the shock and scandal it had caused, not least with her grandparents. But her mother was, she knew, such a warm-hearted and kind person that very quickly she had been accepted and embraced by the villagers. Her father had often said he thought the village looked upon her as slightly different, a bit exotic, but very much part of the fabric. Rural communities might be largely cut off from much of the rest of the world, he would say, but they're not a closed shop.

Everything had changed with Carin's category B classification. Of course, word had got out. Rumours had begun circulating – that all her family were in the SS, that she had links to Hitler himself. A few days before Christmas, Doris Sandford had accosted Carin in the village stores and told her she had a nerve to show her face. 'An enemy in our midst,' she had said. Margaret and Donald Pierson had leaped to Carin's defence, but the damage had been done. Sides had been formed between those who thought the category B classification an outrage and those who deemed it an outrage that Carin still had most of her freedom. Her mother had become a cause of division.

The family had rallied – of course they had – as had the Varneys, the Greadys and other local friends. Letters had been written to the local MP, to other MPs, to anyone of influence known to the family. Replies had come back too, some sympathetic and others accusing the family of making a damaging fuss at a time of national emergency. Yet whether sympathetic or hostile, nothing, it seemed, could be done. There was no right of appeal, no recourse, no second opinion. So her mother had been obliged to report to Constable Jack Allbrook in Middle Chalke once a week, but she had otherwise withdrawn almost entirely from the village community. John, her father, normally so cheery and *laissez-faire*, had been furious ever since. He'd even addressed the entire workforce at the brewery and told them all, in no uncertain terms, what he thought of how his wife had been treated and warning them that if so much as a whiff of negative gossip reached his ears the culprit would be out of the door faster than he could throw them.

Stork, too, had done the same one morning just before Christmas. It was, he told them, a gross injustice, a decision of grotesque over-caution by one man who knew nothing of Carin or the community in which she lived. 'We – all of us here – know what she is really like,' he had said. 'A kinder, more honest person I've not met. It's a cruel by-product of this war, but none of us should think any the less of her for this or treat her any differently. She is still the sister-in-law I love. But we also all know what gossip is like – how it can be used to distort the truth and spread lies. So I want you all to stick up for her and my family. I want you to be deaf to any slanderous comments. I know you won't let me down.' Elsa had felt the eyes of the farm workers looking at her and had squirmed inwardly with embarrassment and shame, yet she was still glad her uncle had said his piece. 'And please make sure you don't,' he had said, eyeing them all in turn. Then, satisfied he had said enough, he had clapped his hands together, and added, 'Right, let's hear no more about it. Ever.'

But it was there, a malign presence made worse by the winter, by the war, by the growing number of privations imposed by an uncommunicative government. Everything had changed. Alvesdon had been tarnished. She had started to question herself. She was half German. Her mother's relatives were her relatives. Small barbs of guilt began to prickle her that she shared the blood of the enemy. The certitude of childhood and all that she had loved about home had been challenged and she could not untangle these conflicting thoughts.

And she missed Ollie so desperately. On Saturday another letter had arrived from him, written from HMS *King Alfred*, the on-shore training base in Sussex. This was not a ship, he had explained, in an earlier letter, but rather had been a large public swimming pool in Hove that was still under construction when the war had broken out. The Navy had swept in, requisitioned it and expanded it into a shore-based training camp for a thousand officers like himself from the Royal Navy Volunteer (Supplementary) Reserve. 'Apparently,' he had written, 'holiday camps and hotels up and down the coast have been pressed into service as new training bases for the Navy. Wellington might have thought that Waterloo was won on the playing fields of Eton, but I think this war will be won at sea in converted seaside hotels.' That had made her laugh. This latest letter was about his three days in a British submarine. He was praying he'd never be expected to board one again. 'I wasn't seasick,' he wrote, 'and I could survive the claustrophobia. But the smell – no, thank you!' He missed her desperately and wished he was back with her. He was due to finish and be posted to a ship as a sub-lieutenant sometime in March, assuming he passed his exams. Then he'd be given a little bit of leave and would, of course, head straight to

Alvesdon and to her. 'It's not so very long, I suppose, darling Elsa,' he'd written, 'but seems interminably so to me as I write this now.'

He sounded like her Ollie right enough in his letters but she also worried that he'd be changed by his experiences, and that she'd changed too in the months since she'd seen him. He'd not even been home at Christmas, which had been the most sombre and dispiriting she could ever remember. She was lonely, she had recently realized. All her life, people had been around her: parents, siblings, grandparents, uncle and aunt, cousins, school friends, Ollie. She'd been so fortunate and she'd felt loved and cared for. Suddenly, though, she could find very little to feel cheerful about. It did not do to wallow, but she missed the life she'd had. Her mother had withdrawn, her father had lost his normal *joie de vivre* and her younger brother and sister were away at school. The cousins were away. Ollie was in the Navy. She had tried to be friendly to the land girls, but there was a gulf between them and her that she could not bridge, even though they were often sent off to work together. 'I'm relying on you to show them the ropes, Elsa,' Uncle Stork had told her. Well, she'd tried, but in truth, they didn't seem terribly grateful or indeed interested.

Jill and Hattie were older than her, and that didn't help. Elsa had only left school the previous summer, but Hattie, whose family were well-to-do and from London, had spent a year in Paris. Jill was from Birmingham and her father was the headmaster of a school in Sutton Coldfield; she had also won a scholarship to study at Oxford and had finished her degree the previous summer. Only Susie was more down-to-earth and closer to Elsa in age. She was from Crewe; her father worked on the railways.

Despite the difference in their backgrounds, Hattie and Jill had clearly decided to take Susie under their wing; after all, they had been sent to Alvesdon together and the three of them were living in the old servants' attic quarters at the manor, which had become vacant again after the evacuees had gone and Edie had moved out. There was a rapport and camaraderie between the three girls. Knowing glances, in-jokes and phrases, and gentle ribbing of Susie's accent were symbols of a fellowship into which it was clear Elsa was not invited.

'So, girls,' said Claude, eventually, 'I'd like you to help feed the dairy herd on Don's instructions, then assist with the mucking out of the byres. That should take you a little past dinner, and then you can help load up one of the pneumatic tyre wagons with manure, take it up to High Elms and get started on that.'

'With Thor?' asked Elsa.

'With the Fordson, yes.'

'I'm taking the larger wagon, though,' said Smudger, then added, 'if that's all right with you, ladies?'

'So use the one that's in the cart shed,' said Claude. 'Put your backs into it and you won't be cold.'

Elsa turned to the girls and, with what she hoped was a cheery smile, said, 'Well, we'd best get to it.' Silently, they followed her to the byres, which were within a large old tile-roofed tithe barn that stood a little way beyond the yard and next to the hayricks. The barn had been given a concrete floor a few years earlier and had been divided into byres with wooden stalls, each roughly the size of a tennis court. For much of the year, these were used for storage and as maintenance areas but for the three or four winter months, with no grass left to feed them and when temperatures dropped, the herd was brought in, all eighty or so, cows and calves in one byre, the two bulls in another on their own, and the rest of the milking cows in the others. Chaff from the previous harvest was laid on the floor, to which sliced and pulped mangolds were added in metal mangers along with some cake. Sweet treacle, thinned with hot water, was poured over the mixture, so the tithe barn was filled with a sweetly savoury aroma of molasses, pulled root crop, straw and dung.

The dairyman, Don Smallpiece, was inspecting the calves as they entered the barn.

'If you girls could clear number four byre,' he said, 'but give them a feed first.'

Elsa nodded. 'Jill and Susie, you get the mangolds and treacle, and Hattie and I will see to the cake.'

Jill and Susie saluted her and Hattie smirked.

'Come on, Hattie,' said Elsa, ignoring them.

The cake shed was across from the tithe barn on its own, standing on staddle stones, with wooden steps leading up to its old door. A hessian sack lay on the hearth and, standing on it, Elsa wiped her gum boots. 'Best wipe your feet too, Hattie,' she said. 'You know how particular Mr Timbrell is.'

'I know,' said Hattie. 'Honestly, Elsa, how many times have we done this now?'

'I'm sorry,' Elsa answered, 'but it's easy to forget.'

'Ah, there you are,' said Claude, coming up the steps and entering behind them. 'Let me get you sorted.'

The cake crusher was beside the door. Claude turned a starter handle once, then twice, and the little engine coughed and sputtered into life, a small cloud of dust filling the shed and making the floorboards vibrate. Hattie coughed.

'All right?' said Claude.

Hattie nodded as Elsa picked up one of the slabs of cake piled to one side and, gasping under the weight, brought it over to the crusher. In moments it had been reduced to small bite-size chunks that dropped into a waiting sack. When it was half full, Claude idled the belt and watched Hattie replace the first with a second. Then the crusher started up again.

'Will that do for you, ladies?' asked Claude, as the last of the slab was spat out.

'Perfectly, thank you,' said Elsa. Then, squatting over one of the sacks, she hoisted it onto her shoulders. 'Cheerio.' Outside, they staggered back to the tithe barn, Elsa breathing heavily as she reached the byre and began pouring the crushed cake into the mangers.

'This will be the death of me,' said Hattie, as Jill and Susie reappeared with wheelbarrows of mangolds.

'An' me an' all,' agreed Susie.

'On the recruiting poster I saw,' added Hattie, 'it was sunny and the girl in the picture was smiling. No one ever mentioned lugging enormous great sackfuls of animal feed around in the freezing cold.'

'Or clearing cow shit,' added Susie.

Jill feigned shock. 'Defecation, Susie.'

'Yeah, that too.' They all laughed except Elsa.

'It's jolly hard work, I agree,' she said, but none of the other girls appeared to hear her.

Feeding the cows in number four, then clearing the chaff into the muck heap behind the farm buildings took them until lunch, as the first break was called, at 9 o'clock. Jean Gulliver had prepared the girls a cheese sandwich each and a flask of hot tea, while Elsa had brought her own. The girls ate inside the barn where the heat from the cows ensured the air was really quite warm.

'I honestly don't think I'll ever get used to these peculiar mealtimes,' said Hattie.

'You always say that,' said Jill. 'Just think of it as breakfast.'

'I don't care,' added Susie. 'I'm starving, me.'

'I'm with you, Susie,' said Elsa. 'I'm ready for something about now. We've done a good hour and a half of manual labour, after all.'

'You can say that again,' said Hattie. 'And now we've got to freeze our derrières out in the fields.'

'Spreadin' defecation,' said Susie.

Jill laughed.

'Oh, the glamour,' sighed Hattie.

When twenty minutes had passed, Elsa said, 'Right, let's get Thor running and load up the wagon.'

'Yes, sir!' said Jill.

Before Elsa could think of a pithy reply, Hattie said, 'You know, I might have a go at starting the Fordson.'

'There's quite a knack to it, Hattie,' said Elsa, 'and we don't want to waste lots of time.'

'You seem to manage it all right.'

'Oh, come on, Elsa,' said Jill. 'Give her a chance. You're awfully bossy, you know.'

Defeated, Elsa said, 'Very well.'

'I've watched you do it,' said Hattie. 'You prime the paraffin tank first for the ignition, then switch to petrol. Anyway, we're here to learn as well as toil.'

They stood by the Fordson, which was parked in one of the bays of the long, low-roofed cart-shed. The air was cold and sharp but there was still a strong smell of dust and oil. Susie sneezed.

'Here,' said Elsa, moving her hand towards the primer.

'I know,' said Hattie, sharply, moving her own hand to it instead.

'Now's the tricky bit,' said Elsa. 'The crank. Make sure you tuck in your thumb.'

Hattie rolled her eyes as she moved to the front of the tractor. Leaning over, she turned the crank, only for it to snap back and make her start.

'Please,' said Elsa, 'let me.'

'Give me a bleeding chance!' said Hattie.

She tried again with the same result, then again, this time completing a full turn, but still the engine failed to fire.

'I'm not beaten yet,' she gasped. She tried again, and this time the engine spluttered into life. Hattie looked up, triumphant, but moments later it died again.

'You didn't switch to petrol,' said Elsa. 'I thought you knew how to do it. Now it's probably flooded and we'll have to wait ten minutes. Here, let me.' She pushed past Hattie and the others, primed the paraffin again, moved to the front, turned the crank and, much to her relief, managed to get it started again. Quickly, she moved back and switched tanks. Thick fumes spluttered from the upright exhaust, but despite the shaking and rattling, the Fordson continued to run.

'Now, let's get going.'

'Gosh,' muttered Hattie, 'I can see the German in you, all right. *Jawohl, mein Führer.*' Jill and Susie smirked. Elsa shot a glance at Hattie but said nothing, and instead clambered up into the seat. She could feel tears pricking at the edge of her eyes. She wanted to scream, to leap at Hattie, scratch her elegant porcelain face and wipe away the knowing smirk. If her uncle had heard that, Hattie would have been sent packing, yet Elsa also knew that this was her battle to fight. She would not be bleating to Uncle Stork.

She breathed in deeply. She wished she could think of something clever and withering that might put Hattie in her place but her mind was confused by the stinging hurt she felt. 'I'm sorry, Hattie,' she said at length, 'if I seem bossy. I don't mean it. And for what it's worth, no matter what blood I have, I feel a hundred per cent English.'

14

Good Going

SOME HUNDRED AND SIXTY MILES TO THE SOUTH-WEST FROM Alvesdon, the Wiltshire Ranger Yeomanry was carrying out a full-scale exercise that same frosty January morning. A Squadron, with two troops of C Squadron, were to battle against B Squadron, similarly reinforced. The objective of the two sides – for the purpose, now renamed with conspicuous originality, 'North' and 'South' – was to capture each other's headquarters, which were respective farm buildings at either end of the Roseland Peninsula.

The splitting up of C Squadron meant that Peter Delafort and Edward had been pitted against Mike Horsley and Monty Trethowan.

'May the best side win,' Monty had said, with a wry smile, as they'd set off in the freezing darkness of pre-dawn, their horses clattering down separate roads.

'We simply have to win this,' Edward said, as he trotted up beside Peter.

'Of course,' agreed Peter. 'A matter of deep pride. Our honour is at stake. Although,' he added, 'I wouldn't want anyone to think we'll be trying any harder than last time.'

'God forbid.'

'After all, this is an important training exercise for war.'

'Absolutely.'

A couple of hours later, however, as the first pink streaks of dawn spread over the Roseland, and the assembled officers of 'South' gathered in the yard of their Tactical Headquarters for their O group, Edward was not convinced the A Squadron commander, Major Donny Moberly, was approaching the challenge with quite the right level of guile.

'We'll keep two troops here to defend Tac HQ,' he said, as he crouched over a map spread out on a trestle table. In one hand was a burning cigarette, the other a red crayon. He circled the HQ with a flourish. Warm clouds of breath and tobacco smoke mixed together. 'We'll use scouts and attack in two thrusts. We want them to think the first is the main assault, which will draw off their defenders. Then, while they're distracted, the primary thrust will charge and take their colours.'

'So which thrust is which, sir?' asked Lieutenant Tom Meddows, one of the A Squadron troop commanders.

'Plenty of woods near Philleigh,' said Moberly. 'The feint will come from Ruan High Lanes – here.' He drew a large arrow-headed line on the map. 'This thrust can use the woods to the north-east as cover. The rest will use the wooded valley from Veryan to reach the coast, then move up through Trewithian and attack through these large woods to the south of Philleigh – here.' More arrows, scrawled on the map with an imprecise flourish.

It struck Edward that both approaches seemed rather obvious. 'And what if the enemy use the same routes but in reverse?'

'That's why we're sending recce troops forward, Edward. That's where you come in, all right? If you see anything fishy, send back a dispatch rider.'

The details were thrashed out. Moberly would lead the main assault, with Peter's troop providing the diversionary attack from the north-east via Ruan High Lanes. Edward's men were to provide the reconnaissance screen for the main thrust.

'Right,' said Moberly, lighting another cigarette. 'Everyone clear?'

Edward looked at the map, now desecrated by a mass of confusing red lines, then glanced at his own, folded neatly in his hand.

'Everyone got their red armbands?' asked Moberly. 'Good, then let's get cracking.'

Edward split his men into fours, then told them to operate in pairs, spaced well apart but within sight of each other. Taking the lead, he saw nothing as they passed north of the village of Veryan, but then, instead of taking the wooded valley down towards Carne Beach, as instructed by Moberly, Edward decided to stick to the high ground, using the hedgerows as cover and from where, with liberal sweeps of his field glasses, he could see any enemy troops moving towards them.

He paused at the edge of a field, careful to keep his horse close to the high hedgerow, and signalled to the three men with him to do the same. It was a still, clear morning, the sun rising dimly. His horse snorted, clouds of steam rising, and he stroked its neck and shushed it before listening carefully. Not a sound. Not a breath of wind. But then, *yes, something*: a faint chink. He cocked his ear. There it was again. Dismounting, he climbed a desolate oak tree and, with the low sun behind him, lifted his field glasses again. Horses. Quite a few. At least thirty. He felt his heart quicken.

'See anything, zir?' called Sergeant Smithers.

'Yes, as a matter of fact, I can,' Edward replied. 'Two troops heading down towards Carne Beach. Come up and have a look.' Smithers had been a jockey in civilian life, working at a successful stud and stables at Whitsbury to the south of Salisbury. Edward had won quite a lot of money on Smithers in the past at various point-to-point races and was glad to have him in his troop. In a regiment where horsemanship counted, the diminutive Smithers was among the most-valued men in the entire Wiltshire Rangers.

He now nimbly hoisted himself into the branches and looked out with his own binoculars. 'Lumme,' he said. 'This'll be inneressin'.'

'Hmm,' said Edward. 'So, this is what we'll do. You ride back and tell Moberly. Keep a good look-out, obviously, but you should have a clear run. Two to one the rest of the North are also using the same route Lieutenant Delafort's using. Then catch me up. I'm going to scout wide of that lot and head pretty much straight for the woods south of Philleigh. Meet me there, by which time I'll have a plan ready.' He clapped Smithers on the shoulder. 'Fun, isn't it?'

Smithers grinned. 'Not 'alf.'

Twenty minutes later, as Edward and his troop reached the southern edge of the woods south of Philleigh, they heard distant firing behind them. So, he thought, the two sides had clashed near Veryan. He wondered whether Smithers had got to Moberly in time. Moments later, his troop sergeant reappeared.

'There you are, Smithers. How'd you get on?'

'I warned the major, awright,' Smithers told him, as he drew up alongside. 'But it were a close-run thing. Couldn't tell 'e who's besting who, mind.' He nodded in the direction of the shooting.

'All right, well, good work, Smithers,' Edward told him. 'Let's carefully push on through these woods and see if we can't get within spitting distance of Philleigh.'

Widely spread apart, the sixteen men moved cautiously through the woods. Although most of the trees were bare, there were large thickets of brambles and ivy, which offered some cover. Thick frost covered everything: the trunks and branches of the trees, last year's leaves on the ground, rotting logs, the undergrowth. In the depth of the wood the light was curious too – daytime, but still dim, half awake. Here, the sun had not penetrated. A cock pheasant cried out not far away, then shook itself down.

Edward glanced across at his men. Smithers was closest, but the furthest four were almost out of eyesight. He was not quite sure what to do but, as troop leader, knew it was vital he appeared decisive. The wood was large but seemed so empty that he was aware he was being lulled into a false sense of safety within its depths, as though it were an invisible cloak shrouding their approach to the village.

Suddenly, there was the sound of galloping hoofs and a shout went up to his right. His horse whinnied and he turned to see a lone trooper stop some hundred yards away, turn and try to head back in the direction from which he had come. Spurring his horse, Edward hurried towards the man but by the time he neared, others had caught him and begun to circle him, closing around him. It was, Edward now saw, Lieutenant Murray, who had only recently joined the regiment and was a troop leader in A Squadron.

'Bang, bang,' called Edward, his rifle drawn to his shoulder, 'you're dead.'

'No, I'm not!' Murray replied, and, slipping down from his horse, made a dash for it, running between the trees and making for a large thicket of box.

'Bloody nerve!' muttered Edward. 'Go and get him, chaps.'

Several of his troopers turned their horses towards the thicket, then dismounted. As Edward trotted up, his men had begun using their sabres to slash at the box, prod and poke the dense foliage.

'Careful,' he said. 'We don't want to skewer him.'

'C'mon out, zir!' called Smithers, now dismounted too. Murray suddenly shot out a little way to the right, like a trapped rabbit, and began running again, but this time he was easily rugby-tackled to the ground.

'All right,' said Edward, as a sheepish Murray, covered with still-frozen dead leaves, was brought before him, 'so you're not dead but you are a prisoner. What were you doing here?'

'Five nine six one four two seven,' Murray replied.

'What?' said Edward.

'I'm not obliged to tell you anything other than my service number.'

Edward laughed.

'Shall I rough 'im up a bit, sir?' asked Trooper Tomlinson, who was standing beside the prisoner.

'No, of course not, Tomlinson,' said Edward. 'But you can tickle him.'

'You can't do that!' exclaimed Murray.

'Of course we can,' Edward told him. 'Take off his boots and tickle his feet.'

Murray tried to kick out but, swiftly overwhelmed, was forced to the ground, his cavalry boots removed and his feet tickled. At first, he writhed, teeth clenched, but eventually it was too much.

'All right, all right!' he cried out at length. 'I was taking a message and due to scout the woods.'

'How many are guarding your HQ?' Edward demanded.

'I don't know.'

Edward nodded and the tickling began again.

'A troop!' he gasped.

'All right,' said Edward. 'That's enough.' Tomlinson, who had been holding Murray down, looked disappointed. Edward was too: Murray had told him nothing he couldn't reasonably have guessed. It now occurred to him that while this little episode had been taking place, they'd forgotten to keep watch. Murray could have been a decoy and with all of the troop milling about they could have been very swiftly rounded up to a man. He chastised himself, but it had got him thinking. There might be some merit in using a decoy.

At the northern edge of the wood, he paused his men again and consulted with Smithers. Up ahead, just two fields away, and perhaps five hundred yards, was the village, the tower of its church and several roofs clearly visible. Stretching west from the village and lined by thick hedge, was the road and, from that, another hundred yards to the north and a little way to the west was the farm that was the enemy's HQ. He raised his field glasses again. There was no sign of movement. He wondered whether he should wait for Peter's attack from the north and for Moberly and his men. But what if Moberly had been waylaid or even defeated in the clash they'd heard earlier?

Smithers was now alongside him, his nose and ears red with the cold.

'Here's what I'm thinking,' Edward said, glancing at his watch. 'The feint from the north is due to go in at ten thirty – that's a little under twenty minutes away. I strongly suspect all timings have gone awry, but we'll wait for that, and if we hear nothing, we'll go and storm the enemy's HQ ourselves.'

'Seems awful still up there, don' it, zir?' said Smithers.

'Maybe, but they're there, all right. We're going to use a decoy. We'll send some men back through the wood to give them a bit more distance, then two can begin a wide loop to the west and two more a loop to the right of the village. Make sure they move at a decent distance, sticking to the hedgerows, so it looks like they're trying to hide their approach, but where they'll definitely still be seen. Hopefully, that'll draw the enemy after them. Meanwhile, the rest of us will dismount and approach the farm on foot. Can't think of a better plan, can you?'

'Not really, zir,' said Smithers.

They looked out across the fields. Low winter sunshine bathed the landscape before them with a soft, orange glow; it made the frost twinkle as millions of tiny crystals were caught in the light.

'Reckon they'm got summon up in that church tower, zir,' said Smithers, training his field glasses.

'You can bet your life on it,' agreed Edward.

Edward pulled back into the woods and briefed the men, then went back to his place of watch. Seeing it was now after ten thirty and with no sound of any attack from the north, he decided it was time for his decoy troops to get moving.

Sure enough, about ten minutes later, the two moving towards the eastern side of the village were spotted. Edward heard cries of alarm from the village and soon after saw eight men gallop out of the village towards them. Edward turned to Smithers and grinned. Then they saw more enemy horsemen heading out of the farm along the road to the west.

'Hook, line and sinker,' said Edward. 'Can't be many left at the farm now. Come on, let's go.'

A narrow, hedge-lined field extended south from the village, so with the western hedge on their left, they half crouched, half crawled: twelve men, swords left with their horses, clutching only rifles and, in Edward's case, his revolver. Reaching the road as it left the village, they crossed, one man at a time, then sticking carefully to the hedge of the next field as it arced round to the back of the farm, they continued their progress until they were almost at the edge of the outbuildings. Signalling to the men to halt, Edward beckoned Smithers over to him.

'This hedge is almost too thick,' he said. 'I can't see through into the farm itself.'

'Wait on, zir,' he said, scurried a few yards, then disappeared among the blackthorn, alder and dog-rose. Edward smiled to himself and started as he heard rifle shots ringing out not far to the north. Peter's feint? Shouts came from the yard.

'Keep a damn good watch to the north, boys!' someone called.

Monty, thought Edward. *Even better.*

Smithers reappeared. 'Reckon there be 'bout five men of Twelve Troop, zir. Colours are in the zentre of the yard.'

'Excellent,' said Edward. 'That must be Peter's mob – I mean Lieutenant Delafort – firing to the north.'

Smithers nodded.

'We should attack now, while they're distracted, don't you think?'

'Whass the plan, then, zir?'

'Crawl along the northern side of this field, hope we don't get spotted and then charge the yard. A bit crude, but we've no fire support and I can't think of an alternative.'

Firing continued to the north, but as they inched closer to the farm, it was clear they had not been seen and were not expected. Crouching at the north corner of the field, an open gate led down a ten-yard-long track to a staddle-stone-mounted barn. From there, the track turned ninety degrees and led directly into the yard.

Edward took a deep breath, glanced back at his men, then was up through the gate, and down the track. One of Mike Horsley's troopers turned and, with a look of utter bewilderment, was pounced on by Smithers before he had a chance to cry out. Without pausing for further thought, Edward now stood up and ran, around the corner, spotted a second man, pointed his revolver and, firing a blank round that snapped loudly in the cold still air of the winter morning, shouted, 'Bang, you're dead!' then charged on, vaguely aware of others following. A blur of images: the farmhouse ahead to the left, a long barn on the right and another directly ahead, and there was the flag, in the centre of the yard. There, too, was Mike, an expression of grim determination on his face, running for it.

'Bang!' Edward called again, and fired another round, but Mike continued to charge the flag, grabbed it, then turned back, away from him. But in doing so, he lost speed, and Edward was able to keep running, sprinting towards his quarry until he was close enough to dive, tackling his legs and bringing him to the ground.

'Damn you, Edward!' gasped Mike.

Snatching the flag, Edward got to his feet and looked around.

''Ands up!' Smithers was saying, as Edward's men corralled the defenders to the centre of the yard. Edward grinned and held out a hand to Mike, still lying on the ground.

'Victory to the South, I think!' he said, as Mike took his hand and allowed himself to be pulled to his feet.

The regiment adjutant, Major Archie Pickering, in his late thirties and already going a little grey at the sides, now emerged from from one of the barns.

'Ah, good morning, sir,' said Edward, still clutching the colours.

'Well done, Edward,' he said, taking his pipe from his mouth and replacing it with a hunting horn. He sounded it, a series of mournful blasts that seemed to ring out across the Roseland. 'I'll get Carter to radio back to your Tac HQ, but that's a fine victory for the South.' He chuckled benevolently. 'Good sport, eh?'

'Very,' said Edward, taking a hip flask from his breast pocket and giving himself a well-deserved tot.

Across the English Channel, between Lille and Armentières in a small bulge in the River Leie, B Company of the 2nd King's Own

161

Royal Guards were holding a stretch of the front line along the French–Belgian border. For much of the time, the days were largely humdrum: route marches, patrols, the digging of a large anti-tank ditch and improvements to their own slit trenches, and a raft of other dreary training exercises.

Conditions were far from ideal, especially now that the weather had turned so cold. Most of the men were billeted in barns, with straw for bedding, and only their gas capes, serge greatcoats and each other for warmth. Outside, in the yard, there were braziers, but the chill was getting to the men, especially since shaving and washing mostly had to be done in the river that ran a couple of hundred yards from the farm buildings. Two days earlier, one man had succumbed to frostbite and had been packed off to the hospital. There had also been consistent cases of flu and colds that had ensured the battalion was never at full strength. On the other hand, the men were given three meals a day and occasional evenings off, and Armentières was close enough to enable them to head into town and make the most of the bars and brothels; certainly, most of the men in Tom Timbrell's platoon seemed to spend their meagre two shillings a day in the town.

Tom had joined the 1st Battalion in December after six weeks' training in England. Captain Woodman had been as good as his word. It seemed remarkable to Tom that a casual conversation at the end of a cricket match in Alvesdon the previous August had led him to serving under Woodman, who was second-in-command of 2 Company, on a four-hundred-yard stretch of the British front line in northern France some four months later. He had settled in quickly, however. He liked the men in the platoon and especially those in his section of ten men, even though most of them were from London, not the country.

He had also swiftly discovered he was quite good at soldiering, and was a better shot than anyone else in the platoon, as well as being bigger, fitter and stronger than most, and good at fieldcraft too. It had meant that when, ten days earlier, his section commander had fallen ill, he'd been given the job and with it a single stripe. If any of the others resented it, they neither said nor showed it. Providing them with extra food also helped: a rabbit shot here, a pigeon or two there, which he would skin, or pluck, fillet and take to the field kitchen. Tom had recognized that such additions to the diet cheered the men up a bit.

No one believed they'd be staying put if the balloon went up but, rather, would cross the river and advance into Belgium. So why had they been digging slit trenches and anti-tank ditches here? What had been the point?

A number of enemy aircraft had flown over during the past few nights, and the previous day two bombers had roared over low, machine-gunned some vehicles and even dropped bombs on a stretch of the line being held by the neighbouring battalion. Word soon reached them that one man had been killed and several wounded. Whether this was the start of anything, though, no one could say. Some thought the Germans would attack in the spring, others that it would fizzle out into a negotiated peace. Whether either of these views was correct, Tom was conscious of being a very small cog in a machine that was completely out of his control.

Now, that Monday morning, as Tom and his men stood smoking around one of the braziers in the yard, he saw Captain Woodman and Lieutenant Ashton, his platoon commander, approach.

'Morning, Tom,' said Captain Woodman, genially, as Tom and the others snapped to attention and saluted. 'At ease, chaps.' He held his hands over the fire and rubbed them together. 'I've a little job for you tonight, Tom,' he said. 'We've had reports of fifth columnists operating round about. Flashing torches into the sky to signal to the Luftwaffe, and whatnot. God knows whether it's true, but we've been tipped off they're just in the wood the other side of the border. I want you to take a patrol up there tonight.'

'Yes, sir,' said Tom. 'How will we cross the river?'

'We've a couple of punts for you. On the QT, the Belgians are happy to turn a blind eye, so long as we're not too obvious about it. So, there won't be any issues about being in their backyard.'

Captain Woodman produced a map from the large trouser pocket on his thigh and circled the wood on the map lightly with a pencil. 'Here. Ploegsteert Wood. Known as Plugstreet in the last show. I don't need to tell you that you'll have to keep a bloody good watch out. But it's only a couple of miles and as we know, the Belgian Army are nowhere to be seen.'

Tom nodded.

'What time do you want us to get goin', sir?'

'Not too early. Seems unlikely anyone would be getting their torches out until most others were in bed. Don't you agree?'

'I do,' said Ashton. 'So, around ten o'clock?'

'Something like that.'

'And how many men?' asked Tom.

'Oh, take the entire section,' said Woodman. 'It'll do them all good.'

'An' if we see anythin', sir?'

'Bring them in, Tom. Get your heads down beforehand, if I were you. Might be a long night.'

Tom managed to sleep for a couple of hours after supper, so felt fresh enough by the time they got going. It was bitterly cold and he could feel the edge of his ears throb and the icy air stab his nostrils as he breathed. All the men were grumbling, particularly Lofty Small, who was carrying the Bren light machine-gun.

'Once we're across the Leie we can allus start runnin' if you like, Lofty,' suggested Tom. 'Warm us up a bit.'

'It's all right for you, Tommo,' said Lofty. 'You're used to livin' rough like this, but for us lads brought up in the city it don't seem natural.'

'I like the country,' said Sid Parkinson. 'I reckon when this war's done, I'm movin' out o' Lunnon. All them fields and open space – beats the bloody East End, I can tell you.' He breathed in deeply. 'Feel that fresh air.'

'Bloody freezing,' grumbled Lofty. 'I'm worried for the state of me man'ood it's so bloody cold.'

'An' I'd hardly call our billet fresh, Parky,' said 'Jammo' Tompkins.

'Well, not anywhere near you, obviously, Jammo. You stank out the whole barn this mornin' with your bloody farting.'

'That wasn't me.'

'You're a bloody liar, and you know it.'

They reached the river and crossed it, using the punts that were tied up and waiting. There was a half-moon and the sky was filled with a million stars, the Milky Way clear and mysterious high above them, giving plenty of light for them to see their way. Ahead across the frozen fields was the wood, darkly silhouetted against the sky. Tom had been told the front line had passed through here in the last war and he'd even seen piles of rusting shells dumped in the corner of a number of fields in the time he'd been out there; it had occurred to him that it was no wonder it had taken so long last time around – after all, any enemy could be seen coming for miles. He could see now why machine-guns had cut down those who'd ventured out of their trenches. Perhaps, he thought, it would be like that again.

They reached the wood, still young, although it included plenty of quick-growing spruce and hazel as well as ash and sycamore. In between, though, there were occasional shattered trunks, dead but still upright from where they had been blasted more than twenty years earlier.

'You're not making us go through there, are you, Tommo?' asked Lofty.

Tom clapped him on the shoulder. 'Course. Don't want to be seen approaching, do we?'

'But it's dark in there. We'll get lost.'

'And might get gobbled up by wolves, eh, Lofty?' said Parkinson.

'Wolves an' goblins an' all,' added Tompkins.

'Leave off, will yer?' said Lofty Small. 'How we gonna see anything?'

'I've spent 'alf my life in woods, Lofty,' Tom told him. 'We'll be jus' fine.'

Tom found his way through easily, even though the ground was still pockmarked by shell craters. Most were not deep and his eyes quickly got used to the dimmer light from the moon and stars. In any case, he could still see the North Star for much of the time, something he'd learned about as a small boy. He couldn't help thinking of home and Tippett's and Mistleberry Woods, which seemed so ancient by comparison: some of the trees were hundreds of years old. He knew every part of those woods and he suddenly yearned to be back there and in his hut in the clearing in Tippett's. His thoughts turned to his time with Coco. Then he thought of Edie Blythe. He'd had several letters from her since he'd left Alvesdon. He could hear her saying what he was reading; her letters were full of funny observations, about Susan Smallpiece's gossiping, about the treatment of Carin Castell by some of the villagers, about Smudger and his young sidekick, Davey. He'd written back too, but had felt keenly the inadequacy of what he had scribbled: he lacked her way with words, and he was unsure how to spell some he wanted to use, which he found frustrating. Then an image of Hannah entered his mind, as she inevitably did when he was thinking of home. He'd had no letters from her. No news of her at all.

An unseen stone made him stumble and nearly fall. Time to con- centrate rather than daydream. From studying the map before they'd set off, he reckoned it was about half a mile across the wood, so after about ten minutes of walking, he guessed they should be now getting close to the far side. Bringing them to a halt in a small clearing, he said, 'Right, let's keep it quiet from now on. We're get- ting near the north side of the wood and that's where these jokers are supposed to be.'

They walked on, one man tripping over, Jammo Tompkins bump- ing into Lofty. Gasps and curses. On they went, sticks snapped underfoot, kit chinking. In the still, ice-cold night air, sound carried, and every noise jarred horribly. Tom couldn't imagine how any fifth columnists could possibly not have heard them coming. But, so far, there was no sign of any flickering lights, or torches or any other indi- cation that a single person was anywhere in the vicinity but them.

They reached the far side, but Tom kept them within the trees at the edge of the wood. Beyond, there was an open expanse of coun- tryside. Away to their right, the wood spread outwards before arcing back again – if the map was correct – while to their left it jagged out and ran briefly along a track before folding around the edge of more fields.

'Right,' he said, in a low voice. 'We're goin' to patrol along the edge of the wood. Keep in line with the trees but from now on we need to be dead quiet. No messin' about. An' no smokin'. Got it?'

He led them left first, along the western half of the wood. Noth- ing stirred, except some tawny owls calling to one another. To the north he saw the silhouette of a village, which he reckoned was St Yvon, and then the ground began to climb towards a ridgeline. It occurred to him that if any fifth columnists were making mischief, they'd be fools to do so quite so close to a village so led them back the way they had come and on towards the eastern side of the wood.

They had moved around the edge of the slight bulge that pushed out when Tom saw a finger of trees extending out into one of the fields. He paused, watching and listening. Behind him he heard the

166

heavy breathing of the men, the moving of feet up and down to keep warm and the blowing of warm air onto frozen hands.

'Jus' wait 'ere,' he said.

'You're not leaving us?' said Lofty, alarm in his voice.

'No. I jus' want to listen without you lot right behind me. Now, don't move.'

He crept forward until he could hear nothing. There was not a breath of wind. Some way to the north a dog barked but was soon silent again. He sighed. What the hell were they playing at? Out in the freezing cold, the wrong side of the border, looking for people who probably didn't exist and were nothing more than a result of gossip and tittle-tattle.

But then he heard something. Something that jarred his ears. He strained and then, *yes*, there it was again. A chink of something moving – over near that finger of trees. He inched forward, then heard a very faint, low murmur and the faintest orange glow perhaps seventy yards away. Then a second dot-like glow. Two men smoking.

'Well, I bloody never,' Tom muttered to himself. It was now nearly one in the morning. Deftly, he moved forward, crouching, keeping low, until he was no more than forty yards from the men. He'd not expected to see a thing, and now suddenly, away to the east, he heard a low rumble. Aircraft. He tried to think. Now he had them in his sights he didn't want to risk losing them again. But could the rest of the lads be sufficiently quiet to get anywhere close enough before they were heard? They had been like a herd of elephants going through that wood. On the other hand, he didn't want to start firing unless he absolutely had to and, he realized, the sound of the aircraft would probably smother any sound of their own. So, then. Decision made.

He sped back and was relieved to find the men where he had left them. No time for explanations. 'Follow me,' he said, in a low, urgent whisper. 'And be bloody quiet.'

The sound of the aircraft was getting louder, and now the two men in the trees turned on their torches and began flashing a signal: two beams, pointing skywards, on and off.

'Bloody 'ell!' said Parkinson.

'Right, we've got to move quick,' whispered Tom. 'Stick to the tree line. When the aircraft is overhead, they'll be distracted, an' lookin' up. We'll charge 'em. An' no shooting unless you see them pull a weapon. I'll go first.' Without waiting for a response, he hurried forward. Up above, the aircraft was nearing, circling low. Tom glanced up and saw it black and low against the sky: twin engines and double fins at the tail, menacing in shape and with its thunderous roar. A quick glance back to see the men were following, and then he was running, sprinting along the tree line, rifle in his hand and pulling back the bolt as he did so. The two men flashed their torches again as the aircraft circled one more time. Forty yards, thirty, his lungs straining, twenty, and then one of them saw him, utter astonishment on his face, frozen to the spot, but the second man now turned, and Tom saw he had a pistol.

'Hands up!' Tom called, as the second man raised the handgun. Tom aimed the rifle at the man's arm, squeezed the trigger and fired, the single shot cracking across the night air but, he hoped, muffled by the roar of the enemy plane. The man cried out and dropped the pistol, and now the others were upon the two men, holding them fast. The wounded man cried out in pain, clutching his forearm with his good hand.

'You bloody well shot him, Tommo!' said Lofty.

'Jus' nicked 'im,' said Tom. 'He'll be fine.' He looked up and saw the plane flying on and waggling its wings in acknowledgement. 'What the hell was that all about?' he asked their new prisoners.

'They are bloody fifth columnists!' said Parkinson. 'Stone me!'

'Come on,' said Tom. 'We need to get back. Let's gag them both first and quickly bind 'is arm.' He pulled out some field dressings and hurriedly gagged the first while Parkinson did the same for the second. Then Tom strapped up the other man's arm; as he'd thought, he'd just caught his forearm. *Good.*

Both men looked terrified, as well they might, thought Tom. He looked around and strained his ears again. Nothing, not even a dog barking. It was time to get back, but this time, he reckoned, around the edge of the wood, where the ground was more level and visibility was better. Speed, he reckoned now, was of the essence.

'Well, I don't mind telling you,' said Captain Woodman, once they were safely back at their billets, 'I'm absolutely dumbfounded. I didn't think you'd see a thing.'

'What'll happen to them, sir?' asked Tom, as he stood warming himself by a brazier. It was just after two in the morning.

'They'll be handed over to the French and questioned, then locked up or possibly even shot.' He shrugged. 'Bloody silly thing for them to be doing right under our noses. But well done, Tom. I knew you'd be a good man to have in this battalion and I wasn't wrong. Now go and get some rest.'

But he didn't feel like sleep: his heart was still racing from the night's excitement. Relief coursed through him that he had done what was asked of him and brought the lads back safely. Taking a hurricane lamp, he found his corner of the barn and sat smoking a cigarette. His thoughts turned to Hannah. He wondered how she was getting on and whether she had some suitor or other by now. Reaching into his pack, he pulled out a pad of letter-writing paper and the pen his father had given him. He would write to her – and perhaps she would write back, and then he would have something from her. Something he could keep. A glimpse of hope.

Dear Hannah,

I hope this finds you well. It's bitterly cold here but I expect it is the same for you. We're doing all right, though. Army life is very different to the one I had on the farm, although at least I already know how to use a rifle and look after myself. I wonder how you are getting on? Are you well? How is life at the manor? I hope Mr Castell is getting better. Please do write to me if you have a mind.

Yours, Tom Timbrell

He read it through. Really, it said nothing at all and he cursed himself. What was he thinking? Mad, crazy thoughts. He was getting above himself. He drew on his cigarette, then scrunched up the letter, got up, stepped back outside and threw it onto the still-burning brazier.

15

Easter

Thursday, 14 March 1940

MID-MARCH AND A BEAUTIFUL DAY, FULL OF PROMISE. HIS MORNING chores and paperwork complete, Stork decided to saddle up and take Jorrocks, his auburn gelding, for a trot around the farm. Smudges of green had already begun to colour the hedgerows while the road leading to Farrowcombe was lined with brilliant yellow and white daffodils. Birdsong filled the air each morning with the resurgence of life now fully under way. The days were lengthening too – noticeably so as they neared the equinox. In a couple of weeks, the clocks would move forward and then it would be light past seven in the evening, finally a cause for cheer. He trotted up the track that led to the top of the downs, marvelling, as he did each year, at the very first of the blackthorn blossom starting to appear, and he breathed in deeply, his lungs filling, then leaned forward and patted Jorrocks's neck. The horse snorted contentedly.

Spring, then summer – *Ah*! But with that thought his mood darkened. The longer days and drier ground marked the start of the traditional campaigning season. These were now modern times and war had become a more mechanized, technological beast, but he had no doubt that the onset of spring would still jolt the conflict into action. Tess was always tight-lipped and, of course, she had to be, but he knew neither Britain and France nor Hitler and his generals would sit out this phoney war for too much longer. Soon enough the balloon would go up. He was sure of it. Even Tess had admitted as much.

Half a year of operations at sea, of factories furiously building tanks, guns and aircraft while the British and French armies sat along the Belgian border waiting for one side or the other to make the first move. Just that morning Claude had shown him a letter from Tom. He was doing fine, it seemed, but was anxious for something to happen. ''E's bored,' said Claude, then whistled. 'Wants some action! He should be careful what he wishes for.'

Stork had agreed. He hoped Tom would be all right. He hoped all the young would be all right. At least the farm was in good fettle, as they all were along this valley and the next. The War Ag committee was pleased with the progress made. More ground had been ploughed than they had been required to sow. On their own farm, the two new Allis-Chalmers had proved a godsend. Even the land girls were proving their worth. Nor could he fault Elsa. She was a determined one, he thought. He was inordinately fond of his niece, all the more so since the horrible jolt they had all received.

Reaching the Ox Drove he turned west along the top of the great ridge of chalk and saw a lone figure and a dog several hundred yards away, which he soon realized was Carin with her lurcher. He dug in his heels and brought Jorrocks to a canter, then drawing up beside her.

'Hello,' he said, sliding off the saddle and kissing her affectionately on the cheek.

'Hello, Stork. There was no need to get down.'

'Well, I thought I might walk with you for a little while – unless you'd rather be on your own?'

She smiled. 'That's kind. Some company would be nice. I wondered whether I might see Elsa.'

'She's down at the farm today. You should be proud of her, Carin. She's been quite wonderful.'

'Dear Elsa.' Carin smiled. 'It's been hard for her. She misses Ollie terribly.'

They were silent, until Stork said, 'No news, I take it?' Both he and John had written to their MP and anyone else they could think of who might help get Carin's classification downgraded.

She shook her head sadly. 'No, I am afraid not. Another reply yesterday, "We regret that at the current time . . ." et cetera. Like the others, all very polite. All full of regret. Regret but unable to do anything.' She looped an arm through his. 'Who knows? I'm trying not to think about it and to get on with life. There are worse places to be. Especially on a day like today.'

'And the villagers are all right, aren't they?'

'There are still those who cross the road when they see me. No one is rude, but in the shop everyone still goes quiet when I enter. I've learned to go only when I absolutely have to and when there are likely to be fewer people there.'

'Well, we won't give up. It's even more ludicrous now than it was when the decision was first made.'

Two days later, on Saturday, 16 March, the officers of the Wiltshire Rangers Yeomanry were all invited to a grand dinner at Sir Richard Farriday's home, Tregarrick Hall. It was a fine Regency house with views out across the Fal estuary. Such dinners had not been infrequent: one to celebrate All Saints' Day, another just before Christmas for Advent, then a further one in February to mark Candlemass. They had all been riotous affairs, as might be expected when some thirty-nine like-minded dressed-up men, most well under thirty, were plied with plenty of food, fine wine, port, brandy and whisky. The CO, Lieutenant-Colonel Vere 'Dasher' Cowper, set great store by such events: they were, he liked to remind the men, vital for morale and 'regimental cohesion'.

Edward was rather fond of Dasher. Although he owned an estate north of Devizes, which included a large part of Salisbury Plain, his dedication to the regiment was total. Older than the rest of his officers, with grey flecks in his otherwise dark hair, and a trim military moustache, Dasher was never less than immaculate, even when drunk. His nickname, originally given because of his passion for foxhunting, suited him perfectly. He spoke fast, walked fast, and ate fast. Without the patience to write more carefully, his handwriting was a largely unintelligible scrawl. He took training seriously but, Edward had soon realized, had never imagined a time when the regiment might be asked to discard their horses. So, although he was the right side of forty, Dasher seemed to be a relic of an age that was rapidly being superseded.

Even at this latest 'Easter' dinner, Edward had sipped his champagne in the magnificent marble-floored hallway of Tregarrick and wondered how many more evenings such as this would take place. Much though he was still thoroughly enjoying himself, he could not see there being a place much longer for mounted cavalry – not in an age of giant aircraft carriers, modern battle cruisers, big twin-engine bombers, super-fast all-metal fighter planes, like the Spitfire his little brother Wilf was flying, tanks, trucks and tracked Universal Carriers.

Before they were called in for dinner, Dasher chinked his glass and called for quiet.

'Gentlemen,' he said, 'once again, we are indebted to our hosts, Sir Richard and Lady Farriday, for inviting us to dine here in their magnificent home. I had feared we'd already outstayed our welcome, but it seems their generosity knows no bounds.'

'Oi, oi,' muttered Peter, who was standing with Edward and Mike, 'a speech before dinner. Something's up.'

'Now, before we eat and drink any more and make merry, I just want to share some very exciting news.'

Edward turned to his friends and raised a quizzical eyebrow.

'I have had confirmation this morning that we are soon to be deployed.'

'Really?' whispered Mike. 'On horseback?'

Edward felt his spirits sink. *Brenda*, he thought.

Dasher beamed happily. 'We have been posted,' he said, then paused for full dramatic effect, 'to Palestine.' He grinned, as a murmur of approval rippled through the assembled officers. Pausing briefly to take in the excitement, he nodded, then said, 'Yes, I know. It's terrific news and wonderfully exciting. A great and singular honour. And we'll be taking our trusty steeds too. We'll be entraining to Marseille then sailing to Haifa. First, though, there will be embarkation leave, which is good news for all those hoping to see family this Easter. And before that, dinner tonight. Gentlemen,' he added, raising his glass, 'to the success of the Wiltshire Rangers Yeomanry.'

Edward ate, drank, and banged his fists on the table in time-honoured fashion during the post-dinner games, but he didn't make as merry as usual. Of course, this idyll in Cornwall had had to end, but he'd rather hoped it might last a few months more. He had optimistically assumed that eventually they would become mechanized and that such a conversion and the necessary training would take a fair few months. With any luck, the war might then be over. As far as he was aware, the chance of any Germans attacking them in Palestine was remote: it was such a terribly long way to go. A different world. When would he next see Brenda? The thought of it was unbearable.

Later, once returned to their billet and lying wide awake in bed with Peter and Mike snoring drunkenly in the beds next to his, he wondered whether he should try for a transfer. It was an idea swiftly dismissed – he could not let down his fellows – his good friends – so abjectly. But as he finally drifted off to sleep, the thought remained with him.

The following days were hectic as the regiment prepared to move back, first to Wiltshire, from where most of the men would begin embarkation leave. Then would follow the long journey to Palestine. Thankfully Brenda readily accepted his invitation to spend his leave with him at Alvesdon. 'You can meet my family,' he told her. 'See whether you like the cut of their jib.'

'I'm sure I shall,' she told him, over dinner in Falmouth. 'They sound like absolute poppets.'

'They have their moments. You'll miss Wilf, I'm afraid, but Tess is planning to come down for Easter, so long as no crisis flares up. But I really can't wait for them to meet you, beloved. They're going to adore you.'

'As I adore you,' she said. 'And now, Mr Pooter, you can take me dancing.'

Edward loved dancing and so did Brenda. He had always been light on his feet and had learned early, recognizing it was a very good way to make himself popular with the opposite sex. But there was something about feeling her hand in his, and his other against the small of her back, and looking down at her slender neck and shoulders that was especially entrancing. During the slower numbers, she rested her head against him and he breathed in her scent, promising himself that, no matter where he was in some fly-infested, heat-ravaged, God-forsaken desert in the Middle East, he would never, ever forget it.

Edward left Cornwall with the regiment on the Thursday and was picked up by his father, who, conveniently, had an appointment with the War Ag in Devizes that very day.

The following day, Good Friday, Brenda arrived by train at Tisbury. Thanks to the ration on petrol, Edward had taken the trap to meet her. It took longer but Edward did not mind. It was a sunny, warm spring day, with green already flecking the hedgerows, and once Brenda was sitting beside him, they had an hour and a half or so in which to be alone together; a precious time in which he could introduce her to the valley he loved.

She folded her arm through his and leaned her head on his shoulder, the trap creaking and squeaking as they made their way through villages and past farmsteads until they crossed the main Shaftesbury to Salisbury road, rolled past the recently sown Cuckoo and Spittle at the very northern edge of the farm, and finally began climbing the great escarpment of chalk.

'It's so peaceful.' Brenda sighed. 'How can we really be at war?'

'Maybe I should resign my commission. Join the farm.'

'Could you?' she said, sitting up.

He smiled sadly. 'I don't think so. Got to do my bit. Like everyone else.'

They turned the hairpin and the road eased its gradient. 'Easy there, boy,' said Edward, soothingly, to the horse. 'It's hard work for him getting up here.'

'It's beautiful, Edward,' said Brenda, gazing back down at where they'd come from.

Edward smiled. 'Just you wait.' They crested the ridge and there, stretched before them, was the valley. A deep combe dropped away, while a little ahead was Mistleberry Wood. Beyond, in the distance, was the southern ridge of chalk. Sunlight shone in shafts through the cloud, casting vivid light on patches of the farmland.

'Goodness!' exclaimed Brenda. 'It's Heaven.'

Edward pulled on the reins and the horse drew to a standstill, shaking his head impatiently. They gazed out, taking in the view. A scent of horse, leather, wood and dust. A flock of goldfinches skirted manically across the road in front and disappeared towards Mistleberry.

'Where's your farm?' asked Brenda.

175

'All this,' he said, with a sweep of his hand. 'To the right of the road, down into the valley and up the other side. See that copse on the ridge the far side?'

Brenda nodded.

'That's where Dad keeps his plane. In a hangar the far side of the trees. He bought her after the last war,' he said. 'She's called Dorothy. It's simply the most wonderful thing flying over the valley. When this nonsense is all over, you'll have to get him to take you up. It's such a thrill, I promise you.'

'I'd love that.' She kissed him on the cheek. 'Do you want to take this over one day?'

'One day, perhaps. It's a wonderful place to live. To grow up. And now that we're at war, I think I'm even fonder of it than I was.' He smiled. 'But I'd like to give being an artist a shot first. My uncle in the South of France thinks I should go out there and paint murals for the rich and glamorous of the Côte d'Azur.' He turned to her. 'Am I making myself more, or less, irresistible?'

'I'd say you're doing rather well.'

'Oh, good.' He grinned at her, flicked the reins, and they trotted on, down the road that led into Alvesdon.

Debbo wanted them all to dress for dinner, something they'd not done since Christmas, and everyone was happy to acquiesce.

'It's so lovely having Tess and Edward home,' Debbo said to Stork, as she sat at her dressing-table at Farrowcombe that evening.

Stork, trying to fit his shirt studs, cursed. 'Blast, I've a smudge of oil on my shirt front.'

'Never mind. You just need to be a little less slapdash, Stork, darling. If I can get rid of the varnish on my fingers, I don't see why you can't clean your nails.'

'A point well made and taken firmly on the chin, my darling,' said Stork, leaning over and kissing the top of her head. 'And, yes, to answer your question, it's wonderful to have them home. And to meet Brenda. She's very beautiful, isn't she?'

'Stunning. And clever too. You know she was at Cambridge? She can speak God knows how many languages.'

'Quite a catch.'

'So is Edward.'

'Of course.'

'He's depressed at the thought of having to leave her.'

'I don't doubt it. But I'd far rather he was going to Palestine than France.'

'I'd far rather he came home and farmed.'

'Darling, you know he can't do that.'

'Why can't he? You're run off your feet with the War Ag. He could help here instead of gadding off with his blasted Yeomanry.' Debbo stood up and turned to face him. 'Or what about becoming a war artist? Paul Nash and Laura Knight have already been recruited so perhaps they could do with some younger blood too.'

Stork finished knotting his tie then put his arms around his wife's waist and drew her towards him. 'You know it's not up to us, my darling. Let's try to make the most of him while he's here.'

'Yes,' she said, picking a thread from his jacket. 'You're right. It's funny. It was always me playing the pragmatist when the war broke out, but now Edward has actually been posted, I don't feel stoical at all. It seems so very final, doesn't it? I get a dull ache in the pit of my stomach every time I think about it.'

'I know. It's ghastly.'

'I worry about them all so much.'

He kissed her. 'Come on. We should go down.'

Stork liked all the rooms at Farrowcombe but he was especially fond of the dining room. In summertime, it was wonderfully bright, with large windows that looked out over High Elms, the field that ran down towards the river, and the curve of the downs. Now, the lush pale green velvet curtains were drawn, and although the room was spacious, it felt cosy and intimate. A fire burned at the far end, while a large picture of the children in the garden at Farrowcombe, painted by Debbo, hung in the centre of the long wall, above a walnut sideboard they had bought at a house sale soon after they'd moved in. The floor was parquet and creaked comfortably, while the room had a perpetual smell of wax floor polish and woodsmoke that Stork found particularly agreeable.

And here they all were, thought Stork – apart from Wilf – sitting around the table again, together for Easter. That was definitely something to raise the spirits.

Glancing at Debbo, he caught her eye and she smiled. *Good*, he thought, relieved to see her looking cheerier. There was no further talk of Edward abandoning the regiment and instead mother and son began discussing art and her latest commission, a portrait of the Bishop of Salisbury, until having overheard Stork and Tess bombarding Brenda, Edward cut in.

'You don't need to interrogate poor Brenda, you know,' he said, then turning to her added, 'Tess has always been terribly nosy.'

'You rotter,' said Tess. 'That's not true at all. I'm just interested.'

'We're having a very nice conversation, Edward,' said Brenda, and returned to her tales of travelling in Europe every long vacation during her time at Cambridge. 'With my parents abroad, I thought I might as well try to improve my French and German. They've been very generous with me, you see. Probably felt a little guilty about abandoning me.' She smiled with not a trace of resentment. She loved France especially, she told them, but Germany she had found terrifying.

'There was a perpetual air of menace,' she said. 'Superficially, everyone was perfectly friendly, perfectly polite, but then one would see the swastikas everywhere and more men in uniform than one would think possible. You'd see SS men, all in black, with their shiny boots and breeches, pistols at their waists, and one couldn't help thinking about what they were doing to the Jews. Even ordinary Germans aren't free – although I have to say they all seemed absolutely in thrall to Hitler. One would be talking quite normally, then suddenly it would creep into the conversation and one would be left thinking the most peculiar thoughts about someone who seemed so nice but viewed a man like Hitler as a good thing. It's awful that it's come to war, but he does have to be stopped.'

'Of course he does,' said Stork. 'One can question the morality of many wars but this one, I think, is different.'

There was a pause and Stork regretted having made his remark. He didn't want any of them to be thinking about the war.

'But tell me about Farrowcombe. Edward says it was derelict when you moved in.'

Stork laughed. 'Well, I don't know about that. It was certainly in a bit of a state.'

'I thought the gamekeeper lived here back then,' said Tess.

'He did,' said Stork. 'Well, in a bit of it. But we wanted to move here, get on with life, and your mother, Tess, wove her magic. I'm jolly lucky to have married a woman with such artistic talent. What this house has become is entirely her vision. I can take no credit.'

'Well, I think it's lovely,' said Brenda. 'It has a wonderfully warm feeling to it.'

'Thank you, Brenda,' said Stork. 'We're very fortunate. But you must get Edward to show you all around and take you down to see his grandparents at the manor.'

'He told me the best way to see Alvesdon is in Dorothy.'

'I told her you'd take her up one day, Dad,' said Edward.

'I'd like that very much,' said Stork. 'Sadly put out to grass for the duration, but the moment she's back in service, you have my word, Brenda.'

'Something to look forward to,' said Brenda. 'I've never been in an aeroplane before.'

The conversation turned to the farm.

'Is all the sowing finished, Dad?' asked Tess.

'Yes. Thank goodness. March is always a tough month,' he said, turning to Brenda. 'We finish the lambing and threshing, and then it's time to put the dairy herd out and start the spring sowing. We've lost a lot of men, you see.'

'But you've more tractors, Dad,' said Tess.

'And land girls,' added Edward.

'Both true enough. And thanks to both, we've managed it and double the amount we did this time last year too.'

'You're rather pleased with yourself about that, aren't you, darling?' said Debbo, then added, 'He feels he's got to set an example.'

'And so I have.'

'And what about Elsa?' asked Tess. 'Is she all right? I've been worrying about her. I wrote to her and she replied but she said very little, really. It was so unlike her. Usually one can't get her to stop once she starts.'

Stork sighed. 'It's been a bruising time for them. It's so awful.'

'It's downright wrong,' added Debbo.

'Of course it is,' agreed Stork. 'But we'll get it put right. I'm sure of it. She's had her confidence knocked, the poor darling.'

'I know she's worried sick about Ollie,' said Tess.

179

'And then there's been the land girls,' said Debbo.

'What about them?' asked Tess. 'Dad?'

'Well, I don't want to overblow things,' said Stork. 'They're good workers, but Hattie and Jill are a bit older than Elsa, both quite self-assured, Hattie especially, and Elsa was – well, Elsa was probably bossing them about too much.'

'Oh dear,' said Tess.

'I can just imagine it,' said Edward. 'Honestly, Brenda,' he said, turning to her, 'Elsa is wonderful. And I want you to meet her – we can all go over and see them tomorrow – but she's a person who knows her own mind.' He looked to the others. 'Is that fair?'

'She's also jolly good,' said Stork. 'Elsa has been able to start that ruddy Fordson when no one else but Smudger could. She ploughs as straight a furrow as anyone, works as long hours as anyone, and I don't think I've ever heard her complain about a thing. And it's been a damn hard first three months of the year. Lambing was absolutely the worst I can remember, it was so cold, and I can assure you that sitting on an icy tractor all day with an east wind hurtling down through the valley is no fun for anyone.'

'You're making me feel rather guilty, Dad,' said Edward. 'I can't even begin to tell you how much fun it's been in Cornwall.' He beamed at Brenda.

'I'm glad,' said Stork.

'Of course I'll be getting my comeuppance soon. I rather suspect I'll be dreaming of frost and snow when I'm out in Palestine.'

Tess, however, had not finished with the subject of Elsa. 'But what are you going to do about her, Dad?' she asked.

'What do you mean?'

'You can't have her at loggerheads with the land girls.'

'Oh, I see.' He grimaced with one side of his mouth, as was his way when perturbed. 'Well, I've kept them rather separate recently. Split them up. Made sure they weren't lambing at the same time and so on.' He had rather hoped matters would just resolve themselves.

'Far be it from me to tell you what's what, Dad,' said Edward, 'but in the troop I've tended to do exactly the opposite.' He put down his knife and fork and wiped his mouth with his napkin. 'I mean, suddenly everyone was being thrust together. The odd week-end and a summer camp was one thing, but we've all been together since the beginning of September. The men need to work together, though, so where there were flare-ups and people not getting on, I always made a point of giving them tasks to do together. That way, they simply had to put differences aside.'

'And did it work?' asked Brenda.

'Actually, for the most part it has done, yes. Couldn't find a happier bunch of lads.' He chuckled. 'Well, that might be a bit of an exaggeration, but everyone in the troop rubs along, as it happens. Which is just as well when one thinks of what's around the corner. But it strikes me that the farm is no different. Fourth line of defence and all that.'

Later, with dinner over and everyone gone to bed, Stork was sitting up reading through some papers as Debbo slid in beside him. 'Edward spoke a lot of sense, you know, darling,' she said.

'About what?'

'Elsa.'

Stork put down his papers. 'Quite a thing to hear my son giving me advice. It always used to be the other way around.'

'Well, I hope you'll take it all the same. I think Elsa's lonely. Lonely and a little unsure of herself. She really could do with making friends of those land girls.'

'I can't make them become friends, Debbo. Some people just don't get along. That's all there is to it.'

She rolled over and turned off her bedside light. 'I think you should listen to our son.'

Stork put away the papers and switched off his light too, but for a while sleep eluded him. Maybe Debbo was right, he thought. On the other hand, he didn't want to make the situation worse or lose his land girls, who were finally starting to become indispensable after five months' working on the farm. Soldiers were given orders and had no choice but to do what they were told. The same was not quite the case with farm workers.

He felt for Debbo's hand and linked his fingers with hers. In the darkness, he felt her give his a gentle squeeze.

On Tuesday, 26 March, with Tess returned to London, Edward and Debbo persuaded Brenda to sit for them. In truth, she needed little goading. It would be an honour, she told them, to be painted by a

181

fellow of the Royal Academy and portrait painter of such repute as
Debbo. 'And it's about time you painted me, Edward,' she told him.
'You've been talking about it for ages.'

'In my defence, I have been rather busy with the regiment,' he
said. 'Now, however, is perfect.'

They set up in Debbo's studio, which smelt of oil, linseed and
turpentine, and placed Brenda on the old chaise with views out to
Farrowcombe.

'But is that right?' Brenda asked. 'Oughtn't such a view be the
preserve of the mistress of the house?'

'Perhaps you will be one day,' said Debbo, and Edward was
thrilled to see Brenda blush.

'Well,' she said hastily, 'it really is the most divine view. I do think
you're incredibly lucky to live in such a beautiful part of the world.'

'We are,' agreed Debbo. 'And I feel rather proud of the place,
really. It's like someone saying something nice about one's children.'

'I'm very happy to say nice things about them too,' said Brenda.

Debbo laughed, then paused, paintbrush held aloft, and looked
out towards Farrowcombe. 'I think it's something about chalk. It's
soft, somehow, and rather ancient. I was born and brought up in
London and wasn't sure about living in the country at all. But when
Stork brought me here all those years ago, I fell in love with the
place instantly.'

'I can understand why.'

'Edward tells me you were brought up in Kenya. That's rather
exotic.'

Brenda smiled. 'Well, it was in a way, I suppose. But it was rather
lonely, because my parents were busy having a gay time, and no
sooner had I become attached to my older brother, Christopher,
than he was packed off to boarding-school in England. I was five. I
barely saw my parents – I had a nanny I adored – but then it was my
turn and from the age of seven I saw my parents every three years
when they were home on leave. Now I'm rather fonder of my uncle
and aunt than I am of my parents, although that's probably a terrible thing to say. So, I'm rather envious of Edward being brought
up here – and of how close you all are as a family. I barely see Christopher, these days. We're a pair of gypsies, really, flitting from one

place to another. I can't think of anything nicer than putting down roots and never leaving again.'

Edward felt an overwhelming mixture of relief and happiness at the way in which Brenda was embracing his family and home. She and Tess had warmed to one another from the outset. 'She's wonderful, Edward,' Tess had said, before she'd gone back to London.

In turn, Brenda had said, 'I think your sister and I will become firm friends.'

His parents had been charmed by her and she had made a great fuss of John, Carin and the cousins; she had bowled over his grandfather and been most attentive to Maimes. And he had liked the way both Brenda and his family had accepted that she was more than a passing fancy. There was an assumption of permanence he found rather thrilling.

As he sat sketching Brenda his giddiness began to melt away. In just ten days' time he would have to leave her, Farrowcombe and his family for God only knew how long. It could be for years, he thought. For all his talk of launching a career as an artist in the South of France he had always assumed he would live much of his life here, in Alvesdon. But what had previously been a rather opaque notion in the back of his mind had been given a clarity he'd not considered before. He knew now just how precious Farrowcombe, the farm, the valley were. Suddenly, a future lay before him: a life, here, with Brenda. It seemed so obvious and he knew, to his very core, that this was what he wanted. Yet just at the very moment it was within reach, it was about to be snatched away from him.

'You're very quiet, darling,' said Debbo, at length.

'I'm concentrating,' he said. 'I need to make sure Brenda is every bit as utterly lovely on this canvas as she is in real life.'

And at that moment, Brenda turned to him and smiled with such extraordinary radiance that he wondered whether his heart would burst.

After lunch on Monday, 1 April, with the sun out and warm, they walked up Farrowcombe, past the rapidly fattening lambs, and near the top sat on the grass, leaning against a large and spongy anthill.

'It's been the most marvellous time,' Brenda told him. Edward

183

had an arm around her shoulders. How good it felt to have the warmth of her body against his, her ebony hair touching his cheek.

'You haven't had too much of my family? We could go away for this last week, if you like.'

'No, let's stay. I think it's utterly heavenly here and your family are adorable. They've all been so kind. Anyway, there are the portraits to finish.' She leaned up and kissed him. 'My darling Edward. I'm going to miss you more than you can ever know.'

He felt completely overwhelmed. This person, who had so recently entered his life, had become his life. He wanted never to be apart from her. The thought of leaving her, waving goodbye from a train and not seeing her for God only knew how long seemed suddenly impossible. He couldn't bear it. He ran his arm down hers, felt the soft, delicate hairs where her cardigan was pushed up her forearm, and twined his fingers into hers. She squeezed, the gentle pressure of her hand against his.

And then it was so clear. If they were to be forced apart physically, at least they could be together legally – and spiritually. A union in the eye of the law and the eye of God. That would be something, wouldn't it?

He remembered a conversation from last summer: Tess had asked their father how he had known when to propose to their mother. 'I just knew,' he had said. 'I can't explain how, but I just knew she was the person I wanted to spend my life with.' Well, Edward knew too. He *knew*.

'Marry me,' he said suddenly. 'Will you? Will you marry me?'

She turned to him and he saw tears in her eyes but she was smiling too. Then she laughed. 'Yes,' she said. 'I will marry you, Edward. I'd like that more than anything.'

16

Spring Wind

Monday, 8 April 1940

EVERYONE HAD BEEN THRILLED ABOUT THE ENGAGEMENT. ELSA WAS pleased that Edward was so happy with Brenda and she had to admit she seemed very nice and was clearly devoted to her cousin. Even her mother's spirits seemed briefly to rise. None the less, seeing them together was a reminder of just how much she missed Ollie. She had seen him for three days only during the second week of March between his passing out from HMS *King Alfred* and joining his ship. A flurry of letters had arrived immediately on his return to the Navy but since then he had been out at sea, God only knew where, and unable to post any, even though he had vowed he would continue to write almost every day. 'I'll arrive back on land and post them all,' he had told her. 'You'll get a torrent all of a sudden. You'll be bored stiff of me.'

She hated not knowing where he was and having only the vaguest image of what he might be doing. And she also hated seeing her parents so unhappy. Everything had changed. Elsa felt as though her entire life had not been turned upside down but twisted and contorted. This bloody war! One day she had felt so angry that half-way across a field she was ploughing she had stopped the tractor, jumped down and repeatedly kicked the rear tyre in frustration.

Now it was April and at least the biting, bitter cold of winter had gone. The previous day, a Sunday, had been warm and sunny. Out walking the dogs she had passed daffodils in full bloom, seen the hedgerows flecked with green and blackthorn dripping with dense white blossom. On the Ox Drove up to the downs she smelt the wild garlic that had miraculously burst forth from the banks and heard a chiffchaff calling its strange two-note discordant cry. Then, up on the downs, the air had been rich with the astonishing trill of skylarks, twittering so hard she thought it a wonder their lungs didn't burst. Clover was springing from the ground amid daisies and buttercups, and for the first time all year, she felt the gloom that had seemed to shroud her and the entire valley start to lift.

Now, it was the beginning of a new working week. Elsa was awoken by the dawn chorus outside her window, as loud as she had ever heard it, with thrushes, blackbirds, robins, blue tits and even a green woodpecker vying to be heard. For some weeks she had been strongly considering leaving Alvesdon and joining one of the women's services – the ATS, perhaps – but with spring here at last and a long summer ahead, she was not so sure.

In the yard, she no longer stood with the land girls. She'd never told Uncle Stork what Hattie had said to her that day back in January, but she and the other girls had barely worked together since and had avoided each other as far as possible. It had been better that way. Elsa hadn't wanted friends in any case – she'd wanted to be left alone.

She looked around. Everyone was there, caps on their heads, most with a small knapsack over their shoulders. She glanced up at Stork, standing beside Claude Timbrell; her uncle was a handsome man still, she thought, with those pale eyes and still-dark hair. Beside him, Claude was quite different: a balding head underneath his battered felt fedora, and the bristling moustache now mostly grey. Quite different from Tom, his son. She wondered where he was now; somewhere in France, she supposed. Then she thought of Ollie, with his gentle face and fair hair, and yearned for him. She so wished he would come home.

Claude cleared his throat. 'There's an old saying,' he said to them all, 'that when the blackthorn blossoms white sow the barley day an' night.'

'We all know that one, Claude.' Alf Ellerby chuckled.

''Mazed if the girls 'ave 'eard it,' said Sid Collis, one of the ploughmen.

'There, you see,' said Claude. ''Ave you, girls?'

'No,' said Hattie. 'But I can guess it means we've got our work cut out.'

The men chuckled and exchanged glances.

'It does, Hattie, yes,' said Stork. 'It means we've got to hurry up and finish sowing as quickly as possible. I'm afraid to say that for all of us, now that we've got more land under the plough, there's even more sowing to do. So that's our priority this week and, sad to say, we'll have to work late till it's done.' He began allocating tasks and fields, then said, 'Elsa, you can sow Airfield with Hattie.'

'With Hattie?' said Elsa.

'Yes, please. Take the Fordson and pick up the seeder.'

After the briefing, Elsa walked over to the cart sheds and waited for Hattie.

'It's been a while,' said Hattie, as she ambled towards her.

'Would you like to drive?' asked Elsa.

'All right,' said Hattie.

Elsa stood back, itching to start Thor but resisting the urge. She watched as Hattie checked the oil and fuels, then moved the throttle on to five notches and checked the gear stick was in neutral. She pulled out the choke fully, moved to the crank and gave it one turn, then a second, and the engine gave a slight splutter. Hattie pushed the choke in halfway, then turned the crank a couple more times and the engine fired into life.

'There!' she said, only for the engine to die again. 'Blast. Now, why's that happened?'

'I don't know,' said Elsa. 'Maybe too much choke. It's quite warm today.'

Hattie pushed in the choke a bit further, returned to the crank, and after a few more turns the tractor once again spluttered into life. Hattie looked at Elsa, as though expecting the engine to die again, but it didn't.

'Phew!' she said, scrambling into the driver's seat as Elsa hopped up beside her and sat on the mudguard. 'Onwards! To the seeder!' Putting Thor into gear, she lifted the clutch and jerkily they moved off.

A short while later, they were trundling down the lane from the manor and turning into the village, the seeder hoisted behind them. There was the village hall and shop, and opposite, on the other side of the road, the pub. Jack Sawcombe, the son of Bill Sawcombe from the garage, was walking towards them with two other boys. Seeing Elsa he stopped, put one finger under his nose to imitate Hitler and gave a Nazi salute. Elsa was so shocked she was unable to speak, but without a word, Hattie stopped the tractor, jumped down and ran towards him. The boy, startled, turned and fled, the other two watching, but Hattie quickly caught him by the back of his pullover, cuffed him over the head, grabbed his ear and marched him back to the tractor.

'Ow! Ow!' he squealed. 'Get off me, you're hurting!'

'You'll hurt a lot more if I ever see or hear you do that again!' scolded Hattie.

Standing before Elsa, she still held the boy's ear tightly. 'Apologize,' she said. 'Apologize and promise you'll never, ever do that again.' She twisted his ear again so that he let out a further yelp of pain.

'Sorry,' he mumbled.

'Louder.'

'Sorry!' said Jack. 'I promise I won't do it again.'

Hattie leaned down. 'I mean it, Jack Sawcombe,' she said. 'If I see or hear you or any of your friends do anything like that again you'll wish you'd never been born.' She eyed the other two boys, who were watching incredulously. 'Now scram!' All three ran off. Hattie watched them go, then jumped back onto the seat of the Fordson.

Silent tears streamed down Elsa's cheeks, but wiping them she managed to mumble, 'Thank you.'

'Well,' said Hattie, 'they needed to be taught a lesson.' She put the tractor into gear and they moved off again, down the track to Farrowcombe and on to Airfield. Only at the newly erected gate did they stop and Hattie faced Elsa. 'Look,' she said, 'I'm sorry. I should never have said what I said to you that day. It was mean and cruel.'

'I deserved it,' said Elsa. 'I was being horribly bossy. I see that now.'

'Well, I want you to know I've felt bad about it ever since. And I'm also grateful you never told.'

'I'd never have done that. But forget it. It doesn't matter any more.' Elsa was so relieved by Hattie berating Jack Sawcombe that morning she had been only too happy to forgive her entirely. Delving into her knapsack, she said, 'Shall we have some tea quickly before we start? I've biscuits too.'

Hattie nodded. 'Why not?'

Elsa poured two cups using her enamel mug and the lid of the Thermos flask and passed one to Hattie, then offered shortbread.

'You've a sweetheart in the Navy, haven't you?' said Hattie.

'Yes. It's no excuse for being such a grouch but I do miss him terribly.'

'My fiancé's also at sea. He's serving in the Mediterranean Fleet.'

'Gosh,' said Elsa. 'I had no idea.'

'You never asked.' Hattie smiled. 'And I've an older brother in France. It's why I joined the WLA.'

'Yes, but why not the Wrens or the ATS or even the WAAF?'

'I did think about it. But I've lived so much of my life in cities. My people are still in London and I spent a year in Paris, but I was feeling so wretched about Steve that I decided a complete change of scene would be good for me. Maybe, later on, I might want to live in the country, you see. I thought this would be a good way to find out.'

'And?'

'If you'd asked me a month or two ago, I'd have told you no, but now I'm not so sure. Look at this view. It's wonderful.'

'That's the Isle of Wight over there,' said Elsa. She pointed far to the south and there, in the pale distance, the chalk mass of the western end of the island could be seen faintly.

'It's bloody awful, though, isn't it? This war, I mean.'

Elsa nodded.

'I have absolutely no idea when I'll next see Steve. Perhaps I never will.' Hattie shrugged. 'Who knows?'

'Where did you meet?'

'In Paris. He was working for a shipping company. But he was in the Volunteer Reserve and was called up in August. And off he went.' She sipped her tea. 'I really adore him and really do want to be married to him. I've been in a peevish mood ever since and I'm afraid you've been on the receiving end of that. I am sorry, Elsa.

We've all been flung together and we should make a better fist of things.'

'Actually,' said Elsa, 'I've been in a dark mood too. I've always been such a happy person. But with Ollie going off to sea and what's happened to Mummy – it's so unfair and we've got no way of over-turning the ruling so she's stuck with it. And although those who know her are perfectly aware of how absurd it is, for others there are now these horrible doubts.' She paused. 'But it's spring and I need to snap out of it. I miss Ollie so much but I can't spend my life pining for him.'

'You're only nineteen, aren't you?'

'Yes.'

'And I'm twenty-two. I feel exactly the same way. Shall we do our level best to try to enjoy the summer? And at least try to have some fun?'

Elsa laughed, which she hadn't done in a while. 'Yes, do let's,' she said.

Hattie held out her hand, which Elsa took.

'Good,' said Hattie. 'Now, we've got a field of barley to sow.'

It was half past five in the morning on Tuesday, 9 April when Tess was woken by the telephone ringing. She had been in a deep sleep, dreaming, and the shrill sound had become a part of the dream until she realized it was real. She stumbled into the hall, reaching the receiver as Diana emerged blearily from her room.

'Hello?' said Tess.

'Miss Castell?' It was the duty officer at the War Cabinet Office. 'You're to come in at once. The general needs you for a meeting at six thirty a.m. in his office.'

'What on earth has happened?' she asked.

'The Germans have invaded Denmark and Norway.'

Tess hurriedly dressed, her mind whirring. So, the Germans had made a move after all. Reports had been coming in the previous day about enemy naval activity but no one had seemed unduly perturbed. Outside, London seemed still, quiet, the air fresh. As she half walked, half trotted along Millbank, the barrage balloons still floated above the city's streets, and the tugs and river barges continued to flow serenely past as though nothing had changed. She wondered what

190

this meant for Alex in France and for Ollie at sea. Perhaps, she thought, Edward and his regiment might now be recalled from Palestine.

She was in the office by six fifteen and was followed moments later by General Ismay. By six thirty, all the service chiefs as well as Field Marshal 'Tiny' Ironside, the Chief of the Imperial General Staff, had appeared. Britain's most senior military figures. Tess had long since overcome her initial awe at working amid these men, but as she sat at a desk in the corner of Ismay's office, she was keenly aware that she was witnessing a potentially significant moment in the country's history. Cigarette and pipe smoke filled the room as the men all sat around the walnut table that dominated one half of Ismay's office.

'I'm afraid,' said Ismay, as he opened proceedings, 'that I did not see this coming. The Germans have seized Copenhagen and also Oslo. Troops are being landed and the Luftwaffe has captured the cities' airfields. Paratroopers have also been used.'

'It's the very devil,' said Ironside.

'We had thought Hitler's next move would be an assault on the Low Countries or France or even an air assault on the British Isles and I freely confess that an operation of this scope and scale had never entered my head.'

'None us thought it possible, Pug,' said Admiral Pound, using Ismay's nickname. 'You'll remember we all agreed an enemy seaborne operation against Norway would be largely impracticable and that the reports of *Glowworm* yesterday suggested a limited operation to forestall our own plans to mine the Leads at Narvik. We've been caught out. But the key now is to work out what we're going to do about it.'

'And quickly,' added Ismay, 'because the truth of the matter is we don't have the slightest vestige of a plan to deal with it.'

A knock at the door.

'Come!' said Ismay. A maid entered with a trolley of coffee and tea; it seemed incongruous that, at this moment of crisis, the meeting should temporarily pause, but Tess was glad of it as for once she was struggling to concentrate. Her job was to record this conversation word for word, in shorthand, then type it up. Once signed off, the minutes would be distributed to the War Cabinet and act as a record

191

of what Britain's military leaders discussed on this momentous day. So far, she had managed to keep concentrating and note the conversation verbatim, but she was shocked by what she was hearing. Shocked by the outrageous assault on neutrals but also by how badly these men had been caught off guard. She had heard Ismay talk a lot about 'grip'; it meant controlling a situation by the scruff of its neck, decisively and with a clear vision of how to proceed. 'Grip', however, was clearly lacking this morning and she was taken aback by it. She wondered what might happen if they were duped again. *Alex*, she thought.

'Surely, though,' said Ismay, once the maid had left the room and Tess was jolted back from her thoughts, 'we have the means for an effective counterattack? Our naval superiority is overwhelming, after all.'

'I'm wondering whether we might harry the German forces stationed along the Norwegian coast and quickly, before they're able to install anti-aircraft defences,' said Ironside.

'We would need to assemble our naval forces very quickly,' said Pound.

'And what about some kind of landing of our own troops? It's the Narvik area and Trondheim that are key if we want to hurt the Germans,' said Ironside. 'Interrupting the flow of iron ore down the coast to Germany was, after all, the whole point of mining the Leads. At least now we can be seen to be going to the aid of Norwegians rather than embarking on a hostile act against one of our friends and neighbours. At the very least Hitler's move has swung the moral high ground back in our favour.'

'The trouble is, the Luftwaffe will now have airfields,' said Sir Cyril Newall, the Chief of the Air Staff. 'We can't possibly hope to match the Germans in the air with just the Navy's aircraft carriers.'

'As far north as Narvik?' questioned Ironside.

'We need to offer a series of viable plans of action to the War Cabinet, gentlemen,' said Ismay.

'But much also depends on the French,' said Ironside.

The meeting continued, the discussions swirling round and round. It seemed to Tess that even by ten o'clock, when it finally broke up, no firm conclusions had been drawn, although a sketchy tentative plan had been proposed; it would be placed before the Prime Minister and the War Cabinet for immediate consideration.

With the Chiefs of Staff gone, Tess put away her notebook, then stood up before Ismay, who was seated at his desk, rubbing his forehead.

'Is there anything else, sir, before I type up the minutes?' she asked.

'I'm afraid,' he said, looking up, 'you've just witnessed one of the least edifying meetings I've ever sat through.'

Tess was unsure what to say. 'I appreciate everyone has been caught off guard, sir.'

Ismay chuckled mirthlessly. 'I think that's understating it. But what to do? Amphibious operations, especially over long distances, are devilishly difficult to put together. They require highly trained personnel, a wide range of technical equipment and a detailed knowledge of the enemy. We have none of those elements. Most of our army is in France, so any troops we use will have to come from our territorial battalions and they'll have to be sent across the North Sea in quick order – under-trained and, no doubt, under-equipped and -prepared. Normally, one would expect to take months to mount such an operation, but we don't have that luxury.' He sighed. 'We shall have to see what the War Cabinet decides and what the French suggest, but it's a bad business, Tess, and no mistake. If only one could make purely military decisions, life would be easier, but for all sorts of political reasons we will have to help Norway, I'm sure. I can't say that makes me feel very sanguine, though.'

Tess felt a growing anger rise within her all day and was in a rare foul mood by the time she got home later that evening, slamming the front door behind her and throwing her keys onto the small side table in the hallway.

'You sound cross,' said Diana, as Tess joined her in the kitchen. 'I've heard the news. It's astounding.'

Tess sat down at the small table as Diana stood by the gas stove preparing their dinner. It was almost the smallest room in the house yet the girls rarely ate in the dining room next door; they preferred the kitchen because of its window and glass-panelled back door that allowed them to look out onto the narrow strip of garden.

'So, too, is everyone else,' said Tess. 'I'm so livid. I can't help it. Not just about what Hitler's done, although that is utterly despicable, but also about what we haven't done. Argh!' She smacked a hand on the table.

'What about a drink?' suggested Diana.

'Good idea. We've still got some gin, haven't we?'

'We have. And sweet vermouth. Two gin and Its coming right up.'

'Thank you.' Tess rested her head on her arm and sighed. 'You know, Churchill first suggested we mine the Leads off Narvik back in September last year and no one could make their minds up. One minute the French wanted to land a force and capture the Swedish iron ore fields and the next they didn't. Then they were going to mine the German shipping routes and then they weren't. They finally decide to do so and now it's too late and no one – not a single person as far as I can tell – saw it coming. We've had all this time to get ready yet nothing has happened. What have they been doing these past months? I just can't believe it!'

'Whose fault is that?' asked Diana, as she wielded the cocktail shaker.

'Oh, I don't know. Partly the French who can't decide on anything and partly the lack of grip by our own government and Chiefs of Staff. I've always thought Chamberlain was a decent sort but I'm not at all sure he's the right man to be leading us now, when we're at war. And it's our boys who will pay for it. Poor Ollie Varney is out at sea at the moment. Elsa is going to be worried sick. And Alex is in France, plus God knows how many others, and I just worry that no one at the top really has a plan – not a good one at least.' Diana passed her a drink. 'Oh, thank you. You're a lifesaver.'

'It can't be as bad as all that,' said Diana.

'I hear some pretty extraordinary things, I can tell you.' She took a sip of her drink. 'You won't breathe a word of this, will you? I've not betrayed any secrets or anything but I'm not being frightfully discreet.'

Diana held up her hand. 'I swear.' She sat down beside her. 'I know it's terrible news, but maybe now Hitler's invaded Denmark and Norway he won't attack France. Perhaps this is a good thing. And maybe there'll be some sort of peace deal after all. Then Alex and everyone can come home.'

Tess looked at her sadly and took her hand. 'Oh, Diana,' she said. 'If only. But I have a horrible feeling that this is just the beginning.'

Far across the Channel, in France, the train containing the Wiltshire Rangers Yeomanry was trundling south towards Marseille. It was a journey of repeated stops and at two the following morning, 10 April, the train ground to a halt yet again, apparently near Auxerre. Edward had been sleeping but was awoken by one of his troop who wanted him to check on a horse that was acting peculiarly. Wearily, Edward got up, jumped down onto the track and walked along in the cool night air to the wagons where the troubled horse was stabled. It had simply lain down, and although Edward was no vet he knew enough about the animals to be able to give the mare a rudimentary health check, and could find nothing wrong.

'The poor animal's exhausted,' he said. 'And I'm not surprised. It's been rather discombobulating for them all, don't you think?' Together, they managed to get it back onto its feet only for the train to jolt, hiss, and start moving again, which meant both men were forced to travel with the eight horses in the wagon all the way to the next stop, which was Lyon, by which time it was daylight.

Back on the platform and walking stiffly to his carriage, Edward saw Peter and Mike.

'Oh, there you are!' said Peter. 'I was half worried you'd left us and were heading home.'

'Sorely tempting,' said Edward.

'Have you heard the news?' asked Mike.

'What news?'

'The Germans have only gone and bloody invaded Denmark and Norway.'

Edward whistled. 'So, what does that mean for us?' he said, his spirits rising. 'Are we turning around?'

'Not according to Dasher.'

'Oh,' said Edward.

'Come on, cheer up!' said Peter, putting an encouraging arm around him. 'There's eggs and bacon in the dining coach. Let's have some breakfast. You know, I never would have guessed you'd become the lovesick sort.'

*

Afterwards, as the train got going again, Edward returned to the cabin he was sharing with Peter and lay down on his bunk, as exhausted as the horse had been and, he suspected, a hundred times more miserable.

He'd had a fair few girlfriends in his time but he had never been in love before. Now this affliction was tearing his heart to pieces. He pined. He grieved for Brenda's loss to him. He could barely stop thinking about her. Making love to her that last night – it had been perfect: a lovely clear night, and she had crept into his room and dropped her nightgown and there she had stood, naked, her creamy skin lit only by moonlight, her dark hair falling about her shoulders. He had been careful to remember every moment, every caress, every word murmured, knowing that it would have to sustain him for months, possibly years. *Years!* If they had had another week – even a few days – they could have been married in Alvesdon Church and she would have been locked to him, entwined with him for ever. But the time had been too short, the telegram of approval from her parents in Nairobi had taken too long, and with his precious embarkation leave running out there had not been time. 'We can marry the moment I'm back,' he had told her.

'I'll wait. I love you, Edward,' she had whispered. 'I'm going to love you always.'

17

All at Sea

Tuesday, 23 April 1940

THE THREATENED PILE OF LETTERS FROM OLLIE ARRIVED AT ROSE Bower that morning, some eighteen in all, written in the time since he had gone to sea in March. Elsa arrived home in the evening to discover them waiting for her.

'So, you see,' said her mother, 'he hasn't forgotten you after all.'

Elsa hurried up to her room to read them. Some were short, others were pages and pages long, all in his immaculate handwriting and with the fountain pen she had given him before he'd gone. In the letters, he repeatedly told her he was fine; he had been pleased to have been posted to a modern Tribal-class destroyer but had found his new life bewildering to begin with. As a sub-lieutenant, he was expected to learn fast and had spent much of his off-duty time studying and testing himself. It had been exhausting and he had rarely had more than four hours' sleep each day.

Very quickly, though, he had become used to it. Phrases and acronyms that had seemed like Greek to him initially had become familiar and so had the rhythms of the ship. He wasn't suffering from seasickness, which was more than could be said for a number of the men. The captain was a fine man, who was vastly experienced and whom everyone trusted totally. Ollie reckoned he was lucky to serve under him.

Then the tone of the letters changed abruptly. They were no

longer on patrol duty but had been sent to Narvik. The sea had been rough and it had been bitterly cold. They'd joined the mighty battleship, HMS— (he'd left the name blank) along with nine other destroyers. A battle had already raged there three days earlier. One of their destroyers had hit and blown up the German flagship and then a second ship. When Ollie's flotilla had arrived with the battleship, they had entered the fjord and opened fire on the remaining German destroyers. All five had been sunk. It had been extraordinary; he had found the battle both terrifying and exciting, although he told her he hadn't been in much danger. He couldn't help thinking of all the German sailors who had been killed in those icy waters as a result, mostly young men like he was. He'd been trying not to dwell on it, but it was hard not to.

Elsa simply couldn't picture the gentle, nature-loving Ollie she knew standing on the bridge of a warship as gunfire was thrown down the length of a Norwegian fjord. She read and reread that particular letter and was brought suddenly out of her reverie by the sharp ring of the telephone.

'Elsa!' called her mother a moment later. 'Quick!'

It was Ollie. She knew it. Running downstairs she saw her mother in the hall, smiling, holding the receiver.

'Ollie?' said Elsa. 'Is that really you?'

'Elsa!' he said. 'It's wonderful to hear your voice. I just had to speak to you.'

'Are you all right? I've been reading your letters. Was Narvik very terrifying?'

'A bit, but actually, I was quite calm when all the firing was going on. But I'm going back to Norway. We're leaving at dawn tomorrow, so I've only got this one evening briefly ashore. Tell me, though, are you all right?'

'Yes,' she said. 'Much better. Your letters arrived. The land girls are much friendlier. I'd say we're actually friends. I even went to the Three Horseshoes with them a few nights ago.'

'I'm so glad. I'm sure I'll get some leave soon and then I'll come and see you. I can't wait. I've missed you terribly.'

'Do you promise?'

'Of course I do. I love you.' There was a crackle of static. 'I've got to go.'

'Be careful, Ollie!'

'I will. Cheerio, Elsa.' The line was cut, replaced with a dialling tone. He was gone.

She put the receiver down, and leaned against the wall, banging her head gently against it. This was hard, she thought. A snatched conversation, across a telephone line fizzing with clicks and static. But it was better than not hearing from him at all. Eighteen letters and barely a minute's telephone conversation. She would have to be careful, she thought, not to gloat about that in front of Hattie, who hadn't heard a word from Steve for more than six weeks.

'So?' asked her mother. 'How is he?'

'He's been in Narvik. In a battle. They sank lots of German ships, and now he's got to go back there.'

'Oh, darling,' she said. 'How terrible it all is. But he will be all right. I know he will.'

'I hope so, Mummy,' said Elsa. She breathed in deeply and went back up the stairs to her room.

HMS *Iceni* had completed another escort duty and had pulled into Scapa Flow for victualling on Saturday, 27 April, only to be given orders to head back out to sea that same night, part of a flotilla of eight destroyers leaving the Home Fleet's base and heading back to Norway.

At 6 p.m., the weather being fine, the captain, Lieutenant Commander Stuart Bertie RN, ordered divisions, which, Ollie had discovered, was a comparatively rare occurrence. It was, however, a chance for the captain to speak to all 190 men who made up the crew, many of whom, because they were divided into different functions of signallers, seamen and stokers, barely saw or had much to do with one another. And, as Ollie had quickly learned, although the officers shared a wardroom, and the petty officers another, the rest of the crew ate and slept in their divisions. Each division had its own officer and petty officers, who were there not only to ensure the men did their job efficiently and effectively but were also responsible for their welfare and any difficulties, quarrels or domestic complications.

Of course, Ollie had been given a brief overview of the Navy's organization while at HMS *King Alfred,* but it had not been until he had spent some time aboard *Iceni* that he had understood how the system worked or how a ship's crew effectively functioned. It had struck him as a very sensible system. As a sub-lieutenant in the Royal Navy Volunteer Reserve, it was his job to learn the ropes – to understand the various roles of the ship's officers, to take his turn on watch, and to learn about each of the destroyer's disciplines, from gunnery to torpedoes to navigation. So far, he had found it utterly stimulating – it was mentally challenging and exciting too. If he was honest, in his letters to Elsa he had rather downplayed how much he had been enjoying himself, and especially now that he'd been at sea for the best part of six weeks. Although still the new boy, he was learning quickly. As he'd stood on deck, lined up beside his fellow officers, he found it hard to believe he had passed out of *King Alfred* just the previous month. It seemed a lifetime ago.

Fortunately, he had scored highly in his exams, which was one of the reasons, he supposed, he'd been posted to one of the new Tribal-class destroyers. He and those of his fellows who had passed had immediately gone back to their quarters and put on their new, smart and rather dashing uniforms: double-breasted black jacket and trousers, white shirt and tie, with a single wavy gold stripe around the cuff that told the rest of the Royal Navy that he was now an acting temporary probationary sub-lieutenant. Emerging transformed in his new attire, the sentry at the door of the wardroom had immediately snapped to attention and saluted. Ollie had been thrilled.

And now, seven weeks later, here he was on the deck of *Iceni*, a ship to which he had already become devotedly attached. Ollie had known destroyers were among the fastest of the Navy's warships, but *Iceni* could make thirty-six knots when needed – that was over 40 miles per hour, an astonishing speed for a ship some 125 yards in length. When he had first experienced her at full throttle, he had felt like laughing with exhilaration. And she was bristling with armoury too: quick-firing high-velocity guns and cannons but also torpedo tubes and a stash of depth-charges.

Standing on the bridge, Ollie had felt invincible. He had now witnessed those guns in action too, both against enemy aircraft and, in what had been a day he would never forget, against the German destroyer force at Narvik. The awesome power of the weapons – the rapid rate of fire, the noise, the stench, the accuracy – had dumbfounded him.

Throughout that battle, Lieutenant Commander Bertie and his number one, the senior lieutenant aboard, Jimmy Malone, had shown a degree of imperturbability Ollie had thought incredibly impressive. That level of cool-headedness and sangfroid was, he had instinctively understood, what he had to aim for himself.

And yet Bertie was only thirty-one; Malone twenty-seven. In terms of maturity, however, they seemed a generation older to Ollie. None the less, both men had also been welcoming. 'We're thrilled to have you join us,' Bertie had told him in the wardroom on his first night aboard, and had poured him a large tot of rum.

'The best ship in the world, a destroyer like this,' Jimmy Malone had said.

'That's true enough,' Bertie added. 'A big warship looks impressive, but as a sub-lieutenant aboard such a vessel, you're only ever a very small cog. On *Iceni* you'll play a much bigger part and learn a heck of a lot about all aspects of naval seamanship. Steering more than two thousand tons of steel at night through inky dark waters at thirty-five knots is a task that requires every inch of your attention, I can promise you.' He had grinned and raised his glass. 'And because everyone has to pull their weight and trust one another, I insist on all us officers, especially, treating each other like brothers. I'm the oldest and can boss you younger ones around when I need to, but it's important we enjoy each other's company too. We don't mind a bit of horseplay on this ship, do we, Jimmy?'

'It's been known from time to time.' Jimmy had smiled. 'And don't forget to ask questions. We don't expect you to be the finished article. But you'll learn a hell of a lot quicker if you ask questions. We'll rib you mercilessly, of course, if you ask something daft, but you'll get used to it quick enough.'

Now, though, as Bertie joined the crew on parade around the X-Gun on the rear deck, the levity of that first night had gone. There was certainly not a hint of a smile on Bertie's face now.

He cleared his throat. 'Gentlemen,' he said, 'although the Royal Navy has given the Kriegsmarine a whipping, fortunes have been somewhat reversed on land. The situation is now critical. The expeditionary force sent to central Norway has been overwhelmed by enemy air forces and the superior firepower of the Germans on the ground. They are pulling back to the coastal town of Åndalsnes.

Our task will be to help with the evacuation and bring them home. We need to be on constant watch for enemy warships but especially the Jerry air force. Central Norway might be lost, but it's now up to us to bring as many troops back as possible so they can fight another day.'

Ollie felt a dull ache of dread in his stomach as he listened to the captain's grave but matter-of-fact talk, a feeling that increased as they slipped out of port at around ten o'clock that night.

'All right, Ollie?' Henry Wymer, the number two and a former Royal Navy Reserve officer had asked him, as they stood on deck and watched the flotilla proceed out of port.

Ollie nodded. 'Yes,' he said. 'A few nerves perhaps.'

'Well, get your head down. You've got the dog watch, and I don't suppose any of us will get much kip tomorrow.'

Ollie had done as Henry had suggested and, for once, had put his books and studies to one side. Just before four in the morning, he'd woken and wearily got out of his cramped bunk, shaved, dressed and staggered along the companionways, then up the metal-runged ladders to the bridge, where he found Jimmy Malone.

'Good man,' he said. 'Nothing to report at the moment. We're making decent progress.'

'And no swell,' said Ollie.

'Flat as a millpond,' agreed Malone. 'Let's hope it stays that way. I'll send you up some tea.'

Sure enough, a steward from the wardroom appeared soon after with a tray of tea and a sandwich, which Ollie drank and ate gratefully as dawn gradually spread and lit up the flotilla on its way towards Norway.

Ollie had been on watch again as they had neared the Norwegian coast later that afternoon, gliding first into Midfjorden, mountains towering either side and then to the narrows of the Romsdalsfjord. Action stations had been called, with the seamen at their guns and those not on duty still ready on the lower mess decks. The tension was rising. Beside him were Bertie, Charles Crawley, the gunnery officer, and Patrick Brooks, the navigating lieutenant. Ollie was keenly aware that the bridge, open to the elements, and with nothing other than a shoulder-high wall of thin steel, offered almost no protection. Jimmy Malone had cheerfully told him the protective wall would probably not stop even a machine-gun bullet.

There were no enemy forces anywhere near this part of the coast and they'd not spotted a single Kriegsmarine warship, but Ollie couldn't help feeling that the mountains were watching them.

'Course one-one-five,' said Bertie, into the voice pipe.

'Steady on course one-one-five,' came the reply from the navigation officer.

'Very well,' said Bertie. He turned to Crawley. 'Make sure your gunners keep scanning the skies. Who's on look-out?'

The question was directed at Ollie, the watch officer.

'Able Seaman Skinner, sir.'

Bertie nodded. 'Make sure he's got his glasses trained.'

Ollie picked up the telephone to the masthead. 'Skinner?' he said.

'Yes, sir?'

'Keep the sharpest look-out.'

'Yes, sir.'

It was less than fifteen minutes later that Skinner reported aircraft approaching.

'Masthead,' said Skinner, as Ollie picked up the receiver. 'Enemy aircraft bearing nor'-nor'-west, green three-four-zero.'

'How many?' asked Ollie.

'Perhaps half a dozen – wait – yes, six, I think, sir.'

Ollie relayed the information and sounded the red alert, the klaxon ringing around the ship. All the officers on the bridge brought their binoculars to their eyes.

'Yes, there are the bastards,' said Bertie. 'Twin-engines. Can't tell what type.'

'Dornier, sir,' said Ollie.

Bertie glanced at him and raised an eyebrow. 'Very well,' he said, with a slight smirk.

Crawley now clambered onto the gun director and the four 4.7-inch guns followed as did the anti-aircraft quick-firing pom-poms. Ollie watched, his heart quickening. A faint, low rumble could now be heard. Yes, six Dorniers – he could see them clearly through his binoculars, approaching low over the mountains to the south.

Maybe a minute passed as they watched, from their exposed bridge, the German bombers drone towards them. Eight destroyers, their guns all trained towards them. Some fifteen hundred men held their breath.

And then they opened fire, the pom-poms bom-bom-bomming, tracer fizzing through the sky, and then the big 4.7-inch guns joining in. The ship rocked from the recoil. The formation of six bombers peeled off, each aircraft targeting one of the destroyers below. None seemed to be heading for *Iceni,* but bombs soon began falling, whistling down and hitting the sea, followed by huge plumes of water rising hundreds of feet into the sky. Spray cascaded over the bridge, showering the officers as the quick-firing guns of the eight destroyers continued to pound, pumping shells into the Norwegian sky.

One of the Dorniers banked and a moment later its engines spluttered and skipped a beat. Smoke was gushing from its starboard wing, thick, black and oily, and then Ollie saw flames streak out, vivid in the evening light. How high was it? No more than a few hundred feet, he guessed. It continued to bank, then flipped over and dived towards the sea. Moments later it hit the water with a loud crash that he could hear even above the firing of the guns. When the eruption of water subsided, the aircraft was gone. Within less than a minute there was no sign that either the Dornier or its crew had ever existed. The deep, dark waters of the fjord had provided a veil of finality. Shocked, Ollie gripped the edge of the bridge guard to steady himself. A Dornier or a destroyer. That could have been them, he knew – gone for ever, their grave unknown to any who loved them, down in the dark depths of the Romsdalsfjord.

The surviving bombers banked, turned south and soon were gone. None of the ships had been hit. A strong stench of smoke and cordite wafted back across the bridge. Ollie felt nauseous.

'Good shooting,' grinned Bertie, as Crawley reappeared on the bridge.

'One–nil to us, I'd say,' said Crawley, lighting a cigarette. He offered one to Ollie. 'You all right, Varney? Look like you could do with a smoke.'

'No, but thanks all the same,' he replied. He had never smoked a cigarette in his life and was determined not to start. 'That was quite some show.'

Bertie clapped him on the back. 'Damned difficult for a bomber to hit a moving ship, like a destroyer. We look like wriggling pencils from up there. Always remember they look a lot more troublesome than they actually are and especially so when we're firing God knows how much ordnance at them.'

'I'd certainly far rather be here than in a bloody Dornier,' agreed Crawley.

'Anyway,' added Bertie, 'that was merely the hors d'oeuvre. Look.'

The ship was turning a bend in the fjord, beyond which was Åndalsnes. They could not yet see the town, but above, as the evening began to darken, a dull and flickering red glow lit up the sky.

'Hmm,' said Bertie, lighting a pipe. 'That doesn't look too clever now, does it?'

'What is it?' Ollie asked, although he knew already. Ahead the light began to deepen and brighten, and then there it was, Åndalsnes, straight ahead of them, several miles away, already burning, angry flames rising into the sky.

'Into the jaws of hell we sail,' said Bertie.

Yes, thought Ollie. That was exactly what it was like, the fjord as the River Styx. He swallowed hard, wondering whether any of them would ever emerge or whether this was it, their very own Götterdämmerung.

18

Inferno

Tuesday, 30 April 1940

AS OLLIE'S SHIP WAS HEADING DOWN THE ROMSDALSFJORD, TESS was hurrying down Whitehall towards Westminster Underground station, past besuited men, a nanny pushing a pram, young men in uniform, two women paused deep in conversation. She wondered what they were all thinking. Was this just another normal day or did worries over what was going on in Norway crowd their thoughts as they did hers? A bus rumbled past. Sandbags covering the Cenotaph. Sandbags at the entrance to Downing Street. Sandbags all around the entrances to just about every building along Whitehall for that matter. Above, silvery barrage balloons swaying gently at the end of their wires. It was evening but still light. Summer on its way.

A little breathless, she reached the platform just as a train pulled in and, despite the evening hour, managed to find a seat. The train jolted on its way. She looked across at a young soldier, head lolling backwards with sleep, his mouth ajar. An older man, in a suit with still-polished shoes, sat next to him, upright, clutching a briefcase, staring ahead.

A general feeling of dismay and mounting despair appeared to be the trend. People couldn't understand why things were going so very badly on land in Norway. Blame was being directed at the political leaders rather than the troops. Tess couldn't shift the profound sense of impending doom that consumed her. She wanted to walk down the carriage, shake people by the shoulder, and tell them to wake up and listen. *Don't you realize what's going on? Don't you understand the threat?* She felt as though she had crossed an invisible dividing line between worlds: on the one side was her old life, the peaceful England of her childhood and all the certainties she had taken for granted, and on the other was this new reality, in which everything was now horribly, unthinkably imperilled. The Germans would not stop. Hitler would not stop. More attacks, more bloodshed, more war. *Snap out of it*, she told herself, biting her bottom lip.

At Notting Hill she got off and, out on the street, rummaged in her bag for Brenda's instructions: *Right down Pembridge Road then bear left and keep going until you reach Ledbury Road. We're at number 82.* Tess was looking forward to seeing her; curiously, it made her feel a little closer to Edward. He'd been posted to Palestine, but was he there? She could picture him but not him in Palestine, a place that seemed so far away as to be on another planet. What was he doing? Where was he sleeping? Was he fit and well? She had no idea. None of them did. A letter would presumably arrive in the fullness of time, but until such time, her brother had vanished into an unknown world. An unknown existence.

It was the same with Alex. Those last days of August had been so perfect, so intimate, their lives briefly entwined, and yet already she was thinking of him less. Letters had arrived from France fairly regularly but that wonderful closeness had vanished. His world of his regiment was not hers; it was literally unimaginable to her. Words, the ink on a page of paper, were something – a link, she supposed – but a very poor substitute for physical presence.

She wondered whether Brenda was having similar thoughts. Whether their love would endure. She hoped so for she adored Edward and was already fond of Brenda. At Farrowcombe they'd promised to meet up in London but Tess had singularly failed to make contact, so when Brenda had rung her one evening she'd felt pleased and guilty in equal measure. Tess had suggested meeting for dinner in town; Brenda had insisted she come to her. 'I'd love to cook for you, Tess,' she'd told her. 'I've the time on my hands, after all.'

A ten-minute walk and she was there. An elegant three-storey house of pale London brick, steps leading up to a dark blue front door. She knocked and heard Brenda call, 'Coming!' from inside, and a moment later the door opened.

'Tess!' She smiled. 'I'm so glad you're here!'

Tess was ushered inside. It was as elegant within as without, although Brenda told her she was only using four rooms: the drawing room, the first-floor bedroom, the kitchen and bathroom. 'Although I've laid up the dining room in your honour.'

The house belonged to her parents. It had been rented for years ever since her mother and father had moved to Kenya, but the tenants had left after war had broken out, so since Easter she had been rattling around in it on her own. 'It's far too big for one person,' Brenda told her. 'I need to get a tenant, but I don't know who. All my girlfriends have either got their own flats or homes or have fled London too.'

'Why don't you advertise?' asked Tess. They were in the drawing room, each perched at one end of a sofa, but turned towards one another and clutching glasses of gin. Brenda had one leg tucked under the other.

'I suppose I should,' said Brenda. 'But I don't know. I feel so . . .', she looked towards an ill-defined spot, '. . . restless. And what if the person who comes to stay turns out to be an absolute rat or dreary dull? It's not always easy to tell on first impression and one can hardly demand a trial run.' She smiled. 'But how are you, Tess? I've been thinking of you often with your general, at the heart of things. Is everyone terribly worried?'

Tess nodded. 'They are, rather. Everyone's been so caught out. There's lots of talk about us having missed the bus.'

'Oh dear, poor Chamberlain. He rather shot himself in the foot with that one. Do you think Italy will enter the war?'

'I hope not. Actually, the general told me a funny story yesterday, which apparently had been told by Signor Bastianini. Apparently Mussolini had said, "Germany is trying to drag me into the war by the hair, but luckily I'm bald."'

They laughed. 'How funny,' said Brenda. 'I never knew Fascists had a sense of humour. He's such an odd-looking little man, though, isn't he? It's baffling how the Italians, who one thinks of as such romantic people, can be so in thrall to him and all that chest-puffing. Well, I'll try and take some comfort from that.'

Tess gently touched her arm. 'Are you missing Edward?'

'More than I can say. You know, it's just so odd. I was really quite content with my life before he entered it but now I can't imagine it without him, yet here I am, living on my own, pining for him and feeling so blue I can't seem to work up the energy to do anything. It's hopeless.'

Tess thought the supper delicious. Soup, followed by plaice and vegetables, all seemingly cooked effortlessly and with Brenda only making brief forays to the kitchen.

'How do you do it?' Tess asked her. 'You weren't packed off to finishing school, were you?'

Brenda laughed. 'No, I was trying to be a learned young scholar at Newnham. The cook at home in Nairobi taught me. My parents were often out – they were frightfully sociable – and Daddy was at work during the day, so I spent a lot of time in the kitchen with Maria. That was the cook's name. She was lovely. And very patient.'

They chatted on. Really, Brenda was so easy to talk to. Later, Tess insisted on helping her clear away dinner. In the kitchen, she dried while Brenda washed.

'I just don't know what to do,' Brenda told her. 'I've been thinking I should join one of the women's services. I've a reasonably good brain, and I would like to help. Do something worthwhile. Perhaps the Wrens or the ATS. I suppose I've felt a bit of an orphan for a long time but now I especially feel as though I don't quite belong anywhere. Or, rather, that I don't have any purpose. You've cheered me up no end but much of the time I'm feeling too wretched to do anything. It's ridiculous. I'm wallowing in self-pity, I know. I need to snap out of it but, oh, Tess, I can't help feeling so terribly blue.'

'What about Alvesdon? Debbo and Stork would love it if you went down there. Dad always needs more help on the farm. You could be an unofficial land girl like Elsa.'

Brenda smiled. 'My parents would laugh to see me driving a tractor and wiping sweat from my brow.'

'Really?'

'Yes. My father liked me to sit up straight, never talk too much, and to act the refined young lady about town. No mess. Mess, dust, dirt were not to be tolerated.'

'Goodness. What would they think of the farm?'

'They'd take a dim view.'

They both laughed, then Brenda said, 'It's been so lovely to see you, Tess.'

She left soon after; it didn't pay to stay up late or drink too much when the working day began at seven, but on getting back to the house in Pimlico, she did write to her parents: 'I think Brenda is rather lonely and needing direction,' she told them. 'I suggested she come and help on the farm and live with you. A rather brilliant idea, don't you think?'

She wondered whether anything would come of it. On balance, probably not. Brenda, she thought, seemed rather set on the Wrens.

Standing on the bridge beside Stuart Bertie and Jimmy Malone, binoculars to his eyes, Ollie wondered how on earth they were going to lift anyone from the wreckage of Åndalsnes. High mountains loomed at either side, the fjord impossibly narrow with barely any room to manoeuvre. *Iceni* felt small and even fragile. Vulnerable. They were being shoehorned into a narrow channel. Ahead, at the far end of the fjord, Åndalsnes burned, thick black smoke rolling like Cornish breakers into the sky. He could smell it on the air and they were still several miles away: wood smoke, no longer gentle and warming but harsh, choking, the stench of destruction. Not a single house appeared to be standing; only brick chimney stacks, pointing forlornly into the sky. Could men still be there, living through this hell? He lowered his binoculars and glanced at Malone who had paused to light a cigarette. He noticed the number one's hands were shaking a little as he struck and cupped a match.

A gaggle of Junkers bombers suddenly appeared in the valley, as though out of nowhere. Ollie started at the sudden roar of their engines, then cursed himself. He'd been so transfixed by the town up ahead he'd forgotten to keep alert. The raft of anti-aircraft guns of the cruiser HMS *Manchester* opened fire, followed a moment later by those of *Southampton* and the destroyers. The Junkers swooped towards them. Bombs falling. Mountains of spray, the evening sky pockmarked with black smudges of flak. *Iceni*'s own guns finally opened up. *Pom-pom-pom-pom-pom-pom-pom.* An explosion, a ball of flame, and an aircraft was plunging in pieces, each on fire, until enclosed by dark waters. More men gone, just like that. Ollie swallowed hard and his hands gripped the edge of the bridge.

Now the remaining bombers were rapidly becoming dots, melting away into the darkness, the sudden immense din over. Bertie went hurriedly from one side of the bridge to the other, glanced around and said, 'Can't see any hits. Good job those Huns can't aim very well.'

A buzz from the voice pipe and Bertie swung around.

'Message from *Manchester*, sir,' came Henry Wymer's voice from the signals room. 'Proceed to pier behind *Delight*. Evacuation to commence straight away.'

'Very well,' replied Bertie, then brought his binoculars to his eyes again. 'Although there doesn't appear to be much pier left. This might prove a tad challenging, gentlemen.'

They continued forward, and only as they cleared the headland at Klungnes did they realize they had been looking at Isfjorden, at the very far end of the fjord, burning and not Åndalsnes, which lay mercifully intact, nestling on the southern shores a couple of miles further on. The pier remained hidden until they cleared the promontory of the town and then there it was, but already swarming with men.

'Look at them all,' muttered Malone, as they waited for *Delight* to moor. The town was more of a village – a collection of wooden houses crammed along the shoreline, a squat-towered church overlooking the flock beneath it and a mass of fishing warehouses. Isolated, remote, presumably a place that for centuries had been rather left to its own devices, thought Ollie, but now the scene of a crazy evacuation, with the Germans literally snapping at their heels.

He looked up at the mighty mountains, still covered with snow, looming over them. He longed for the open sea once more, a sensation of claustrophobia and mounting dread weighing down on him. They now inched in towards *Delight*, to moor alongside, even as *Inglefield,* a third destroyer, slipped in behind to move alongside them. Even so, he wondered how they were going to lift the reported four thousand men now waiting.

The heat from the burning Isfjorden could be felt on the air, the smoke darkening the evening sky, a thick pall spreading over the eastern end of the fjord.

'Think of it as a protective shroud,' said Bertie, following Ollie's gaze. 'Now head to the stern, Mr Varney, and help with the troops coming aboard. They'll move directly onto *Inglefield*.'

'Then us, sir?'

Bertie nodded. 'We'll deposit our load on one of the cruisers, then return for a second helping.'

'Aye, aye, sir,' said Ollie, and hurried to the ladder that led down from the bridge to the main deck.

It was getting dark. Ropes were being thrown across to *Delight* as *Iceni* eased alongside, nudging the other destroyer so gently that Ollie barely noticed the contact. *Inglefield* was now pulling alongside them in turn. Shouts, barked orders, glances at the sky. Men still at their guns, watching, waiting. No one liked being stationary when the skies belonged to the enemy.

Now the first troops were boarding and being ushered straight across towards *Iceni*, but stopped at the guardrail at *Delight*'s stern, which was a couple of feet lower than that of the Tribal-class destroyer.

'Come along,' said Ollie, but the men looked at him with blank disbelief. 'Come on!' he urged. 'Just climb over.'

Still the men hesitated, and Petty Officer Goodchild was now beside him.

'Come on, come on!' bellowed Goodchild. 'Get bloody moving!'

Gingerly, the first climbed over and jumped down onto *Iceni*, just as the two vessels lurched. On *Delight,* the men moved back from the rail in horror.

'Bloody jump to it!' yelled Goodchild.

At this, Ollie nimbly leaped over the guardrail of both ships, thinking how much easier it was than vaulting a gate back home on the farm.

'Now come on,' he said, 'you've fought off Germans, you can surely jump a guardrail.' He jumped back over again. 'You!' he said, pointing to one of the men. 'Jump to it.'

The young man did so, and the rest followed, rather like sheep, Ollie thought. It had been drummed into him at HMS *King Alfred* that officers were to lead by example, and he'd always had an image in his mind of storming some vessel rather like Nelson at Cape St Vincent. Vaulting a guardrail had been the last thing he'd expected to have to do. Soon they were clamouring to climb over, all fear replaced by a sense of urgency to get onto the next ship and away as quickly as possible. Then a young lad tripped and fell, crying out, and several others stumbled too and collapsed on top of him. Ollie moved to help them up, while Goodchild cursed and roughly grabbed a man by his greatcoat, yanking him to his feet.

'Easy, mate!' said the man.

'Don't you "mate" me, sunshine,' said Goodchild, 'now get a move on before Jerry gets here.' The petty officer glanced briefly at Ollie: *No time for pleasantries, this.* It was a challenge to him, Ollie knew. Goodchild thought him a bit wet behind the ears. He might have been too soft but he wasn't going to start rough-handling exhausted troops. Instead, he said, 'Carry on, Mr Goodchild,' and hoped he'd done so with sufficient authority and assurance.

It was nearing dawn when they finally left, having first deposited several hundred troops on *Southampton*, then returned to the pier for a second batch. They now had 132 men aboard, double their normal complement, and filling, it seemed, every gangway, lower and upper deck space. Men unshaven, men dirty, men exhausted.

There had been a hold-up getting the first load of men transferred aboard *Southampton* as *Delight* had struggled to close in alongside in the darkness of night. Frantic and increasingly angry signals from the cruiser did nothing to speed matters up. Even once alongside, it took time to transfer more than four hundred weary troops and then *Iceni* had to repeat the process. Lieutenant Commander Bertie had been becoming increasingly incensed: he couldn't understand why they were not able to come alongside *Southampton*'s port side while *Delight* disgorged to starboard; but the cruiser was the senior ship, and the captain senior in rank. They'd had to wait their turn, then hurry back to Åndalsnes.

Now, as they sailed away at nearly thirty knots, dawn was lightening the eastern sky as Ollie reported to the bridge.

'There you are, Sub,' said Jimmy Malone. 'The captain's in his cabin. All the soldiers all right?'

213

'Yes, Number One,' Ollie replied. 'And grateful for the tot of rum.' He paused. 'It's getting light very quickly, isn't it?'

'Too bloody quickly,' said Malone. 'Need to get to that open sea as quickly as possible.'

'But the evacuation's not over,' said Ollie. 'Perhaps the Luftwaffe will focus on the town and the ships still there.'

'Perhaps. Look here, Sub, do another prowl around, will you, and make sure those Army bods are either making themselves useful or out of the way?'

Ollie toured each of the four twin 4.7-inch main gun turrets as well as the twin Bofors and the anti-aircraft machine-guns. He spoke with several of the gun crews and had to shift a few soldiers but was satisfied all seemed well and that none of the soldiers was in the way. At the Y Turret at the stern of the ship, he found a lieutenant he'd spoken to earlier. It was now light, the sun's first rays straining to break through the pall of smoke still hanging over Isfjorden. Above, the sky was perfectly clear, the air fresh, clear and sharp once more, while behind them *Iceni* left a long, perfectly white wake that contrasted with the smooth, inky darkness of the Romsdalsfjord.

'You and your men all right?' Ollie asked him.

'As well as can be expected.' The man smiled. He introduced himself as Michael Harrington. 'Second lieutenant.' He offered Ollie a cigarette. It turned out Harrington was from a farming family too – near Melton Mowbray. He'd only joined the Territorials for a bit of fun and because a number of his friends had done the same. Suddenly they were on a ship to Norway and now here they were, only a week later, evacuating and with most of the battalion wiped out. It had been bewildering. Quite terrifying at times.

'I wonder what will happen next,' said Harrington. 'Hopefully we're a bit better organized in France.' He hoped he'd be given some leave when they got back. It was his birthday the following week – his twenty-first. 'My family were planning to make a bit of a fuss,' he told Ollie. 'Now they might be able to after all.' He grinned.

'Well, happy birthday in advance,' said Ollie. Then a faint hum, and he immediately looked back down the fjord. The hum rose, a deeper buzz, then the sound of guns and explosions.

214

Harrington sighed. 'Crikey,' he said. 'Thank goodness we're out of it.'

Ollie was thinking of the seventy miles they still had to go to reach the open sea when the sound of aircraft grew louder.

'Oh, Lordy,' said Harrington.

The ship's alarm sounded over the Tannoy and in the same moment Ollie saw them: four dark dots hurtling towards them, low, skimming over the water below the depression of the destroyer's guns.

'Hide yourselves!' shouted Ollie, urging the soldiers to shelter behind the gun turrets, cannon and searchlight mount at the stern of the ship. Men were getting to their feet, some just woken, expressions of alarm and panic. Harrington was beside him, pulling men to their feet. 'Come on! Come on!' he called out. 'Get up! Quick!'

Ollie glanced back, shocked by how quickly they were upon them. Four twin-engine aircraft – he recognized them as Messerschmitt 110s. A moment later, stabs of orange from the noses and a rattle and clatter of tearing metal and a hiss as several machine-gun bullets and cannon shells fizzed past him. *Christ, that was close.* Their own pom-poms and machine-guns booming, smudges in the low sky. Immense noise and the first Messerschmitt hurtling past at deck height. Fleetingly he saw the pilot. Then another clatter of bullets. Harrington gasped and fell against him as another aircraft roared past. Ollie grabbed his shoulders, clasping the serge of the greatcoat and saw the young man's face just inches from his: eyes wide, in shock and blood already pouring from his mouth.

'I've been hit,' said Harrington.

My God, thought Ollie, the two of them collapsing onto the deck, port side of the Y Turret.

'Quick!' he yelled. 'I need dressings!'

One of Harrington's men now crouched beside them, fumbling as he tried to tear open a field-dressing pack.

'Where's he been hit, sir?' Panic on the man's face. Guns still firing, but the sound of aircraft becoming thinner.

'I've been hit,' muttered Harrington again.

'It's all right,' said Ollie. Harrington was still clasped to him, Ollie's arms around his back. He was trying to think. It was all happening too quickly. His hands were wet. Sticky. He lifted them and

215

saw they were covered with Harrington's blood. 'He's hit in the back. Let's get his greatcoat off.'

It was hopeless. Harrington was still slumped against Ollie and blood was seeping over the deck.

'I don't think this bandage is going to do much good, sir,' said the soldier.

'Call for a bloody medic!' said Ollie, angrily. 'Can't you see he needs urgent help?'

Other men crowding round, looking down on the scene. Ollie was faintly conscious of a sergeant crouching down, then yelling, 'Medic!'

'Don't let go of me,' mumbled Harrington.

'I won't,' said Ollie. 'It's going to be all right.'

'I'm cold.'

'Sssh.' Ollie looked down. The pool of blood spreading, thick, dark, running across the deck. He could feel it seeping into his trousers as he knelt there, holding the boy, who was barely older than him.

Suddenly Harrington lifted his head. Tears were running down his face. 'This is it, isn't it?' he said softly.

Ollie looked at him, then clasped his head and held him to his chest. He felt a gasp and a shudder, then Harrington was still.

'He's gone, sir,' said the sergeant, who now knelt and gently pulled away the dead man. Ollie nodded, saw Harrington's lifeless eyes still staring at him, turned and got to his feet. He staggered and grasped the railings, then looked down at the blood covering his hands and still spreading across the deck so that it reached his shoes and ran around the soles.

'Here.' A small bottle of rum was handed to him. Ollie glanced up and saw Lieutenant Commander Bertie beside him. 'Drink this.'

Ollie nodded and took a tot, the liquid scouring his mouth and throat.

'All right?' said Bertie.

'I think so.'

'Good. Now, go and get yourself cleaned up and report to me on the bridge.' He patted Ollie on the back.

Harrington was buried at sea later that morning as they finally reached the open waters of the North Sea. He'd been the only man killed in the attack, although four others had been wounded. Ollie had watched as the body, enclosed in canvas and weighted down, had been tipped overboard, the bosun piping his whistle. An eerie, melancholic sound, Ollie thought.

Later, as he lay in his bunk, he struggled to clear the image of Harrington's face, wide-eyed, bloody-mouthed, staring at him. He tried to think of home instead, and of Elsa. The riverbank. Summer. Anything. He knew he was going to cry and didn't want anyone to see him, so he turned over, facing the metal wall of the ship's side and let the tears run down his cheeks.

19

The World Ablaze

THAT MORNING STORK DROVE OVER TO A FARM JUST TO THE SOUTH of Salisbury. The farmer, Alf Beresford, had a 130-acre concern that ran from the higher ground around the old hill fort of Clearbury down to the River Avon. Beresford had been recently categorized C after repeatedly refusing to plough more land, in particular three fields that encircled the old hill fort. That put him at odds with the district committee and a local land agent called Mr Reginald Drewitt, who had clearly embarked on an increasingly personal battle with Beresford and who had written to William Price suggesting the War Ag confiscate the farm. This, the War Ag had agreed, seemed a little precipitous, so Richard Stratton had asked Stork to make a visit and report back with his own assessment and recommendations.

As Stork pulled into the yard he saw three men already there: Beresford, smoking a pipe, talking to one of his men, and Drewitt, arms folded, a few yards away, turning with what appeared to be relief at the sight of Stork's car. It was the kind of yard Stork had seen countless times: a little run-down, the main house behind looking as though it needed a lick of paint, the sheds and stables surrounding the yard missing tiles on the roofs. At the far end was an old cart, abandoned, surrounded by nettles and dock sprouting up through the wheels. A half-dozen swallows were darting in and out of the stables, while from somewhere beyond he heard the two-note call of a cuckoo.

'Morning!' he called, as he got out of the car, then strode over with what he hoped seemed an affable smile on his face. Hands were shaken, acquaintances renewed and made as Beresford introduced his ploughman, Charlie Stott.

'A fine day,' said Stork. 'And the first cuckoo I've heard this year.'

''E's been here a few days now,' said Beresford. 'Here to make his mischief.' He shot a glance at Drewitt.

The land agent cleared his throat. 'Shall we get down to the matter in hand?'

'Them fields are not suitable for the plough,' Beresford jumped in. 'I don't know how many times I need to say it.'

''S right,'agreed Stott. 'Never was, never 'as bin.'

'You can't ignore government instructions just because something has never been done before,' said Drewitt. He was a tall man, very thin, with a pale ginger moustache that was neatly trimmed. With his immaculate tweed suit he gave off an air of meticulous efficiency. Stork knew both men only slightly, but looking at Beresford, in his collarless shirt, old and filthy dark suit, tanned, lined face, and two-day grey beard, felt certain the farmer was unlikely to hold much truck with a desk-man like Drewitt.

Stork watched the swallows, still swooping and pirouetting about the yard. How best to bring Beresford round? 'Always a lovely sight,' he said.

'They are,' said Beresford. 'We've house martins too, busy under the eaves of the house. It don't bother them that there's a war on.'

Stork chuckled. 'No, thank goodness. Anyway, how about we all go and have a look at these fields, Mr Beresford?'

'We can,' said Beresford, pushing his cap onto the back of his head, then scratching his neck. 'Not that I can see what good it'll do.'

'All the same,' said Stork, 'I'd like to see them. I imagine there's a fine view worth seeing from up there, even if nothing else.'

A horse and trap was brought round and the three of them set off, jolting up a track from the farm. Stork breathed in deeply, filling his lungs with the sweet scent of the verges and the musky smell of the horse. The field on the right-hand side of the lane was pasture, home to heifers awaiting their first calves. To the left was a field of very young corn. A pair of lapwings were circling and crying mournfully over the heifers.

'Yer see,' said Beresford, nodding towards the wheat field. 'I already ploughed this up when afore it were just pasture for the cows.'

'And it looks like it will be a good crop,' said Drewitt.

Beresford grunted. 'Ah, well, iss good enough soil 'ere, down on the lower half of the farm, but wireworm's playing merry hell.'

'There's a lot of it about,' said Stork. 'What did you have on it before?'

'Been sheep on it ten year now,' said Beresford.

'It's a curious thing,' said Stork. 'We've ploughed one thirty-acre field that had a beef herd on and the barley on it is doing just fine. Another where we used to fold sheep has got wireworm something rotten. I'm not sure why that should be. Have you rolled it?'

'Not yet.'

'Well, I'd get rolling it and keep rolling it while it's still this young. And if you can, add some nitrogenous fertilizer.'

'Tha's all very well, but it costs a pretty penny, Mr Castell.'

'We should be able to help you there,' said Stork. 'We're all in this together, you know. The role of the government and the War Ag is to ensure we produce as much food as possible. If people are struggling, there are ways and means by which we can help.'

Beresford grunted again.

They presently climbed up an old holloway and emerged near the top of the hill, the track continuing to the hill fort, its embankments still high despite the centuries that had passed since they'd first been dug and built. Long ago, there would have been a palisade atop the circular mound, protecting tribesmen and their animals, but now there was a copse of beech, at least a hundred and fifty years old, Stork reckoned, and now just starting to leaf.

'Whoa there,' said Beresford, pulling on the reins and bringing the trap to a halt. He paused a moment, looking around, then fetched a pipe and a pouch.

'An' the government's not helping,' he said, 'putting up the price of tobacco like that.'

Stork said nothing but jumped down and looked around. Ahead of him lay the Avon valley, the river snaking its silvery way southwards, while to the north, the spire of the cathedral stood sentinel over the city, nestling in a hazy light.

'It doesn't disappoint,' said Stork. He squatted down and took out a long sword bayonet left over after the last war from the canvas knapsack he'd brought with him. The grass looked thick enough, a few flints around. Gently, he slid the blade of the bayonet into the soil, pressing firmly but without exertion until he reached resistance, then pulled it out again and examined the blade.

Drewitt snorted. 'There's nothing wrong with this soil, Mr Beresford.'

'It's not right for ploughing,' Beresford insisted.

Stork rubbed his chin. 'This bayonet is thirteen inches long, Mr Beresford, and I pushed it in this far.' He held it up. 'What's that? At least ten inches.'

'Well, you got lucky. It's not all as deep as that. An' try the other fields.'

'It's not good enough, Beresford,' said Drewitt. 'These fields are perfectly sound enough to plough. There's a war on. A national emergency and—'

'You're quite right,' said Stork, interrupting him. 'But we all know that on farms such these there are other considerations, aren't there, Mr Beresford? One has to think about how fields ploughed up for arable are going to be harvested. How many men do you have here?'

'Twelve,' said Beresford. 'I've got my dairyman and two lads that work with him, but he's seventy and the boys only sixteen. I've Charlie, and a shepherd, a pig man, and seven others for all the ploughin', drillin' and harvestin.' I've lost two good lads who've gone off to play at being heroes and doubt they'll be the last.'

'As I told you before,' said Drewitt, 'those losses can be made good with land girls.'

'No, they can't,' snapped Beresford. 'They're from all over, most have never lived on the land and it's not in their blood. I dunno who's training them but my neighbour's had two on his farm and says they're ruddy 'opeless. 'E's got to train them up, see, and he hasn't got time for that. I haven't got time for that. Last harvest it was hard enough getting it in, and that was afore we ploughed up another forty-five acres. We're not an arable farm, Mr Castell. Oats an' some barley an' that's it. An' we ploughed up as we were told in the last war an' what good did that do us? Nearly broke us, that's what.'

'I understand, Mr Beresford,' said Stork. 'You've a tractor, though? A Fordson?'

'Well, that's another thing,' said Beresford. 'I got one on the government scheme – which we can ill afford – and the darned thing's broke. No good to man or beast.'

'What about getting it fixed?' said Drewitt.

'Did once, but it bust again. It's the devil to start, allus playing up. You know where you are wi' horses.'

Stork remembered his father's scepticism when he'd first proposed mechanizing the farm – and it wasn't just his father, but many of the farm workers too. People were suspicious of change, and particularly the kind that boasted of offering the power of twenty horses. It required new skills; machines were very different beasts from horses. Worse, it threatened their livelihoods and with it their lives. These fears were understandable, but he'd not laid off a single man in the years since their first tractor had arrived; rather, as he'd pointed out to his father, their farm had become more efficient, more profitable and, as a consequence, had made the employment of a large workforce even more secure.

He suspected such reassurances would cut little ice with Beresford, whose financial situation was already clearly precarious. Nor was it helping to bully a stubborn old farmer with threats.

'All right, Mr Beresford,' he said, at length. 'We can head back down to the farm now. Let me have a think about how we might help. If we can iron out some of your worries, then we can have another think about these three fields up here.'

Beresford re-lit his pipe. 'Well,' he said, 'it's nice to be offered a bit o' help for a change, I'll not deny it.'

Stork gave him a light pat on the back. 'You've a fine farm, Mr Beresford,' he said, 'and I'm certain we can sort things out easily enough.' He turned to Drewitt. 'Wouldn't you say so, Mr Drewitt?'

It was Carin's birthday and John had invited Stork and Debbo over for dinner that evening, Maud and Alwyn too.

Certainly everyone was doing their best. They'd all dressed for dinner, a habit that had been dropped in recent times, and the younger children, Maria and Robbie, had been allowed to stay and join them alongside Elsa and the other adults. Stork thought Carin looked as lovely as ever, although there was a wistfulness about her. He so wished he could do something to help sweep it away but his

222

letters had achieved nothing. He understood the reasoning thrown back at him but it seemed to him that common sense was needed too, and that this was badly lacking. Any number of people would be prepared to vouch for Carin.

John was most attentive, raising a toast over drinks in their drawing room and bustling around pouring wine once they had sat down to eat. But how diminished they were, thought Stork, sadly, all trying just a little too hard to have a good time.

'Any news from Tess or Edward?' asked Maud.

'No,' Debbo replied. 'Not a squeak from Edward but letters will take a little while from Palestine.'

'They ought to be quicker after the hike in postage prices,' said John. 'Have you seen the cost of stamps since the budget? Daylight robbery!'

'Everything is going up,' said Stork. 'It's bound to, with the war on.'

'But letters,' said John, 'they're so important for morale. I can't imagine how I'd have got through the last war without all the letters that reached me.'

'Well, I'm not sure increased postage cost is why we've heard so little from Tess,' said Stork. 'Her general works her frightfully hard.'

'But we did have a letter from her last week,' added Debbo. 'She had had dinner with Brenda. It seems Brenda's somewhat at a loss, with Edward in Palestine and living on her own in London. Apparently, she's thinking of joining the Wrens.'

'Then she might bump into Ollie,' said Carin.

'I suppose she might,' said Debbo, 'but, actually, Tess wondered whether she could come down here and help on the farm.'

'I'd love that,' said Elsa. 'Do you think she could, Uncle Stork?'

'We can always use extra hands, as you well know,' Stork replied. 'But we've not heard anything since.'

'I've written to her,' added Debbo, 'telling her that of course she can come and live with us if she would like to and posted it with an expensive stamp!'

Everyone laughed.

'Any news of Ollie?' asked Maud.

'He's back from Norway,' said Elsa. 'Safe and sound. He's been helping the evacuation.'

'Good for him,' said Alwyn. 'He's a fine young man, Elsa.'

'Any leave on the horizon?' asked Debbo.

'Oh, I do hope so, but not at the moment. He's in Scotland still.'

'Dear Ollie rang, didn't he, Elsa, darling?' said Carin. 'You said he sounded all right.'

'I think so,' said Elsa.

The conversation turned to what had happened in the House of Commons that day. Debbo had been to the village stores earlier where there had been much chatter over whether or not Chamberlain would survive.

'They'd be bloody fools to get rid of him now,' said Alwyn. 'Not the time to change a prime minister.'

'I'm rather hoping Churchill takes over,' said Debbo. 'He's what we need now. A bit of charisma.'

'The man's a damned liability,' said Alwyn. 'Always backing the wrong horse. If Chamberlain does go, I'd rather see Halifax in charge. He's a sound fellow.'

'How was the farm you visited this morning, Stork?' John asked, changing the subject.

'I felt rather sorry for the farmer,' said Stork. 'He's a bit scared. Scared of change, scared of ruining himself. Doesn't trust the government. And he's had a Salisbury land agent threatening him.'

'The poor lamb,' said Debbo.

'So, what are you going to do?' asked John.

'First of all I'm going to send Smudger over with some spares and get his Fordson working. He can show Beresford's chaps what to do. And I've suggested to Richard Stratton that we send him some fertilizer and do all we can to help. There's nothing wrong with his farm. He just needs a bit of support. If he can see we're trying to help rather than hinder he might be willing to plough the extra fields that are causing all the trouble.'

At nine o'clock they paused to listen to the news on the wireless. Men aged nineteen to thirty-six were now being called up – a little younger and older than had previously been the case. Chamberlain was holding on as prime minister, despite a humiliating debate in the House about Norway, and Churchill had made a speech calling for unity.

'Mark my words,' said Alwyn, once the wireless had been switched off, 'there's trouble brewing.'

Tom Timbrell was woken at around four thirty the following morning, Friday, 10 May, with the sound of aircraft thundering low overhead. Hearing the roar of engines, Tom had immediately jumped up from his straw palliasse, pulled on his boots and hurried outside the barn as a second wave of aircraft hurtled over, barely a thousand feet above them, in the thin light of dawn. *Dorniers*, he thought, looking up at their twin engines and twin-fin tail planes. And there, under each wing, was a large painted black cross, which, after all the news reels, all the studying of aircraft recognition charts and all the talk of the unseen enemy from Nazi Germany, was rather startling to see. A moment later, anti-aircraft guns opened up, the ground pulsing gently with each shot.

The bombers were over and gone in a flash, the rumble of their engines disappearing as quickly as the tailing-off of anti-aircraft fire. Tom wandered out into the yard, in his shirt and trousers, breathed in deeply and scratched his chin. A few others were up now too and sleepily ambling outside.

'Jesus!' said Parkinson beside him. 'Were those Jerries?'

Tom nodded and went back into the barn. 'All right, you lot,' he said, 'everyone up. Stand-to in three minutes.'

Groans, grumbling and grouching but most were already awake. Tom hurried to his spot near the double door at the barn's entrance and put on his battle blouse, belt and webbing. Finally grabbing his rifle, he stepped back outside only to see Lieutenant George Ashton hurrying over from the farmhouse.

'Ah, well done, Sergeant,' he said. 'There you are.'

'I've ordered stand-to, sir.'

'Good man. Battalion's trying to find out what the orders are.'

'Advance into Belgium?' suggested Tom.

Ashton smiled. 'Very possibly. If this is it, that is.'

To the south they heard a dull, distant thud of exploding bombs followed by more anti-aircraft fire. Tom pulled out a cigarette and lit it. A lovely late-spring morning, the sky clear. The men emerged, most still pulling belts together or adjusting webbing. Tom formed them up and brought them to attention. A loud drum on the ground as thirty-six pairs of boots were brought together.

'Thank you, Sergeant.'

'Platoon . . . ease!' called Tom. Another thrum of feet.

'Well, chaps,' said Ashton, 'I'm afraid I don't have much to tell you. Clearly, those were Jerry bombers that flew over and equally clearly they were dropping bombs so that suggests the balloon has gone up, all right. But until we get our orders through, there's not much we can do. Let's keep alert and be ready.' He looked around, as though hoping for some last-minute news to reach him. 'Er, right. Um.' A glance at Tom. 'As you were.'

Tom ordered them to fall out. The men began brewing tea and chuntering about having got up for no reason. Everyone seemed a bit fed up. Tom felt a bit browned off too. The inaction of the past weeks had been tedious. The men were restless and Tom was surprised by how much he wanted this to be it, for them to move off and meet the enemy. Of course, he didn't want to die or be wounded, but he was sick of hanging around, twiddling his thumbs.

The 1st Battalion of the King's Own Royal Guards was now based to the south-east of Lille, still on the French–Belgian border, but a shift of around twenty miles from their positions earlier in the year. Why they'd been moved, Tom had never been told; they just had. Orders had arrived one day in April and that was that: into trucks, a long, tedious trundle through Lille, and out the other side until they'd stopped at a farm just outside the village of Mouchin. The new farm was much like the last: barns and stables around a yard and a farmhouse next door. In many ways, it wasn't so very different from Manor Farm back home in Alvesdon. Tom had watched the farm workers sowing the corn in the fields opposite, and the dairy herd slowly plodding by twice a day for milking, and had felt moments of yearning for the life he'd left behind.

Since they'd arrived, there had been much talk of a German attack, although one day had followed another without even a faint hint of enemy activity; the Germans might have been making mischief in Norway, but Tom had begun to think nothing would ever happen here. It had all been so quiet. The men had become a little restless too. There were only so many route marches the lads could be sent on, and only so many times rifle practice and other drills

226

could be carried out. After the platoon sergeant had been invalided out with pneumonia at the end of March, Tom had been promoted and had taken over. If any of the longer-serving lads had resented it none of them had said so: the capture of fifth columnists on the night patrol had won him some respect within the company as much as the platoon, but most of the lads had grown up in cities and didn't share his affinity either with the land or his prowess with a rifle. A country upbringing, he'd discovered, was a good starting point for an infanteer.

Tess was woken at 6 a.m. by the shrill ring of the telephone. It was Bill Elliott.

'The Germans have invaded the Low Countries,' he told her. She was needed immediately.

Alex, she thought, then realized with a lurch in her stomach that Wilf might soon be sent into action too. Dressing quickly, applying only the lightest amount of make-up, and making a marmalade sandwich, she was out of the door in just twenty minutes and walking as fast as she could to the office at Richmond Terrace. She felt exhausted. The past ten days had been the hardest of her life – ever since Mr Churchill had been put in charge of the Military Co-ordination Committee. 'Mr Churchill is an extraordinary man,' General Ismay had warned her, 'but unconventional too, and that goes for his working hours.' Just this past week she'd worked fourteen hours on Monday, fifteen on Tuesday, twelve on Wednesday and the previous day fifteen again after a late-night meeting at the Admiralty where she'd been required to take notes. It had been nearly midnight when they'd left.

Churchill had said nothing about the two-day Norway debate or commented on whether Chamberlain might resign, and Ismay hadn't asked, but as they had walked back to Richmond Terrace, he had told her to get a good night's sleep.

'I won't call you early,' he said, 'but we may well have a new prime minister tomorrow. And, if so, I pray it might be Winston.'

There had been no lie-in, though, and now that the Germans had invaded, she supposed Chamberlain would stay on. She sighed. She had understood why Ismay had been so in thrall to the First Lord of the Admiralty: Churchill, despite his age, was the most energetic

227

person she had ever met. Ideas poured from him, all laced in the most incredible language, with references drawn from poetry one moment, history the next. He wanted more expertise in the Military Co-ordination Committee, which Tess thought seemed a very sensible idea. It was unorthodox but, as Mr Churchill had pointed out, war was not the time for niceties of political decorum. It was the time for dynamic action.

But what would happen now? It was hard to think straight. The lack of sleep, the enormity of the unfolding events both in the Commons and now on the Continent, and the sheer dizzying complexity of the situation in which she unwittingly had gained a ringside seat were impossible to digest with any kind of clear-headedness.

And yet, as Tess climbed the few steps up to 2 Richmond Terrace, she felt a frisson of excitement. Guiltily she chided herself, then stepped inside.

In northern France, by one o'clock Tom Timbrell had still not moved an inch. They had been given a series of coded warning signals that they would soon be heading forward into Belgium to take up positions along the River Dyle. This, Tom reckoned from looking at his maps, was about seventy-five miles away, to the east of Brussels. News was trickling in: that Holland, then Belgium, had been invaded and that the Germans had used airborne troops to secure bridges and other key targets.

Later, Tom had been called to a company O group in another large barn that had been taken over as company headquarters, and included all officers and senior NCOs such as himself.

'The BEF is moving into Belgium, all right,' said Major Alastair Burnham-Browne, the company commander, 'just as sure as the Huns are sweeping through the Low Countries too.' Burnham-Browne was a handsome, clean-shaven, sandy-haired man in his early thirties and a career soldier who seemed utterly wedded to the regiment. Everyone knew him as 'Toast'. 'The Guards Brigade will be in reserve,' he continued, stabbing a map he'd pinned to the wall of the barn with his stick – small tears were appearing in the paper – 'so we'll be behind the rest of the 1st Division and not actually on the D-Line itself. So, we'll be departing at Z plus twenty-eight hours.'

'And when is Z-hour, sir?' asked Alex Woodman.

'Thirteen-hundred hours today, as per the alerts earlier.' He looked at his watch. 'So, we move off at seventeen hundred tomorrow.'

No one appeared to bat an eyelid at this, but Tom was rather taken aback. *Bloody hell*, he thought. *Late afternoon tomorrow.* He couldn't understand it. Why the wait? Why not get going straight away?

'Got to give the rest of the division a head start,' Burnham-Browne told them. 'Don't want to get the roads log-jammed. It's seventy-five miles we'll be advancing and there are a lot of vehicles in Two Corps, with comparatively limited roads.' A steady and methodical advance was what was needed. 'Don't forget,' he said, turning to them all, 'it was the tortoise that won the race, not the hare.'

Afterwards, just as Tom was about to head back to his platoon, Alex Woodman called him over. 'Can you believe it?' he said. 'This is it at long last.'

Tom kept his counsel. 'I don't really know what to think, to be honest, sir.'

'I know what you mean. I'm quite excited but a little apprehensive too, I don't mind admitting.'

That was about right, Tom thought, as he lit a cigarette and headed back to see how the packing up was going. Even so, he wasn't sure that the commander's line about the tortoise and the hare was the right way to look at it. Time, he supposed, would tell.

At nine o'clock that evening, Stork switched on the wireless in the drawing room at Farrowcombe to listen to the news. He sat down beside Debbo and felt her take his hand as they heard Chamberlain's voice. The same slightly reedy tone that, back in September, had told them the country was at war with Germany. Now he told them, in an equally sombre tone, he had decided that in light of recent events it was time for a new, national cross-party government, and a new prime minister too. That afternoon, he said, he had visited the King, and offered his resignation. It was his duty to inform the nation that Mr Churchill was to be his successor.

'Goodness,' said Stork. 'You got your wish, my darling.'

But Debbo just looked at him, her face ashen. 'Oh, Stork,' she said. 'I can scarcely believe what is happening to us. Whatever next?'

20

On the Move

AS THE GERMANS SWEPT INTO THE LOW COUNTRIES AND WINSTON Churchill took over as prime minister, Edward Castell and the rest of C Squadron of the Wiltshire Rangers Yeomanry were moving cross-country, oblivious – at that moment – of the dramatic events taking place closer to home. Their destination was Latrun, a Palestinian hilltop town perhaps thirty miles inland; it was due to be the regiment's home for the immediate future. C Squadron was the advance guard, so ahead of the rest of the regiment, and the men were all mounted on their horses, fully armed with rifles, pistols and swords.

They had set out from Rehovot just before 11 a.m. and, despite the month-long journey by ship, train, then ship and then, from Haifa to Rehovot, a further – and most uncomfortable – train journey, the horses seemed in remarkably good fettle and so, too, the men, as far as Edward could tell. And it was good to be back in the saddle, with the familiar smell of Byron, his horse, the squeak of leather and the feel of the animal's muscles working beneath him. The heat, though, was intense, unlike anything he'd felt before, so they made sure they moved slowly, careful not to over-exert the horses on this first outing in a strange and foreign land.

After a few miles they passed through a village, which looked exactly how Edward had imagined a biblical village, with its flat-roofed houses, donkeys and mules, street vendors selling large hessian sacks of beans, seeds and boxes of fruit.

'A far cry from Devizes, zir,' said Sergeant Smithers, riding along-side him.

'The land of Our Lord Jesus Christ, Smithers,' Edward said. 'The Israel of the Bible, of the Virgin Birth, miracles, holy deeds, feeding the five thousand. You remember the Bible stories, don't you?'

Smithers tutted. 'Never been much of a one for religion, sir.'

'You might need it, though, before this war is done.'

Smithers looked doubtful. 'I wouldn't know about that, zir. Just seems ruddy hot, dusty and squalid to me.' He glanced around in disgust. 'Never seen such filth.'

Edward laughed at his troop sergeant's discomfort. *Mad dogs and Englishmen go out in the midday sun.* One could take the Englishman out of England, he thought, but not England out of the Englishman. He glanced back at the pink-skinned troop following behind, one man wiping his brow on his sleeve, another flapping away flies. Others glancing at the scene around them with equal distaste. It might take a little while, he supposed, for them to acclimatize. After all, before the war, the majority of the men had barely left Wiltshire.

They stopped every hour to check the horses and just after one o'clock paused for a lunch from rations and a brew. Flies followed them, and as he ate, Edward found himself whisking them away constantly. Around him settled a soporific, sticky heat, a permanent clicking and ringing of insects and, out in the country, the dry, sweet scent of herbs and vetch. Adding to the discomfort was the webbing they wore and the amount of kit they carried with them; Dasher had even insisted they bring gas masks. Once moving again, they were climbing gently, and as they neared the top of a ridge, Edward looked back and saw the column stretching several hundred yards. He couldn't help feeling a small swell of pride.

They reached Latrun just after four o'clock and Edward was relieved by what he discovered. There was a large abbey of pink stone and a terracotta roof around which swifts were careering and screeching, a clutch of umbrella pines, palms, olive groves and the remains of a crusader castle, all ideal subjects for painting. Around them, the countryside was hilly and rolling, much greener than it had been closer to the coast. And another cause for cheer: at their prepared camp, he and the other officers were all given individual bell tents, complete with a camp bed, simple chest of drawers, a wash bowl, a folding table and chair. Their heavy trunks would not be with them for a few days but Edward had kept his small, framed photograph of Brenda in his personal kit and placed it on the table next to his bed. She would be his first sight in the morning, his last before he went to sleep at night. It was a particularly good one, he thought, taken by his mother on the downs above Farrowcombe. She was smiling bewitchingly, her pale eyes twinkling, her dark hair buffeted by the breeze. It had been that wonderful Easter weekend, a lifetime ago, he thought wistfully.

Lying down briefly, his arms behind his head, he breathed in deeply. A smell of dust, dry grass and canvas, then lit a cigarette and gazed at Brenda's photograph again. A telegram from her at Marseille in response to his and that was all, even though he'd written almost every day and she had promised to do the same. At Haifa they'd been told their new address was WR Y, Palestine, and that letters should take about a week by airmail. That had improved his mood enormously but now he was here, at camp in Latrun, he wondered how on earth airmail would get to and from the plane that would bring it back and forth between England and Palestine. They'd also been told that Barclays Bank in Jaffa would cash cheques, but Jaffa was at least twenty-five miles away and he couldn't imagine they'd be dashing there any time soon. He sighed, then drew on his cigarette and watched the blue-grey smoke curl and swirl above him before dispersing against the dun-coloured canvas.

Wednesday, 15 May, and the usual weekly meeting for Stork, John, and Dick Varney. Superficially, much was the same: Stork sat behind his desk in his study in the converted barn-end, Dick and John in the leather armchairs opposite. On the wall opposite, the clock still ticked rhythmically. Morning sunshine poured through the window so that the shadows of the horse-chestnut outside, now in full leaf, danced gently on the wall. Stork noticed a beam of dust motes.

'You've heard the news, of course?' said John.

'Yes, I can scarcely believe it. The Germans seem to have a worrying knack of rolling over countries in next to no time. Hard to believe the Dutch are out of it already, isn't it?'

'Actually, I didn't mean that,' said John. 'I was thinking of Eden's call for a Local Defence Volunteer force. It was on the wireless last night.'

'Oh, I see,' said Stork. 'Well, I'm not sure how much good will come of that, are you?'

'We've both signed up,' said John.

'Went into Wilton this morning,' added Dick. 'Got to do our bit.'

Stork sat back in his chair and rubbed his eyes. 'You don't think you're already doing your bit? What about the farm and the brewery? How are they going to run themselves if you're in the new militia?' He knew he sounded irritated, but couldn't help it.

'We'll have to make time,' said John.

'And you didn't think to check with me first?'

'Oh, come off it, Stork,' said John. 'This is a national emergency. Holland has surrendered, the Belgians will probably be next. Our country is in terrible danger. There's talk of the Germans sending over paratroopers.'

Stork snorted. 'I rather think Hitler's got his hands full at the moment without sending paratroopers to us.'

'The Germans have already shown us what happens when neighbours become complacent,' muttered John.

'Look here, Stork,' interjected Dick. 'Eden wouldn't have made a call for defence volunteers unless the government thought it necessary. Who are we to judge from here in the valley? We've done some soldiering, and God knows when the last show was over, I was eternally grateful and determined to put away my uniform for ever. But these are truly extraordinary times. We have some military training and a lot of experience, and if we can put that to good use and help in some way in this national emergency I feel I have a duty to do so. I'm sorry if you disagree, but that's all there is to it.'

Stork sighed and eyed them with the lop-sided grimace he tended to pull when troubled. 'Very well,' he said. 'And I'm sorry for pouring cold water on what I can see are the best of intentions and most noble of instincts. I just hope this doesn't end up taking more time than you can afford. Defending the valley might be important but so is feeding the nation. We're losing men as it is, the demands on us are greater and we have to become self-sufficient in food production. Don't forget that in 1938, we imported more than eighty per cent. Eighty-four per cent, to be precise. So, we've a huge job on our hands. The figures are sobering. As it is, I'm wondering how we're ever going to have the manpower for this year's harvest.'

'I do understand,' said Dick, 'but we're volunteers. I'm sure it won't be overly onerous as we're not alone in having full-time jobs to maintain. Most are going to be in the same boat. And if Wilton is anything to go by, there'll be a lot of us. The queue outside the station was already pretty long when we got there and even longer by the time we left. I'll bet the authorities are going to be pretty swamped. We didn't mention it to you, Stork, because we'd both gone to Wilton quite independently – we'd had the same thought after hearing the broadcast last night. And, if I'm perfectly honest, I thought you have more than enough on your plate as it is.'

Stork smiled weakly. 'Very well,' he said again. Then he glanced at John. His brother looked utterly wretched. 'I'm sorry,' he added. 'I had no right to question you and this is no time to quarrel. Please forgive me.'

John raised a hand, and sighed. 'This bloody war,' he muttered.

That evening, Elsa arrived at home to find her mother sitting on the bench by the stream at the end of the garden. It was a tranquil evening, the sun lowering but still shining strongly, the garden bursting with life, and a nightingale singing its strange mêlée of notes somewhere not far away.

'Mama?' Elsa called, as she walked along the brick pathway towards her.

Carin smiled. 'There you are, beloved Elsa.'

'Has something happened?' Elsa asked her, sitting down next to her.

Carin passed her the folded newspaper. 'Just horrible letters.'

Elsa read. A Mr Digby from Stourbridge was demanding that the government do more. Of course, he wrote, there were some perfectly decent Germans living in the country today, but surely the government could not afford to take the risk. With the concerns of parachutists and fifth columnists at large the time for niceties was over. Hard though it undoubtedly would be on a proportion of many peaceable and law-abiding foreign aliens, there was only one thing to do: lock up the lot.

'Oh, Mama,' said Elsa, putting her arms around her.

'They've started rounding up the men already,' she said, and Elsa

234

saw a single tear break from her eye and run down her cheek. 'Next it will be the women.'

'Of course it won't.'

Carin stroked her daughter's cheek. 'Darling Elsa. I'm sorry you have to find me like this. I just can't help it. Not just that I might be forced to leave you all but because of what is happening. I went to the church earlier and prayed. Prayed for all the young men and for Ollie.'

Elsa held her tightly. She couldn't think of a single thing to say.

Later, in bed, she struggled to sleep. The novel she was reading didn't help because she couldn't concentrate on the words. Outside, all was still – the only noise came from the owls calling from the beech trees. Then, at a little after two in the morning, she heard her father come in from his first night patrolling up on the downs. Putting on her dressing-gown, she went downstairs and found him in the hall, taking off his coat, his shotgun leaning against the wall.

'Elsa!' He turned suddenly. 'You made me jump!'

'Sorry. I couldn't sleep. Did you catch any parachutists?'

'No. Didn't see a thing. It was almost as though there wasn't a war on at all. We just walked up and down the Ox Drove and chatted mostly. Actually, it was rather magical, the moon shining down and the ground smelling sweet and fresh.'

They were silent for a moment, then Elsa said, 'I can't stop worrying. I'm worried about Ollie and I'm worried for Mama. What if they lock her up?'

'They won't do that, beloved.' He kissed her forehead. 'Now, go back to bed. We've both got work tomorrow. All will be well. You'll see.'

Elsa went upstairs and slipped back under the covers. Not long afterwards she heard her parents talking in low voices, then her mother crying, convulsively, and her father trying to soothe her. Elsa wanted to scream, to jump up and down and hurl something at the wall. Instead, she turned over, put her pillow over her ears, shut her eyes and tried hard to think of something different. Tomorrow she would be going with Hattie and Smudger to Alf Beresford's farm. Her uncle wanted them to show the farmer what land girls could do. *Think about that*, she told herself, *Think about that instead.*

*

Hannah Ellerby was out in the yard fetching the eggs when Mikey Mundy, the paper boy, cycled up to the manor to deliver the Castells' copies of *The Times* and the *Daily Express*.

'I can take that,' Hannah told him.

'Got any spare eggs?' Mikey asked. He was the youngest son of Reg Mundy, the blacksmith.

'Cheeky boy!' said Hannah, but after furtively looking around, handed him two. 'Don't tell and don't break them, Mikey.'

She watched him cycle off, then wandered back towards the kitchen, horrified by the headlines in the *Express*. The Allied lines had been broken in three places over the River Meuse. Sedan was in German hands. The French line was collapsing.

'You look like you've seen a ghost, my love,' said Jean, as Hannah placed the eggs on the kitchen table.

'It's the news. The Germans have crossed a river and taken Sedan.'

'Wherever that is.'

'But that's not the point, is it? The Germans are winning. Tha's all that matters. It's awful.'

'Best not to think too hard about it.'

'But what will happen to all our boys out there?'

Jean squatted down by the range and pulled out a tray of bacon and kidneys. 'You mean Tom Timbrell.'

Hannah felt herself redden. 'Not just Tom Timbrell,' she said quietly. 'All of 'em. I worry for all of us. What's to become of us if we lose?'

'Here,' said Jean, 'these need taking to the dining room.' She stood up, leaned backwards to stretch, then said, 'We won't lose. Mark my words. We might have a few hiccups along the way but we'll come out in the end.'

'But how can you know that?'

Jean shrugged. 'I don't know. I just feel it. In my bones.' She nodded to the dish. 'Off you go. Their nibs'll be waiting.'

They were not, though, so after setting down the dish, then returning for the pot of tea and the rack of toast, and finding the dining room still empty, she paused to look again at the newspapers. *The Times* seemed a little more optimistic. The French, she read, were counterattacking at Sedan and the BEF had repulsed heavy German attacks. More than a hundred enemy aircraft had been destroyed. A hundred! She couldn't imagine so large a number. Just about the only aircraft she had ever seen was Mr Stork's.

'Ah, good morning, Hannah,' said Maud Castell.

'Oh, sorry, ma'am,' said Hannah, hurriedly putting down the paper.

'It's quite all right.' She came over and took first the *Express*, then turned to the teapot. 'Such a worry. We've been desperate for word of Denholm and his family over there in France. One feels so helpless. And, of course, the others out there too. Dear Tom Timbrell. No doubt he's in the thick of it, along with Tess's beau.' She sat down. 'It all comes flooding back, rather – the worry, you know.'

'Yes, ma'am.'

At that moment, the master appeared.

'Looks like the French are making a hash of it,' he said, barely looking at Hannah. 'Total collapse along the Meuse front. We need to get hold of Denholm, Maud. Tell him to get out while he can.'

'Do you think it's as bad as that, Alwyn darling?'

'Mark my words. The French have been humbugged.' He picked up his *Times,* flicked through the pages until he found what he was looking for. 'Here,' he said, laying the paper beside his wife and jabbing a finger at a map. 'Just been speaking to the general. Why I'm a bit late. He says we've all rushed into Belgium to meet the German thrust, but a second enemy strike has come around the back. And now they're across the damned Meuse and sweeping west. Hate to say this, but he reckons we're in danger of becoming surrounded. Huns have got everyone on the run this time around.'

'Surely it can't be as bad as that.'

He helped himself to breakfast from the sideboard. 'Need to get a message to Denholm,' he muttered. 'Tell him what the general said.'

Hannah had heard enough. 'If that'll be all?'

'Ah, apologies, Hannah,' said the master. 'Didn't see you there.'

She returned to the kitchen, her mind reeling. What did it mean? Would they really be invaded, as she'd heard people in the village suggesting? Mr Pierson, the ARP warden, had been telling anyone who would listen to look out for enemy parachutists and even Mr John and Dick Varney had signed up for the LDV. In the shop the previous day it seemed as though no one could talk of anything else. Even her father had been muttering about it being his 'duty' to join the LDV and do his bit. She simply couldn't imagine Germans descending on Alvesdon.

Later, her morning chores done, Hannah took a mug of tea out into the yard as it was such a warm, sunny day and she wanted some fresh air. She prayed Mr Denholm would not end up back at the manor although he was no longer at the forefront of her worries. The general was an old friend of the master's – she'd seen him a number of times, on shoot days or at a dinner at the manor. He was retired now but only quite recently. She'd heard the master say that General Bartholomew was 'in the know' and that he could be relied upon. Was he right? She couldn't stop thinking about Tom. She wondered where he was and whether he was in danger.

Around her the chickens scratched and pecked, birds sang from the trees, swallows darted around the yard and the sun shone down. A scene that was as familiar to her as any. It was unimaginable that this could be under threat yet that was what people were saying. Who was she to question them? And she felt a strange longing in her heart, a wistfulness she couldn't shift, that perhaps their lives were about to fall in around them. She thought of all the things she had wanted to say to Tom but never had, and regretted those opportunities she'd missed. Pride, embarrassment, and the fear of being made to feel a fool had stopped her letting her heart speak.

She still had an hour or so to herself before she needed to be back for lunch so decided to go to the village shop. Thankfully, it was quiet with no one about, other than Mrs Pierson behind the counter. Hannah found a writing pad and some envelopes and placed them on the counter.

'Just these, please, Mrs Pierson.'

Was that a knowing look Mrs Pierson gave her? Hannah could feel herself blushing but if Mrs Pierson noticed she said nothing. Mr Pierson, Hannah knew, would not have let it pass. Mr Pierson always made comments.

'That'll be two and six,' said Mrs Pierson.

And that was all. Hannah handed over the coins, thanked her, and walked out, bumping into the doctor, who made a joke about it being a fine day for parachuting, briefly asked after Mr and Mrs Castell, then went on into the shop, leaving Hannah to walk to the post office, where she bought half a dozen stamps. A quarter of an hour later, she was back in the kitchen. Still with plenty of time to herself, she sat down to write.

Dear Tom, she wrote in the copybook script she'd been taught at the village school.

I am sitting here at the kitchen table in the Manor and wondering where you are and what you are doing, but hoping you are safe. I have no idea whether this letter will ever reach you out in France but I hope it will.

She paused and thought.

The village is not the same with you and some of the other boys gone, although it looks just as it has always done. It is pretty now that summer is on the way. Please write if you can.

Yours, Hannah Ellerby

Folding it carefully, she put it into the envelope and addressed it to *Tom Timbrell, King's Own Royal Guards, British Expeditionary Force, France.*

Would it ever reach him? She remembered Susan Smallpiece telling her that when she wrote to her Billy that was all she put on the envelope: his name, unit and the BEF. Perhaps it was different now the British Army were fighting. None the less, as she put the letter in the postbox, she felt a strange charge of excitement. For the first time in her life she had allowed her heart to win over her fears. A small flicker of personal hope on a day of otherwise foreboding news.

21

On the Defensive

Monday, 20 May 1940

THAT EVENING TOM TIMBRELL AND THE REST OF THE 1ST KING'S Own Royal Guards were digging in along the western banks of the River Escaut, some sixty-five miles from the Dyle. Fortunately, the soil was fairly soft despite the dry weather of the past couple of weeks, but even so, the men of 4 Platoon were exhausted and in a cantankerous mood.

'Still glad you joined, Baby?' said Sid Parkinson, as they sweated in the evening sun.

'No,' said 'Baby' Glover. His name was William but he was only eighteen and looked younger. 'Could be at home now with me feet up.'

'Or doing your homework,' said Corporal Souch.

'Very funny, Corp,' muttered Glover.

'Jesus!' exclaimed Parkinson, standing and stretching his back. 'I've had just about enough of this.' He madly whisked a hand around his head. 'And the bloody midges! Christ! This place is a shithole and, as far as I care, the sodding Jerries can 'ave it. In fact, they can 'ave it on a silver fuckin' salver.'

'You all right, Parky?' said Tom. 'Woke up the wrong side this morning?'

The others laughed.

'Don't remember waking up, Sarge,' said Parkinson, 'because I can't remember the last time I was asleep.'

''Ere,' said Tom, jumping down into the half-finished slit trench. He'd already finished his own: four foot deep, big enough for two, the soil piled in front. He began digging alongside Parkinson and Souch. 'Get this done, help bring up some ammo, and then you can get yer 'ead down, Parky.'

'Thanks, Sarge. Makes me feel much better.'

The sun had gone down and the light was fading by the time they were done a couple of hours later. Guards had been posted while the rest of the platoon finally got their heads down. It was hardly comfortable squatting in a hole in the ground, surrounded by earth, legs bent, but most of the men were so tired they were able to sleep no matter the position. Tom accompanied Lieutenant Ashton on his rounds, then slipped into his own foxhole. At least the smell was familiar: earth, grass, the distinct aroma of water from the canalized River Escaut in front of them. A row of poplar trees, each perhaps twenty yards apart, lined the bank, and the emerging leaves rustled gently on the evening breeze. Tom lit a cigarette and gazed out into the gloaming. A number of ducks flew in for the night, skidding noisily on the water. He wondered where the enemy was and when they might appear on the far side. Tomorrow? The day after? Would that then be their first proper action? Or would they be ordered back again before the Germans emerged. The ground on the far side rose gently so at least he'd be able to see them clearly as they crested the low ridge beyond.

He had a feeling that a terrible fiasco was unfolding. So far, they'd advanced almost to the River Dyle, reaching there only five days after the Germans had first attacked into the Low Countries. He'd accepted the reasons they'd been given for the slow advance but the following day new orders had arrived to pull back to the Escaut. After packing up, they'd got going around one o'clock in the morning of 17 May. Their task had been to cover the withdrawal of the whole of the 3rd Infantry Brigade, which meant they, along with the 3rd Grenadiers, were last in line.

Over the next three days, they'd headed back sixty-five miles, sometimes in trucks, but for a lot of the time walking. Refugees clogged the roads and the vehicles simply couldn't get through. Other times the trucks were needed elsewhere. The men had been grumbling ever since. During the advance, they'd been cheered by

Belgian civilians at every turn, given flowers, food and wine and treated like heroes come to rescue them. The return could not have been more different. Now, those Belgians who turned out to watch this ignominious retreat stared blankly or wept quite openly. In one village, several women shouted, 'Cowards!' Tom had never felt more humiliated. They'd all felt a sense of shame that they were letting the Belgians down. The colonel had tried to explain: the Dutch had surrendered so the Belgians on their left and the French on their right had started to pull back. Therefore the British in the middle had had to fall back too. It was a filthy business, Toast had told them, but he, for one, hadn't chosen Britain's Allies and they were all to make the best of it.

Three gruelling days, the roads heaving with fleeing civilians and the rest of the brigade. Enemy aircraft had frequently thundered over, although No 2 Company had lived something of a charmed existence; several times, Tom had watched them hurtle over only to attack a mile or two ahead. On the second day, Tom had seen a number of Stuka dive-bombers screeching towards the road perhaps three miles further on. He'd heard the bombs, seen the clouds of smoke and dust rising and swirling, and wondered who had been unlucky enough to be underneath the mayhem. They'd discovered soon enough when, some time later, they'd passed the scenes of devastation: several burned-out trucks, blackened corpses charred to a crisp, and a number of civilian cars hit and blasted. A Belgian family lay dead at the side of the road, one young girl with a leg blown off, a boy with his guts half ripped out. Several of the men had vomited. A suitcase had been blown into the hedgerow, its contents flung far and wide. Tom had picked up a small, knitted rabbit in a blue top. The boy's, he had thought, and placed it by the dead child.

Now, in his hole in the ground, he thought of the farm and of his father. He could picture him coming into the house, taking off his boots, sitting reading by the hearth with his pipe; his father did like to read. Tom could smell the scene in his mind: the sweetness of the tobacco mixed with the faint aroma of bread. Then he thought of Hannah, picturing her in the yard at the manor, her auburn hair glowing and her sweet, shy face gazing at him with that guarded look. *To hell with it*, he thought. If he ever made it back from this mess of a war, he'd throw caution to the wind and simply sweep her

into his arms. He smiled to himself, took one more drag on his cigarette, then closed his eyes.

The attack, when it came, surprised everyone. Tom had woken early
to discover a low early-summer mist covered the Escaut and with it
the far bank, but although he'd listened hard, he had seen and heard
nothing, save the ongoing birdsong of the dawn chorus; birds, he
knew, could easily be discouraged from singing when confronted by
unusual movement. Some of the boys had even begun shaving and
preparing breakfast when suddenly, at seven thirty, the world in
front of them erupted with the whine and hiss of incoming mortars
and their subsequent explosions, fountains of earth, grit and stone
showering them. There were shouts, a scream, the sudden drill of
enemy machine-guns and stabs of orange tracer spitting across the
water. Tom ducked as a shell landed nearby, felt the clatter of stone
and earth on his tin helmet, then was aware of German voices
coming from the direction of the river. *Christ*, he thought, his brain
struggling to comprehend the sudden hammering of bullets, shells
and danger. *Think*, he told himself, looking around. Morrison, the
Bren gunner in Souch's section, had ducked into his slit trench leaving the Bren on the earth parapet in front of him. Bullets were fizzing
nearby but they appeared to be high and he realized that in the mist
the enemy were firing blind.

With a deep breath and his heart pounding, Tom scrambled out
of his own foxhole and hurriedly crawled the ten yards to Morrison
and Guardsman Hitchen's slit trench, snatched the Bren and several
extra magazines, then crawled on fifteen yards ahead to a poplar
near the towpath.

In front of him, he saw faint, indistinct shapes in the mist and
opened fire with several short bursts. Change the magazine. Pull the
bolt. Finger on the cold metal of the trigger. The jolt and judder of
the Bren. Bullets spewing, the stench of explosive charge and a
scream from in front of him, a splash, frantic voices. Tugging a
grenade from his belt, he now pulled the ring-pin, waited a second,
then threw it. An explosion ahead, another scream, and then he
hurled another.

Jesus, he thought, *what am I doing?* He stood, fired another
magazine down into the river, then ran back. Mortars were still

243

coming over but they were too deep, landing behind their lines of slit trenches and so, half crouching, half running, he went back along the platoon, yelling at the men. 'Get up! Get up! Get shooting!'

A second Bren now opened fire along with single rifle shots.

'Keep shooting!' he shouted, through the din, and hurled another grenade. The mist was thickening with smoke and dust. He crouch-ran back to Morrison's slit trench. Hitchen was firing his rifle, one shot after another, but Morrison was slumped next to him, the side of his face slick with blood.

Damn it! thought Tom, as he slid back into his own hole and swung the Bren out in front of him, its bipod clattering on the ground. Bolt back, and he fired again: short, sharp, angry bursts. Another hiss and whine of bullets coming back at him, but now their own mortars were firing and overhead he heard a whistle of shells screaming towards the far side. Frantically, he tried to work out what was happening. Heavier firing was coming from their left, beyond No 4 Company. Was that where No 1 Company was or was it the Grenadiers, the next battalion in line? He wasn't sure but was conscious that the attack directly in front was quietening, until, five minutes later, the mortaring had all but stopped.

Lieutenant Ashton was suddenly there, slipping noisily into the slit trench beside him. 'Jerry's launched a major attack across the river,' he said. 'They've got over between the Grenadiers and the Coldstreams.'

Tom nodded. 'I think we've stopped them here. Morrison's been killed.'

'Morrison? Christ, we were talking to him just an hour ago.' His eyes were darting from side to side, his breathing heavy.

'What are the orders, sir?'

'I'm not sure. The line to battalion was cut by a mortar shell, but I've sent Butler as a runner. For now, hold our positions like grim death.'

Tom glanced at his watch and was surprised to learn almost an hour had passed since they'd first come under fire. Another salvo of shells whined over from behind them, a ripple of explosions follow-ing seconds later. Then, briefly, all was quiet again in their sector, although Tom could hear furious fighting continuing away to their left. He continued to peer into the mist, wondering how many were lying hidden in the waist-high corn beyond the river. How many had he just killed and wounded? He was overcome by a sense of relief. He'd not panicked. He'd kept calm, had done what was needed, and was still alive and breathing, his heart hammering in his chest. *Morrison*. The unlucky one.

Tom sighed. The air was sharp, the stench and smoke like sandpaper grating the back of his throat. Furious firing grew to a crescendo some way to their left. The Grenadiers? Or the Coldstreams? It was hard to tell, but one of their fellow battalions in the brigade was facing the full brunt of the attack.

'I wonder if Jerry's got across?' said Ashton.

'If they have, we need to be careful, sir. Whole brigade'll be rolled up if we can't kick 'em back.'

'All a bit of a bloody shower, isn't it?'

In more ways than one, thought Tom, wiping soil from the back of his neck. The mist was now clearing and he raised his head gingerly to look at the cornfields that rose gently from the far bank, the young green corn easily waist height. Beyond, on a low hill, a small wood. The enemy would be in there, he reckoned. Probably in the corn too. He spotted a number of dead on the far bank and wondered whether he'd killed them with the Bren. He glanced along at the rest of the platoon, a few helmeted heads protruding but still low enough not to be spotted above the spoil in front of them.

Tom took out another cigarette and bent his head to light it with a cupped match when suddenly a fizz zipped sharply just above his head.

'Jesus!' said Ashton, as Tom slumped into his slit trench, heart pounding. 'A bloody sniper! Are you all right, Sergeant?'

Tom nodded. So, he'd been correct. The enemy was out there. He thought of the times he'd been in Tippett's Wood hunting down foxes and waiting, rifle at the ready, for one to stray into his line of sight. The grim sense of satisfaction when he'd hit and killed the beast, the frustration when it had slipped back into the shadows. *Tippett's Wood*, he thought, and leaned back against the edge of his hole in the ground. *What I'd do to be back there now.* He felt as though he'd been snared like any of the vermin he'd trapped back at Alvesdon. Snared, and with little chance of escape.

*

245

The same morning, Denholm Castell was pulling into the Gare de Lyon in Paris, a long, two-day journey finally over. It hadn't been entirely unpleasant and he had at least had a *wagon-lit* to himself. He'd also enjoyed a half-decent dinner before turning in for the night, but it had been a reminder of the vast scale of France, and it had seemed to him incredible that all of it was now threatened by the catastrophe of imminent defeat.

Earlier that morning, as the dawn had risen over the French countryside, he'd been awake and looked out, marvelling at the huge expanse of fields and woods, winding rivers, occasional villages and hamlets. It was so different from England, he had mused, with its small fields, hedgerows, church towers poking through the trees and sleepy villages. Yet despite France's size, the Germans were clearly making short work of the Army and l'Armée de l'Air. He'd predicted as much before the balloon had gone up, not that it gave him any satisfaction to have been proved correct.

As the train halted amid much hissing and swirls of steam, he grabbed his suitcase and stepped out onto the platform. The Gare de Lyon pullulated with people hurrying towards other trains. He spotted plenty of uniforms but families too – his eye caught two young children clinging to their father's legs, the mother's face lined with tears. People fleeing. From the war, from collapse, from the Nazis. From a city that had lost faith.

He took the Métro to the Gare de l'Est, relieved to discover the trains were still working perfectly, then stepped out into the early-summer morning air. It looked much like Paris had always done, he thought. The tables of the cafes still spilled onto the street, the pigeons swooped and pecked at crumbs just as they always had, posters were pasted to walls and to the sides of newsstands and *tabacs*.

Then a quick stride across the street to the rue de Nancy and to number 21: a tall townhouse of pale stone, six storeys high. He rang the bell, was let in by a porter and directed to an electric lift that was narrow, dusty and jolted as he stepped in, pulling the metal gate across in front of him. With another jolt and a whir it moved up, each floor in turn passing until he had reached the fourth. Stepping out, he took a staircase up a final flight until he faced a dark blue door.

Denholm knocked lightly, and a moment later the door was opened by a good-looking middle-aged man in a double-breasted navy suit, with a cigarette between his fingers.

'Ah, there you are, Denholm,' he said. 'Come in, come in.'

'Good to see you, Biffy,' said Denholm, shaking the hand of Commander Dunderdale and following him inside.

The main room of the flat was pleasant but sparsely furnished: a rectangular table and six chairs, a sofa and two armchairs, with doors leading off. No pictures on the walls, no books. A set of French windows led to a narrow balcony and a metal railing and Dunderdale led him outside to where a second man, lean-faced, early forties, with laughter lines stretching from his eyes, was looking out over the city. *Commander Kenneth Cohen*, thought Denholm. He'd not seen him in years.

'Ah, Denholm.' Cohen smiled, extending his hand. 'Good to see you. Been a while.'

'Well,' said Dunderdale, 'I know Dansey liked to keep all his Z men apart, but things are a little different now.'

Denholm gazed out over the city.

'Looks peaceful enough, doesn't it?' said Cohen.

'Very,' agreed Denholm. He could see the Eiffel Tower in the distance and the rooftops of a thousand houses, grey slate and stubs of terracotta chimney pots. 'Such an extraordinary number of chimneys in Paris.'

Cohen chuckled. 'Yes. The Parisians like their winter fires although whether there will be enough coal to go around once the Nazis are here is another matter.'

'What a ghastly thought,' muttered Denholm.

'One soon to become reality. Two weeks, maybe more. But France has lost. There is no way back.'

'It's true, I'm afraid,' said Dunderdale. 'The Germans have reached the coast.'

'Already?' said Denholm. 'I hadn't heard that.'

'Yesterday,' said Dunderdale. 'The whole northern front is trapped in a giant lozenge. And that includes the BEF. The rate the leading panzers are going, the whole lot will be encircled before we know it. At the moment, we've still got the Channel coast at our backs but for how much longer is anyone's guess.'

Denholm sighed. 'So,' he said, 'what's to be done?'

'Menzies has given me warning,' said Dunderdale. 'He's going to pull us out.'

'For God's sake,' said Denholm. He thought of Lucie, of his villa, of his business. What the hell was he to do? His entire life was here. 'Can't Menzies wait a bit? See how things pan out? We have no idea what the settlement might be and we may well find it's far more useful for us to have me in situ here, rather than starting all over again from London. Me and other SIS men. What do the Deuxième Bureau boys think? You're both in regular contact with Rivet and Co., aren't you?'

Cohen sighed. 'I saw Rivet yesterday as it happens. He thinks Reynard will be forced out and that the old generals will take over. Apparently, conversations are already being had with Pétain.'

'Pétain? But the old boy's practically ga-ga. That's absurd.'

'He's getting on, I grant you, but he and his chums still have immense clout. They're the generals who delivered victory in the last war. People get very hot under the collar about the Communists, but the vast majority of French are conservative to the core. They've had enough of fractious politics, of Jewish prime ministers, of the constant state of flux. I'm Jewish and, trust me, the French are an anti-Semitic bunch, which chimes with the odious ideology of Hitler and his mob. One has to understand that what most French want above all is certainty and stability.'

'And they don't want a bloodbath,' added Dunderdale. 'They sacrificed everything last time and they're simply not prepared to do it again.'

'Just think about it for a moment, Denholm,' added Cohen. 'They sue for peace – not next week but, let's say, sometime soon after. What does that look like? There'll be a German occupation to begin with and the Nazis will probably insist on a puppet government. Part of the armistice will be allowing the Germans to use the Atlantic coast and probably their armament factories too. There will be a few troops garrisoned here but otherwise the French will be left to run things themselves.'

'And the price will be the end of democracy,' said Dunderdale.

'Certainly. Some kind of military dictatorship is my best bet.'

Denholm took out a cigarette, lit it and inhaled deeply. If he was

248

a betting man, and he was, he'd say Cohen was bang on the money. He'd just not been expecting to be recalled to London. The situation was unravelling so damned fast.

'And, of course, we can't know what our friends in the DB will do, although we have to prepare for the worst. Friends becoming enemies and so on. They know who we are and if we stay we could well be rounded up in a trice. Diplomatic immunity won't count for anything once the Nazis are here.'

Denholm drew deeply on his cigarette again, then nodded. 'Yes, yes, I do see that. Although I know a good number of people in the south who will never willingly succumb to that kind of thuggery.'

'And we'll undoubtedly need those people,' said Dunderdale.

They were silent for a moment. 'The battle is lost,' said Cohen at length. 'It's as Reynaud said. France is going to be defeated, and the BEF is going to be defeated. The only question is what can be salvaged. If Britain can hold out and fight on, and assuming we do – I believe we will – then how do we best continue? We'll need to rebuild, establish networks of agents and work out how we can undermine the enemy ever more effectively until he's beaten.'

'And we'll need men like you, Denholm,' said Dunderdale, 'who have had long careers in the service, with contacts and connections here in France, to help rebuild and continue the fight. But you're no good to us on the Côte d'Azur, no matter how much you might wish to stay there. You'll be needed in London.'

Denholm flicked away his cigarette and gazed out over the city.

'Look,' said Dunderdale, 'this war is a huge inconvenience. D'you think I want to leave Paris? Of course, I don't. But it's also a national crisis. What's happening is a fucking catastrophe. It's a threat to everything: to Britain, to the Empire, to our lives. To all that we hold dear. We're all going to have to do what we can to get rid of that Austrian upstart, bring the Nazis to their knees and safeguard the freedoms we all want to continue to enjoy.'

Denholm turned to face them both. 'Yes,' he said at length, 'I see that.' His mind was racing. 'How long have we got?'

'Two weeks. A month perhaps. Get your affairs in order, Denholm, and be ready to get yourself back to England as soon as we give you the word.'

*

The following morning he was on the train steaming south. He'd caught up with an old friend for dinner and both had promised not to talk of the war; perhaps the conversation had been a little forced to begin with but they'd soon transported themselves back to another time when the future was full of hope. Edmée had even come back with him to his hotel room – after all, her husband was away with his regiment, safe and sound, she had told him, along the Maginot Line. Why not? he thought. For old times' sake. He wouldn't tell and neither would she.

Back to reality now, though. He stared out of the window as Paris thinned and disappeared. The compartment was full – no *wagon-lit* until Lyon: an older couple, a middle-aged woman, who began knitting the moment she sat down, a young mother and her three children. Their collective luggage filled the racks above them. These people were part of the exodus; Paris was emptying. They'd lost hope. That much was obvious.

The long journey gave him time to think. Lucie would not like it, and neither would Coco. For goodness' sake, he didn't like it. But they had no choice. He could put the contents of the villa into storage, then, when the time came, shut the place up. Étienne could be trusted with the boatyard; he hoped there might be something left to come back to, but he told himself not to waste time worrying about such things. War threw everything up into the air. When it was all over there would be the chance to build it up again. Or not. There would be other opportunities. The most important thing was to get them safely back to England. That in itself would require some planning, some pulling-in of favours; he could, of course, sail from Cannes, but it was a long way round Spain. Better to get to the Atlantic coast. Get a berth from there. Denholm closed his eyes and let the sun beat down through the glass onto his face. A lot to think about. A lot to worry about. But later. Now, he thought, he would get some much-needed sleep.

Far to the north, Tom Timbrell was also closing his eyes after a long night. The Grenadiers had managed to push the enemy back across the river and, although they were shelled and mortared into the evening, there had been no further attack along the brigade's stretch of the line that day. Even so, Tom had spent most of the night

250

watching, waiting, expecting another enemy attack across the river at any moment. He was better used to the dark than most of the men and felt it was his duty, despite the posting of pickets, to keep awake and alert for trouble.

He awoke with a start as enemy guns from somewhere on the far side opened fire, shells screeching over, sucking the air, slamming into the fields behind and exploding. The ground shook, ears rang, helmets clattered as soil and stone showered down on them. Air thick and choking, the river disappearing behind the swirling wall of smoke, then more shells screeching over, deafening, numbing. Tom sat crouched in his hole in the ground thinking of home, of the farm, of Hannah, and wishing more than anything he had ever wished for that he might be back there right now, safe, secure, and away from this carnage, this storm of death.

'You'll not get me, Jerry!' someone yelled nearby. *Parky*, thought Tom, and raised his head to see Parkinson standing up in his slit trench shouting, arm raised, hand in a fist. Tom could see the veins on his neck, the grime and soil on his cheek. And then another shell came over. Parkinson disappeared and Tom felt himself pulled from his hole, hurled into the air, saw the sky darken with soil and clods of earth and stone, then blacken altogether.

22

On a Wing and a Prayer

Saturday, 25 May 1940

AT 2 RICHMOND TERRACE, TESS WAS NOT FEELING OVERWORKED, but certainly overtired from the long hours she had been keeping for the past month. She and the other girls now worked shifts and this last week she'd been on lates, arriving at noon, but very often not getting home until after midnight. General Ismay had been to France twice in the past week and, although she knew he always made every effort to appear cheerful and upbeat, the mask had slipped on more than one occasion.

She often thought of Alex, and of Tom Timbrell, but so far neither had been on the casualty lists she'd seen. That was something. Mostly, though, she found herself worrying about Ollie and most especially Wilf, even more so now that squadrons from Fighter Command were daily being sent over. It was only a matter of time, she knew, before it would be the turn of Wilf's squadron.

She had just finished typing a letter and was gazing out of the window towards the War Office. Outside, the plane trees were now in full leaf, lush and luminously green in the May sun. It seemed so entirely wrong that in such a beautiful early summer terrible things could be playing out across the Channel. She'd written to Alex at the start of the week but had felt frustrated by the banality of her words. She couldn't tell him anything of any interest and nothing about her work or what she had heard. Instead she stuck to lines she'd written before: that she missed him, wished the war would end, that she was working hard and that London was bursting into leaf. There was no excitement at being young and in love in what she wrote, no shared secrets, no plans for the future – not of an upcoming weekend or a planned escape to Suffolk . . .

The door opened and Ian Jacob appeared. 'Tess, you're needed. The PM wants Ismay.'

She nodded, picked up her spare typewriter, already in its case, and followed Jacob out of the door.

'It's looking bloody,' said Jacob. 'Calais is surrounded.'

Tess said nothing. What was there to say? But she felt her heart hammering in her chest and a new kind of breathlessness as they picked up Ismay, then trotted down the stairs and out onto the street, warm still in the lunchtime air. A pigeon swooped towards them and flapped its wings noisily as it rose again; Tess envied its simplicity and ignorance.

Up Whitehall, past the Cenotaph, the memorial to the nearly million British dead in the last war, on beyond the Banqueting House, where Charles I had lost his head on a chilly January morning nearly three hundred years earlier . . . Then they crossed the road to Horse Guards, the sentries in battledress, no longer their pre-war finery, and into the Admiralty. Churchill should have been in Downing Street, but he'd told Chamberlain not to be in any hurry to leave. Tess knew that Ismay was worried about the old man. Chamberlain seemed tired, short of breath. Churchill had picked up on that too. For the time being, the new prime minister had kept his home at the Admiralty, which, after all, was a finer building in every way than No 10.

Into the courtyard, guards clicking to attention, and into the great building itself, and then up the staircase to what had become the Upper War Room, with its portrait of Nelson and other naval heroes of a bygone age. It was nearing two o'clock but the Prime Minister was sitting at the long table in pyjamas and an elaborate floral silk dressing-gown, a long cigar clamped between his teeth.

'We have to hold out at Calais as long as possible,' he growled, without any greetings. 'I'd like you to look at this draft signal for Brigadier Nicholson, Ismay.' A secretary Tess had not seen before handed over a sheet of typescript. 'Calais is of the highest import-ance,' he said, reinforcing his words as Ismay read. 'It occupies a large number of the enemy's forces. Nicholson must make his defence of Calais one of the great stands in our island's long history. A Corunna of this new age.'

Tess had already been ushered to a side-desk and was taking shorthand notes.

'Prime Minister,' said Ismay, 'Lord Gort has signalled this evening that tomorrow morning he intends to order the BEF to fall back to Dunkirk.' Churchill puffed out a large cloud of cigar smoke. There was a half-full glass of wine and an empty plate beside him. The sides of the glass, Tess noticed, were smudged and the rim edged with small bits of food. 'It means he's vetoing French orders, of course.'

'The French show no inclination to move with anything like the necessary urgency. The entire German Army will have enveloped France before Weygand can organize his forces into a counterattack.'

'This is rather Gort's thinking too.'

'Then we must endorse his decision wholeheartedly,' said Churchill. 'Pray that Nicholson can hold Hitler's panzers for as long as possible and we must then prepare for evacuation, Ismay.'

'Have you told the First Sea Lord?'

'He has been informed.' He puffed on his cigar and stared up at the portrait of Nelson. 'Calais,' he said at last, 'is the crux.'

'The panzers appear to have been ordered to halt,' said Ismay. 'God only knows for how long.'

'I doubt God is any the wiser. The decision, it seems, is that of Herr Hitler, and what lurks inside that dark mind is hard to fathom,' muttered Churchill. 'We must hope for long enough to allow the BEF back to Dunkirk. In between such decision-making, Ismay, we should all pray. I need not tell you of the perilous situation in which we find ourselves, and far be it from me to deny any succour God might provide us in this hour of need. To wit, the King is announcing that tomorrow will be a National Day of Prayer. We're all to be at the Abbey at ten a.m.'

'I suppose it can't do any harm,' said Ismay.

'Time will tell,' said the Prime Minister, then took another gulp of wine. 'Time will tell soon enough. But God can be capricious and I have a sickening ache in my stomach that so far He seems unwilling to alleviate.'

*

The following morning, 26 May, in the parish church of St Mary's, Alvesdon, the Reverend Charles Trubshaw was giving his Sunday sermon. He had clearly made a few minor adjustments to refer to the King's call for all to pray together that day. Stork watched him, the vicar's hands clenching and relaxing, then clenching again, gripping the aged oak of the pulpit, as he tried to find the words. The country faced an unprecedented existential threat, the vicar told them in his ponderous, precise tone, yet Britain had been imperilled many times before and had prevailed. God would protect them again; the forces for good and for righteousness would prevail. They must all trust in the Almighty.

Stork's eyes wandered. There was a marble tablet honouring one of the Liddell brothers who had been killed in the last war; it was now nearly twenty years since it had been clamped to the wall and was as familiar as any other part of the church. The old pews creaked whenever the congregation shifted. A smell of wax and brass polish, the eagle lectern shining gold in the bright morning light. The whole village, it seemed, had turned out, while the Liddells, their farming neighbours, and all of the Castells who were still at home were there too, even Carin.

He glanced up at the great silvery stone arch above him at the end of the nave. Sometime in the Victorian age three banners had been pasted to the wall there: *Love the Brotherhood*, *Honour the King* and, in the centre, *Fear God*. He'd never really understood them or why anyone had thought to put them there. Honour which King? Jesus? Or George VI, the man now calling them to prayer? And which brotherhood? Of Christianity, or the world, or their little community here in Alvesdon? Yet what had always troubled him the most was the instruction to fear God. If God was all good, why should anyone be afraid of Him? Yet Stork was fearful of what lay around the corner. For his family. For his community. For the country.

Stork wondered how much the government was really letting people know. Boulogne had fallen, a Channel port, which meant France had been cut in two, and the Germans had also overrun Holland and much of Belgium so the BEF was now sandwiched in the middle, with its back to the coast. His father had confidently told him the Germans were likely to encircle the lot. 'The general says they'll have to pull 'em out of Calais and Dunkirk or else the whole

255

damn lot will be in the bag.' For once, Stork thought, the general might actually be right.

He realized he'd stopped listening to the sermon as Debbo, on his left, and Maimes on his right, stood for the next hymn, 'Lord of All Hopefulness'. *Of course*, thought Stork. On a wing and a prayer. Had it really come to that? The organ played the opening bars, its reedy flutes pumping out the familiar tune. The service was supposed to give them all a lift but Stork felt a sense of helplessness and hopelessness. He glanced up again. *Fear God.* It wasn't God he feared. It was bloody Hitler and his Nazis.

Sunday lunch at the Manor. Maud had invited them all and all had agreed to go, although Stork and Debbo had done so with little enthusiasm and, from the look of John's brood, none of them seemed eager to be there either.

'Mrs Gulliver has pulled out all the stops,' she told them, as they drank sherry in the drawing room beforehand. 'Roast pork and your favourite, John, Queen of Puddings.'

John smiled. 'Well, she's a marvel and you're very good to me, Maimes, indulging me like this at my age.'

Maud's best efforts did not prevent long silences as they sat around the dining table, cutlery chinking against the plates. *This is awful*, thought Stork.

'And what news of the children?' Maud asked Debbo and Stork, after another protracted silence. 'Any word from Edward?'

'Yes, actually,' said Debbo. 'They're camped at some hilltop town in Palestine. If he weren't mooning over dear Brenda he'd be having a marvellous time of it.'

'Seems to be playing a lot of cricket,' said Stork.

'Well, he'll enjoy that. At least he's safe enough over there.'

'He's not in France, that's true,' said Debbo.

'And what of Brenda? Wasn't there some thought of her coming down here?'

'I did write to her,' Debbo continued, 'and she thanked me and said she was thinking of joining one of the services. That if Edward was doing his bit she thought perhaps she ought to do hers.'

'But we've told her she's welcome here at any time,' added Stork.

'And dare I ask about Tess and Wilf?'

'Tess is working all God's hours and doesn't appear to be able to tell us anything, and Wilf is still at Debden.'

'He thinks they might be called upon to fly to France soon,' said Debbo. 'I can hardly bear to think of it.'

'He'll be all right,' said Stork. 'He's a good pilot, plenty of hours in that logbook of his.' He smiled at them all while a wave of nausea swept over him. It made him wonder how he was going to finish the dish in front of him.

'And Elsa has had a letter from Ollie, haven't you, darling?' said Carin. She smiled, but, Stork thought, looked so sad. Defeated almost. A number of German women had been rounded up over the past few days; he'd read it in the paper. He knew Carin must be aware of this. They'd written so many letters, had had so many conversations with supposed men of influence in the county and beyond, yet Carin remained classified as a 'Category B Alien', a grotesque stamp issued with ignorance that made him feel ashamed of his country.

'Oh, good, Elsa,' said Maud, clapping her hands together. 'And he's fine and well, no doubt?'

Elsa nodded. 'He seems to be, thank you, Maimes.'

Hannah was at the door and waiting expectantly.

'Ah, Hannah,' said Alwyn. 'Everything all right?'

'Excuse me, sir, ma'am,' she said, 'but there's someone for Miss Elsa.'

Stork glanced at Elsa. They all did. Stork saw his niece's face drain of colour, and Hannah was clearly alarmed. 'Oh, no, it's nothing like that, sorry, miss,' she said.

Elsa looked baffled, but Maud said, 'You'd better go, Elsa. How very mysterious.'

Elsa pushed back her chair, smiled uncertainly at her parents, then hurried out with Hannah.

'Goodness!' said Maud.

Stork hoped Elsa's visitor was who he thought it must surely be.

''E's in the yard, miss,' said Hannah, as they walked swiftly towards the kitchen.

Elsa could think of nothing to say, her mind reeling. She barely noticed the corridor or the kitchen and was only vaguely aware of Mrs Gulliver smiling benignly at her. And then when she opened the door to the yard, there he was, not in uniform, but in old trousers and a flannel shirt, looking just as she remembered him from last summer.

'Ollie!' she cried, and ran to him. He grinned at her and held out his arms, and then they were around her back and her lips were on his and her hands feeling his hair and the warmth of his skin. She hugged him, her head leaning against his chest, his arms enveloping her. 'I've missed you so much,' she said.

'Not half as much as I've missed you.' He laughed.

She found herself laughing too, and crying at the same time. She couldn't help it.

'You are funny,' he said, then wiped her cheek and kissed her again.

'Oh, Ollie, I can't believe you're really here!'

'Well, I'm very lucky. The ship's in Portsmouth having her engines looked at and taking on supplies so we've been stood down for thirty-six hours. I didn't think I was going to be able to get home in the time we've been given but Jimmy Malone took pity on me and lent me his car. He lives in Southsea so said he wouldn't need it and that I could take it. So here I am.'

'I think I like the sound of Jimmy. He's your number one, isn't he? You see, I read all your letters then reread them and read them again. I can't believe you're here!' she said again. 'It's the loveliest surprise I've ever had!'

'I wish it was for ever.' He kissed the top of her head and she felt him breathe in deeply. 'I'm so glad I found you quickly. Dad said he thought you'd be here.' He pulled away. 'I suppose I'd better let you get back to your lunch.'

'I'm not leaving you now,' said Elsa. 'They'll understand. Oh, Ollie, I've missed you so much.' She hugged him again. 'I can't tell you how I have.'

'I wanted to see you first, without anyone else,' he said, 'but don't you think I should say hello to them all? And ask if you can be excused?'

She laughed. 'Probably. They'll all be wondering who was waiting for me.'

Elsa led him into the dining room where the mood lightened at his appearance. Cutlery dropped onto plates, chairs were pushed back, hugs and handshakes greeting the returning hero.

'Welcome home, young man,' said Alwyn. 'We're all very proud.'

'We most certainly are,' agreed John.

'A national day of prayer,' said Carin, 'and here you are, dear Ollie.'

Ollie grinned bashfully, answered some questions about Norway – 'It was a bit startling but I can't say I was in much danger' – explained again that his ship was in Portsmouth, and Elsa asked if they might be excused.

'Of course,' said Maud. 'Make the most of it.'

Elsa and Ollie headed down the track to Tippett's Wood and went on towards the water meadows. Along the banks of the stream the willows were already in leaf. They lay down on the grass beneath their favourite tree and watched the swallows darting about above the water, catching insects and calling to one another as they swirled and dived.

'Were you ever scared?' Elsa asked him, her head on his chest.

'Honestly?'

'Honestly.'

'Yes. So many times. You see a plane get hit and it plunges into the water and you can't help thinking of the crew on board, probably alive when it hits the water and knowing they're going to die. It's terrible.' They were silent. Elsa didn't know what to say to him.

'And at the same time, I couldn't imagine anything happening to me. It's odd. I honestly believe I'll be all right, Elsa.'

'I don't want you to have to see such things. I just don't. I want you to be here, with me, and for the rest of the world to leave us alone.'

'Believe me, I want that too.' Another pause and he sighed heavily. She felt his chest rise as he did so.

'What is it, Ollie?'

'There was a soldier. An officer. On the ship. One of those we evacuated. I was talking to him and, I suppose, befriending him. And then we were attacked and he was shot and killed. He . . . he . . .'

She felt his chest rise again and held him a little more tightly.

'He died, Elsa. In my arms. I watched his life draining away.'

Elsa felt the tears running down her cheeks. The sadness of it. Sadness for the young man, sad that her beloved Ollie had had to witness such a thing.

259

'It's a bloody awful thing this war,' he said, his voice cracking. 'Absolutely bloody awful.'

Tess woke early on Monday morning, 27 May. She had been sent home at 9 p.m. having finished typing up some more minutes. The general had earlier gone to dinner with the Prime Minister and with Anthony Eden, the Secretary of State for War. She had had a brief drink with Diana, eaten some cold food, then gone to bed, sleep coming quickly.

It had not lasted long enough, and it was around five in the morning when her eyes opened and her mind was instantly filled with a cascade of conflicting thoughts. She wondered where Alex was, whether he was safe. She remembered the brief image of him on the newsreel they had seen the previous autumn. It had been him all right, but grainy, distant, not the Alex she remembered in Aldeburgh last August. A lifetime ago. Now the Navy was preparing to bring the BEF home. Operation Dynamo had been authorized late the previous afternoon. Then had come the news that Calais had fallen, with the whole brigade defending the port captured. So much for praying, she had thought. She knew everyone at the office was shocked and knocked sideways by the calamity that was unfolding. She also knew that Lord Halifax, the Foreign Secretary, was talking to the Italian ambassador about opening peace negotiations; she'd heard Ismay discuss this with Ian Jacob and Bill Elliott.

'Winston must prevail,' she'd heard Ismay say. 'What Halifax doesn't seem to appreciate is that once the door is ajar it'll blow wide open and that will be that. The Prime Minister is determined to fight on but he has to carry the War Cabinet with him. Attlee and Greenwood are the new boys, while Chamberlain and Halifax have been friends and colleagues for decades.'

'Did the PM ask you about estimates for the BEF?' asked Jacob.

'Yes. And I had to tell him the truth, of course. If we get forty thousand home, we'll have done well.'

Tess had hardly dared believe what she was hearing. Was this really it? Was Britain on the verge of collapse? It was too terrible, too fantastical, yet that conversation had played over and over in her mind. She'd tried to read a novel but couldn't concentrate on that either so had lain there, the familiar sheets covering her, wondering

260

whether this really was the end and whether Alex would be one of the lucky ones to escape or among the bulk of the British Army soon to find themselves prisoners of the Germans. And what would that mean? What happened to prisoners of war? She had no idea. They were staring down the barrel of catastrophe.

As she lay there, staring at the ceiling, her thoughts turned to home, as they so often did. After eventually getting up, dressing and making herself some toast, she decided to telephone her parents, to whom, she realized, she had not spoken in over a week. She knew they would be worried too.

It was her mother who answered. 'Tess, my darling, how lovely! How are you? Are you all right?'

'Yes, I'm fine,' she said. 'A little tired but otherwise all right. Working hard. I'm sorry it's been a week or so.'

'Don't worry. It's just lovely to hear your voice.'

She paused, wondering what to say. 'And is Daddy all right?'

'I think so. A bit worried, as we all are.' Debbo talked on – there had been letters from Edward, Wilf had rung and was on standby but so far hadn't been over to France. They were all worried about Carin but everyone was hoping for the best. Praying for some kind of good news.

Hope. Prayer. How many times had Tess heard those words over the past few days?

She rang off, promising to be down just as soon as she could. A little later she left the house and headed for Millbank. High above, a squadron of fighter planes flew over, little more than dots but the roar of their engines loud enough even from that height.

She wondered whether they were going to France. Perhaps it was Wilf up there; she shuddered, then felt sick at the prospect of the day's events. The evacuation begun, Churchill's battles with Halifax. The fate of the BEF. She had been so thrilled when she had got the job working for Ismay but now she rather wished she could turn back the clock: she wasn't sure she wanted to know all that she did.

Tess walked on, past the Houses of Parliament, across Parliament Square and on to Whitehall, a dead weight of dread sitting heavily in her heart.

23

Darkest Hour

AS TESS WAS HEADING TO WORK, WILF AND THE REST OF THE
599 Squadron officer pilots were eating breakfast in the mess when
Wing Commander Walker came in, excitement on his face.

'Well,' he said, pausing behind CO Pete Partington's chair, 'this is
it. Rat-a-tat-a-tat-a-tat! Action at long last!'

'Is that supposed to be a machine-gun, sir?' asked Bluey
Thompson.

'Yes.' Walker grinned. 'A whole squadron's worth!'

Wilf looked at his fellow pilots, none of whom seemed quite as
thrilled as Walker, then dipped a finger of toast into his boiled egg.

'France?' asked Partington.

Walker nodded. 'You'll be flying down to Rochford later this
morning and then over to Dunkirk, you lucky devils. They're evacuating the BEF and we're to help provide cover.'

Sim Delaney whistled. 'Things must be bad.'

'They are,' said Walker, 'but it's our chance to prove that Fighter
Command is superior to anything the Luftwaffe can throw at us.
You're all extremely experienced pilots with a mass of hours under
your belts. Show the Hun what you're made of, chaps.'

The entire squadron flew down to Rochford, all twenty-two
pilots and Spitfires, the great curve of East Anglia to their left, the
leg of Kent stretching away and France clearly visible on the far
side of the Channel. As they circled over what was to be their new
home for the duration of the evacuation, Wilf thought how small

the airfield looked; the CO had warned them it was a tricky place to land because it was only around a thousand yards wide from east to west and even narrower across. A railway embankment ran along the eastern end, which made an approach from that direction awkward and presented a wall should anyone overshoot from the other. Despite this, they all touched down without mishap, and it wasn't until later when Wilf was told he would be among the first twelve pilots to fly over to Dunkirk that the first flutter of nerves swept over him.

'How are you feeling?' Sim asked, as they walked across the grass to their waiting Spitfires.

'All right, I think,' said Wilf. 'You?'

'Nervous as hell. This is it. I can't believe the moment has arrived after all this time.'

Wilf grinned at him. 'You're a good pilot, Sim. We'll be fine.'

And he had still felt calm enough as they'd taxied and taken off, heading up into the early-evening sky, no more nerves than if he'd been going out to bat. It was around six as they headed out over Shoeburyness, the sky suddenly a little cloudier to the east, the sun behind them casting a warm, bright glow over the canopy ahead. They climbed quickly to twenty thousand feet and then as they crossed the Channel Wilf was confronted with a view unlike any he'd seen before. Up ahead, black smoke rose high into the sky, some twelve thousand feet and more before it merged with the cloud and the haze and spread laterally southwards towards Calais covering the French coastline. Something major on fire, he thought. Fuel depots? His heart began to thump.

Pete Partington was ahead, no more than forty yards in front, while on his right, also in Red Section, Sim glanced across at him and waved. Wilf turned his head. Yellow Section behind and a little to port, then two more vics, Blue and Green, of B Flight, also behind but on his starboard side. Twelve Spitfires flying in near-perfect formation. Flying into combat.

Moments later they were over Dunkirk. It was hard to make out what was going on below – snatched glimpses of ships beneath the haze, smoke and cloud, and they circled, somewhat aimlessly, somewhat anticlimactically, before Bluey, leading B Flight, spotted a Heinkel, flitting in and out of the haze.

263

'This is Snapper Leader,' he heard Pete say over the R/T. 'Attack, Number One, go.'

The squadron was manoeuvring into line astern, one behind another when, swivelling his head once more, Wilf saw a number of dots away and above them, bearing down from the north-east. *Messerschmitts.*

'Bandits, one o'clock!' he called.

'This is Snapper Leader,' he heard say Pete calmly, his voice crackling and faint with static. 'Green Section, attack the big job below, the rest turn into the little jobs.'

Yellow Section peeled off into a dive while Pete ordered the rest into Fighter Attack No 6.

Wilf cursed to himself as he pushed the stick to port and back into his stomach, then opened the boost. His Spitfire turned and climbed but, he knew, not fast enough, and now he saw the Messerschmitts bearing down on them with the twin advantages of height and speed. 'Damn it!' he muttered.

Flashes from the wings and noses of the leading enemy planes. Stabs of orange fluorescence pumping across the sky and then a clatter as something hit his fuselage. He felt himself gasp, then saw Pete flip over and drop, white smoke pouring from his engine. *Glycol. Damn it!* Two machines sped over him, their silvery-grey undersides streaked with oil. Head turning frantically. There was Sim, *good,* and the enemy aircraft continued to dive, out of the fray, so Wilf now banked, dropped a wing and followed. But the enemy fighters had gone as quickly as they'd appeared. He and Sim circled briefly, seeing little, then climbed once more. Fuel was already getting low – it really didn't take long.

Where was the rest of the squadron? And what had happened to Pete? Wilf continued to glance around him as they sped back over the Channel at around twelve thousand feet. His heart was still racing and his body tense. It had been a shock. He had been confident in his flying ability – he had over five hundred hours in his logbook, for God's sake – but air combat had been so different from how he'd imagined. So much faster. Christ, he'd even been hit and hadn't once fired! His Spitfire still seemed to be flying perfectly well, though, so that was something. He'd been lucky. An inch here, a few feet there, and it might have been a different story. It might

264

have been him plunging downwards. *Hell, Pete gone. The CO!* He found it hard to fathom. *Really?* But he'd seen it. Seen Pete drop out of the sky. *Concentrate,* he told himself, swivelling his head.

Only once he was over the Kent coast did he think again about what had just happened. The attack formations they'd trained in weren't quick enough. Visibility had not been as good as it might have been. Straining forward, making the most of the small amount of give in his harness, he had only just been able to see his tail plane. They needed rear-view mirrors; he would take one from a car and fix it in place.

Then there was Rochford, homely in the late-May evening sun, and the soothing calm of the ground controller in his ears. Wilf let Sim head in first, then dropped in behind him. Brakes and throttle back – mind that embankment – and then he was taxiing to Dispersal, his first combat sortie over France done. Pulling out his radio and oxygen leads, he took off his flying helmet, wiped his brow and paused, head against the cushion behind him, closing his eyes. He felt exhausted.

'Welcome back, sir,' said Davies, his rigger, as Wilf pushed himself out of his seat, and dropped down onto the wing root.

'Thanks. 'Fraid I didn't get a single shot off.' He slid off the wing on his backside and jumped onto the grass with a sense of relief.

'You'll get your chance, sir.'

His fitter, Gregson, now joined them.

'Need to get a mirror in there,' said Wilf. 'A car rear-view mirror would do it. There must be a garage in Rochford somewhere.'

'There is,' said Bingley. 'Right on the high street.'

'Good. I might pay it a visit as soon as we're stood down.' He grinned. 'I know it's after hours, but apparently there's a war on.'

Sim joined him and together they wandered back to Dispersal, a wooden one-room building that reminded Wilf of the cricket pavilion at his old school. Inside there was an assortment of chairs and old armchairs, a couple of trestle tables, a dartboard and aircraft recognition posters pinned to the wall. Flight Lieutenant 'Holly' Hollister was grilling each of the pilots, so Wilf flopped into an armchair to wait his turn. It seemed that Pete had bailed out – several had seen his parachute open, but which side of the lines he'd fallen no one could say. One other, Sam Parnell, was missing, last spotted heading back across the Channel trailing smoke. Bluey Thompson had stuck with him but had lost him in cloud.

Several had opened fire but not a single pilot reported shooting down an enemy plane. Everyone, Wilf thought, looked a little stunned by the experience. He felt a bit shocked too.

Sim came over and perched on the arm of Wilf's chair. Cigarette smoke filled the air. 'Christ,' he said. 'Not quite what I'd expected.'

'No.'

'Feels like we've still a bit to learn. I thought all our training would be enough. Now I'm not so sure.'

Wilf scratched his chin. He needed to think. They could all handle their aircraft well enough; really it was just a question of applying that skill more effectively. But he was determined they should never be caught out like that again.

At the same time, Tom Timbrell and the rest of the King's Own Royal Guards were resting near Ploegsteert Wood and Lieutenant Ashton was telling him that his father had fought there during the last war.

'They called it Plugstreet Wood,' he told Tom, 'not that there was much left of it at the end. Shattered stumps mostly.'

It had recovered well, thought Tom, although the trees were still obviously very young, but pine and even ash grew relatively quickly.

Fatigue swept over him. Having been ordered back from the Escaut the previous evening, they'd walked overnight and not stopped since. Orders were to make for Dunkirk. It was now evening and everyone was hungry as well as tired; they'd not had any rations since the previous morning. He also still had a splitting headache from being blasted the previous day – a spot of concussion, the MO had told him. The same shell had obliterated Parkinson – they had found nothing of him, just a crater in the ground. *Wouldn't have known a thing,* Tom told himself, but that didn't make it any less shocking. The battalion CO, Lieutenant-Colonel Mallory, had also been wounded; Tom had seen him at the regimental aid post and he'd looked in a bad way – shrapnel wounds all down one side. It meant Toast was now acting CO and Captain Woodman commanding the company.

Tom rubbed his eyes. All he wanted to do was sleep. He was lying on a grassy bank by the edge of a dirt road when Ashton nudged him and Tom looked up to see Captain Woodman and Major Burnham-Browne approaching.

'Ah, there you are,' said Burnham-Browne. 'Change of orders. It seems Jerry's got across the Ypres-Comines Canal near Comines so we and the 3rd Grenadiers are to put them back over the other side. We're to be temporarily attached to 5th Division.'

Ashton's face drained.

Tom watched a cricket hop onto his leg, pause, then spring away again. He wished he could disappear as effortlessly.

'It's a hell of an ask,' said Alex Woodman, 'but there are bigger things at play. We've got to hold what is a pretty fragile line. Do this and then we'll be heading to Dunkirk and, with a bit of luck, embarking for home.'

'What are the timings, sir?' asked Ashton.

The colonel looked at his watch. 'We'll move up through the wood now and start our attack at twenty hundred.'

'So much for a rest,' said Ashton, once they'd moved on.

Ten minutes later, they all marched off. Not for the first time, Tom wished he'd never been so stupid as to leave the farm.

A golden evening, the sun setting behind them, a vast disc of burnished orange that cast a warm glow across the open fields, copses and farmsteads of Flanders. Tom looked at the dairy herds mindlessly eating grass in the pastures; birds still sang. It was quiet in the air too – not a single aircraft flew over. In the distance guns could be heard and a faint pulse detected through the ground but otherwise it seemed more like a training exercise than anything else. No 2 Company was on the left of the advance, now only around ninety men strong; nearly forty had been lost since they'd set off into Belgium a fortnight earlier.

Innumerable fences and hedges held them up, so that at 8 p.m., when the sky above them suddenly filled with the scream and whooshing whine of their own artillery shells, they were still short of their start line for the attack. Then they met a winding stream south of the village of Houthem that wasn't on the map; it was only about five foot wide but was at least four foot deep, and wiggled its way between them and 3 Company on their right. It took their neighbours what seemed an age to cross.

With the light fading, the guns behind them had stopped firing and now the enemy opened fire in turn as mortar shells began raining down and the air was cut apart by machine-gun fire. Everyone hit the ground, the attack stalling immediately.

'Now what do we do?' said Ashton, beside Tom.

Ahead the stream cut across them, the ground sloping up gently towards the canal and a railway embankment immediately beyond it. There was a farmhouse just this side of the canal, no more than five hundred yards away; Tom saw stabs of machine-gun fire coming from one of the upper windows.

'Got to knock out that farmhouse,' he said to Ashton. 'We need to crawl as close as we can, then get a couple of Brens on it to keep Jerry's head down and charge it.'

'You make it sound so easy,' said Ashton.

A Bren chattered now, followed by the rip of the German machine-gun. More mortars crashed nearby, showering them with dark, rich soil.

'Well, we can't lie 'ere. Need to get off our arses, sir. Come on. Let's get to the hedge line of the stream and take it from there.'

Ashton nodded and together they got up, still crouching, and urged the rest of the men.

'Come on, up yer get!' called Tom. At least the light was fading. That was something. He glanced back at Ashton as they scurried forward across the lush grass. Rifles and machine-guns clattered tinnily. Mortars whined and crashed; smoke hung heavy on the air and offered a little more cover. Ashton smiled at him. Tom saw one man fall and another was blasted by a mortar burst and disappeared. *Who?* he wondered, but there was no time for that. Something nicked the side of his cheek but he hurried on, crouch-running, and then somehow he was at the stream, dropping down beside a clump of hawthorn, gasping. The men were drawing up alongside him. How many were down? He couldn't say, then looked back and saw Ashton just behind him. At that moment a bullet hit the lieutenant in the side of his head, straight through his tin helmet, and he crumpled to the ground.

Tom was so shocked he could say nothing. *Christ!* Ashton gone, just like that. Tom had dropped countless deer just like that: single shot to the head – they just fell, legs gone, to the ground.

Someone was clutching his shoulder and Tom turned to see Captain Woodman squatting beside him with Lieutenant Robbins of 5 Platoon.

'You're platoon commander now, Tom,' said Woodman. 'We need to get to that farmhouse up ahead.'

Tom nodded. 'Yes, sir. I was just saying that to Lieutenant Ashton.'

'We'll keep four Brens on the stream so that we have a constant rain of fire. That should keep their heads down. And the rest of us will charge. Unless you've a better plan, Tom? I'm afraid Two Company is the closest and Three Company have lost their commander and two I/C. So, it's up to us. I'll brief the mortar platoon to pour fire onto the farmhouse too.'

'I'll get our Brens ready, sir,' said Robbins.

'Good, and you'll get your men briefed, Sergeant.'

Tom scurried between bushes priming the section Bren gunners, then hurried back to Captain Woodman. Robbins reappeared and Woodman blew his whistle. Their own mortars whined, the Brens began to chatter and Tom took a deep breath, then urged his men forward, plunging out across the stream. Jammo Tompkins was struggling so Tom grabbed his shoulder strap and hauled him clear, then ran, no longer crouching but sprinting, across the open field. Behind him the Brens continued to fire but another German machine-gun was also firing nearby, its faster rate peppering the darkening sky.

A flare crackled as it burst, casting fresh light over the battleground. Bullets whistled past him, fizzing and zipping, slicing through the air, like the swish of a sword, and suddenly he was no longer conscious of any sound at all except his own beating heart and heaviness of breath. A tightness in his chest, a gasp, and then he was at the farmhouse, a grenade in his hand. He pulled on the ring, felt the pin come clear and hurled the missile through one of the ground-floor windows, then took another from his belt as he reached the edge of the house and the first exploded. Screams, shouts from inside and, with his back to the brickwork, Tom threw in another, scampered around the corner, and tossed in a third. Others were now beside him, Corporal Souch and, he saw, Captain Woodman. More shouts, and he raised his rifle, drew back the bolt and carefully inched around to the rear of the building. Germans

269

were running, fleeing towards the canal and he shot one, then a second and even a third, *one, two, three,* just like that. Like felling skittles, just dark shapes against the fading light.

More men were now in the house so Tom hurried back and found Captain Woodman there, sitting on a chair. The faint light of a kerosene lamp cast a glow over a room of shadows, dust and debris. Woodman was being helped out of his battle blouse by one of the men, his shirt dark with blood.

'Sir?' said Tom.

'A bullet through the shoulder,' he replied, grimacing. 'At least it went clean through. I'll be all right.'

Firing continued beyond the farmhouse and away to their right. The room smelt heavily of sweat, smoke and cordite.

'There's a wooden footbridge across the canal,' said Tom. 'We should blow it up.'

'Where are the bloody sappers when you need them?' said the captain. He turned to Souch. 'We need to send a runner to Battalion HQ. Tell them we have the farmhouse and that we've cleared the canal along this stretch. Ask for some sappers. Where are Robbins and Five Platoon?'

No one knew.

'And we need to bring up the reserve platoon. Sergeant, send a runner, will you?'

Tom sent back Lofty Small, purely because he was the shortest and slightest. Having given him a hastily scribbled note and sent him on his way, he then went back into the hallway and took the stairs. In one room he found two dead Germans and their machine-gun by the south-facing window, then scouted the rest of the upstairs area. Men needed to be posted. Bren gunners ought to be swiftly positioned up here. Looking out, he saw another house, perhaps half a mile further along the canal towards Comines, blazing in the night, and watched as tracer continued to stab the sky, little pulses of coloured light. He thought about Ashton, presumably lying where he had fallen, and wondered how many others had been killed or wounded. *Jesus.* He wondered how he'd been spared. *And now the captain*, he thought.

Alex Woodman was now stripped to his trousers as one of the men pressed field dressings to both sides of his shoulder and another

270

wrapped bandages around it. Tom glanced at an old mirror and only then saw blood on his face. He touched his cheek. A graze, nothing more. He'd been lucky.

There were now a dozen men in the house but no sign of reinforcements. Where the hell were they? Tom scraped a boot on the flagstone floor, then turned to Jammo Tompkins. 'Come with me,' he said, and carefully led him to the wooden bridge. The battle was dying down at last but small-arms could still be heard, and further down the canal the house was burning more fiercely than ever.

At the end of the bridge he discovered a small area under which he could wedge a grenade before the bank dropped down to the water. *Good*, he thought. Placing his last two grenades on one side and a third that Tompkins had in his haversack on the other, he felt his fingers fold around the rings.

'Got yours, Jammo?' he whispered.

'Yes, Sarge.'

'Fingers around the ring?'

'Yes, Sarge.'

'Right, pull on three and then we run.' He counted in a low whisper: 'One, two, three.' He pulled the pins clear, then turned and sprinted back towards the farmhouse. Seconds later, an explosion. The night was ripped apart by a flash of orange, bits of wood hurtled into the air, then rifle and machine-gun fire opened up once more from the far side, bullets whipping and fizzing past him.

He reached the farmhouse with Tompkins panting behind him. 'Blimey! That was a bit bloody close!'

Yes, thought Tom. But they had got the bridge. That was something, but there was still no sign of any reinforcements and it was now after ten o'clock.

'How's the captain?' Tom asked Souch.

'He's lost a lot of blood.'

It was dark in the house – just the faint glow of the lamp – and desolate. Tom thought about the dead men upstairs, about how isolated they were without reinforcements. That Captain Woodman was wounded and needed help. Where the hell was everyone? He wondered what to do. With the captain now drifting in and out of consciousness, he was in charge. He could see the others were looking to him. Back on the farm, he'd taken instructions from Mr Stork

271

and occasionally from old Mr Castell, and sometimes even his father, but otherwise he had been left to his own devices. And he'd liked it that way. He had been his own man. But that had been a lifetime ago and now here he was, in this God-forsaken house, seemingly cut off from the rest of the battalion and with the enemy just the other side of the canal, barely two hundred yards away. He took a deep breath and pulled out a cigarette. After lighting it, then exhaling, he said, 'Right, I want men upstairs and pickets outside. Souch, you stay with the captain. We'll take it in turns to get our 'eads down.' *And hope for the best.*

Upstairs, crouching on the floor by the window, with his rifle ready, he stared out into night, his eyes already acclimatizing to the dark. The darkness had never held any fears for him, but there'd been no Germans lurking in Tippett's Wood. Outside, the sky flickered with an orange glow to the south-east. He wondered how many they'd lost in the attack. Wondered whether help was on its way. And wondered whether he'd ever see another dawn or ever, somehow, get home to Alvesdon.

24

Despair

THE YARD AT ALVESDON MANOR WAS LOUD WITH SHEEP BAAING, now briefly back in the sheds for their annual shearing. Wool, as Claude Timbrell reminded the girls, was the first crop of the year to be cut. It meant that Gilbert Rose was down at the farm, a comparatively rare sight. Elsa had always enjoyed talking to him, recognizing that for all his lack of formal education he was a man of wisdom and knowledge. While she waited for Alf Ellerby to bring up a couple of horses, she wandered over to watch him working alongside Frank Ellerby and Sid Collis.

'Morning, Mr Rose,' she said.

Gilbert paused, looked up and winked. He had a ewe held by her forelegs, her back against his own legs, as he used a set of hand shears, the blades seemingly gliding through the wool of the surprisingly calm and benign beast. In different pens, Frank and Sid were using electric cutters, the faint whirr dimly heard over the bleating of the waiting animals.

In no more than a few minutes, Gilbert had finished, the ewe on its four feet once more, immaculately shorn and led into a different pen with the others already done. Dust, dung and lanolin were heavy in the air – a not unpleasant smell, Elsa thought.

'She looks so beautiful,' she told him. 'Is it very difficult to do? You do it so much more neatly than Frank and Sid.'

Gilbert paused and lit a pipe, the swirls of sweet smoke curling up towards the rafters. 'Well,' he said at length, ''tis amazin' what practice can achieve. I got nothin' against electric clippers but I reckons I can do the job better by my own fair 'and an' quicker besides.' He sucked on his pipe again, came over and leaned on the wooden stockade. 'An' 'ow are you farin', Miss Elsa?'

'Oh, all right, I think.'

He looked at her. 'Not sure, then?'

Elsa looked down, wondering whether she should say anything, but found herself looking back at him, at those twinkling, kindly eyes, and said, 'Ollie's gone back to sea and I worry about him a lot. And I'm very worried about Mama. That she'll be sent to some horrid camp for being German.'

'People don' like change and they definitely don' like shock. They're roundin' up Germans and Eyeties an' the like because they're panicking cos of what's 'appenin' in France. But France is next to Germany and a land border is a darn sight easier to cross than a stretch o' sea. Those Germans, Miss Elsa, knows 'ow to fight in Europe but they don' know 'ow to fight agin an island. And don' forget, your man is part of the world's largest navy. 'Itler's navy's no match. Takes decades to build up experience. I's like I said, 'tis amazin' what practice can achieve, but I dun reckon the Germans bin practising much with their navy. Not enough to cross the Channel, anyways.'

'I hadn't thought of it like that. They just seem so unstoppable.'

'On the Continent, mebbe. We jus' need to 'old our nerve. An' Mr Churchill ain't for quittin'.'

'Do you really think so?'

He smiled and relit his pipe. 'I'm not a bettin' man, but if I 'ad to wager, I'd put good money on me standing 'ere this time nex' year an' shearin' again.'

'And Mama?'

'Once the panickin' passes, all will be well.' Alf Ellerby was bringing the two horses into the yard at last. 'Looks like you're needed, Miss Elsa.'

'Thank you, Mr Rose,' she said. He raised a finger to his cap, winked once more, and turned back to his sheep.

'Here you go, Elsa,' said John, as the three other land girls came over. Increasingly, Elsa had been paired with Hattie while Jill and Susie were put together and today it was horse-hoeing.

'Let's get it over and done with then,' said Hattie, leading Samson by the bridle.

'You finishin' off Blindwell, then?' said John.

Hattie nodded. 'Jill and Susie will go back to Triangle. Is that all right?'

'Right enough,' said John.

The four headed down the track together until it split, with Jill and Susie turning left up over the shallow saddle that led to Triangle, Elsa and Hattie continuing towards Tippett's Wood.

Elsa told her what Gilbert had said. 'He rather cheered me up,' she said.

'That's all very well, but now the Belgians have surrendered the situation's even worse.'

'Yes, but that's because they're on the Continent.'

'And so is the British Army. What happens if most of them end up as prisoners? D'you think Churchill will be able to keep on fighting then?'

Elsa was silent a moment. 'I don't think we should ever surrender.'

'What about your cousin and uncle? I thought you said they were bona-fide signed-up Nazi Party members?'

'I think they must have gone stark raving mad, but they can be Nazis in Bavaria if they so wish, just not here.'

Hattie laughed.

'What's so funny?' asked Elsa.

'I can just imagine you telling them that with that look of outraged indignation on your face.' Elsa scowled. 'Actually,' said Hattie, 'I couldn't agree with you more. And maybe Gilbert is right. Let's hope so, at any rate.'

They reached Blindwell and harnessed Samson to the horse-hoe, a simple task that took only a couple of minutes.

'Front or back?' asked Hattie. 'Shall I lead to start with?'

'All right.'

Hattie sighed. 'I know we've done worse jobs, but this is one of my least favourite.'

Elsa went to the back and took the twin arms of the horse-hoe. 'I don't mind it,' she said, as she lined up the twin hoe-blades between the drill-lines of the mangolds. 'It's mindless but it's a nice day and at least you and I get to talk to one another.'

'Mindless but still requires concentration. Bending over looking at the ground, making sure we get the weeds and not the crop.'

'Well, we've half done it. Not much more to do.'

'And I suppose it could be worse. We could be in France.'

Hattie clicked her tongue and led on Samson as Elsa felt the hoe-blades bite. She thought of Tom Timbrell and wondered where he was; they'd passed his old hut in Tippett's Wood not ten minutes earlier. She hoped he was safe, Tess's Alex too. Her uncle had high hopes for Tom, she knew. Then she thought of her beloved Ollie. What was he doing now? It had been so wonderful to see him and he had been so reassuringly the same, but then she'd had to let him go again. An urgent telegram – *Return to ship* – and off he'd gone, a hug, a kiss, then a wave from his friend's car. She'd watched it disappear down the road so that all she had was the memory of just a few precious hours, the warmth of his skin and the touch of her hands in his hair. She wondered how long that would have to sustain her.

Wednesday, 29 May 1940

Ollie Varney was standing on the bridge of HMS *Iceni* when, later that afternoon, they approached Dunkirk for the second time that day. If anything, it seemed more chaotic than it had earlier. Not for the first time, it struck him as extraordinary that he could have been lying with Elsa on the riverbank just three days ago and now here he was, in the midst of this mayhem. A half-sunken ship lay off the beaches, while on the sands lines of men could be seen, some milling in bunches, others among the dunes. Peering through his binoculars, he saw one man stagger down from the dunes, a bottle clutched in his hand, then stumble and fall. *Good grief*, he thought. Abandoned or wrecked vehicles and artillery pieces dotted the beach too, along with boxes, clothing and a mass of other detritus.

Distant guns boomed dully, almost metronomically, somewhere beyond the town and the dunes. Thick smoke still billowed from the bombed fuel depot the far side of the port, but its noxious and depressing canopy had now merged with the thick blanket of natural cloud that had descended over the Channel and coastline, like a protective shield. Really, they had all agreed, it was something of a miracle: ten-tenths cloud in the nick of time and barely a flutter of wind. It was raining – light, persistent drizzle – but the sea around them was as flat as a board.

They had first reached Dunkirk at a little after 5.30 a.m., following the I-class destroyers, *Icarus* and *Ivanhoe*, to the East Mole, a long harbour breakwater that extended for the best part of a mile from the seawall. It was not, and never had been, a quayside, but Dunkirk's port was blocked, ruined and inaccessible, and this long, straight finger, built of concrete lattice and with a narrow wooden walkway on top, had become a makeshift jetty. A ship had then been brought alongside and, lo and behold, successfully berthed. A potentially transformative discovery.

'Smart thinking,' Commander Bertie had said, as they'd gingerly inched alongside that morning. Ollie had watched them draw in; the mole had looked horribly fragile to him and he had expected it to collapse the moment they attempted to nudge against it. Yet Bertie and the helmsman had remained imperturbable.

'Course one-three-five, cut throttle,' Bertie had said calmly, and through the voice pipe, the helmsman had repeated the instruction and gently, so very gingerly, they had slipped in behind *Icarus*. The slightest of jolts and they were there. Ollie had just sighed with relief when a huge explosion behind them had made them all jump.

'Good Lord!' exclaimed Bertie, and they had leaned over the edge of the bridge to see *Mona's Queen*, a passenger steamer they had passed not five minutes earlier, engulfed in flames and angry black smoke and already rapidly sinking.

'Must have been a mine,' said Jimmy Malone.

Bertie nodded, his face grim. 'We need to be careful. Let's make sure we've got men scouring the sea every time we leave. Mines really are the very devil.'

They had taken on more than five hundred troops, most tired, dishevelled and hungry. Ollie had been sent off to oversee the mess team's best efforts to give the men something to eat, a mug of hot tea or cocoa and a shot of rum. They'd been lucky: they'd got away quickly and had avoided the Luftwaffe. Two hours later, they'd pulled into Dover, unloaded and, after taking on more fuel and supplies, had set off again, dog-legging on a frustratingly long route to avoid minefields and French coastal guns now in enemy hands.

'Signal from SNO Dunkirk,' came Henry Wymer's voice up the pipe now, as they neared the port again. 'Proceed off Bray-Dunes and pick up troops from beaches.'

Bertie cursed and Ollie felt a wave of nausea sweep through him.

Bertie leaned into the voice pipe. 'Course one-zero-five, Mr McAllister. Make eighteen knots.'

'Aye, aye, sir,' answered Lieutenant McAllister, then repeated the order to the helmsman.

'Very well,' said Bertie.

Ollie felt the ship tremble and the metal plate beneath his feet vibrate as *Iceni* increased speed. It was some seven miles or so to Bray-Dunes from Dunkirk but all along the stretch of beaches he could clearly see what remained of the British Army. How on earth were they going to get any men aboard? A destroyer could not get close enough to the beach and they had only a brace of whalers and a single small motor launch. They could lower those, of course, and drop netting over the side but they would only be able to lift men at a trickle. It would take hours to get even a hundred men aboard. They'd be sitting ducks.

At that moment, a swarm of Stukas emerged from under the cloud base. Bertie ordered McAllister to increase speed and to zigzag. A whistle and a scream, then a second's silence, followed by one explosion then another, huge columns of water erupting and rising high into the air between them and the beach. In and around the dunes, Ollie saw men diving and falling flat, then disappearing behind fountains of sand as more bombs fell. A cacophony of noise: of their own pom-poms firing, of aircraft thundering over, of bombs exploding, then a further roar as two Spitfires emerged through the cloud and hurtled over, machine-guns chattering. A Stuka was hit; Ollie watched it, almost stationary mid-air as it tried to climb once more, then a brief flash of flame, and it flipped over and dived into the sea. All that remained was a line of smoke stuck on the air that had followed it down. Aboard *Iceni* the men cheered.

But not Ollie. He stood on the bridge open-mouthed, wondering how they were ever going to get away again. He felt trapped, pinned out in the open and with nowhere at all to run.

Thursday, 30 May 1940

At Richmond Terrace, Tess was now on the early shift, which meant she was due in the office at 7 a.m. to go through the mass of signals, memos and mail that had arrived overnight: memos from the Prime Minister and other ministers, reports from Lord Gort's headquarters in France, naval reports, briefings from the RAF, from the Joint Intelligence Committee, reports on morale taken from around the country and filtered through the Ministry of Information, and other notes besides.

'You're not expected to read any of it,' Mary Chambers, one of the other secretaries had told her, 'just organize it. PM at the top, then into groupings.' She told Tess that she always separated the three services, then ministries, and finally any other matters.

That had been two days ago, and on that first morning the weight of different papers on her desk had been enough to make her head spin. None the less, she had managed to organize it all more quickly than she had at first anticipated and had also begun to skim-read many of the more interesting items, so that now, on this Thursday-morning shift she had decided to come in earlier, at six, and look through the mass of papers more carefully still. She was keenly aware of her privileged position, the access her job gave her, and had the wit to realize that the more she understood what was going on the easier it would be to organize, prioritize and pass on. As Colonel Bill Elliott had told her, it was vital that Ismay and his team had as clear a picture of what was going on as possible, and especially so in these days of peril with so much happening all at once.

But more than that, she was curious to know more. The news that was reported on the BBC or in the newspapers was, she knew, only part of the picture. The public had not been told of the Admiralty's decision to comb the entire coast from Portsmouth to Great Yarmouth for every available shallow-draught powered boat to sail to Dunkirk to help lift troops. This, like the evacuation itself, remained part of a new embargo. No one was to know. Sometimes this knowledge – these secrets – was hard to bear, although she was generally working such long hours, and spending most of what time she had at her house asleep, that there was little opportunity to share what she knew.

Diana was wonderful about not asking questions. It only became harder when she spoke to her parents. They would fish so. 'Of course I know you can't tell me anything, darling,' her mother would say, while Stork would make some claim and then add, 'Although, no doubt, you know a lot more than me.' She desperately wanted to tell them what she knew but, of course, she could not; when she had signed the Official Secrets Act it had been made absolutely clear to her, in no uncertain terms, that any such betrayal of that oath would be regarded as treason.

Now, with the rain gently falling and London rumbling into a new day, she sat at her desk scanning the documents and organizing them into piles. What a week it had been already; she had never seen General Ismay – normally so bright and indefatigable – look so downcast, despite the Prime Minister successfully averting any further talk of opening peace negotiations.

'Winston's won that battle,' she'd heard Ismay say, but then had come the news of the Belgian surrender and the seemingly hopeless situation of the BEF, which appeared certain to be entirely cut off. Even as troops were streaming back to Dunkirk, no one had thought it possible to lift an army off the beaches. And yet the day before, Wednesday, there had been a faint chink of light: rather than laboriously ferrying the men from beach to ship in whalers and other small vessels, ships could dock against a jetty breakwater known simply as the 'East Mole'. She was looking at the evacuation statistics now, sent in from the Admiralty: 47,310 had been brought back the previous day alone. An incredible figure! That was more in one day than Ismay had predicted for the entire operation. Now a mass of little boats was also heading across the Channel and she wondered, with a jolt of hope, whether something could be salvaged from this terrible defeat after all.

More memos, more letters, more reports. The RAF had shot down more than forty enemy aircraft. She wondered whether Wilf had flown over there yet. She prayed not. A list of naval vessels involved. She ran her finger down a list of destroyers. *Yes, there:* HMS Iceni. *Ollie's ship.* A Ministry of Information morale report. *The shock of the news is still apparent,* she read, *but people are, if anything, calmer. Bad news has had a sobering effect.* Tess couldn't help smiling at that. Had people been drunk with panic? She wondered who wrote these reports. People at typewriters in offices at the Ministry, she supposed.

And then she came to a buff folder, opened it and saw the heading, 'Casualty Reports BEF up to 2300 29 May 1940'. She held it for a moment, hardly daring to turn the page. She knew she must, though. Her first thought: *So many names.* The losses were typed up by corps, then division, then brigade and then individual unit. It didn't take her long to find a column of losses from the King's Own Royal Guards. A list that was far too long, she thought. What had her Alex been put through? Casualties were listed by date. One in March, two in April, then a mass of names on 21 May. Frantically, she scanned them but there was no mention of Alex. A handful of losses in the days that followed, and she felt a sense of mounting relief until she turned the page and saw another long list for 27 and 28 May.

She gasped out loud. There he was: *Woodman, Capt. A. E. R., MIA.* Missing. What did that mean? Was he dead? Or prisoner? And there was another entry that now caught her eye: *Timbrell, Sgt. T. E., MIA.* Were they together? What had happened? Tess held up the sheaf of paper, staring, then realized her hands were shaking and her heart was racing. *No!* she thought. No, this couldn't be. And yet there was Alex's name, and Tom Timbrell's too, typed out by some secretary just like her at the War Office. Missing in action. *Missing.* Gone.

That evening, Stork rode Jorrocks to Middle Chalke to see John and Carin. It was cloudy and drizzling, the fine weather of the previous weeks gone for the time being, but the air was still fresh and beautifully scented. May had always been his favourite month. The month he'd met Debbo, during leave from the front in the last war; the month their first child, Edward, was born, and always a time of hope. The start of summer. Of renewed life as the trees and hedgerows burst into their annual and astonishing spurt of growth. In the trees the birds sang, over the river the mayflies rose, on the farm the winter was behind them and they could all afford to take matters just a trifle easier, before the long days of harvest time. Now, as he trotted down the road he marvelled, as he always did, at the abundance of cow parsley lining the verges, and a mass of other grasses

281

and wild flowers, dormant over the long winter but which had now blossomed with such miraculous fecundity once more. As he passed a small wood he heard a nightingale singing, its strange jumble of notes, shrill and impossibly complex one moment, long, drawn-out and hollow the next, vividly clear despite the rain.

No matter what was happening in the world, no matter how weighed down he felt, there was still joy to be found in his surroundings. He was determined to hold on to these crumbs of comfort.

He wondered what Edward was doing, far away in Palestine. Or Wilf. They had had a letter that morning. He was fine, Wilf had assured them, and with the rest of the squadron was now carrying out a number of patrols over the Channel. They had had a bit of action and the CO had been lost, although he was believed to be a prisoner of war. The poor fellow, Stork thought. *Honestly, I'm fine*, Wilf had written, then added, *Dad, I've added a car rear-view mirror to my cockpit and am learning a lot. So, no need to worry!* And that had made him feel a little better. In the last war, a lot of good pilots had been lost because they had become over-confident. He knew Wilf was a natural pilot so it reassured him to learn his younger son was not being complacent. 'You must always be willing to learn,' he had told Wilf, more than once. It seemed he was listening.

John and Carin were at home, as he knew they would be; it wasn't John's night to be on duty with the LDV and these days Carin barely left Rose Bower. How sad it was, he thought, when she had been such a popular figure and had so wholeheartedly thrown herself into village life. She seemed pleased enough to see him, though.

'How are you, Carin?' he asked her, as John went to fetch drinks.

'I am all right, thank you, Stork.' She paused. 'Well, if truth be told, I am very worried.' She sighed. 'But my worries are no worse than yours or anyone else's, I am sure. Tell me how you all are. What news of Tess and of the boys? And how is the farm?'

Stork told her what he knew and about Wilf's letter that morning.

'I've always thought he's the most sensible of the lot of us,' said John, reappearing and handing Stork a Scotch.

Stork smiled. 'You may well be right.' He raised his glass. 'Here's how.'

Elsa now joined them. 'Uncle Stork! How lovely! I had such a heartening talk with Mr Rose this morning. He's a wise old bird, isn't he?'

'Very,' agreed Stork.

'I felt so cheered it quite spurred me to finish the horse-hoeing.'

Stork laughed, then said, 'Actually, John, I had a thought about your LDVs. Want to put something to you.'

'Oh, yes?'

'I wonder whether you could do with some kind of hut up on the downs. Where you and the chaps can get your heads down if you need to. Have it as a sort of base.'

'Go on.'

'Well, there's Tom's hut down in Tippett's Wood. There's no shoot any more and Tom is off doing his bit, so it's sitting there doing nothing.'

'Don't you think Tom might be a bit miffed if he comes back and finds it gone?'

'I think he'd be glad it's being used. I had a look in it earlier. It's got very musty, needs an airing, but I could arrange for it to be brought up onto the Herepath or the Ox Drove.'

'I think that's a terrific idea,' said Elsa.

John smiled. 'All right – thank you, Stork. Very thoughtful of you.' He suggested it would be best on the Ox Drove, where the Bockerley Road crossed the downs. They always mounted patrols up there because one could see across the Chase and all the way down to the coast, thirty miles away. And so it was settled. Elsa even offered to tow it with Thor.

'A splendid idea,' agreed Stork. 'We can do it in the morning.'

'I say,' said John, now looking at his watch, 'it's getting on for half past six. I might switch on the wireless and catch the headlines, if you don't mind?'

He glanced at Carin anxiously and Stork saw her nod, then John went over to the wireless that stood amid the bookshelves that lined one side of the room. The newsreader's voice entered the room, mid-sentence, a little quietly, so John adjusted the volume. The voice was calm, unemotional. *These are the facts.* Hard fighting was continuing for the BEF in Flanders. It had been another day of successful operations for the RAF in the air; the Luftwaffe had suffered grievously. Naval operations in the Channel and in Norway were ongoing. A different voice then announced a broadcast by Sir Neville Bland, British Minister to the Court of the Netherlands.

There was a brief pause then Bland's voice entered the room. He had experience of fifth columnists operating in the Netherlands, he said, and wanted to share his thoughts and observations. The British public needed to be vigilant; the fifth column seemed like ordinary people but were working for the enemy. Spying, feeding information. He confessed he had had many German friends in the past and hoped, one day, to have German friends again. Stork saw Carin put a hand to her mouth and fear in her eyes. 'I hate to have to say this to you,' said Bland, 'but I find it my duty to say it and say it I will: be careful now at this moment how you put complete trust in any person of German or Austrian connections.'

'What absolute rot!' said John. 'I'm going to turn off this tripe.'

'Keep your eye on them,' Bland continued. 'They may be perfectly all right – but they may not, and today we can't afford to take risks.'

John switched off the radio and muttered, 'For God's sake.' Carin now got up and hurried out of the room, John swiftly following.

'Wretched man,' said Stork, then glanced at Elsa, who sat perched at the edge of the sofa, staring at some indistinct spot, a single tear running down her cheek.

'Poor Mama,' she said. 'I hate this war. I absolutely hate it.' She looked up. 'What's going to happen to her, Uncle Stork?'

Stork grimaced and ran a hand through his hair. 'Let's hope this madness passes quickly, Elsa. What a world.' He, too, felt like crying. He'd not fought through the last war just so the world could be in similar turmoil twenty years later. Would they ever learn? In generations to come, would man still be fighting man? And over what? Nothing! It was always over so little. Hubris. Greed. Hate. All such terrible things.

He stood up. 'I'd better get back.' Leaning over Elsa, he kissed the top of her head. 'You have all your mother's best qualities, Elsa. I'm sure all will be well and that this nonsense will stop.'

Elsa nodded silently.

He sighed and left her, letting himself out of the house. It was still raining but he barely noticed as Jorrocks clopped his way back down the valley road. The nightingale still sang but for once Stork took no joy from the magical sound. Rather, he felt sick at heart and filled with foreboding.

25

Deliverance

Friday, 31 May 1940

IT WAS A LITTLE AFTER MIDDAY AND THIS TIME THE SQUADRON HAD the advantage of height. They could manoeuvre themselves so that the sun was behind them. And there they were: nine Me109s around six thousand feet under them, twinkling in the midday sun and below them perhaps two dozen Heinkel bombers. Once again, Wilf had spotted them first; he was proving quite the eagle eye. Bluey Thompson led them down, not in any prescribed attack formation but with instructions for A Flight to clobber the fighters and for B to dive straight on and hammer the bombers.

Wilf lowered his goggles and made sure he didn't look at the sun reflected in his mirror, now welded at the top of the windscreen. He then peeled over, following Bluey, feeling the lurch of his stomach as his ears popped. The airframe seemed to be juddering with the increased air speed, which, he noticed, was creeping up to over 400 miles per hour. Below, getting closer, the enemy fighters. Those boys had still not seen them. How could they? If they looked up all they'd see was the blinding sun. Getting closer. A thousand feet. Eight hundred. And still the German pilots had not spotted them. Closer, closer, starting to fill his gunsight. Wilf now lined up a Messerschmitt that was a little back from the leading fighter – the Germans flew in wider formations than they did, he had noticed, and in fours rather than vics of three. Five hundred feet. Four hundred. Start to level out. The stick heavy as he pulled it back towards him, engine screaming. Wilf let his target fill his gunsight, flicked the gun button to 'fire' and pressed down. Bullets spat from his wings, the airframe juddered from the recoil, and from his guns' stabs of tracer he saw them converging on the 109. Strikes across the port wing and engine cowling, a puff of flame and smoke and the Messerschmitt flipped over and dived as Wilf hurtled past.

And now he kept going. No point climbing and losing the precious advantage of height. He quickly glanced behind and saw the enemy formation had already split. A second Messerschmitt dived past him trailing smoke and above him the mêlée had already begun as aircraft twisted, turned and pirouetted in their individual battles. But Wilf was already gone, he and B Flight speeding together towards the Heinkels for a second bounce. How big they were in comparison, he thought, and although this time the enemy spotted their attackers before the Spitfires reached them, they were slower, more lumbering, and Wilf soon had one in his sights, a machine that was pulling away slightly from the rest. Tracer was spitting towards him from the bomber's rear-gunner but it was arcing wide and Wilf applied a bit of rudder to yaw the plane so it appeared to be turning more than it was. Thumb on the gun button, the Spitfire juddering. Again he saw strikes across the enemy aircraft, this time over the fuselage and starboard wing. Wilf swept over the top, hurtling through the rest of the scattering formation, then banked and turned, coming around for a second run at the bomber. Swivelling his head frantically. *No fighters. Good.* He spotted his Heinkel, diving away from the rest, trailing smoke from its starboard engine, desperately heading for the cloud base, and Wilf followed, giving the stricken bomber another burst.

Something caught his eye. A glance in the mirror and, yes, a Messerschmitt was speeding towards him. Below him the cloud. Wilf headed for the carpet of grey-white, just a thousand feet below, but already the first darts of tracer were flashing past his canopy and port wing. *Christ, they dive fast!* Air speed rising. Wilf rolled and fired at the Heinkel again just as it disappeared but he was right behind it and suddenly enveloped in cloud. He could see nothing – his Spitfire shrouded in white. Where was that Messerschmitt? He turned his head this way and that, glanced at his mirror and wondered when he would emerge from the wall of cloud. A look at the altimeter; now down to just three thousand feet. He throttled back and pulled the stick towards him; it would be careless to emerge and plunge straight into the sea.

Fifteen hundred feet, twelve hundred, a thousand. Still engulfed in white vapour. Then sudden thinning, vague shapes, and he was out and miraculously flying parallel to the coast. Wilf grimaced as he pulled the stick back towards him and felt the Spitfire strain, but it levelled out at no more than three hundred feet and there, just up ahead, was a Messerschmitt – *the same Messerschmitt?* – and Wilf opened the throttle. Before the German pilot had spotted him he drew up to just two hundred yards and opened fire. Much to his surprise and relief, he saw bits of aircraft spewing into the air, then smoke. The Messerschmitt dropped into a shallow dive and plunged into the sea. Below on the beaches men were raising their arms and Wilf grinned, hurtled along the beach, then banked over a destroyer approaching the port and sped out to sea and for home.

Ollie Varney was watching Wilf shoot down the Messerschmitt. He had been out on the bridge alongside Jimmy Malone as HMS *Iceni* approached Dunkirk. Ollie had been training his binoculars on the mole when he'd heard shouts from the crew and seen arms raised, fingers pointed. It all happened very quickly, the Messerschmitt plunging into the water no more than three hundred yards off their starboard bow and the Spitfire hurtling almost over them before heading for home. The men had all cheered.

Without lowering his own binoculars, Jimmy Malone had said, 'One less to worry about, I suppose.'

Ollie had fleetingly wondered whether it had been Wilf – the only Spitfire pilot he knew – then dismissed the notion. After all, what were the odds? Hundreds to one, he supposed. Instead he peered at the mole, then along the beaches.

'Still a lot of men over there,' he said. The wind was getting up and the haze that had covered them was starting to disperse. He watched some of the small boats struggling in the swell.

Malone leaned over to the voice pipe. 'Number One to signals officer. Anything from the SNO, Mr Wymer?'

'Signals officer to Number One. Message just coming in.'

'Very well,' replied Jimmy.

Orders from the senior naval officer ashore – orders that would tell them whether they would be pulling up to the mole or repeating the order of three days earlier when they had been kept hanging about off the beaches for almost five hours. Ollie looked at Malone, then briefly stepped into the pilothouse. Everyone was tense. Wallis, another of the subs, was chewing his nails. Lieutenant Charlie Sweetman, the navigation officer on watch, was smoking and drumming his fingers. Ollie stepped back out onto the bridge. Sitting off the beaches had been an ordeal. They'd been attacked four times that day, successive waves of Stukas and twin-engine bombers diving down or sweeping over them. Ollie had been put in charge of one of the whalers, heading to the beach with a crew of six oarsmen taken from the crew. It had taken an hour and a half just to reach the shore and all the while Ollie had wondered whether he'd ever set foot on *Iceni* again. Every time he glanced around, she was on the move: forward, backward, then circling, out to sea a little, then back again, in an effort to dodge the bombers. Bombs had to fall within fifty or so feet to cause severe damage to a ship; several times *Iceni* had disappeared entirely from view as exploding bombs prompted eruptions of water that rose high into the air and Ollie had feared the worst. Miraculously, she had come through unscathed. On the whaler, he and the men had nearly been swamped twice by spumes of water terrifyingly close by and then, as they finally neared the shore, by too many soldiers trying climb aboard, the wooden craft rocking dangerously.

Ollie had ordered his men to row back out, away from the mob, then had told the soldiers on the shore he would take them only if they did as they were told. It made little difference.

'Show them your pistol, sir,' one of his men had suggested.

Ollie had looked at him incredulously, then realized he was serious, so he pulled out his revolver and fired a shot into the air. Much to his surprise it did the trick. The soldiers moved away, allowing the whaler to reach closer to the shore, steady itself and allocate the men they were going to lift, which amounted to just twenty-two. Only two hours later, after a Dutch skoot had come alongside *Iceni* and transferred more than four hundred men did they finally turn back for England.

On the return leg they'd been attacked again out at sea, *Iceni* avoiding the bombs by zigzagging at over thirty knots. Half the men aboard had been sick; Ollie had never seen so much vomit in his life. Once at Dover, one of *Iceni*'s boilers had been in need of urgent attention; the entire ship had to be cleaned up and supplies taken on board. It had taken them two full days to be ready to sail again.

And now here they were, back at Dunkirk for their third trip, and everyone anxiously praying they would not have to sit off the beaches a second time. Ollie peered through his binoculars. A large number of small craft were now shuttling between the beaches further along at Bray-Dunes and Malo-les-Bains, most ferrying to several Channel steamers lying off-shore.

'Signal for you, Number One,' came Wymer's voice at last.

'Yes?' said Jimmy.

'SNO Dunkirk to *Iceni*. Proceed to East Mole.'

Relief. Ollie felt his shoulders relax.

'Reply, "*Iceni* to SNO Dunkirk. Your last. Affirmative."'

They glided in and drew up alongside the East Mole, if anything more gently than before.

'Get down there, will you, Sub,' said Malone, 'and make sure they come aboard in an orderly fashion. Five hundred and fifty and not a man more, all right?'

'Aye, aye, sir,' said Ollie. He hurried down the metal steps of the superstructure and out onto the deck as *Iceni* was being lashed. The mole was rammed with troops, but naval officers on the jetty were barking orders and warning the men to board in an orderly fashion. A gangway was lowered and on they came, some ashen-faced and exhausted, others laughing at their good fortune at getting a passage home.

A little under half an hour later they had their quota and Ollie ordered the gangway to be drawn back. The next in line were pleading to be allowed on.

'There are other ships coming,' said Ollie. 'Let us go now and we've a better chance of coming back.'

'Please,' said a man, his hands clasped together, beseeching him to allow him aboard. 'Please. I've got to get home to my wife and daughter.'

Another tried to scramble over the railing but was pulled back.

Ropes were hauled in, engines run up and then they were pulling away. Ollie turned to the deck, now packed with soldiers. There was a noticeable stench of sweat and grime and filth.

For the most part the men sat quietly, some anxiously scanning the skies. A number were walking wounded, bandaged heads, arms in slings, others brought in on stretchers. He thought of Michael Harrington and wondered if the image of that young man's death would ever slip out of his mind. It was horribly vivid still yet seemed a lifetime ago. In fact, it was only a month past.

After checking on Lieutenant Markham, the medical officer, Ollie headed back to the bridge to report to Malone.

'The men seem settled, Number One,' Ollie told him. 'The MO has everything under control.'

'Usual drinks issued?'

'Yes, sir.'

Malone sighed. 'We've evacuated troops from Norway and now Dunkirk. I wonder whether this will be the last evacuation we do, Sub.'

'No more troops left to evacuate, are there, sir?'

Malone laughed. 'After this lot, probably not. A good point, Sub.'

Shortly after, Ollie came off watch and headed down to his cabin. Only as he lay down on his bunk did he discover how exhausted he was. Around him, the ship continued to plough its way back to England; he could feel the turbines rumbling dully, the entire vessel throbbing. He wondered whether they would be attacked again, but he was beyond caring.

He turned over and stared at the painted steel wall of the ship. Alvesdon felt a long way off and all the more so because he was fairly certain this was just the beginning, that the war would not end any time soon and that the day, in the future, when he could go back and be with Elsa for ever, was so distant that there was almost no point in even thinking about it.

Around the same time that *Iceni* was sailing away from Dunkirk, Tom Timbrell was deposited at the King's Own Royal Guards' command post with eight other stragglers.

'Here you go, gents,' said the Carrier driver, cheerfully. 'And now I'd better get back to what I was supposed to be doing or else I'll be for the high jump.'

'Thanks,' said Tom, and shook his hand. The driver winked, turned the Carrier on a sixpence, and sped off again.

Tom and the others spotted the RSM, Blondie Barker.

'Bloody hell!' he said, hurrying over from a large barn in which a number of men were resting. 'Tom Timbrell as I live and breathe!'

'Sergeant Major,' said Tom.

'Where the hell have you been?'

Others were emerging from the barn and gathering around, the men behind Tom lighting cigarettes, shaking hands and clapping backs.

'Bit of a long story, to be honest, sir,' said Tom.

'All right. Well, you'd better come and tell the colonel.' He paused and ordered some food for the newcomers. 'We're on half rations,' he told Tom, as he led him to the farmhouse, 'but the lads will give them something.'

The farmhouse was a two-storey brick building with a steep-pitched roof. Tom noticed a hole in the tiles and signs of damage on the southern wall but otherwise it appeared to be more or less intact. Inside, around a kitchen table, were the battalion clerks. Rifles stacked up in a corner, ammunition boxes, rations, and in the dining room, maps spread out alongside a radio transmitter and receiver. Guns were booming to the south and Tom felt the building tremble as they fired, then heard the faint whistle and whoosh of passing shells.

Blondie led Tom into a back parlour in which a trestle table had been set up and behind which sat Major Burnham-Browne. Blondie saluted. 'Look who the cat brought in, sir!'

Tom saluted and came to attention.

'Sergeant Timbrell – good Lord! At ease, man.' He stood up and shook Tom's hand. 'Welcome back.'

'Thank you, sir.'

'What happened to you?'

Tom told him about how they had attacked the farmhouse by the canal, that Lieutenant Ashton had been killed and Captain Woodman wounded. How he and Guardsman Tompkins had blown the bridge and they had then sent Guardsman Small for reinforcements.

'I'm sorry to say that Small never reached us,' said Burnham-Browne. 'He's missing, just like you chaps have been.'

'I started to realize that, sir. We were very exposed. Jerry was on the other side of the canal and in numbers, and we were increasingly certain no other platoons were in line with us. We were badly hidden and reckoned that once dawn came, with no reinforcements and our own ammo runnin' low, we had no chance.' The decision weighed heavily on him, he told the colonel, but at around two in the morning, Captain Woodman came to and agreed they should pull back, although he was in a bad way from his shoulder wound and too weak to walk. They took two curtain poles from the farm-house, fed these through the arms of a pair of greatcoats and that way made a stretcher for him. Then they sneaked out of the farm-house, and went back across the stream, looking out for signs of their own lines. But there was no one – not a sign.

'I'd ordered the battalion back behind that little river you crossed. Both Two and Four Companies had taken a hammering that night and were simply too exposed on the canal. But it was a hastily pre-pared line, in darkness, and you must have inadvertently passed through a gap.'

Pickets probably asleep, thought Tom, but said, 'Yes, sir. So, we walked on and made for Messines. We paused and tried to get help for Captain Woodman. Some engineers had an MO with them and he redressed his wounds, gave us a proper stretcher and told us we should get him to one of the field hospitals at Dunkirk as quickly as possible.' Tom had told them he was looking for his battalion, but the Royal Engineers captain had said they were most likely already en route for Dunkirk. 'And if you don't get this fellow help soon,' the doctor had added, 'he's not going to make it.'

'Well, sir,' Tom told the colonel, 'Captain Woodman was awake at this point so I told him what the sappers had told me and he agreed that since we couldn't find the battalion that was what we should do. 'E didn't want to hold us up but obviously we weren't goin' to leave 'im.'

They got a lift to Poperinge but the roads leading out of the town were clogged with military traffic and hordes of refugees, and soon after they were attacked by German fighters strafing the road. They all leaped out of the truck, taking the captain with them, but Guards-man Hitchen was struck and killed. The truck was also hit and began to burn. They left Hitchen and the flaming Bedford and con-tinued on foot.

Everyone was exhausted, and Tom made them all rest in an abandoned barn. They dressed Captain Woodman's wounds again and, having slept a few hours, decided to make the most of the night and clearer roads to try to reach Dunkirk. They passed through Bergues early on the Wednesday, 29 May, and pushed on. Tom didn't mention the long road of smashed and broken vehicles, abandoned and destroyed. Or the shelled and bombed houses, the wreckage in the town. It had shocked them all.

They stopped anyone coming from the direction of the coast. Did they know where a hospital was? Where was the nearest casualty clearing station? Eventually an ambulance driver told them there was one at Bray-Dunes in the casino on the seafront. Could he take them there? Tom asked. The driver told him he had to be joking. He couldn't head back for just one man: he had an entire ambulance to fill from the front. They finally reached Bray-Dunes around midday on the Wednesday and found the casino easily enough but there was no sign of the hospital and the stores had been looted. Tom had never seen such a mess. A Navy beach officer told them the No 8 casualty clearing station had been ordered up towards Malo-les-Bains. All this time, Captain Woodman was getting weaker, slipping in and out of consciousness. There were so many men on the beaches, all heading towards the mole, that it was hard to make progress, but later in the afternoon they finally reached a warehouse just behind the Corniche where the remnants of 8 CCS were now based and waiting their turn for embarkation.

'And we had to leave Captain Woodman with them,' Tom told the colonel. 'I didn't like to but they gave him some morphine and cleaned the wound. They were concerned it was going bad.'

'And they agreed to take him with them?' asked the colonel.

'The doctor promised. Major Martin, sir, 'is name was.'

Burnham-Browne was grim-faced. 'You did the right thing, Sergeant. Well done. So, that was Wednesday and it's Friday now.'

'Yes, sir. We learned you were still in the line, so we've been trying to find you ever since. Eventually got picked up by a brigade Carrier on his way back with some ammo, sir. 'E knew where you were and gave us a lift.' He didn't mention the night in the empty house they had found or the wine they had drunk and the food they had eaten.

'Well, I have to say that's very noble of you, Sergeant. I think most men in your position might have got on the next ship home.' He stood up and put his hands on the table. *Interview over*, thought Tom. 'Well, we're due to move to Malo-les-Bains this afternoon so, with a fair wind, we'll be on our way back to Blighty soon. Possibly even tonight. We will, of course, do all we can to keep tabs on Captain Woodman's whereabouts, and, fingers crossed, his speedy recovery.'

As he was leaving, one of the clerks accosted him. 'Sergeant Timbrell?'

Tom turned. *Yes?*

'There's some post for you.'

'Here?'

The clerk chuckled. 'I know. Beats me. Anyway, here. Three letters.' Tom saw the first was from his father, so tucked it and the other two into his battle blouse, then went back out into the yard and found Lieutenant Robbins. The battalion had lost half its number over the past ten days and 2 Company had been merged with No 3. Robbins was now acting combined company commander.

'So, as you can imagine,' said Robbins, 'I'm delighted to see the eight of you. Almost doubles my men.'

Ahead, no more than a mile away, Tom guessed, heavy firing could be heard: machine-guns and rifles, tinny on the afternoon air, while the thunder of the guns continued, the ground pulsing with each blast and ripple of fire.

Tom found a quiet spot in the orchard beyond the barn and sat down under an apple tree with some dry rations he'd been given and a packet of smokes. The cloud that had descended over Flanders was clearing at last and warm sunshine shone down on him. Despite the boom of battle, a bumblebee buzzed past him and a thrush was singing somewhere nearby. Tom smiled to himself, then remembered the letters. He'd assumed they'd all been from his father but one was addressed to him in unfamiliar handwriting. Carefully, using his clasp knife, he slit the envelope, took out the single sheet of folded paper, and began to read, his heart quickening. 'Blow me!' he mumbled to himself. *Hannah*. And, for the first time in an age, Tom's spirits soared.

Saturday, 1 June 1940

The squadron were back over Dunkirk again, and for the first time, Wilf could look down from clear skies at the entire battleground. Black smoke still billowed from the fuel depots beyond the port but he could clearly see the long finger of creamy sand stretching far into Belgium. Even from twenty thousand feet he spotted ships in the water and a line of vessels heading across the sea.

He continuously turned his head, glanced in his mirror and scanned the skies. What a lot he'd learned during this week of fighting: that one had to get in close before firing, far closer than the 450 yards prescribed in training; that it was jolly bad luck on poor Pete Partington, but that Bluey Thompson was a far better squadron commander. He was more open to new ideas, and less wedded to older fighter tactics that had been valid in the biplane days but were hopeless when applied to modern fighters. That close formation was helpful when trying to stick together but needed loosening the moment enemy aircraft were spotted. And the vital need for concentration at all times and keeping one's eyes peeled. It was the aircraft one didn't spot that was the greatest threat. It had occurred to him that while chance always played a part and one might get an unlucky bullet, skill and common sense would unquestionably improve his chance of survival, perhaps more for a fighter pilot than in any other form of air combat. He didn't want to be caught out through carelessness.

He now spotted a formation of bombers heading in low along the coast, but they were too far away; in any case, a second squadron was operating several thousand feet below him and was better placed to deal with them. Sure enough, he spotted them peel off and dive. Another scan around the sky for any fighters, but he could see nothing. They circled for a further twenty minutes, then headed for home. He glanced at his watch. It was nearly 7 p.m.

Waiting in the dunes at Malo-les-Bains were the King's Own Royal Guards. It had been a frustrating twenty-four hours: they had been about to depart for Dunkirk the previous evening when they'd been called up to help plug a hole in a canal line where the enemy was

295

threatening to break through. Off they'd headed, back into the fray, everyone muttering and grumbling. After all, it wasn't the first time they'd been recalled and then flung into battle; no one needed reminding about what had happened four days earlier.

They'd taken up positions around a barn and a farmhouse overlooking the canal and almost immediately found themselves fighting off another attack. It was during this fight that Tom had been hit as he'd been signalling to his platoon. He'd held up his arm and suddenly been stung, a searing, stabbing pain. As soon as he'd looked, he saw a bullet had gone straight through his left forearm and out the other side. It had bled a lot and hurt like hell, and the back of his arm was a mess, but the MO had administered an anti-tetanus shot, a sulphonamide pill, a mug of sugary tea, then bandaged him up and given him a sling. 'You'll need surgery on that,' the MO told him, 'but you'll do for now.'

Not long after that the fighting had died down. The Germans didn't like fighting at night, apparently. Then had come orders to move to Malo-les-Bains after all, so they had all trudged off, the Carriers and what trucks were left taking all their kit, remaining ammunition and rations, leaving the men to head off on their own two feet.

They'd been in the dunes at the edge of the town to witness not only a beautiful sunrise but a scene of utter desolation and mayhem as half a dozen Heinkel 111 bombers had swept in low just as four destroyers were leaving Dunkirk. Three of the ships were hit, thick, angry smoke billowing from them, their pom-poms and main guns booming and spattering the sky with smudges of flak to no avail. All three went down soon after. Tom had watched them sinking; they all had. The screams of the men burning, drowning, floundering in the water, had drifted across to them on the morning breeze.

Tom had seen the beaches once already but then his mind had been on getting Captain Woodman to safety and they had been thronging with troops. Now, those to the east were empty as the perimeter had shrunk. In the far distance, he spotted the remnants of a makeshift jetty of abandoned trucks. Other vehicles littered the sand. The tide was out, and in front lay a beached destroyer, its back broken so that its bow stood split and bent as though a giant axeman had sliced off its head. Other boats, most smaller, lay sunken, some weighed down by sand, others in pieces. Everywhere he looked there was detritus. He saw a body being rolled about by the breakers at the edge of the sea. *Bloody hell*, he thought. No one said much. What was there to say?

A naval officer came around and told them they would be called to move up to the mole when they were ready to embark them. Until then, he said, they should keep their heads down and try to get some rest. Tom had prayed they would wait until dark when they might be protected by the cloak of night. As the morning wore on, more bombers came over. They had watched as a hospital ship neared and was straddled by bombs so that the vessel entirely disappeared from view. When the bombs and water subsided they watched her turn and sail away again.

Tom saw two of the little boats ferrying men from the beaches disintegrate and parts of them – and men – blasted into the air by a cluster of bombs that fell on and around them. A Spitfire was shot down, but so, too, were a number of enemy aircraft. A Messerschmitt and a Spitfire streaked over, machine-guns rattling, then disappeared. And always the guns, booming, thundering, shaking the ground. Bringing ever more destruction.

During a lull in the afternoon, Tom took the opportunity to check on the warehouse where he'd left Captain Woodman. Corporal Souch offered to go with him so together they picked their way through the back-streets, clambering over the rubble and dodging bomb craters. Collapsed buildings. Shells of houses. Telegraph poles askew and blasted, cables snaking like eels on the road. They stepped over them carefully, even though all electricity had been cut off. And everywhere abandoned vehicles: burned-out trucks, bomb-damaged trucks, trucks in half, trucks with their tyres slashed and radiators staved in.

'Jesus,' muttered Souch, but soon after they found the warehouse they'd been to two days earlier. No one was there. A few empty boxes of medical supplies and rations, a shredded and abandoned stretcher. A stench of blood and death. But that was all. No sign of Captain Woodman.

'I wonder if he's back already,' muttered Tom.

'I hope so after all that effort to keep the bugger alive.'

'I liked him,' said Tom. ''E were a good sort.'

'I reckon I'll be dead soon if I don't get something to drink,' said Souch. 'I'm bloody parched.'

Tom still had a bit left in his water bottle. ''Ere,' he said, passing it over. 'Don't drink it all, mind.'

They left the warehouse and wandered back through the streets, looking into the empty houses for food or drink, but clearly other troops had been there before them. Their scrounging had taken them on a different route back onto the dunes, and lying beside a crater they found two dead French soldiers. Souch immediately dropped beside them, took a water bottle from the first and drank greedily. The second man's flask was also almost full. 'One good turn deserves another,' he said, throwing it to Tom.

They had then rejoined the rest of the men. The urge was to get onto the beaches, closer to the mole, but Tom realized that so long as he lay flat whenever an aircraft came over and kept himself clear of any blast as far as he could, only a direct hit would do for him. Again he prayed they wouldn't be called until after dark. Until then, he told himself, he'd lie low. And then he'd get on a ship. Come what may. He looked down at his bloodied arm. It hurt like hell, but it occurred to him it might well be a ticket home, so maybe he'd been lucky after all.

It was just after midnight on the morning of Sunday, 2 June that *Iceni* pulled in alongside HMS *Windsor*. Ahead, another destroyer, *Icarus,* was lashed against the Channel steamer *Maid of Orleans*. Lieutenant Commander Bertie had been clear: the evacuation was being accelerated during the hours of darkness. This was their seventh trip and they were now old hands. 'No time for complacency,' he'd told the entire crew over the ship's Tannoy as they set sail, 'but we need to be quick and efficient. We get the men on board and get the hell out of there.'

Ollie was on watch and on deck as they lashed up against *Windsor*. Ahead, the town of Dunkirk was burning, glowing orange in the night; he could see the cathedral and town buildings silhouetted jaggedly against the sky. What a tragedy, he thought.

On the mole, officers were barking orders.

'Straight across, now! Keep going!'

The first men crossed the gang plank from *Windsor*, dark figures, faceless in the night, only the flicker of the burning town casting any light on them. The crew were on hand to usher them to left and right and down into the wardrooms.

'That's it,' said Ollie. 'Keep going. Sooner you're on the sooner we can leave.'

'I recognize that voice.' A tall man paused beside him, clear of the others clambering aboard.

'Tom?' said Ollie.

Tom laughed. 'Mr Ollie! Well I bloody never!'

'It's very good to see you, Tom,' said Ollie, and was about to shake his hand then saw his sling.

'Anything serious?'

'Hope not.'

'You're still standing at any rate.'

'Come on, keep going there!' called an officer aboard *Windsor*.

'You'd better cut along,' Ollie told Tom, 'but I'll come and find you. Head to the bow.'

It was just after half past midnight that they started engines again, pulled in the ropes and moved away from *Windsor*. Gently, they reversed out and, once clear of the mole, turned. Once more Ollie felt the turbines open up and *Iceni* start to speed away. Down in the wardroom he grabbed a flask of cocoa and some corned-beef sandwiches, then picked his way through the men until he reached the bow. Tom was sitting beneath the forward X-Gun mount but stood up when he spotted Ollie.

'Here,' Ollie said, handing him a sandwich.

'Thank you.'

Ollie watched him eat hungrily. 'How bad is the arm?'

'Bullet clean through. A proper Blighty wound. Should be all right, I reckon. To be honest, I'm hoping it'll lay me off soldiering for a little while.'

Ollie smiled, envying him. He turned to look back at the port, Tom following his gaze.

'I don't mind telling you,' said Tom, 'I'll be happy if I never see that place again.'

'Yes. Seven times is plenty for me.'

Tom whistled. 'You've got everyone off, then?'

'Pretty much, I think. A miracle, really.'

'I tell you what,' said Tom. 'There's only one place I want to go right now.'

'Alvesdon?' said Ollie.

'Yes,' said Tom. 'Home.'

26

Matters of the Heart

DIANA WOODMAN HAD LEARNED HER BROTHER WAS MISSING. TESS had arrived home to find her in tears, although had struggled to weep herself. Somehow, she supposed, she had already got used to the idea. She felt sad, depressed even, but it had been such a long time since she had seen him and their time together had been so very brief. She remembered when he had first kissed her – it had been at a party when she had first come to London. That had been the beginning of August last year. Then they had had dinner several times and gone dancing, and she vividly remembered the intense excitement and thrill of such a handsome and likeable fellow treating her with so much attention. It had been all so new. And then had come Aldeburgh and that last weekend at Alvesdon before the war. That was it. She'd felt in love, and he was in her thoughts constantly, but there had been so much to think about since then.

'But what does it mean?' Diana had asked her. 'Missing?'

'It means he's become separated from the rest of his unit,' Tess had told her, sitting next to her on Diana's bed. 'I know it's hard, but we must try not to worry too much until we know more. And we certainly mustn't think the worst.' Did her words give any comfort? Tess wasn't sure. She knew that if Wilf or Edward was missing she would be inconsolable. Far more so than she was about Alex, at any rate.

Yet the following Sunday, she returned to the house in Pimlico to find Diana in jubilant mood. 'Oh, Tess, he's alive!' she said, running to her and flinging her arms around Tess's neck the moment she opened the door. 'I can hardly believe it! He's been wounded, but he's going to be all right.'

And at that moment Tess felt a strange swell of emotion, from deep within her, sweep up through her body and she knew she could not control it. 'That's – that's the most marvellous news,' she said, and really it was. Then she put her hands to her face and began to sob. She couldn't help it. In truth, she couldn't understand it either.

'It's all right,' said Diana, clearly rather dumbfounded but holding Tess to her.

'I'm sorry,' blurted Tess. 'I don't know why I'm crying, it's just . . .' She stopped trying to talk and wept some more, clinging to Diana until she gradually began to recover.

'Are you all right, Tess?' Diana said at length, peering at her.

Tess nodded.

'Let's have a drink. A little brandy.'

Tess nodded again and went into their little kitchen at the back of the house. 'Oh, my goodness,' she said, wiping her face as Diana handed her a small tumbler. She took it, sipped, felt the spirit burn her throat and, sighing, felt a little better. 'Honestly, I don't know what came over me.' She forced a smile. 'It's wonderful news. I think it was the relief. That he's all right, that the Army is all right, that the evacuation has been such a miraculous success.'

'You're also overtired,' said Diana. 'You're exhausted, Tess. Think of those hours you've been doing.'

'I am tired,' she admitted.

'I never like to pry, but I'm sure you must see all sorts in your job. And with a lot of responsibility. The pressure to get things right.'

Tess rubbed her eyes again. 'I must look a sight. But it's the most wonderful news. Where is he?'

'At Guy's Hospital apparently. Will you come with me to visit him?'

'Don't you want to see him alone?'

Diana took her hand. 'No. I'd rather you were with me.'

'What about your parents?'

'They're planning to come down from Yorkshire tomorrow.'

Tess nodded. 'All right,' she said.

She really didn't feel all right, though. She felt upset and something else besides. And then, as they sat on the bus together, crossing Lambeth Bridge, she realized what the uncomfortable sensation in her stomach was. She was nervous about seeing Alex again.

The last time Tess had been in a hospital was when her mother had given birth to her at the infirmary in Salisbury. Now she was struck by the calm efficiency of the place and the almost overpowering smell of carbolic. It appeared spotless and she wondered how much time must be spent cleaning and scrubbing the place from top to bottom.

'You can't stay long,' the ward sister told them. 'He needs rest and there are others to consider too.' She looked at her watch. 'Twenty minutes. No more.'

The heavy ward doors swung open and they followed the woman. It was a long room, with a high ceiling and a linoleum floor. There were wounded soldiers in every bed, one with so many bandages around his head that all Tess could see was a nose and mouth. Some were asleep; others sitting up. One man said, 'Have you come to see me, ladies? Come and sit by me. Please?' Tess felt herself redden.

'Pipe down there, Mr Lawrence,' said the sister.

Alex was at the end and asleep. He looked pale and tired, thought Tess, but otherwise much as she remembered him. She couldn't see his wound, which was covered by his pyjamas. The sister drew a curtain around them, then woke Alex with a gentle shake of his left shoulder. He blinked, looked at them both with shock, then grinned. 'My two favourite girls! What a treat!'

'I'll leave you to it, then,' said the sister. 'Twenty minutes.'

'Alex,' said Diana, 'are you all right? You've had us all so worried.'

'I was a bit worried myself,' he said. 'I can't tell you how good it is to see you.' He made a move to sit up.

'No, don't,' said Diana. 'Where are you wounded?'

He tapped his left shoulder and winced. 'Good job I'm right-handed.' He shuffled himself up and Diana lifted a pillow for him.

'Sorry,' he said, the pain obvious, 'this is damnable.' He sighed, smiled, and said, 'Please, both of you, do sit down.'

There was a chair beside him so Diana took it and Alex motioned to Tess to sit on the bed. She did so gingerly, feeling unaccountably shy. He extended his hand towards her, and Tess took it, feeling its warmth in hers. 'What happened, Alex? Was it very terrifying?'

He sighed. 'It was bloody. We lost a lot of good chaps. First defending a river. Well, more of a canal really. And then when the Belgians surrendered, we had to fill a gap in the line and throw back the enemy. We were trying to take a farmhouse and I got a bullet through the shoulder.' Tess didn't know what to say, so she gently squeezed his hand.

'I don't remember too much of that night. It was Tom Timbrell who saved me.'

'Tom?' said Tess. But she knew he was missing too.

'Yes, I knew he'd make a damn fine soldier. And I wasn't wrong. He's been the outstanding man in the company. I'm afraid I wasn't much good for anything after I'd been hit but somehow he got us out of that farmhouse and back to Dunkirk. Honestly, I don't remember a lot of it. I was pretty groggy, I don't mind admitting. But he got me to Dunkirk and found a doctor, who patched me up and got me on a boat home. I owe Tom and that doctor my life. I don't even know whether he made it back. I hope he did.'

'I suppose we'll know soon enough,' said Tess, thinking she would try to find out the next day at work.

'My poor brother,' said Diana. 'Does it hurt terribly?'

'It's not too bad. Doped up to my eyeballs. I'm trying to look on the bright side. I'm alive, they tell me I should make a full recovery and I'm going to have to spend a bit of time getting back to full fitness.'

'Of course! The Army can't have you back for a while.'

'Yes,' said Alex. 'Some time off.' He looked at Tess, smiled and squeezed her hand. 'I've missed you.'

Tess knew he was waiting for her to say the same. She put her hand on his cheek. 'I'm so glad you're safe. That you've come back to us.'

'And you'll come again?'

'Of course.'

He closed his eyes. 'I'm sorry – I'm not much company.'

'We'll let you get some rest, Alex,' said Diana. She got up and kissed his head.

'But you'll come back?' he said sleepily.

'Yes. Every day.'

Back out on the street, the sun shone on a glorious summer's day, the plane trees on the South Bank in full leaf and casting dappled shadows on the promenade. People were out and about. A tug passed down the river. Pigeons swooped and fluttered, looking for scraps around a street hawker selling nuts. Diana chatted happily but Tess barely heard her.

'Are you all right, Tess?' said Diana, stopping and turning to face her.

'Yes, yes, fine,' said Tess. 'Sorry. I don't know what the matter is. The shock of seeing him, I suppose. And it's been quite a week, hasn't it?' She suddenly felt immensely tired and wanted very much to be alone. *Perk up*, she told herself, and threaded her arm into Diana's. 'It's so wonderful he's back,' she said, trying to sound buoyant.

Yet later, lying in bed that night, her mind ran over and over the same thought: that far from feeling ecstatic about Alex's return it had left her feeling unsettled in a way she could not quite understand.

Tuesday evening, 4 June 1940

The wireless was on in the kitchen at Alvesdon Manor. It was a small Bakelite model that Alwyn Castell had presented to Jean Gulliver in an act of tremendous benefaction shortly after the German attack on Norway. 'You need to be able to hear the news in these historic days,' Mr Castell had told her. She had thanked him profusely and professed it was the kindest gift anyone had ever given her.

'No, no, Mrs G,' he had said, 'it's nothing less than you deserve.'

That it had been given to Mr Castell by Mr and Mrs Stork for Christmas two years ago had not been lost on either Jean or Hannah; or that Denholm had given him a bigger, smarter and more ornate model for his last birthday. No matter the provenance, however, both had enjoyed having it in the kitchen with them.

Now, as Hannah helped Jean prepare the evening's dinner, they listened to the six o'clock news in silence. It was dominated by a recording of the speech the Prime Minister had made to the Commons earlier that afternoon.

'An' to think they expected only thirty thousand at most to be rescued,' said Jean. 'It's a miracle. Three hundred and thirty-five thousand, did 'e say? Well, I never did.' She eyed Hannah. 'Wonder where young Tom Timbrell is.'

Hannah said nothing and continued peeling the potatoes. 'Mr Churchill means business, though,' she said, at length. 'D'you think they'll try and invade? I can't believe it somehow.'

Jean shrugged. 'There's no knowin' what goes in 'Itler's dark mind. If someone went an' bumped him off they'd be doin' the world a great favour.' She peered out of the kitchen window at the yard, the fields beyond and, in the distance, Tippett's Wood. 'An' such a beautiful evening. Can't imagine there being a war on at all on a day like this.'

Churchill finished his speech, promising to fight on the beaches and in the hills and never surrender.

''E does mean business an' good for 'im for saying so,' said Jean. 'You got to stand up to bullies, and Hitler and his Nazis are certainly those.'

Hannah thought of Denholm and felt a resurgence of anger. 'Yes,' she said, slicing through a particularly large potato. 'I don't like bullies either.' She stopped a moment, then said, 'Jean, what d'you s'pose will 'appen to Mrs John? She's ever so gentle a lady. I think it's wrong that she's bein' punished for being a German.'

'I dunno, my love. But I agree. Bain't right. Why she might still have a bit of an accent, I s'pose, but she's as English as you or I now in her ways, and those kiddies of hers are lovely children. Why, Elsa's quite the little English rose. They should leave 'er be. Let's 'ope they do.'

The news ended and a programme of music followed. Jean began making her pie and hummed along for a few bars then said, 'Well, I want to know 'ow young Tom is even if you don't.'

'I never said I didn't,' replied Hannah, just a little too quickly.

'So, why is it you always go so silent whenever 'is name is mentioned?'

Hannah stopped what she was doing. All these years she'd held

306

to herself her feelings for Tom and never told a soul. Not one. But sometimes she thought she might burst with the burden of keeping the secret to herself. Should she now confess all to Jean? One part of her brain told her not to, but another urged her to do just that. What if Jean laughed at her? Or told someone else? She trusted her on most things but people did prattle so. What if Jean let it slip to Susan? She wouldn't be able to bear that.

Hannah stared at the chopping board but her eyes were not focusing on it. Another part of her desperately wanted to tell her. Get her advice. Jean was a woman of the world. She might be able to help. *A problem shared is a problem halved*, she was fond of saying.

'Hannah, my love?' said Jean. 'You goin' to stare at that old board all evenin'?'

Hannah shot her a glance and she blurted, 'I wrote to him.'

Jean's face softened. 'Well, that was nice of you.'

'No, you don't understand. I *wrote* to him. So now he knows.'

'Knows what?'

Hannah wiped her brow and looked around the room, exasperation sweeping over her. This was harder than she had thought but there was now no turning back. 'That I'm sweet on 'im.' She looked at Jean imploringly, but she was now placing the pastry on the top of the pie.

'That I love 'im.' She sighed and slapped her hand on the table. 'Oh, what 'ave I said?' She was shaking her head now and could feel herself blushing.

'I know you do, my pet.'

Hannah stared at her incredulously. 'You do?'

Jean laughed. 'Why, yes, of course!'

'How? How could you know?'

Jean walked over to her and put her arms around her. 'I may seem like an old woman to you, but I was young and in love once. I know the signs. I caught you starin' at him many a time. The crossness on your face whenever Miss Edie talked to 'im. That you started blushin' if he ever spoke to you.'

'And you never said nothin'?'

'It weren't my place. You'd tell me if you wanted to an' now you have and I'm very glad.'

'And you won't . . . ?'

307

'Won't breathe a word or tell a soul. What d'you take me for? Think I'd go tellin' Susan Smallpiece, did you?'

Hannah felt rather sheepish. 'I'm jus' scared. Scared of being made to look a fool.'

'So, you'd rather keep it buried inside and not take the risk? Rather deny yourself?'

'No, of course not, it's just . . .' She stopped.

Jean was now pressing down the pastry around the edge of the dish with a fork. 'I reckon you've both been as bad as each other. He's sweet on you too; I seen the way 'e looks at you. And why wouldn't he be? You're the prettiest thing in the entire village, Hannah. And you've a heart o' gold. There's no bad in you. Why, Tom would be mad not to sweep you up and hold on to you for ever.'

Hannah felt a tear prick at the edge of one eye. 'That's the loveliest thing anyone's ever said to me. Thank you.'

'Come 'ere,' said Jean, holding out her arms.

Hannah stood up and let herself be held. She breathed in deeply. 'I don't know if he even got my letter. I don't know where he is or if he's . . .'

'Shush, shush, shush,' said Jean. 'Let's not have none of that talk. Tom's someone who can look after 'imself. 'E'll be all right. And 'e'll be back too. You mark my words.'

Hannah held her a little more tightly. 'Thank you.'

'You're most welcome. And now let's get back to it. We've a dinner to get ready.'

At Farrowcombe, Stork and Debbo had also been listening to Churchill's speech.

'Good on him,' Stork said. 'Of course we should fight on. And of course we should never surrender. Why would we?'

'I heard people muttering about it at Pierson's earlier,' said Debbo. They were in the drawing room, she half-heartedly reading and Stork flitting between listening to the wireless and reading War Ag papers sent over by William Price.

'Really? Saying what?'

'That we were for the high jump and that if France couldn't stop

308

the Germans how on earth were we going to? That it would be better to pack it in now before it was too late.'

'Who the devil was saying that?'

'I forget.'

'No, you don't, Debbo, you know perfectly well. Come on, out with it.'

Debbo sighed and put down her book. 'No. It doesn't matter. And I'm not going to tell you anyway.'

'People like that deserve tarring, feathering and being run out of town.'

'Which is precisely why I'm not telling you. But people are scared, Stork darling. And some believe peace is better than war.'

'Peace is always better than war,' said Stork, 'but slavery is worse than anything. Even death. Anyway,' he said, pretending to turn back to his papers, 'I'm glad Churchill mentioned the sterling efforts of the RAF and the Navy.'

'I do hope Wilf's all right. I can't bear the thought of him flying over there. I've already been through that with you the last time around.'

Stork set aside his papers. 'I know.' He sighed. 'I try to put it all out of my mind and concentrate on work, but it's damnably hard.'

'And what about the French?' said Debbo. 'They're finished, aren't they?'

Stork nodded. 'I fear so.'

'And Denholm?'

'With a bit of luck, he'll stay there.'

'Oh, Stork, you don't mean that! And poor Coco and Lucie? You can't possibly wish them to be trapped there by the Nazis. And it could be very awkward for Denholm – an Englishman trapped in France. You know how worried your parents are about him.'

He got up irritably and poured himself another whisky and soda from the sideboard. 'You want another, darling?'

'Yes, please,' said Debbo.

'Of course,' he said, handing her the drink, 'I don't want him to get into difficulties, and I certainly don't wish him ill, but life is always a lot better when he's not around, as you well know.'

Stork had only heard from his older brother once since last summer and that was a brief telegram acknowledging Stork's own message about Alwyn's stroke. For his part, Stork had written to him three times, as well as sending a card at Christmas. There had been nothing in return. He sat down again. 'But I'd put very good money on him getting out of there. He'll have something up his sleeve.'

The telephone rang, which, in recent weeks, had always made them start.

'I'm sure it's nothing,' said Stork, glancing anxiously at Debbo and getting up. He strode into the hall and picked up the receiver.

'Yes, hello?'

'Stork, it's me.'

'John – are you all right, old boy?'

'No, no, I'm not. It's Carin.'

'What's happened?'

'We've just had Jack Allbrook round. It was good of him, really, to warn us. He says he's been told by the Wilton police that they're sending someone round tomorrow to take Carin.'

'They're what?' He was conscious of Debbo now beside him.

'They're taking her away, Stork. They're interning her. They're taking my darling Carin. Oh, Stork, what are we going to do?'

27

Departures and Arrivals

COCO CASTELL HAD BEEN LISTENING TO THE NEWS AS WELL. THE British Army had finally left, gone back across the Channel, it was reported. A few British troops remained but France was now alone. One by one, her Allies had crumbled, but France would fight on. The French armies were readying themselves for a major counter-attack across the River Somme. Honour would be restored, defeat averted.

Coco switched off the wireless and wandered out onto the terrace under the bougainvillaea that covered much of the front wall of the villa. She found Lucie lying on a lounger reading a novel. It was a warm evening. Ahead of them, not a couple of miles away, the dark blue Mediterranean shimmered in the evening light. Cicadas clicked and whistled in the trees that surrounded the villa.

She walked over towards Lucie and stood in front of her, leaning on the balustrade, looking out over a view so familiar yet, she worried, might now be threatened. 'Where's Papa?' she asked.

Lucie put down her book. She was a striking woman: dark Mediterranean hair, lean face and sharp, neat nose and mouth.

Lucie shrugged. 'Out.'

'He's up to something.' Coco turned to face her stepmother. 'Do you think France is finished?'

'On the battlefield? Maybe. The sooner they sign an armistice the better and then we can get on with life.'

'You can't mean that?'

311

'Why not? The Germans want to humiliate France. They don't want to run the country. What possible benefit could there be to them?'

'But they would surely station troops here, insist on a puppet government and strip us bare?'

'Any government has to be better than the lot we've had the last few years. It's been chaos. You know it has. All those different parties, right wing, left wing, Communists. Now, that's something to worry about. God help us if the Communists were to get into power.' Lucie eyed her. 'Or do you think that would be a good thing? The Communists would take this from us to start with. You can bet on it.'

'And what about Papa? What if Britain is still at war and he's here? What if the Nazis arrest him?'

'Oh, really, Coco! None of this has happened yet. The British will probably make peace too. They have just lost their army, haven't they? Or their guns at any rate. Why spoil a perfectly pleasant evening?'

She didn't feel like arguing with Lucie but the gnawing sense of dread had not gone away. She decided to go for a swim to calm herself, but when her father reappeared she was determined to find out what he was up to. She wanted reassurance but, as she swam the first length of the pool, thought she was unlikely to get it. That was why she'd not talked to her father properly since his trip to Paris two weeks earlier: she was worried she'd not want to hear what he told her.

The detectives arrived at Rose Bower at seven o'clock the next morning. Initially brusque and businesslike, they quickly softened after witnessing the family's distress. John was angry, as angry as Carin had ever seen him.

'You've got a bloody nerve coming here like this,' he told them. 'I fought in the last war to uphold freedom and I've nephews and a godson fighting for freedom at this very moment. But what the hell did I do it for? So England can turn into a police state?'

'I'm sorry, sir, but can we please come in for a moment?'

'No, you damn well can't and my wife's not coming either. She's lived here twenty years and raised our *English* children. This is absolutely ridiculous. It's abominable.'

Carin pulled at her husband's arm. 'John, darling, don't, please. You'll only make matters worse.'

'She's right, sir. Come on, now.'

She had packed a case – a few of her favourite clothes, some photographs and some books. A few trinkets. Precious things. Jack Allbrook had seemed to think that would be all right. Behind her, Elsa was distraught and now pushed through and confronted the detectives.

'Please,' she said, tears running down her cheeks. 'Please don't do this.'

The taller detective softened. 'I'm sorry, love,' he said. 'I don't make the rules.'

'But you can't – you can't take her. She's my *mother*.'

'Oh, God, no!' John clutched his hair, then hugged Carin. 'Don't leave me. Don't leave us.'

Carin had been determined to keep her composure but the finality of this moment, the helplessness and grief of her husband and daughter were suddenly too much to bear. She felt her legs buckle beneath her and she collapsed onto the rug that ran down the hallway and sobbed convulsively. She felt John and Elsa around her and then a tug at her shoulder.

'Come along now,' said one of the men. 'Or you'll start me off too.'

This is it, she thought, her sobs subsiding. She gulped, her chest heaved, and she pushed herself up and back onto her feet.

'I have to go,' she said, to John and Elsa. She hugged John, then Elsa. She could hardly bear to look at them. 'Take care of each other. And have hope. It won't be for ever.' She felt herself pull away from them, felt their touch lessen and separate. So, this was it. John was leaning against the wall, head in his hands, Elsa staring at her, hands to her face, aghast, scarcely believing.

'That's it, ma'am,' said the taller detective. 'Best not to look back.'

Then she was at the car, a black saloon, a door was being opened for her and she got in, placing her case beside her. *Don't look*, she told herself. *Don't look back*. Ignition on, engine rumbling into life. Into gear, brake off and then the car was moving, moving away from her home, from her family. She looked out, a last glimpse of the life she had known for twenty years, the home she had made, the family she had created. And it struck her how very pretty it was, the house with its thatched roof, its brick pathway to the front door, lined by lavender bushes and the roses climbing up the front of the pink brickwork, some already starting to bloom. It was, she thought, so very, very English.

Thursday, 6 June 1940

Tess went into work early as normal but that morning Ismay arrived before either Bill Elliott, Ian Jacob or any of his aides and paused by her desk before he went into his office.

'Those the morning papers, Tess?'

'Yes, sir.'

'Thank you. I'll take them now.' He leafed through them, then glanced down at her. 'Are you all right? Please don't take this the wrong way but you look all washed out. Is that brother of yours all right?'

Tess nodded. 'Yes. He was over Dunkirk but he's still in one piece, thank goodness.'

'I'm very glad to hear it. I expect a lot of you, of all of you, but you've been marvellous, Tess. I'm very grateful. I know it's not been easy.'

'Thank you, sir.' Exhaustion swept over her and she worried she might cry. She'd not had a day off since Norway, but the constant worry, Alex's return and now the ghastly news about Aunt Carin had left her drained and out of sorts. She knew she needed to pick herself up, but her *joie de vivre* had deserted her.

Ismay eyed her and said, 'Is there anything else, Tess? Anything particularly troubling you?'

She bit her lip, wondering whether she should speak to him about her aunt.

'Tess? I'm not going to bite, you know.'

She looked up at him. *All right*, she thought. 'It's my aunt, sir. My uncle John's wife. She's German and she's just been interned. But she's lived here for twenty years, has raised my cousins and lived with my uncle back home in Wiltshire all my life. We're all fighting so hard for our freedom but she's had her freedom taken away. It's wrong.'

'Ah,' said Ismay.

314

'She was classified B at a tribunal because her father and brother in Bavaria are members of the Nazi Party, but she's not like that. She's the loveliest, kindest person I've ever met. We all adore her.'

Ismay was silent a moment, then said, 'I don't need to tell you how serious our situation is at present. We've just witnessed something of a miracle but as you know we now face the imminent loss of our ally and possibly even an invasion. I pray God it won't come to that, and I'm sure if Hitler tries it, we'll prevail. But we've lost nearly all our guns, tanks and vehicles in Flanders. We have an army still but not much with which to fight. It's a perilous situation we find ourselves in. We cannot take any chances.'

Tess nodded. 'I understand that, sir.'

'Of course you do. But I'll admit, Tess, it does sound like your aunt should never have been given a B classification. I can't promise anything, but let me look into it. And I also want you to take a few days off. Go home this evening and don't come back until next Tuesday.'

Tess smiled weakly. 'Thank you, sir. Thank you very much.'

Tess had not visited Alex since Sunday but after work she decided she would pay him another call before she headed home to Wiltshire. She walked over Westminster Bridge and along the South Bank, her spirits rising a little at the prospect of a weekend in Alvesdon.

Above her, the barrage balloons shone silvery in the afternoon sunshine. There were plenty of people out and about and she detected no sense of mass panic for all the invasion talk and warnings on the wireless of how people should react if German paratroopers suddenly descended from the sky. Looking at London that afternoon, people going about their business, it seemed to Tess a fantastical notion.

As had been discussed in a Chiefs of Staff meeting earlier that day, which she had minuted, the Germans could not mount an invasion overnight. They would need shipping, airfields brought up to the Channel coast, and almost certainly have to finish off France first. In fact, it had been the French who were causing the most concern by the time she left Richmond Terrace. According to Ismay, ageing French generals were now running the show. After lunch, she had taken notes on an informal meeting held by Ismay with his team. Marshal Pétain, the old French hero of the First World War, apparently had General Weygand, the French commander, wrapped around his little finger and both were ganging up against Reynaud.

'The French are nothing short of outrageous,' Ismay had told them. 'Without one word of gratitude for all their troops we've rescued from Dunkirk they continue to sling mud at us. And now Pétain is saying that unless we send more fighter planes France will have to capitulate.'

'What the French need,' said Bill Elliott, 'is some young blood. They're all too bloody old. Weygand's in his seventies and Pétain's eighty. They're has-beens, too scarred by the last war.' Ismay had agreed. He'd been spitting – Tess had rarely seen him so incensed, yet had got the distinct impression that none of them thought an invasion to be imminent for all the scaremongering in the press or even for the warning Ismay had given her that morning. In any case, she told herself, she would hardly have been given the weekend off if the Germans were expected to land in the next few days.

She stopped near Guy's to buy Alex some chocolate and a detective novel, then headed into the hospital. 'He's popular today,' the nurse told her, as she led Tess to Alex's ward. Sure enough, a soldier was sitting in the chair beside Alex, his arm in a sling. As she drew near, she saw it was Tom Timbrell.

'Tom!' she exclaimed, a little too loudly.

He stood up and grinned. 'Miss Tess,' he said, holding out his hand.

'Goodness, Tom, how wonderful to see you. What happened?'

'Bullet through my arm, but it's nothing too serious. They've told me I can go home.'

She leaned over and kissed Alex's cheek. 'Gosh,' she said, 'I hardly know where to start.' She gave Alex the chocolate and the book.

Tom said, 'I'll leave you two to it, then.'

'Wait,' said Tess. 'Are you going back to Alvesdon?'

'Yes, miss, I'm planning to take the train.'

'I'm heading down there too. We can go together. We can give you a lift from the station.'

Tom nodded. 'Thank you, I'm much obliged to you.' He looked a little embarrassed, so said, 'You'll be wanting some time together. Why don't I wait for you outside the main entrance?'

'All right.' She turned to Alex. 'I hope you don't mind. I'm only going for the weekend. I'm sorry to abandon you, but I've not been home since Easter.'

'Of course,' said Alex. 'Will you visit again next week?'

'I promise.'

'The doc says I'll be here for a while longer. The wound was going a bit gammy, apparently, so they need to keep a bit of a watch on me.'

'Well, you must do exactly as they say.'

'I know, but when I'm back up and on my feet again, will you let me take you away? We've so much to catch up on, Tess. I can't tell you how much I've missed you.'

She smiled at him and ran a hand through his hair. 'I'd like that very much,' she said. It wasn't exactly a promise. She just needed time. Time to get used to him being back. Time to consider whether she could again find the spark – the intense romance – she had felt before war had arrived and spoiled everything.

Much to his embarrassment, Tess bought Tom a second-class ticket so they could sit together on the way down to Salisbury. He couldn't help thinking how much the war had changed things already. Before it, he wouldn't have dreamed of sharing a carriage with Miss Tess, and he strongly suspected she wouldn't have thought to share one with him either.

They talked a little about the war but he could tell she was trying not to pry and he didn't want to talk of it too much. What had happened out there, he reckoned, he should try to keep out there. Instead, he asked about the family and for news from home and she told him about Carin Castell. He was shocked. 'That's terrible news,' he told her. 'I didn't fight out there for that.' As they passed Andover, his spirits began to soar, and then there was Salisbury, the spire of the cathedral, so impossibly slender and elegant, drawing him like a moth to a flame. They alighted at Wilton and there was Mr Stork to meet them.

'Welcome home, Tom.' He smiled, shaking his hand so hard Tom wondered whether he'd ever let go. 'I can't say how good it is to see you. How long d'you think you'll be back?'

'Not sure, Mr Stork, but it's a terrible wound. Reckon it won't be fixed until well past 'arvest.'

Stork laughed and led them to the car, Tess insisting Tom sit in the front.

'Tess tells me you saved Alex's life,' said Stork, as they pulled out of the station.

'Well, there were eight of us. We all took our turn in carryin' 'im but anyone else would've done the same and he'd 'ave done the same for me. It was mayhem out there. I'm just very glad he got back because when we left him at that casualty clearin' station, we made the doc promise to take him, but there's promisin' an' it actually happenin'.'

'But it all worked out. I'm so very glad, Tom. We're all immensely proud of you.'

Tom smiled bashfully. 'Thank you, Mr Stork, but it were nothin'.' He gazed out of the window as they emerged from Hare Warren Wood and drove over the downs. It was a perfect early-summer's evening, the valley bursting with new life, the chalk downs glowing in the last of the evening sun.

'Weather set fair, I reckon,' he said. 'Haymaking time.' He breathed in the sweet scent of summer as they drove past the hedgerows.

'Yes, and we've already begun.'

Tom grinned. 'It's good to be home.'

Stork dropped him at home with his father who was quite overcome to see him, holding him tightly and weeping openly. Tom had never seen his father cry before.

'They sent a telegram,' he told Tom, 'saying you were missing. I thought the worst. First your mother and then my only son. I didn't tell a soul. Didn't dare to. I thought if I did then perhaps you'd never come back. Superstitious nonsense, I know, so I bottled it up. Three of the longest days of my life. And then when the postman delivered your telegram from Dover ... well ...' He swallowed hard. 'I saw him coming down the path and I thought that was it, Tom.'

'It's all right,' Tom told him. 'I'm here, Father. I'm all right. I got separated from the rest of the battalion for a few days, that's all.'

His father led him into the front room and they sat down, his father in his usual armchair, Tom perched on the other. He looked around at the rows of books and volumes of poetry on the shelves, heard the reassuring ticking of the pendulum clock and breathed in the familiar smells of bread and pipe tobacco. Why was the smell of a place so reassuring? He thought of the farmhouse on the canal and how he'd smelt only death and decay there. *Put it out of your mind*, he told himself.

'And what about your arm?' his father asked him.

'It does 'urt, I don't mind saying. Made a right mess of the back as it exited and it shattered the radius bone. But it'll heal. With a bit o' luck, though, I might not have to go back for a while. If ever. I reckon Jerry might just have done me a favour.'

He went up to his room, which was just as he had left it, took off his uniform and put on an old flannel shirt and a pair of corduroys. 'Good riddance,' he said out loud to himself, folding up the uniform and putting it at the bottom of the chest of drawers. He wondered whether he'd ever have to wear it again.

'You look your old self again,' said his father, 'except for the sling.'

Tom smiled. 'Father, d'you mind if I go out? I won't be long. I just want to . . . well, there's somethin' I've got to do.'

'Of course, but I should warn you. Mr Stork has taken your hut up to the Ox Drove for the LDV.'

Tom had never heard of the LDV.

'To guard against invasion and fifth columnists,' his father explained.

Tom smirked. 'I bet they'd all put the fear of God into any Jerry.'

'They're doing their bit, son. Mr Stork said it was getting musty and needed to be used.'

''E's probably right. In any case, I don't need a hut. Not in summertime anyhow.'

He left his father, walked down the road and turned into the track that led to the manor and the farm. His heart was thumping heavily in his chest. He wondered how many times he'd read her letter. Perhaps a hundred. Perhaps more. On the beaches, in the dunes. On the ship heading back. At the hospital in Dover where they'd X-rayed his arm and stitched it back together, and then at Guy's, where he'd finally caught up with Captain Woodman. He had it in his pocket now. He prayed she was there. Surely she would be. It was now past nine o'clock, the light starting to fade, and she would be clearing dinner, then thinking about going home.

319

He walked on down the track, the verges sweet with the scent of cow parsley. In an elm tree a wood pigeon was cooing soothingly. It was as though he'd never been away, his boots on the grit of the track, crunching in the evening air. There was the house, lights on inside now. He walked past into the yard and saw Jean Gulliver working in the kitchen. *Of course*, he thought, *in that light, she can't see me.* But where was Hannah? And then he saw her enter the kitchen with a tray. He breathed in deeply, looked up to the sky, then went to the kitchen door and knocked.

Seconds passed, then the door opened.

'Well I never!' exclaimed Jean. 'Hannah! Come quick!'

A moment later there she was, an expression of utter shock, and then her face, the sweet, pretty little face he remembered so well, broke into a smile of the purest joy. She pushed past Mrs Gulliver and flung her arms around him. 'You're back! You're back!'

He felt her warmth, her arms around his back, her auburn hair on his cheek. His arm throbbed painfully but he didn't care. He laughed and held her to him.

'I've waited a long time for this moment, Hannah Ellerby,' he said, and she looked at him, put her hands on his cheeks and kissed him. It was the sweetest kiss he'd ever had.

28

Home and Away

Monday, 10 June 1940

IT HAD BEEN A BEWILDERING FEW DAYS. CARIN LAY ON THE HARD palliasse, the light streaming in from the window above, unable to sleep. It was only a little after five in the morning. She felt exhausted, dirty – she'd not changed her clothes since leaving home – and still in shock that the England she had known over the past twenty years could be so cruel.

'This place is not so different from Dachau,' Anna Hartman had told her.

Perhaps the guards were gentler, Anna had conceded, but the privations here at the mill were terrible. Lavatories were buckets lined up in a tent outside in the grounds, a bench with holes above them to sit on. The stench by the end of each day was appalling. Carin was a private person: she found sharing a lavatory intensely humiliating.

She looked across at the other three women in the room. Anna appeared to be asleep. So, too, Brigitte, an elderly lady who had been living in England with her husband, an Oxford don, for fifteen years. Both she and her husband had been interned but separated; as she had told Carin, it had been the first time they'd slept apart since marrying nearly forty years earlier. Now that Carin thought about it, the night after her arrest was the first time she'd not been with John since they had married back in the summer of 1920. Then there was Gretchen, only nineteen, who had fled Austria after the *Anschluss*; like Anna, she was Jewish. Anna had been imprisoned for ten months in Dachau for protesting against the anti-Semitic laws. The *Kristallnacht* pogrom had followed her release and then she had managed to get a visa for England, sponsored by the Quakers. 'I'm not religious,' she had told Carin, 'but if I was I'd definitely become a Quaker.' Gretchen hadn't seen her parents since leaving Vienna. So, really, Carin thought, she'd been lucky.

And it won't be for ever, she told herself again. She had to believe that. The detectives had said as much in the car driving her to Wilton. At the police station she had been put into a cell for a few hours – 'Sorry, ma'am, but we've nowhere else to keep you' – then taken by car to Swindon and put on a train with a number of other internees, including Brigitte. It had been a long journey, with lots of inexplicable stops and military policemen guarding them. 'Enemy aliens' they were called; a grotesque term. Anna and Gretchen were Jewish, welcomed into Britain as refugees from the Nazis. What possible harm could they want to bring upon their adopted country?

Then, in the early hours of the third day, the train had stopped at Warrington and they'd been put onto a bus and taken to an abandoned mill, manned by a territorial battalion of a Lancashire regiment. Brick walls surrounded the old mill, on top of which now stood coils of barbed wire. As they'd shuffled in, they had been told to move forward to a line of trestle tables outside the main entrance.

A bored-looking private sat behind one, and as Carin approached he asked her to open her case and empty everything out. She did as she was told and watched, appalled, as he looked through every item, even her knickers, brassières and wash-bag.

'Who are these people?' he asked, looking at a leather photo frame that opened like a book.

'My family.'

'Then why aren't your children here with you?'

'Because they're English. So is my husband.'

He'd looked surprised. 'How long have you been here?'

'Since the summer of 1920.'

'All right, you can put it all back,' he'd said, and she'd been led into the mill. By the look of it, it had been disused for some years. One half was a three-storey brick building with a tall chimney, while the other was a large, open factory floor. There were perhaps two dozen others arriving with Carin and they were given a tour by a lady in a dark blue uniform. The old factory floor was where they would receive meals. It was high-roofed with cast-iron columns holding up the rafters and a dirty glass ceiling above. More trestle tables had been lined up but there were still relics of old machinery dotted about. The floor, mostly wooden boards, was dirty. A smell of brackish water from a canal that ran alongside, from oil, and from the latrines in the grounds, hung heavy in the air.

They were housed in the rooms of the main building, in hastily built bunks with palliasses, old wool blankets and nothing more. Everything about the place suggested it had been organized in very quick order, with few nods to personal comfort. It would not be for long, the lady assured them, but where they were ultimately to go – or when they would leave – they were not told.

Fortunately, Carin liked her immediate companions well enough. Anna was a musician and had brought her violin, which she played beautifully. Just the previous evening, she had given them 'The Lark Ascending'.

'This is for you, Carin,' she had said, 'and to prove to these ignorant idiots just how Anglicized I have become.'

Carin had listened, transfixed, imagining herself back on the downs at home, hearing the skylarks that lived in such abundance there; it was her very favourite birdsong.

She had clapped when Anna finished; they all had. 'That was beautiful, thank you,' she said, and meant it. Even in a place as squalid and grim as the mill, she reflected, beauty could still force its way through. Anna was in her late thirties and had been a member of the London Philharmonic Orchestra; when she had been arrested they had taken her to Holloway prison before moving her to the mill. 'They even made me wear the prison fatigues,' she told Carin. 'Can you imagine?'

Gretchen was quieter and spent long hours on her bunk, writing and sketching in a journal she kept. She had a brother who had managed to get to America but she had not heard from her parents in more than a year. 'They will have been arrested,' she told them one evening. 'For all I know they might not even be alive.'

Brigitte was nearly sixty, and struggling with the privations thrust upon her and the separation from her husband. 'He is a brilliant man,' she told them. 'A physicist. Britain should be using his brain not shutting him away.' She feared for his health and how he would be coping. 'He has an extraordinary mind,' she said, 'but he is not practical. He's never really had to think about day-to-day life before. That has been my role. I worry about him.'

Carin now turned onto her back and stared up at the ceiling from her position on the top bunk. Below, she heard Brigitte's heavy breathing. Cobwebs stretched across the window and from the ceiling to the single light bulb that hung down. She thought of home, of the subtle scent of the white climbing roses outside the front of the house, and of the crystal-clear chalk stream at the end of the garden. Her John had always been very protective of her; as an outsider coming into his sheltered little community all those years ago that had been only understandable, but she had loved him all the more for it. She knew how much it would be torturing him that he could not protect her now. And poor Elsa, she had Ollie to worry about and now her mother as well.

Yet she also remembered what it was like being in Germany after the last war; how tough times had been. Being swept up by John had been her chance to escape the poverty her family had experienced in those early years after the war and to escape the oppressiveness of Bavaria at that time. So much anger; so much hatred. Those had been dark days, she thought now, but she had survived them. She was determined she would survive this ordeal too.

HMS *Iceni* had completed seven trips to Dunkirk and, although she had managed to avoid a single direct hit, had suffered her fair share of wear and tear. There were jagged holes in the hull and on the superstructure from shrapnel, and the twin turbines were in need of an overhaul; the repairs were expected to take at least three weeks.

'I'm sending you to HMS *Osprey* to do the ASCO course,' Lieutenant Commander Bertie told Ollie. 'It's at Portland and only twelve days but you can have forty-eight hours' leave first.' It was a vote of confidence. The Anti-Submarine Control Officer course was known to be challenging but mastering the ASDIC, the main means of tracking enemy submarines, was of crucial importance for destroyer officers, and to further his career he needed to broaden his skills. Ollie was pleased to have been chosen, although it meant he wouldn't have as much leave as some of the others.

Still, two days at home was something. He was desperate to see Elsa; she had been inconsolable during a brief phone call after Carin had been taken away, and it had troubled him that all he'd been able to do was offer her some banal words of reassurance.

His father picked him up from Salisbury – extra fuel coupons were one perk of being a farmer.

'Very glad to see you in one piece,' Dick told him, as they set off for home.

'Very glad to be in one piece, Dad. It's been quite a difficult week, I'll admit.'

They were silent for a moment. He could see his father was wondering whether to ask more, and Ollie was debating whether to tell him, although it was something he no longer really wanted to think about or share. He didn't want his father to worry more than he already was. Dick had rarely talked about his own experiences in the trenches and now Ollie understood why. One simply didn't want those one loved picturing one in such circumstances of peril and awfulness.

'You know, you can tell me about it if you want to,' his father said. 'If it would help. But if you'd rather not, I do understand. I just wanted to say that, Ollie.'

'Thank you, Dad. I'd rather not for the moment, if that's all right?'

Dick glanced at him, smiled and patted his son's leg. 'Of course it is. Just glad to have you back.'

That evening, John and Elsa joined Dick, Eleanor and Ollie for dinner. They seemed wretched, not even Ollie's presence enough to lighten the mood. John made a valiant effort to chat but Elsa looked more miserable than he'd ever seen her, pushing her food around the plate, her usual *joie de vivre* vanished.

As they were leaving, Ollie said to Elsa, 'Do you think your uncle might let you have the day off? We could take the bikes out. Go for a ride and a picnic.'

A flicker of a smile. 'I'd like that,' she said. She leaned up and kissed him. 'I'll ask.'

Afterwards, he sat with his parents for a little while. 'It's so damnable what they're doing to poor Carin,' his father said.

'It's wicked,' agreed Eleanor, 'and worse because I thought we're supposed to be the force for good.'

'There must be something that can be done,' said Ollie.

'Well, if public opinion is anything to go by there's a lot of people who think the government has been far too heavy-handed,' said Dick. 'After all, why on earth would a German Jew who escaped the Nazis want to spy for Hitler? And how would they do it anyway?'

'What have they been saying in the press?' asked Ollie.

'Mostly that it's one thing locking up known Fascists and Nazis,' said Dick, 'but quite another interning refugees from the Nazis and those like Carin who have been living here for years. A number of MPs have spoken out about it too and quite forcefully. Who knows whether it'll make any difference? I've been up on the hills with the LDV doing my bit, you know, and it's primarily fifth columnists and possible enemy agents parachuting down from the skies that we're watching out for.'

Ollie laughed. 'Really? But the Germans have turned south and are fighting the rest of the French now. I wonder if our leaders have gone a little mad. You haven't caught anyone yet, I suppose?'

'Er, no,' conceded Dick. 'We have stopped a few for driving without the proper papers but that's all. I agree that waiting for parachutists to fall is a bit far-fetched, but I'll have you know we're also training so that if the Nazis do invade there'll be units across the country to take them on.'

'A very noble aspiration, Dad.'

'Armed with shotguns and air rifles,' added Eleanor.

'We've been promised proper rifles and even Bren guns,' said Dick. 'You can mock if you like but I'm prepared to defend this valley if it comes to it.'

'Well,' said Ollie, 'let's hope it doesn't. And fortunately the Germans will have to get past the Navy first and, as I'm constantly being reminded, we have the largest in the world, even after last week's losses.'

Dick lifted his tumbler. 'I raise my glass to that.'

Elsa was given the day off and, as planned, Ollie and she took their bicycles out, riding up through the valley and out towards Tisbury. It was another fine summer's day. In the fields, the farmers were making the most of the good weather and cutting the hay, the sweet scent of freshly mown grass and clover heavy in the back lanes along which they cycled.

They stopped by the ruins of the old castle at Wardour, climbing up the remains of one of the towers, then eating their picnic beneath one of the great cedars in the grounds. Elsa was quieter, though, than was usual and Ollie found himself trying to fill in the pauses in a way he'd not done before. He was conscious of prattling about life on the ship, all of which meant little to Elsa and he sensed she had stopped listening.

'I'm sorry,' he said. He was leaning against the tree, her head in his lap, and gently stroking her hair. 'I'm talking a whole load of rot.'

'I don't mind,' Elsa replied. 'It just doesn't make a lot of sense.' Neither spoke for a moment, then Elsa said, 'I suppose it was inevitable that you should find another life with your ship. But it's a life in which I have no part.'

'Don't say that.'

'It's true, though.' She peered up at him. 'Was it very awful? At Dunkirk?'

Ollie swallowed. 'Yes, it was terrible. A shambles, really. But you don't want to hear about that.'

'Don't I?'

He thought of the screaming Stukas, the bombs exploding with huge fountains of spray. And the men he'd seen drowning when a ship had been hit: their screams, the flailing arms, figures disappearing between the waves. The desperation of the men who had tried to get into the whaler, of him drawing his pistol and firing. The fear in their eyes. The panic. The dead bodies on the beach and in the water.

'It was pretty bloody awful at times,' he said.

She said nothing, and for a little while they remained where they were, Ollie wondering whether he'd said something terribly wrong because she hadn't responded.

'I hate this war,' she said eventually. 'We should get back.'

They cycled mostly in silence.

'I've got to go again in the morning,' he said to her, as they reached her house. 'And I'm not sure when I'll be back again. I'll miss you.'

327

'Off to your world of ships and destroyers.'

'I wish I wasn't going anywhere. I don't want to be in the Navy. I want to be here.'

She hugged him tightly. 'I'll miss you too. Thank you for a lovely day and I'm sorry I've been a bit quiet.'

'I understand.'

She kissed him, then turned and wheeled her bicycle around the back of the house.

As he cycled home, Ollie couldn't shake off a feeling of disquiet. He'd never seen Elsa so low – she'd always been such a bright, sunny person. But today there had been a coolness to her he'd not seen before.

It troubled him.

Tom had been enjoying himself. He'd caught up with old friends on the farm, had been to the pub with Smudger and had not been allowed to buy a drink all evening. Everyone treated him like a hero, and now he was about to spend the day with the loveliest girl in the land. The Germans were attacking south towards the River Seine and closing in on Paris, but Tom couldn't have cared a fig. The sun was shining, the valley looked its very best, and he walked up to Hannah's family cottage with joy in his heart and a lightness of step he'd not experienced once during his time in the Army.

Hannah's mother opened the door. 'Oh, hello, Tom. Hannah's expecting you. Come on in a moment.'

'Thank you, Mrs Ellerby,' he said, taking off his cap.

It was a small cottage, two up, two down, and he wondered how the five of them managed to fit; his own home was a little larger as befitted the foreman of Manor Farm, but Tom had always found the cottage a bit of a squeeze just with the two of them. He supposed Hannah must share a bed with her older sister, who was in service with the Liddells down the road.

Hannah appeared from the kitchen, clutching a basket with a cloth over the top. Kissing him, she bade her mother goodbye and off they went, she looping her arm with his as they walked together through the village. He wondered what Edie would think if she spotted them like this; he hadn't seen her yet. Perhaps, he wondered, she had some other fellow by now.

'So, where are we goin'?' he asked her. 'On this perfect day?'
'Up on to Mistleberry.'

It was one of his favourite spots. From there, he could see the valley and the farm spread out beneath it. He could gaze at the folds of the chalk, at the combes on the far side of the valley, and could see the village nestling below, the church tower peeking up through the cluster of elms and horse-chestnuts. He could see Tippett's Wood and the cricket ground. And on Mistleberry, there were old anthills to rest on, soft with moss and the sweet fragrance of downland grass. He loved it up there. Always had, ever since he'd been a boy.

They chatted all the way up the track, as though making up for the long years of mutual silence. Pausing occasionally to look back, Tom wondered why it had taken them so long. All that time she had never said anything to him and he'd never said anything to her. It seemed so silly now. Damned pride, he thought. Fear of being laughed at. They reached the top, ate the picnic, drank some beer, and then Tom lay back, his head against an ant mound, Hannah next to him, an arm across his chest.

'Why did you suddenly decide to write to me?'

'I don't know. I suppose I just didn't want to die wondering. I think I've loved you since, well, pretty much since I first saw you, but I was scared you might not feel the same. I saw you with Miss Coco and with Edie. Oh, but I hated them then.'

'They were nothing,' said Tom. 'I tell you, Hannah, I was only thinkin' of you.'

She leaned up and kissed him. 'But then I thought, to hell with it. I felt ever so brave sendin' that letter off to you.'

He laughed. 'It made my day. Couldn't believe it. I'd been think-ing of writin' to you. In fact, I did once, but screwed it up and threw it in a brazier. So, you were much braver than me.'

She sat up, resting her elbows on his chest and kissed him. 'What's goin' to 'appen, Tom? Are those Germans going to win?'

'I don't know. I don't take much notice of this invasion talk, though. They're no better than us. One night we stormed a farm-house. I was runnin' across this field, firin' and yellin' – it was when Captain Woodman got hit – and I tell you, those Jerries scarpered. Ran. They're not supermen. And I tell you something else. They might have their Stukas but the whole of our army got away, didn't it? So they can't be that special. That last day in the dunes those Stukas and Junkers and Heinkels must have come over seven or eight times. Not a single man killed. I'm not saying they didn't hit anything, but they didn't hit us. And another thing, they might have their panzers and whatnot, but they've got a hell of a lot of 'orses. Horses tow their guns, horses tow their wagons. Now that's quite old-fashioned in my book. It's not all armoured cars and tanks. I tell you, they're not that special. We only fell back because the French on one side and the Belgians on the other didn't fancy it.'

'So, I can stop worryin' about German parachutists droppin' from the sky, then?'

Tom kissed her. 'I reckon you can stop worryin' about anything right now. This day is too perfect to spoil with worrying.' He looked at her and kissed her again. 'You've made me a very happy man, Hannah.' He sighed and closed his eyes, felt the warmth of the sun on the lids, then Hannah's hand on his cheek and through his hair. 'Who knows what'll 'appen?' he muttered. 'But right now, I want to bottle this moment and keep it for ever.'

In Palestine, the officers of the Wiltshire Rangers had sat around the wireless in their tented mess that evening listening to the news that Mussolini had declared war on Britain and France.

'The bastard!' muttered Dasher Cowper between sips of his gin.

'He's a joke, though, isn't he?' said Archie Pickering, the adjutant. 'I've never had any truck with the chest-thumping they seem to go in for and cockerel feathers in their helmets and whatnot. Looks a bloody sight.'

'Never tempted to join Mosley's Blackshirts then, Adj?' said Edward.

'No, thank you very much. The man's an ass and a class-A bounder.'

They were now at Karkur, their third camp since arriving in Palestine, closer to the coast and further north than they had been when they'd first arrived out there. They were all a little bored. Edward had been on a Bren-gun course, a field-gun course in which they'd learned how to fire old 18-pounders no longer used anywhere else in the British Army, and he'd also attended a signals course in Tel Aviv. The men were restless too. It was hot, the rations were repetitious, there were too many flies and there was only so much training one could do. Everyone could strip their Lee-Enfields blindfolded.

Between courses and training, Edward had written a lot of letters, mostly to Brenda, sketched and painted. Rumours abounded that they were soon to lose their horses and become mechanized. Perhaps the move to tanks would be accelerated. Certainly, Italy probably had more interest in the Mediterranean than Hitler did. Time, they all agreed in the mess that night, would tell.

Edward rather liked Palestine and would have been enjoying himself were he not missing Brenda so much. Absence had certainly made his heart grow fonder, and he found that so long as he had regular letters from her he could just about keep his spirits up. To make matters worse, a couple of the officers had managed to get their wives out to join them – Donny Moberly's wife, Margaret, and Major Digby Howell's wife, Clarissa, had managed to ship themselves out before the balloon had gone up in France and taken houses in the nearby village. It was most irregular, but Dasher didn't seem to mind so long as Digby and Donny spent no more than a couple of nights a week out. Irregular it might have been, but it was tolerated because Digby and Donny were married, not merely affianced.

'Well, I'd better be pushing off to see Mrs M,' Donny had said earlier that evening.

'If only I'd married Brenda before we left,' said Edward to Peter – not for the first time – as they headed back to their two-man tent.

'Cheer up. I'm sure the mail will arrive any day now.'

'Humph,' said Edward.

'Tell you what, let's ride over to Caesarea tomorrow afternoon. Take your mind off things. You've always said you wanted to go.'

Actually, Edward thought that an excellent idea. There was no road that led there and mostly desert in between, so travelling by horseback was the best way to visit. The following afternoon, taking a few men each from their troops, they rode over, armed with bottles of beer and sandwiches, skirting around the desert. Edward trotted amid the ruins of Herod's Palace and the Roman theatre, then tethered his horse, climbed to the top of the semi-circle of stone seating, and began to sketch.

'You know, you should do this professionally,' said Peter, joining him.

'Ha, ha.' It was an old joke.

'Bloody ridiculous, though, isn't it?'

'What do you mean?'

'Nazis swarming over France and the Low Countries, the BEF evacuated, Italy declaring war, and here we are on a gorgeous evening sightseeing and sketching Roman ruins.'

Dusk was falling by the time they got back to camp and, much to Edward's delight, the mail had arrived with letters numbered 33, 34, 35 and 37 from Brenda. Both had agreed to number each they wrote, so what had happened to 36? Of course he didn't know, and took himself off to a quiet spot to read them alone. The first three he read quickly. She was all right. Had seen Tess. Was thinking about joining the Wrens or the ATS and wondering which might be more useful for their future life together. He liked that bit. It was reassuring. Then he opened 37. She began as she always did.

My Darling Mr Pooter,

I have something to tell you. I've been worrying so much about how to write this to you.

Christ, he thought, and a wave of panic swept over him.

I've been feeling odd for quite a little while and then I've been a bit sick too. I thought, it can't be, but it is.

Edward could barely read on.

The thing is my darling Edward, my love, I'm pregnant. There's no doubt about it. With our child. And I just don't know what to do.

Edward read the words, then read them again and a third time. Brenda was pregnant. With his child. *Bloody hell*, he thought, exhilaration coursing through him. And then panic. *No*, he thought, *no, Brenda, tell me you haven't done something stupid.* He looked at the date: 25 May. Only a couple of weeks ago. It had reached him quite quickly.

Please, he thought, *please don't let it be too late.*

29

From Across the Sea

DENHOLM CASTELL HAD RECEIVED THE TELEGRAM FROM DUNDERDALE late on the afternoon of 11 June. *Marjorie sick. Come quick. Expect to see you at hospital in Rouen by 26.* The code book they had agreed to use was Kipling's *Plain Tales from the Hills*, and Denholm quickly had the message deciphered. *Christ*, he thought. *Tours.* That was the best part of six hundred miles away and he needed to be there by the morning of 13 June. Normally, that wouldn't be too much to expect but he was unsure how busy the roads would be, how clogged with refugees. First, though, he had to tell Lucie and Coco. He was dreading it.

He'd not told them a word of his plans – plans he'd been working on since his return from Paris: he wanted to give them as little opportunity as possible to argue against him. He couldn't tell them much in any case because neither knew that he had been working for the British Secret Intelligence Service all these years. Now, though, there was no time for dallying.

Coco was down by the pool, lying on a sun-lounger, apparently asleep, but she turned at his approach and lowered her sunglasses, with a look of mild annoyance.

'Ah, there you are.'

Yes?

He drew up another lounger, sat down and took her hand.

'Must be serious,' said Coco.

'It is. I know you've been wondering what I've been up to this past week or two.'

'I have, as it happens.'

He took out a cigarette, lit it, smoke swirling around him. 'Well, I've been putting our affairs in order. Shutting things down. Putting assets into storage. That kind of thing.'

'Uh-oh.'

'France is losing the war, my darling. Obviously, I've been hoping for the best as I'm sure you have but it's all over. Paris will be overrun by Nazis in a day or two and the rest of the country will follow. Reynaud hasn't a chance against those vultures Pétain and Weygand, and that ghastly old cabal of doddery generals from the last show.'

Coco pushed herself up onto her elbows. 'But there's no fighting going on down here.'

Denholm sighed. 'Life will not be the same.'

'But how can you know what defeat will mean? Won't France sign an armistice and that will be that? It's what Lucie thinks will happen. She's more worried about Communists.'

'If only it were that simple. Honestly, I don't know what an armistice would look like but it'll be pretty ugly. We won't just be able to carry on our lives as normal. The Germans hate the French. Loathe them. Always have done. Do you think Hitler's going to let France off the hook after what happened in 1918? Fat chance. At any rate, I'm not prepared to hang around and find out what the new France will look like. As a Brit, I imagine I'll be rather *persona non grata*. That might well apply to you too.'

'So, you're suggesting we leave?'

'I'm not suggesting, I'm saying. Honestly, what else did you think we'd do? We need to get out of here. Shut up the house and leave. We'll drive north to Brittany. I've a yacht waiting for us at Saint-Malo.'

'We're sailing back?' Coco was incredulous.

'The last boat train left a while ago, Coco, darling. How else?'

Coco sat up. 'Have you told Lucie?'

'No. I was rather hoping you might help.'

'Can I have one of your cigarettes, please?'

Denholm took out one from his case, lit it, and passed it to her.

'My God,' she said, now perched on the edge of the lounger, staring out at the twinkling Mediterranean in the distance. 'I can hardly believe it. I don't want to leave here, Papa. This is my home.'

'I know, my darling. But it won't feel like home if the Nazis have their way. It's adieu not farewell. We'll be back here one day, I promise.'

'We really can't stay?'

Denholm shook his head.

She looked around. 'What if I told you I wasn't coming?'

'I'd say, don't be so bloody silly. This is war. We all have to do things we don't want to do. You love it here because it's home but also because you're free. How much fun would it be with Fascists and Nazis running the show? I won't be here. And I won't have a business that will pay for you to live this life either.'

She turned and hugged him, which rather surprised him.

'All right, Papa.' She pulled away, tears running down her cheeks.

'We'll be back. Come on, old girl. Chin up, eh? Think I want to leave?'

'When do we go?'

'Tomorrow morning. I'm planning to turn in early then get going at four.'

'My God. I can hardly believe it.'

'France is finished, Coco. Staying here won't alter that.'

They left a little after four o'clock, with dawn creeping over the mountains and hills of Provence. His wife and daughter were in tears as Denholm paused the car outside the gates so he could shut and lock them for the last time in God only knew how long. He wondered when he would be back. If ever. At least they were not refugees. And at least he had work to go to . . . work, very possibly, of interesting and challenging importance. A last check of the luggage strapped to the roof. And, as he got back in behind the wheel, a glance at his wife and daughter. 'All right, then?'

No reply from Coco, crammed into the back seat alongside more luggage.

'Come on,' said Lucie, wiping her face with a handkerchief. 'Let's get going before I change my mind.'

They drove in silence. What was there to say? And particularly after the previous evening's hysterics. Denholm had always known that Lucie had a fiery temper but she had more than lived up to her billing last night. After initially refusing to leave, obstinacy had given way to screaming at Denholm and calling him every name under the sun. As he'd pointed out, it wasn't his fault Hitler had invaded France, that the French had made such a pig of things or that he was British. She had known that when she'd married him. She then tried a different tack: she hadn't said goodbye to her brother and his family and couldn't possibly leave without seeing them. 'Étienne already knows,' he told her. 'He's known for several weeks. We have a business together, remember?' That had been a mistake. How dare he tell her brother before he told his wife? So it had continued. Back and forth, back and forth, Denholm dodging the swings and upper cuts, until Lucie had finally given in and agreed to come with him. 'But you'd better look after me,' she had warned him. 'You're not abandoning me in that city of fog you call London.' He'd been more than ready to get to sleep then, but they always seemed to make love after a fight and, if he was honest, it had been the best fun he'd had in bed with her for a long time. As he drove through the mountains, his eyes already stinging with fatigue, he wondered to himself if he'd ever understand his wife. Or women in general.

For the most part the roads were quieter than he'd imagined. Only as they passed through Bourges, Vierzon and Saint-Aignan did they notice more traffic on the roads and nearly all heading south, away from the front. In the heart of France, the country was already on the run, fleeing from the panzers and Stukas and from the Nazi stormtroopers. And here, in Tours, where they arrived late that same day, was the French government, such as it was, now ensconced in the Préfecture.

A night at the Hôtel Colbert, a little dinner, and then, the following morning, Denholm made his excuses. 'I just have to see someone,' he told Lucie, who was still barely awake. 'Tell Coco, will you? Won't be long and then we'll head on up to the coast.'

'Where are you going?' There was a little crease of a frown between her eyebrows.

'Just tedious business stuff. Someone I need to see. Safeguarding the future, sweetheart.' He kissed her. 'Shouldn't be too long.'

At the Préfecture, he was kept waiting while gendarmes checked his passport and papers, then was met by Colonel Georges Groussard. Smooth, lean face, intense expression, single monocle.

'There you are, *mon ami*,' said Groussard, extending his hand. 'It has been a while.'

'A couple of years at least,' said Denholm. 'And I'm sorry to be meeting again in such bleak circumstances.'

Groussard nodded acknowledgement and held out an arm – *this way, please*. 'We're expecting the British contingent any moment, although the Luftwaffe were over yesterday evening and there is some damage to the airfield. Apparently, it will be cleared in time, though. And Dunderdale is here already.'

Groussard led him down a long corridor, up some stone stairs and along another corridor to a large room that overlooked the Préfecture's garden. 'There you are, Denholm,' said Commander Dunderdale, striding over from the window. Denholm shook his hand, glancing around the room. Large, rectangular walnut table, two men in French military uniform, one of whom was imposingly tall, with a trim moustache, Roman nose, somewhat hooded eyes and a small chin. Denholm almost laughed: the garden beyond, with its snaking pond and gravel walkways, was so very French and the figure before him, holding out his hand, could have been no other nationality either. *Le jardin, le château et l'homme,* thought Denholm. A harmony of Frenchness.

'This is Brigadier Général Charles de Gaulle,' said Dunderdale, 'and this is his aide-de-camp, Baron Capitaine Geoffroy Chodron de Courcel. The *général* is the Under-Secretary of State for National Defence and War, as I'm sure you know, Denholm. As you are also no doubt keenly aware, the situation here in France is grave to say the least but we do have something of a plan, do we not, sir?'

'Yes,' said de Gaulle. 'Maréchal Pétain and Général Weygand hold the strings of power and they are defeatist and determined to ask for an armistice. Churchill arrives here shortly but it won't make any difference. Their minds are made up. Of course I am doing all I can to dissuade them, but they think of me as a young upstart, impertinent and talking out of turn. In their world, when a field marshal speaks everyone should listen, should be respectful.'

'And they have spoken,' added Groussard.

'Yes, they have spoken, and they have decreed that France should lay down her arms. That France should surrender. They are, to my mind, traitors and deserve no respect, only contempt.' No one spoke for a moment, but then de Gaulle continued: 'So, France will sign an armistice. Maybe not tomorrow or the next day. Maybe not until Paris is in the hands of the Nazis. But it will happen. However, the flame of the real France must never extinguish. The fight must continue because otherwise we will never recover. We have to give people hope. Defeat now must not and cannot be final.'

'Very well said, sir,' said Denholm. He cleared his throat. 'But forgive me for asking, where is the rest of the government? Here, at the Préfecture?'

Groussard smiled. 'This is just another meeting, Denholm. Meetings, discussions, conversations in corridors. It never stops at the moment. Every man in the government is doing it. You can bet the *maréchal* is plotting somewhere in another part of the Préfecture. Don't worry, we can talk freely.'

'All right,' said Denholm.

'So, we're going to take the *général* to Britain,' said Dunderdale. 'Well, to London, actually. There he will establish the Free French. This will be the start of a resistance movement and the organization around which France can rebuild and eventually overthrow the Nazi occupiers. It will be the focus of hope that the *général* has just spoken about.'

'Glad to hear it,' said Denholm.

'And,' added Dunderdale, turning to Groussard, 'we're also going to establish a French secret intelligence service attached to de Gaulle's organization. We're assuming the Deuxième Bureau will be shut down or, officially at any rate, hostile to Britain, which is why we need a second organization operating in Britain and France. Georges here will be a vital cog, needless to say.'

'I see,' said Denholm, taking out a cigarette and lighting it.

A knock at the door and a steward came in with a tray of coffee. If he was surprised by the company, the steward didn't show it.

'Sirs,' he said, when he was done, nodding deferentially, then slipped out again.

'And this is where you come in, Denholm, and why we need you in London. You'll be working in Naval Military Intelligence for

MI6, but with your knowledge of France and fluency you'll be the liaison between Six and our new show in London.'

'So will Six be funding the *général*'s new intelligence organization?'

'Yes. Dansey will be overseeing this. You'll be working with the *général* and the *capitaine* here and, of course, whoever is appointed to run this new organization.'

They chatted some more, then a telephone rang to tell them that the British delegation was arriving. Meeting adjourned. Back down the corridors, down the stairs and out into the yard just as the Prime Minister was stepping out of a French sedan. Denholm recognized Halifax, Lord Beaverbrook and General Ismay. The Prime Minister was being ushered inside but Denholm caught Ismay's eye.

'Everything all right, Castell?' Ismay asked, walking over to him.

'Yes, sir,' said Denholm. 'I'll see you in London.'

'And you've seen de Gaulle?'

'Yes, sir.'

'Good luck.'

'And to you.'

'I suspect we might need it.' A brief shake of the hand, then Denholm strode briskly away.

That afternoon, Tess had arrived back at her house in Pimlico to find a telegram waiting for her. Telegrams were invariably harbingers of bad news so she hastily tore open the envelope and unfolded the single sheet, with its taped strips of teletext. *Tess darling Please contact Brenda urgently. I'm fine – your loving brother – E*

She showed it to Diana. 'What can he mean?'

'I can't imagine,' said Diana. 'But you'd better do as he asks, don't you think?'

Tess rang but there was no answer. She wasn't sure what to do.

'Why not wait twenty minutes first and see whether she gets back?' suggested Diana.

'Good idea.' She started getting her clothes ready for work the following morning and asked Diana about Alex. Her parents were down and proposing to take him back to Yorkshire in a week or two if it was allowed.

'I'll miss him,' said Diana, 'but I expect that would be for the best.' She looked at Tess, waiting for a response.

'I'd miss him too,' she said, 'but I expect you're right.'

A half-hour had passed before she rang again and this time, much to her relief, Brenda answered.

'Whatever is the matter?' asked Tess. 'Edward sent me a telegram telling me to get in touch. Said it was a matter of great urgency. Are you all right?'

'Yes, well, sort of. No, not really. I – I can't really talk about it on the telephone. I—'

'Would you like me to come round?'

'Would you?'

It was nearly eight o'clock by the time Tess stood outside Brenda's house and knocked on the door, a bottle of wine tucked under her arm.

Brenda opened the door and Tess was struck by how lovely she looked despite her obvious distress and the dark rings of fatigue under her eyes.

'I feel an absolute heel making you come all this way, but I can't tell you how wonderful it is to see you,' Brenda told her.

'You've had me worried sick, Brenda. What on earth has happened?' She gave her the bottle of wine. 'You sounded as though you might need it.'

Brenda smiled. 'I rather think I do.'

Tess followed her to the kitchen where she began to attack the cork with a corkscrew before pausing, placing both hands on the table and looking down. 'I can't do a thing properly at the moment.'

Tess took the bottle from her, pulled out the cork and poured them each a glass.

'Thank you, Tess,' said Brenda. 'Let's go through.'

They sat on the sofa, opposite each other, and Tess wondered whether Brenda was ever going to tell her what the matter was.

'All I know is that Edward sent me a telegram,' said Tess, 'and told me to get in touch as soon as I could. So, here I am. What is it, Brenda?'

Brenda took a deep breath. 'All right,' she said. 'I'm just going to tell you.'

Yes?

'I'm pregnant with Edward's child.'

Tess felt the colour drain from her face. She nearly dropped her glass. *So, that was it.* She felt utterly dumbfounded.

341

'Oh, no!' said Brenda, hand to her face. 'You're appalled, aren't you?'

'No, no – no, I'm not,' stuttered Tess. 'It's just – I just – it wasn't what I expected you to say.'

'It's so awful,' Brenda said, putting down her glass and taking Tess's hand. 'I could not be happier to be bearing our child but he's in Palestine and we're not married. I thought about getting rid of it, but I can't. I just can't. The thought of it and, anyway, I don't want to. But I don't want my life ruined either and nor do I want to ruin Edward's.'

'Promise me, Brenda, you'll not do anything silly. Promise you'll not try to get rid of it.' Tess saw the tears building at the corner of Brenda's eyes.

'Thank you,' she said. 'Thank you for saying that.'

'Don't be silly. I mean it. Have you told anyone else?'

She shook her head. 'Only Edward. I wrote to him and told him.'

'So he sent me the telegram.'

'He sent one to me too.' She took it from her dress pocket and handed it to Tess. *Most marvellous news. For the second time of asking, will you marry me? You've made me very proud. I adore you. E xxxx*

Tess laughed. 'That is so very Edward. Oh, Brenda.'

Brenda dabbed her eyes with the back of her hand. 'But what am I going to do? I can't tell my parents – what would they think?'

'What about your uncle?'

'He'd probably disown me on the spot. If only we'd got married before Edward left. I so want to be married to him but he didn't want me to be tied down and left on my own. Bringing up a baby as an unmarried mother is going to be so very hard. Edward says there are men in the regiment whose wives have joined them. I wondered whether I should do the same – sail out there, get married to him and be with him – but now Mussolini has declared war and France is almost overrun, I fear I'd never get there and the whole situation would then be even worse.'

'Oh, Brenda,' said Tess, for the second time. She wasn't sure what else to say. She tried to think calmly and logically. Glancing at Brenda's flat tummy she thought how miraculous it was that inside a little life was forming – a life created by Brenda and her brother.

'People will think me a terrible slut. It'll be too shame-making.'

'I slept with Alex,' Tess said, hoping a confidence might help. 'And I took no precaution either.'

'Really?'

Tess nodded. 'Will you let me talk to Mama?'

'Debbo? But wouldn't she be horrified?'

'I'm not sure she would. She's really rather modern, you know. Bohemian in many ways. I don't think Mama is very shockable. She misses Edward terribly and I know she'd love to have you stay there. She's very fond of you and you would help her feel closer to Edward. And if she agrees to help, she'll win over Dad. Oh, he'll bluster a bit and say it's not normal and not how things should be done, but there's a war on. We all know Edward would marry you in a trice if he could. These are exceptional times, and in exceptional times there have to be exceptions. And he'll love having you there for all the same reasons Mama will. Of course, there will be mutterings and nudges and glances from the village, but so what? A small price. And down in Alvesdon you'd be looked after and you'd have all the support you could possibly want.' She sat back. 'There,' she said. 'You asked me what you should do. That's what you should. What *we* should do.'

A long and increasingly tedious journey to Saint-Malo. Near Château-briant, the Citroën started playing up, the engine missing a beat, then back-firing.

'I'm sure it's nothing very much,' Denholm told Lucie and Coco. They both had alarmed expressions on their faces: breaking down was simply unthinkable. *Then what?*

At Janzé, he pulled into a garage – they needed more fuel in any case – and paid a mechanic handsomely to replace the spark plugs, strip the carburettor down and put it back together.

It was getting dark by the time they reached Saint-Malo and Denholm was a little apprehensive that his plan might go awry at this point. What if Monsieur Émile Delgrave was nowhere to be found? What if there was no yacht and the deal was off? He'd been half expecting it, which was why he had picked Saint-Malo: far enough away from the front line, but still a decent-sized port where alternative options could be pursued if necessary. At such times, people would always be willing to sell. Everybody wanted cash in a time of war. But he need not have worried. Monsieur Delgrave was at home on the rue d'Alet and expecting him.

While Lucie and Coco waited in the car, Denholm handed over the agreed ten thousand francs in cash. They shook hands and began loading their luggage into the little rowing boat tethered at the quayside. It was dark as Delgrave rowed the three of them out to the yacht, a thirty-five-foot sloop called *Jeanne d'Arc. What else?* thought Denholm. A rising moon and a clear sky, so that the city was silhouetted clearly. The gentle lap of the oars in the water, the slight wobble as the overloaded boat moved away from the quay. The smell of seaweed and brine heavy on the night air.

Then there she was. Delgrave lit a hurricane lamp as he pulled alongside and they all climbed aboard. Delgrave stepped back into the dinghy, passed up the suitcases and they exchanged keys, wished each other luck and bade one another *au revoir.* Denholm stood on deck, smoking, watching the boat move away, then disappear entirely. Relief coursed through him. He'd never been entirely convinced they'd make it but here they were. They'd get some sleep, then, early morning, weigh anchor and set sail for England.

Paris fell the following day, 14 June. That evening, as Maud and Alwyn were listening to the evening news, a telegram arrived. Hannah brought it to them.

'Whatever can it be?' said Maud, opening the envelope. Reading it, she exclaimed, 'Ah! It's from Denholm. He's back, Alwyn!'

Alwyn beamed. 'That's marvellous news! Here, let me see.'

She passed the note.

'"Just reached Weymouth,"' Alwyn read aloud. '"Lucie and Coco in tow. With you shortly."' He clapped his hands together. 'Ha, ha! Marvellous. Thank God, eh, my dear? Thank God. Some good news at last.'

30

Tensions

ONE MORNING, THEY WERE TOLD THEY WERE BEING MOVED, ALL OF them, to a permanent camp. They were to pack their cases and be ready to leave at 9 a.m. They climbed into waiting buses and made a slow journey through industrial towns, dark with soot, and patch-works of open countryside until they reached a larger city, which someone recognized. Liverpool, she said.

'Maybe they're sending us to Canada,' said Anna.

Carin felt her stomach twist. 'Really? Could they do that?'

Anna shrugged. 'They seem to be able to do whatever they like.'

What a dreadful thought that was. The bus rumbled on, along the streets of terraced brick houses, past parks and increasingly large civic buildings, until up ahead loomed the docks with their cranes and derricks. She felt so impotent, as if she were a pawn. Someone had decreed that she should be taken from her family, that she should be placed in a derelict mill and that now she should be sent across the Atlantic to a far-off land.

'You look like you've seen a ghost,' said Anna.

'I'm frightened, Anna. I don't want to be sent to Canada.'

'I'm sorry, I shouldn't have said that. Try not to worry – it hasn't happened yet.'

She hardly dared step down from the bus. Fate: it was not in her hands. Her legs felt weak as she followed Anna and the others to the quayside where a number of vessels of differing sizes and types were moored. A crane hoisted a roped box from one ship, swinging it in an arc and lowering it gently to the ground. Men shouted, trucks moved along the quay. A distant horn sounded, mournful on the morning air.

They paused by a smaller vessel, a passenger ship perhaps a hundred yards long. Across from it on the quayside was a building on which was written 'Isle of Man Steam Packet Company'. So, perhaps not Canada, she thought, allowing herself a sigh of relief.

An army officer appeared, conferred with the head guard, then turned and faced them, feet together, stick under his arm.

'You'll be boarding the ship presently,' he bellowed, above the racket of the dockside. 'The destination is Douglas, on the Isle of Man. At Douglas, you will be met by buses and transferred to a new camp on the south of the island. Are there any questions?'

Someone asked whether there were any derelict mills on the Isle of Man. The officer winced a little and replied, no, not to his knowledge. Someone else asked what kind of accommodation they would be placed in.

'You'll be billeted in houses,' he told them, 'and I can assure you that the south coast of the island is very pleasant, particularly so at this time of year.'

Anna nudged her. 'Feel a bit better? It doesn't sound too bad at all.'

Carin nodded but also felt an overwhelming urge to cry. Really, she thought, she needed to take hold of herself. They would be boarding in an hour, the officer told them. Anyone who wanted to send a letter or telegram could do so at the post office in the hall, but would need these to be checked and censored by him first.

Since her arrest, Carin had been given only one opportunity to make a brief telephone call so now she hurried inside to send a telegram and write a letter.

She dictated the telegram first, had it signed off, then sat down to scribble a hasty note. It was odd, she thought, writing it on the headed paper she had brought from home, with 'Rose Bower' and their Middle Chalke address printed at the top, yet just writing to them, thinking of them – establishing a link, no matter how tenuous – helped calm her.

She passed her letter to the officer. 'I hope you can read my scrawl,' she said.

He read the first few lines carefully, skimmed the rest and handed it back with a kindly smile. 'I'm sorry,' he said, 'this must be very hard for you.'

Soon after, it was time to board. Anna sidled up beside her. 'Let's stick together,' she said. 'Perhaps that way we'll be billeted together too.'

'All right,' said Carin. 'I'd like that.'

On board they were allowed to move around the ship so went to the stern deck. Gulls swirled overhead and they looked out over the port, the many ships at harbour or steaming in and out, at the barrage balloons floating above the city.

'I feel quite the tourist,' said Anna.

Carin laughed.

'It's nice to see a smile on your face.'

Carin clutched her arm. 'Thank you, Anna.' She sighed. 'This is easier to bear with a friend beside me.'

A horn sounded, shouts from the quayside, a cloud of sooty smoke belched from the single funnel and the ship, the *Lady of Mann*, began to pull away from the quay.

Monday, 17 June 1940

Stork slipped the Morris into second with a grind of the gears that made him grimace and reminded him that he was not concentrating properly. He drummed his fingers on the steering wheel, his brow knotted, and clicked his tongue irritably against his teeth.

He was driving back from a War Ags meeting in which tempers had flared. Farmers around the county wanted machinery to help them with haymaking but, of course, they all wanted it at the same time – now, during this spell of fine weather. Haymaking was a tricky business. It could be glorious when the sun shone, and that was the irony, Stork had always thought, because the best-quality hay was the cheapest to make. It merely relied on the sun, which was free to all.

Every farmer was keenly aware of this, as was every member of the War Ag, and local bias inevitably came into the discussions. Frank Spicer, who farmed near Lacock, wanted to make sure his local farmers got their share of the tractors and mowers available but so, too, did Christopher Whatley, a landowner on the eastern side of the Plain. Kenneth Badger, one of the county land agents, pointed out that if agreement couldn't be made during haymaking, how would they reach a consensus when it came to the harvest? Eventually Richard Stratton lost his temper, allocating machinery for haymaking as he saw fit and appointing Stork, William Price and Kenneth Badger to investigate contracting the machinery out to third parties for harvest-time and having them deal with it.

The Morris continued its steady progress up the downs, finally gaining speed as the road began to level out. Really, though, the irascibility of the War Ag committee was the least of his concerns. Far greater worries were bubbling away at home. All this past weekend he'd felt completely torn over what to do about Brenda. He'd been shocked at the news, and everything about Tess's suggestion felt wrong to him. Brenda wasn't their daughter. She was a lovely girl and Edward was very smitten, but he wasn't sure why she should become their responsibility. Not for one minute did he want to abandon Brenda or see her become a social outcast in any way, but at the same time, supporting an unmarried mother and helping her to raise a bastard baby – and he hated the term but that was what it would be – would make life difficult for him. Socially. In the village and in the county. Within the War Ag. And it wasn't the sort of thing one could keep quiet, or pretend wasn't happening. People always talked.

Debbo had been more shocked by his reaction than she had by Brenda's pregnancy. He winced again as he remembered the row they'd had on Saturday morning. 'So, you'd rather let the girl our eldest son has pledged to marry end up on the streets, would you, Stork?'

'No, of course not!' he'd replied.

'Then don't be so bloody pig-headed!' And the awful thing was, he knew she was right: he was being pig-headed, but he couldn't shake his disquiet. His discomfort. That what she was suggesting was upending the social order more than he was comfortable with.

'You're being ridiculous,' said Debbo. 'They'd be married now if it weren't for this stupid war! It's your grandchild we're talking about, yet you'd rather put your social standing in the village and county above the well-being of your son, future daughter-in-law and unborn grandchild. I thought better of you, Stork.'

They'd barely spoken since. He couldn't remember a time when she'd been so livid with him.

He ran the car down the steep, narrow hollow that ran into Dinton, dark under the canopy of sycamores, horse-chestnuts and elms, then emerged into the village, past the cricket ground and over the road where a new RAF ammunition dump was being built.

Stork knew he had to resolve matters with Debbo but now further trouble loomed with the arrival of his eldest brother and family.

'Stork, I've the most marvellous news,' his father had told him on Saturday morning, after the row with Debbo when he'd come down to the farm to escape. 'Denholm's back! How about that?'

'That's tremendous, Father,' Stork had replied. 'So glad he's safe.'

'Yes, he managed to make good his escape, sailing all the way from Brittany, can you imagine? He's got Lucie and Coco with him. Reckons they'll be here tomorrow evening. Got a few things to sort out first, apparently.'

Stork hadn't seen his brother since his arrival, but his father had left a message that they'd arrived safely. The family was invited to dinner that night. Stork wasn't sure what was depressing him more: the prospect of dinner with Denholm or Debbo's frostiness.

As he climbed up over the downs and looked towards the valley and at the farm, he saw they were haymaking in Half Moon. He decided to call in there first, before heading back to Farrowcombe or the manor. Pulling the car off the road by the gate, he took off his jacket, loosened his tie and walked over to where Tom was watching Smudger and young Davey tinkering with one of the Fordsons. On the far side, Sid Collis was moving steadily across the field behind two of the horses.

'Horse versus machinery, eh?' said Stork.

'It's nothin' much this time,' said Smudger, 'some grit in the fuel line, but Davey's just puttin' it back together.'

'Good lad,' said Stork. 'And how are you, Tom?'

'Beats soldierin'. Feelin' frustrated I can't do too much with this arm of mine.'

'Try her now,' said Davey.

Smudger turned the handle and the tractor sputtered into life. He winked at Stork and ruffled Davey's hair.

Stork watched Smudger climb onto the seat, slip the tractor into gear and move off, the rotating forks rolling and churning the hay into a neat line. He wandered over to the far side and Sid brought the horses to a halt.

'Mind if I take the reins, Sid? Just to keep my hand in.'

'Go right ahead. You're the guv'nor.'

Stork took out a couple of sugar cubes he always kept in his waistcoat pocket, gave one to each of the horses, then clambered onto the seat. Picking up the reins, he clicked and said, 'Walk on,' and the rake began to turn with the forward motion of the wheels, picking up the loose hay and churning it to one side. Stork felt himself bounce gently as the horses walked steadily across the meadow. He breathed in deeply the warm mustiness of the animals, the fragrant sweetness of the hay, and a wave of contentment rolled over him. A late cuckoo called from the narrow wood at the foot of Windmill Hill and he felt the warmth of the sun on his face.

He thought about Edward and how much he must be worrying about Brenda. Was it fair of him to add to that worry when his son was playing his part in the war? Debbo had been right: Brenda would not be an unmarried mother if Edward was not serving in Palestine.

He reached the edge of the field, lifted the rake and turned the horses, then lowered the forks once more and began heading back across the length of Half Moon.

And now that he thought of it, he supposed having Brenda at Farrowcombe would be rather fun. It was quiet without the children and having someone a little younger about the place might brighten things up. When the baby arrived, it might be rather marvellous to be a part of its little life and, as he or she grew older, share the farm once more with a new generation. Ahead of him were the curves of Windmill Hill, the contours that snaked in shadowed lines towards the main ridge of the downs. Beyond the far hedge was Village Field, to his left Pinkham, and beyond that Lower Windmill. He'd learned all their names as a boy. It would be a joy to teach them all to Edward and Brenda's child. His grandchild.

Good God, he thought, but he'd been an ass. How could he ever have thought that reputation was more important than the needs of his family? In any case, there was a war on, for goodness' sake. It wasn't Brenda's fault Edward had been posted overseas, and it was no good pretending couples never went to bed together until their wedding night. He had slept with Debbo every time he'd had the chance before they were married – and why not? Every time, he'd expected to be dead a week later. Opinions were changing. They had been ever since the last war and were changing again now in these modern times. Maimes and his father would worry, and it might cause a little awkwardness, but nothing he couldn't handle.

As for Denholm – well, he'd be perfectly civil, try not to rise to any bait and, with a bit of luck, they'd soon be off to London. After completing three more rows, revelling in the sweet smell of freshly turned hay, he pulled up the horses and ambled over to Sid and Tom, who were lounging on the ground by the gate, sharing a flask of tea.

'Got a few things straight in yer 'ead then, guv'nor?' Sid asked him.

'Yes, thank you. Just what the doctor ordered, as it happens.'

He waved at Smudger and Davey, bade Tom and Sid a good day and headed back to Farrowcombe.

Later, as he lay in bed, watching Debbo at her dressing-table take off her earrings and necklace, he felt a new wave of shame about how pompous and crass he had been. He had apologized earlier and told her that of course Brenda must come to stay with them, but now, at the end of what had been a long day, he felt compelled to show his contrition afresh.

'I truly am sorry, Debbo, darling. As usual you were completely right. I wasn't thinking straight. It'll be wonderful to have Brenda staying and even more of a miracle to have her and Edward's child brought into the world here.'

'She might not want to be here by then. She might have had enough of us.'

Stork hadn't considered that. 'Well, that's possible too.'

'I thought you were admirably restrained at dinner.'

'So did I. Actually, I felt rather sorry for them all. Imagine that was us having to flee to France.'

'I did feel a bit for Denholm. You don't how lucky you are being married to me.'

'I do.'

'Well, having Lucie as your wife would be jolly hard work. Brittle as bone that one. At least you don't need to worry about them staying here. If they're here another night, I'd be surprised. She wants to get to London as soon as possible. She's no interest in her husband's family whatsoever. What do you think Denholm will do?'

'Goodness knows. He was sailing a desk at the Admiralty in the last war so I wouldn't be surprised if he winds up doing something in that vein again. Denholm will be all right.'

'And I hope we'll be all right too.' Debbo turned and looked at him. 'I worry so much about Wilf and Edward. And dear Ollie and Tess, of course. It's not fair that poor Edward and Brenda should be apart like this. I just want them all to be safe and happy.'

'It's what any parent wants, isn't it?'

Debbo smiled. 'I suppose it is. And I also want *us* to be happy, Stork. I do love you very much, even though you can be a pompous old bear sometimes.' She walked over to the light and switched it off so that only her bedside light remained. Then she slipped off her gown and, quite naked, climbed into bed beside him.

'Those poor French,' she said. 'It makes us realize we have to make the very most of what we've got.'

He leaned over and kissed her and felt the warmth of her body against his. *Ah*, he thought, *this is good*. How wise she was.

Because it had been Monday, Hannah had had her day off and Susan Smallpiece had been brought in to help Jean Gulliver instead. She and Tom had taken the bus into Salisbury and seen a film, then finished the day with a drink in the village pub. Edie Blythe had come in, seen them together, paused to say hello, then had gone to sit with the land girls. As far as Hannah was concerned, it had been a good end to the day, bettered only when Tom had walked her home, kissed her goodnight and told her he loved her.

She'd not given Mr Denholm a thought until she walked into the yard early the following morning. Another fine day, the air fresh and sweet, a gossamer web on the gate, pricked with dew and shining vividly in the early-morning sun. She hummed to herself, then smelt cigarette smoke on the air and stopped, stock still.

'Ah, my favourite little housemaid,' said Denholm. He was standing in the yard, one hand in his pocket, hair a little unruly and only half dressed. 'How joyous to see you again.'

She felt quite frozen to the spot, her heart hammering in her chest.

Denholm was now ambling towards her. 'What's the matter? I promise I won't bite.' He chuckled.

Somehow, she managed to move again, and without a word, made straight for the kitchen door. 'Good day to you,' she muttered, as she passed him.

In the kitchen she paused by the sink, her heart still thumping and her breathing heavy. Then the door to the yard opened and she turned to see him step inside.

'The offer still stands, by the way,' he said. 'I'm going to be down here from time to time. God knows what the old man pays you, but I promise I'd make it worth your while.' He smiled. 'You really are far too pretty to be a housemaid.' He winked, then said, 'Right, I'll be off. Lovely to see you, Hannah, as always.'

When he'd gone, she burst into tears. She'd felt his eyes undressing her. It had been horrible and she couldn't help feeling threatened physically by his presence. It was as though in listening to his vile offer she was somehow betraying Tom. She couldn't bear it.

She had managed to recover her composure by the time Jean Gulliver arrived and, thank goodness, Mr Denholm had not been in the dining room when she had brought in breakfast and placed it on the sideboard.

'You're awful quiet this mornin', Hannah,' Jean said, as they sat down briefly for their own breakfast at the kitchen table.

'I'm fine,' Hannah said, but no sooner had she said that than there he was again, standing in the doorway, clutching a coffee pot.

'So sorry to intrude,' he said, 'but it's my Continental womenfolk. Not happy with tea. They're demanding more coffee.'

Jean made to get up but Hannah was closest and Denholm paused beside her. He put his hand on her upper arm, almost gripping it.

The door to the yard opened just as Hannah yelled, 'Get away from me!'

'Hannah!' exclaimed Jean, as Tom entered, looked first at Hannah, then at Denholm, and with his good hand, swung him around and then drove his right fist hard into Denholm's jaw. It all happened in a trice, Denholm staggering back, crashing against the dresser and Hannah screaming.

A moment of stunned silence. Hannah put her hands to her face, unable to hold back the tears any longer. Now Tom was beside her, arm around her shoulders, Denholm rubbing his jaw and Tom yelling at him to get away before he did something they might all regret. And then Mr Castell came in.

'What the blazes is going on?'

'Nothing to worry about, Father,' said Denholm. 'A little misunderstanding, that's all.' He rubbed his jaw.

'Tom?' said the master. 'What on earth is going on? What's happened? Explain yourself, man!'

Tom kept himself close to Hannah, unable to look at Denholm. His face was flushed, angry.

'It were nothing, sir.'

'My God, did you just hit my son?' he said, the penny dropping.

'It's all right, Pops,' said Denholm, trying to usher his father away. 'Don't make even more of a scene. As I said, a little misunderstanding.'

But Mr Castell brushed past him, and staring at Tom, said, 'How dare you strike my son? I want you out of this house. Now!'

Tom glared at him and said, 'Come on, Hannah.' He held out his hand and she took it and, her other hand cupping her face, followed him out of the kitchen and into the yard, slamming the door behind him.

'My God, Tom, what have we done?' she said, once they were outside.

'What have we done? What have *we* done? Hannah, that don't matter. Tell me, what has *he* done?'

She looked at him, searching his face, seeing the muscles in his jaw clenching.

'He – he—' But she couldn't tell him and instead put her face to his chest and sobbed. 'Just take me home, Tom. Please, take me home.'

31

Family at War

STORK WAS IN HIS OFFICE WHEN THE TELEPHONE RANG.

'Oh, Stork, darling, I've caught you.'

Maimes. He knew that tone of old. 'What's happened?'

'I'm sorry to say there's been a bit of a scene. Could you come down?'

'Of course, but what on earth has happened?'

'Some ghastly misunderstanding between Denholm and Tom. Your father's incensed and has sent Tom packing. Tom has taken Hannah with him.'

Stork sighed. He could see it all. Denholm leering over Hannah, Tom taking a swing. 'All right, I'll be down shortly.'

He crossed to the house to tell Debbo.

'Can you believe it? He's barely got here and already caused the biggest rumpus since last August. He's impossible.'

'Well, he's probably off to London today,' said Debbo. 'I hope you're going to stick up for Tom if Denholm's been a cad.'

'Let's just see what's what first,' he said.

He took Byron, trotted down the track, and as he neared the village and the row of terraced tenant cottages, he had a hunch that Hannah might now be at home. If so, he thought it would be worthwhile hearing her side of things first. Tethering Byron, he pushed open the gate, walked up the brick path and knocked.

It was Hannah's mother who opened the front door. 'Oh, hello, Mr Stork. There's been a bit of a to-do. She's inside. Come on in.'

She called upstairs for her daughter, who came downstairs a few moments later, her eyes still red and cheeks blotchy. She could barely look at him.

'It's all right, Hannah,' he said. 'I've not been down to the manor yet so I don't know what's been going on, but it would help me if you could tell me.'

'I'll put the kettle on,' said her mother, leaving them together in the front room.

They sat at the table by the window.

'I promise you, Hannah, I'll not betray any confidences, but if I'm to help Tom, I need to know. From the beginning.'

She nodded. 'All right,' she said. And she told him. All of it, including what had just happened.

'I screamed, I couldn't help it. It just came out, and then the master came in and 'e realized what had happened and told Tom to leave. An' Tom took me with him.'

Stork rubbed his brow. 'And do you know where Tom is now?'

'He took me back here, made sure I was all right and then said he needed to go and clear his head.' She put her face into her hands. 'Oh, this is all my fault!'

'No, it isn't, Hannah. If there's anyone who is totally blameless, it's you.'

Her mother came back in and set the tea tray on the table.

'Thank you, Mrs Ellerby,' said Stork. 'Now, Hannah. Stay here today, have a mug of hot, sweet tea and get some rest. I don't want you to worry about anything. My brother – well, I can only apologize but I'll do my best to make things right. You have my word.'

'Thank you, Mr Stork,' she said. 'And will Tom be in trouble?'

'Leave it with me. I think very highly of Tom. He's a fine young man. It doesn't pay to hit people, but I'd like to think if anyone threatened my wife, I'd have the guts to stand up for her.'

He left them and, back in the saddle, rode down to the manor. So, it was as he had feared. It would, of course, cause a God-almighty row, but he was damned if he was going to lose Tom. There was a cottage empty at the end of Windmill Lane and he had it in mind that he might let Tom have it, should he and Hannah decide to marry. Perhaps that was jumping the gun, he thought, but it paid to think ahead a little. Betty Collis had told him some months ago that she was thinking it was time to retire and he knew Hannah wanted to work at Farrowcombe. *Of course*, he thought suddenly. That was why.

He reached the manor, bringing Byron round to the front. He walked through the front door and found his mother in the drawing room.

'Where's Denholm?' he asked.

'In the billiards room, I think, darling.'

He found Denholm leaning over the table. 'Don't say a word until I've potted this ball,' said his brother. 'It's a very tricky shot.'

Stork paused, watched the cue gently come back, whip forward, hit the white onto the red and the ball disappear into the bottom right pocket.

'Bullseye,' said Denholm.

'Good shot.'

Denholm stood up and chalked the end of his cue. 'So, you've heard about my little contretemps.'

'I have, and I've spoken to Hannah, who has told me everything.'

'Ah.'

'You don't deny it, then?'

Denholm shrugged. 'I merely offered. She's very pretty and I thought she might be happy to make a few bob, have a bit of fun.'

'You frightened the living daylights out of her, Denholm. She's a very sweet, good, innocent and shy girl. Her heart belongs to Tom and apparently always has done. What you've done was unconscionable.'

'Well, I admit I might have trodden a little more carefully.'

'You're impossible, Denholm, absolutely impossible, but it's in no one's interest to cause a massive stink. So, this is what I think you should do.'

Denholm lined up another shot, this time aiming to pot the black. 'All ears.'

'Tell Father you've been thinking about what happened. Admit you acted out of turn with Hannah. Tell him you know Tom is a good fellow and that there's no hard feelings. You can lay it on quite thick. How you know that Father has always thought the world of him and you'd hate a little misunderstanding to ruin a fellow's future. Get Father to calm down and forgive Tom, and in return I won't tell anyone what has really gone on. Including Lucie and Coco. I'm assuming this would not play well with them.'

Denholm potted the black. 'It would not.' He stood up. 'All right. I'll do that.'

'And I'm going to take Hannah up to Farrowcombe so that she never has to see you again. I'm assuming you'll be down here from time to time?'

Denholm nodded. 'Probably.'

'And you need to back me up because Father and Maimes won't like it. Those are my terms. Stick to them and I'll not breathe a word.'

'Thank you,' said Denholm. 'And, for what it's worth, I'm sorry. I've been a swine. I can be . . . careless with people.'

'You're selfish, Denholm. Egocentric. I just wish you'd pause to think about others sometimes.'

'All you say is true.' He took out a cigarette and lit it. 'Well, I'll be out of your hair soon. When the ladies are up and about, we'll be heading to London.'

'Where will you stay?'

'Oh, I've something lined up. Old contacts.'

'The Navy?'

'Something like that.'

'And you'll talk to Father? This morning?'

Denholm held up three fingers. 'Scout's honour.'

Stork left the manor hoping a crisis might have been averted. It was ridiculous, he thought, that such dramas still unfolded when the war was so precariously balanced. But, of course, family squabbles, domestic troubles and individual wrongdoings were still the stuff of everyday life, war or no war. And regardless of what followed in this war, he did not want Tom to be punished for taking a swing at Denholm, which his brother had fully deserved.

Having retrieved Byron, he clopped around to the yard and called in first on Jean Gulliver.

'I hear there was a bit of a to-do this morning, Mrs G,' he said, as he came in through the kitchen door.

'You can say that again!' She put a hand to her chest. 'Oh, my Lord!'

'Well, I wanted to apologize on behalf of my brother to you that you had to witness such a thing. I've told Hannah to stay at home. She's rather badly shaken. I trust you'll be able to manage today.'

'Course I will. Poor lamb. There was some terrible trouble last summer, Mr Stork. I couldn't get it out of her what the matter was. She wouldn't say a thing, but she was terrible upset. Caught her in floods the day of the master's birthday party.'

'You're a woman of the world, Mrs G. I'm sure you can guess what was going on.'

'Tried to have his wicked way with 'er, did 'e?' She tutted. 'I did wonder whether it might have been somethin' like that, but she wouldn't say and I didn't want to pry.' She looked at Stork. 'Oh, you needn't worry, I shan't breathe a word.'

'He's behaved abominably. I'm deeply embarrassed on behalf of the family.'

''E's always been a wild one, has Mr Denholm.'

'He has rather.'

'And you can't choose your family.'

'Er, no. Look here, I'm also rather anxious to find Tom. You haven't seen him, have you?'

'Saw 'im going down to Tippett's Wood about an hour ago,' she said. 'It's his second home, bain't it?'

'Of course. Let me see if I can't find him. Thank you, Mrs G. As always.'

He found Tom in the clearing where the hut used to be, sitting on an old beech trunk and carving a stick with a clasp knife, the stick held across his legs with his fingertips while he used the blade with his good hand.

Tom looked up as Stork appeared but said nothing.

'I've been feeling bad about your hut,' said Stork, as he nimbly climbed down from the saddle. 'I've found a couple in a yard over in Sparrowcliffe. Fellow there is happy to sell, so one can be brought back here and we can put the other up on the Herepath for the LDV.'

'So, you're not firing me, then?'

'Well,' said Stork, 'technically, you're in the Army and no longer in my employ, so I could hardly fire you in any case.' He came and sat down next to him on the trunk. 'But, no, of course not.'

Tom nodded.

'I'm only ever going to say this to you once, Tom, but don't ever,

359

ever hit anyone in my family or on this farm again. Is that understood?'

Tom nodded again. 'I just never seen her look like that. She was frightened. I saw that face in France – on some of the men. It was pure fear – and I'm sorry but I saw red.'

'I know, but it's not the way to resolve matters. There's quite enough violence in this world already without adding it to it in the kitchen at the manor.'

'But you'd defend Mrs Stork with your life, wouldn't you?'

'Yes, but it's not quite the same thing as seeing red and lashing out with my fists, Tom.' He sighed. 'My brother spoke out of turn to Hannah. It was very wrong, but he won't be doing it again.'

'And the master?'

'He's like you – got a bit of fire in his belly. Even at his age. He'll calm down.'

Tom sighed. 'The amount of time I've spent in these woods. When I was in France, I'd think about them all the time. There were moments when I began to wonder whether I'd get back here again.' He looked at Stork. 'Lost a hell of a lot of blokes out there. One fellow, he was in the slit trench, about as far away from me as Byron is now, and a shell come in. That was that. Literally nothing left. I've seen enough dead men to last a lifetime and we were only in battle three weeks. I got back here and found Hannah and, to be honest with you, I don't ever want to leave again.'

'How's the arm? What did the doctors say?'

'They think it's unlikely I'll ever get complete use back but reckon I should be able to do everything I want to do.'

'Like fire a shotgun, drive a tractor and a hay cart?'

Tom grinned ruefully. 'I'll make sure I can.'

'Farming is a reserved occupation, you know. I'm sure you could get a medical discharge.'

'I dunno. We'll have to see. I'd like to marry Hannah, but I don't want to if I've got to go back. It ain't fair on her.'

'Isn't that her choice?'

'She's still young, though. She loves me right enough now, but when she knows what I'm really like . . .' He left the sentence unfinished.

'Well, I'm very anxious for you to stay, Tom. There's the old cottage at the end of Windmill Lane. It's been empty since the winter when Mrs Dymock died. I'm going to have it spruced up. It could be yours. How old are you now? Twenty-four?'

Tom nodded. 'Thank you, sir. That's very good of you. Definitely something to think about. I mean, I'd love it, honest to God I would, but I wouldn't want to take a good house off you if I've got to go to war again.'

Stork patted him on the shoulder. 'I must get on, Tom. Don't forget there's also the LDV here. You could farm and still do some soldiering. Once your arm's on the mend. Mull it over. And cheer up. Let's put this morning behind us, eh? Enjoy the lull before the Nazis turn their eyes back on us. And as soon as you can work, I'd like you back on the farm.'

'What d'you think will 'appen?'

'God only knows. But I do know we can only plan for what we can control. I've haymaking to finish, a harvest to bring in. The rest,' he said, as he swung himself up into the saddle, 'is in the hands of those much higher up than you or I.'

Carin and Anna heard the news of the French armistice on the wireless while they were having their tea with Mrs Elsie Galloway in the front room. A daily ritual already: breakfast at eight, dinner at midday and tea at six, listening to the news on the wireless. Elsie liked to have her main meal in the middle of the day, so tea was something simple. Soup, perhaps, or tinned sardines on toast. Perhaps a slice of cake. And always with a cup of tea. They had tea with all their meals. It was so very different from how Carin ate at home, but she could not have minded less. Mrs Galloway was a kindly soul, and it was her house and they were her guests.

'Well,' said Elsie, gingerly placing a bit of kipper on her fork, 'I think we're better off without the French. No one's been able to make their minds up on anything!'

'But surely, Elsie,' said Anna, 'we were better off having France's Army, Navy and Air Force on our side?'

Elsie raised her eyebrows. 'Fat lot of good they've done us, though.'

'Elsie has a point,' said Carin, smiling.

'It's all very well those Nazis sweeping through Luxembourg and

361

Belgium and whatnot,' said Elsie, 'but they'll not find the Channel so easy.'

'What about the Luftwaffe? And their paratroopers?'

Elsie shrugged. 'They'll need a bit more than paratroopers to take the whole of the British Isles. Anyway, whose side are you on?'

'Not the Nazis',' said Anna.

They finished their tea, washed up and tidied everything away, then Anna suggested they go for a swim. Elsie shook her head. 'I cannot imagine why you'd want to do that on a full stomach. My mother would never allow us to swim on a full stomach. Always made us wait. She worried we'd get cramps and drown.'

'We will be very careful,' Anna told her.

The house, one of a terrace of seven fronted with pebble-dash and a slate roof, was on Shore Road. When they'd first reached the Rushen Camp, they'd been told they were being billeted at 5 Shore Road, and Carin and Anna had wondered whether that meant a view of the sea. They'd not imagined it meant they'd be living with only the lane in front and an allotment garden separating them from the beach and the sea. Carin liked sleeping with the window open in her room at the top of the house and hearing the waves breaking against the shore. She woke up frequently, but the sound soothed her back to sleep.

Of course, neither had brought swimming costumes with them so they swam in their bras and knickers. Carin had felt a little prudish to begin with, but Anna flung off her clothes and ran in, laughing. 'I don't care if someone sees me. What will they do? Lock us up?'

Carin had quickly lost any feelings of bashfulness and they now made a ritual of running in and diving. As Carin surfaced and rolled onto her back she couldn't help wondering what a strange war this was. France defeated, German troops presumably swarming over the country and an eighty-year-old field marshal now a puppet dictator. She had read enough about Pétain to know he had been the hero of Verdun, France's great victory, the symbol of defiance and the fight for France's liberty. How ironic it was that he was now turning his back on those liberties, yet, she supposed, no more ironic than the democracy of Britain forcing innocents like herself to be detained without trial or recourse. What a topsy-turvy world it had become.

She turned over again and swam – breaststroke – parallel to the beach. She had tried to explain the unusual set-up of the camp in a letter to John, because it wasn't really a camp at all. Rushen was the name of the parish that incorporated the two villages of Port Erin and Port St Mary at the southern end of the island. The British authorities had simply cordoned off both villages and run coils of barbed wire across the narrow peninsula. All the internees were women and children, billeted either in boarding houses and hotels or with villagers. Elsie told them she'd been only too happy to accept the two guineas a week for having them as house guests.

'And I'm glad of the company, to be frank with you,' she told them. 'I've been a long time on my own.' Her husband, Dougie, had been killed in the last war and her only son had grown up and left the island. 'He's got his own family now.'

How sad, Carin had thought at the time, remembering how miserable she had been at home for months, despite being with her family. The stigma of her category B status had been unbearable and had hurt her acutely. Then, curiously, the moment she was taken away she had actually felt a sense of relief. The waiting was over, her fate sealed. The mill had been so very awful and she had supposed the rest of her incarceration would be much the same, yet now . . . *This is not so bad.*

She had regular letters from home. Just this morning one had come from John. The children were well enough; the brewery was thriving, in spite of or, rather, because of the war. That was something, Carin thought. The LDV had been renamed the 'Home Guard' and some uniforms had arrived – denim battledress. *So, I'm back in uniform for the first time since 1918*, he had written. Contact with home definitely helped, she thought. They'd not seen as much of Brigitte or Gretchen, who were in a boarding house in Port St Mary on the other side of the peninsula, but clubs were being formed and there was sport for those who wanted it. And look at me now, she thought, running into the sea like a child with Anna. And she was living in a very sweet seaside house, with a kindly old widow and a new, interesting friend to keep her spirits up. They could do what they wanted. Anything, except cross the wire. 'It beats Holloway,' Anna had told her, 'and my tiny flat in London.'

Bad luck, good luck, Carin thought. A bad roll of the die had taken her from her home. But good luck had put her with Anna and another lucky hand had kept them together at 5 Shore Road.

As she swam, she alternated between breast- and backstroke, and now turned again, looking up at the evening sky above the cliffs of the bay beyond. Gulls wheeled and cried, and it reminded her of when she and John had taken the children to Lulworth Cove and to Sandbanks. Afterwards, as they dried themselves on the beach, Anna said, 'I've decided I'm going to treat this as an enforced holiday and Rushen as an enforced holiday camp. We're two friends who have gone on holiday.'

Carin laughed. Anna was funny. She had faced so much more hardship than Carin ever had yet she had the gift of seeing everything that was flung at her in the most positive way one could imagine. 'You're a dear friend, Anna. Thank you for being you.'

'What a lovely thing to say,' said Anna.

'I mean it. You're making this bearable.'

Anna looked out to sea. 'I wonder how long they'll keep us here. Honestly, if only they knew how unthreatening we are. I'd be really very happy to help their war effort rather than hinder it by costing them a guinea a week. Think what that could be spent on.'

'You could be entertaining the troops.'

'Yes, that would be fun. Anna the German Yiddler Fiddler. It has a ring to it, don't you think? Maybe I should suggest it.' She put an arm around Carin's shoulders as they walked back to the house. 'Well, however long we're here, I'm determined to make the best of it. And I'm not going to keep worrying about what might lie around the corner.'

'I may be older than you,' said Carin, 'but I do think you are definitely wiser.'

But the next day, a new arrival joined them at 5 Shore Road. Leni Schiffler was not a Jew or married to an Englishman, or a refugee of any kind. She had been interned because she was a German and a Nazi.

32

Waiting

TESS WAS SUDDENLY CALLED TO TAKE MINUTES OF A MEETING IN the boardroom at 2 Richmond Terrace. She'd not seen the visitors arrive so was flabbergasted to find her uncle, Denholm Castell, sitting opposite Ian Jacob and Lieutenant Commander Angus Nicholl, Ismay's naval aide.

'You all right, Tess?' General Ismay asked her, looking up from his seat at the head of the table. 'Look like you've seen a ghost.'

'She wasn't expecting to see her uncle sitting here, General,' said Denholm.

Ismay laughed. 'Of course. I suppose I never mentioned it to you, Tess. I've known your uncle a long while.'

Tess felt herself reddening and, not sure if she should say anything, smiled uncertainly at Denholm, who winked back. She took her seat at the desk behind Ismay. It wasn't a secretary's place to make a scene.

The meeting was to discuss the Prime Minister's demands to get Secret Intelligence Service agents into France as soon as possible now that an armistice had been signed by the French, although to begin with the conversation was dominated by the news from Mers-el-Kébir in Algeria, part of the French Empire. The British had feared that the French fleet there would be forced to hand over its ships to the Germans so demanded they join the Royal Navy or

365

surrender. When they'd refused to do either, the British warships had opened fire. Nearly thirteen hundred French sailors had been killed, one battleship sunk and two more badly crippled.

'As a signal to the world that Britain means business and intends to fight on, it was a very strong message,' said Claude Dansey, the deputy head of MI6. 'But how it will affect our ability to deal with the new French government at Vichy is less clear.'

'It's been a terrible business,' admitted Ismay, 'and I know Admiral Somerville felt dreadful. He was friends with his French counterparts – colleagues before the war. Just terrible, but I'm afraid it had to be done. We couldn't risk those ships falling into German hands.'

'Tragic though it was,' said Commander Dunderdale, 'I don't think it will make the Vichy government any more hostile than it already is.'

'I rather agree,' said Ismay. 'Pétain and Darlan never forgave us for getting off lighter than them in the last show. I met Pétain a few times before the armistice and he was both defeatist and hostile. It was very unpleasant. He's a frightful man. Anyway, be that as it may, how are you going to fulfil Winston's wishes? Destroying the French fleet in Algeria is one thing, but getting agents operating in France is quite another kettle of fish.'

Dansey cleared his throat.

'Yes, Dansey?' said Ismay.

'Thank you, General. We have two potential routes into France. Through contacts of ours now attached to Vichy – on paper at any rate – and also through working with de Gaulle and his Free French. To this end, Menzies has put Dunderdale here in charge of Section A.4 to continue to build contacts through Gustave Bertrand and Georges Groussard. Meanwhile, Cohen will head up Section A.5, which will work alongside de Gaulle's Bureau de Renseignements. We feel this may bear the greatest fruit in the short term because we know for certain that the BR are on our side and because we have greater access to them – and, obviously, their contacts in France – than we do to those in Vichy. It's why I've brought Lieutenant Commander Denholm Castell here today. Most of you already know him. He's been working for Six since the last war but has been living in France since 1919.' He turned to Denholm.

'Yes, I've been building up networks over there for the past twenty years and have accelerated them since last September. Mostly in the south, I should add, but that's all very much to the good now that we know how France has been carved up, with the Germans controlling the north and the Atlantic coast and the central southern part completely in the hands of Vichy.'

'We believe,' continued Dansey, 'that the best way to infiltrate agents is through Vichy France rather than occupied France.'

Tess was listening to this with some amazement. What a dark horse Uncle Denholm was! There were moments when she became so intrigued by what she was hearing that she almost stopped taking shorthand notes and had hurriedly to catch up.

'I cannot stress enough,' said Dansey, 'that we need to recruit agents from the areas in which we want them to operate. We need people to know how to hide what they're up to. As soon as a stranger arrives in an area, especially in wartime, they will stand out like a sore thumb. It's why the networks we already have in place are invaluable.'

The meeting ended a little over an hour later.

'Will you type those up for me this afternoon, Tess?' Ismay asked her. 'I want to get them to the PM and the War Cabinet as soon as possible.'

'Of course, sir,' Tess replied.

Denholm came over. 'I wonder, General, whether before she does you might excuse Tess for an hour?'

Ismay smiled. 'Yes, all right. If you think you can get those minutes done, Tess?'

She nodded. 'I will, sir.'

'Good. Then, yes, cut along with your uncle.'

Once they stepped outside and onto Whitehall, he said, 'Sorry if that shocked you, Tess.'

'It did rather.'

'Look, let's not chat here. We can go to my club. It's only round the corner on Pall Mall and there's a Ladies' Room. We can go in there and have a single course. Does that sound all right? Won't take you long to type up those minutes, will it?'

'I hope not. An hour and a half maybe.'

'And it's only half twelve now. Plenty of time!'

They talked as they strode up Whitehall and into Trafalgar Square. They had a house not far from the office in Maunsel Street, he told her. 'Lucky to get it really. The girls seem to like it. Of course, it's not quite the view they're used to but they're at the heart of things, St James's Park a ten-minute walk, Piccadilly and the bright lights a stone's throw away. Fallen on our feet, really.'

It was only once they were seated at their table that he said, 'Look here, Tess, I know you've signed the Official Secrets Act, but I just want to stress that you cannot mention any of this to Stork or any of the family.'

'Of course not! I wouldn't dream of it – I've not—'

He held up a hand. 'Didn't doubt it for a moment. But it'll have to remain our little secret. I did wonder whether I might see you at today's meeting, but Ismay obviously knew the connection when he took you on and felt comfortable with that.'

Tess looked at him aghast. 'Did he . . . ?'

'Yes, I was in London last summer and he mentioned he was looking for a new secretary so I suggested you. Don't worry, you got the job on merit, Tess. He wouldn't have employed you if he didn't think you were up to it. And you clearly are.'

'Gosh, Uncle Denholm,' said Tess. 'It really is turning into a morning of surprises.'

He laughed. 'So, how's everyone else? Edward's got his fiancée knocked up and Carin's been banged up.'

'Uncle Denholm! Really!'

He held his hands up. 'Sorry, sorry, talking out of turn again.'

'Can't you do something for Carin? She's no more a threat to our security than Maimes might be. It's ridiculous. She's sharing a house with a Jewish refugee who sounds adorable and some horrible Nazi.'

'Febrile times we live in, Tess. People are still nervous about parachutists dropping from the sky. The whole country seems to be waiting for Hitler to make a move, as far as I can tell.'

'But you might be able to help?'

'You may now know where I'm working, Tess, but don't overestimate my influence. I'm merely a very small cog in a big machine.'

'Please try, Uncle Denholm. I did tell General Ismay but he hasn't mentioned it again.'

'Well,' he said, and smiled, 'how's the fish? All right? You know, it really is very jolly to see you. We might do this again. My very favourite eldest niece.' And that was it: the subject was closed.

They parted outside the club, Denholm heading back across St James's Park and she to Whitehall. She could see why her father and her uncle never saw eye to eye. But she was fond of him, none the less. He *was* fun to be around, and, she thought, rather remarkable in his way. Yet she also wondered why he'd so suddenly changed the subject when she'd pressed him about Carin.

HMS *Iceni,* repaired, its various crew back from training, Ollie included, was now on east coast duties, escorting colliers down from Scotland and Teesside to London and back. Each trip was three days down from Rosyth and three days back. Short trips in the big scheme of things, but one could never relax for a moment, not just because of the threat of enemy aircraft, submarines and even fast torpedo boats, but because Britain had its own protective wall of minefields while the Germans had also begun laying increasing numbers of sea mines. The entire eastern coastline of Britain was awash with them. Minesweepers swept ahead but navigation was challenging because the convoy, often up to fifty ships, had to follow a series of light buoys marked out every five miles or so, and it was all too easy to stray.

On *Iceni*'s second trip, Ollie had been officer on watch when a huge explosion not far behind had erupted, making him and everyone on the bridge jump. The collier had gone down in a matter of minutes and they'd only been able to pick up seven men from the crew. Ollie had been shocked by the random violence, by the speed with which it had happened.

Now, on Tuesday, 9 July, they were heading south when a seaplane buzzed over the Humber estuary. Ollie had once again been on watch and quickly identified it as a Heinkel 115. It was painted white and had red crosses on it, which suggested it was air-sea rescue, but it was a long way from home – presumably Norway, Ollie guessed. He was unsure whether to give the order to open fire or not. On the other hand, should he disturb the captain to check? The red crosses persuaded him he should.

'Bridge to captain,' he said, down the voice pipe. 'German air-sea rescue seaplane with red cross markings circling. Permission to open fire?'

'Granted. Shoot the bastard down.'

Moments later, two Spitfires appeared, roaring overhead, and beat them to it, peppering it with machine-gun bullets. Trailing thick smoke, the Heinkel drifted down, the pilot landing safely on the water. Ollie ordered the helmsman to head towards it, his binoculars trained on the crew as they climbed out. In moments they had inflated a rubber dinghy and scrambled in as the Heinkel began to sink. By the time *Iceni* was alongside them, the seaplane had almost disappeared beneath the waves.

Ollie ordered a net to be lowered and the three men came aboard, the first Germans with whom he'd come face to face. Sullen and scowling but otherwise not so very different, he thought. *But of course they're not*, he chided himself. Why would they be?

Bertie ordered Ollie to take *Iceni* into Hull. 'We can hand our guests over,' he said. 'I'm keen to get these vermin off my ship as soon as possible.'

It didn't take long: at full throttle, *Iceni* could make almost four times the speed of the colliers, and a little over an hour and a half later they rejoined the convoy, the prisoners safely deposited with the police.

'Should we be shooting down rescue planes?' Ollie asked, later that evening, as they ate supper in the wardroom.

'Rescue plane, my arse!' said Jimmy Malone.

'But it was unarmed.'

'It was a recce plane.'

'Did you hear a Heinkel was shot down this afternoon?' asked Bertie. 'Soon after you came off watch. *Black Swan* got it. A so-called air-sea rescue plane buzzes over, spots the convoy, sends off a signal and, bingo, Heinkels follow. I'm telling you all now, if you see an enemy plane, whatever type it is, don't wait for permission to open fire, just try to blast the bastard out of the sky, because they're only interested in one thing.'

'Sinking our ships,' said Malone.

'Spot on, Number One. Chaps, I have to say, I think we're in for quite a time of it. God knows what's going on in Hitler's mind but it seems pretty clear to me that now he's got France in the bag he's building up forces. We've got the North Sea and the Channel in the way but it's our job to make sure those swine don't get to England. So, if you see an enemy plane, you give those buggers everything we've got, all right?'

'Damn right,' agreed Jimmy.

'Got that, Sub?' Bertie said, looking at Ollie.

'Yes, sir.'

Later, in his cabin, and before his next watch Ollie reread Elsa's latest letter. That last leave had unsettled him: there had been a barrier between them, invisible, unspecific, but there all the same. Yet the letters had continued to arrive. Her mother was on the Isle of Man and seemed in much better spirits. *We think it sounds rather like a holiday at the seaside and are worried she's now having too nice a time and won't want to come back*, she had written. The hay was in, and they were bracing themselves for harvest. More Spitfires and Hurricanes were flying over the valley. *I always wave if I see Spitfires, in case it's Wilf.* That was very Elsa, he thought. In this letter, at any rate, she seemed more her normal self. Perhaps he was thinking too hard about things. He lay back and closed his eyes. Next watch in three hours. He needed to get some sleep.

Tuesday, 16 July 1940

Early afternoon. Outside it was raining, not hard but persistently, and the skies were sullen. Stork was in his office when he heard the distinctive sound of a motorbike and, looking out, felt a pulse of joy as he saw Wilf pull it onto its stand and jump off.

'Wilf!' he called, from the window.

His younger son grinned and waved. 'I'm on a twenty-four-hour pass!'

Stork hurried down to the house to find his wife embracing her boy.

'Where's Brenda?' Wilf said. 'I hear it's all change at Farrow-combe. Brenda here, Mrs Collis gone, and Hannah now running the show.'

'Brenda will be back shortly,' said Debbo. 'She's just gone down to the post office.'

They migrated to the drawing room.

'Well, the good news is that we've been posted to Boscombe Down,' said Wilf.

'Marvellous,' said Stork. 'Does that mean we'll see a bit more of you?'

'Hope so. It took me less than half an hour to motor over, and we're now being given twenty-four hours off once a week and a forty-eight hour pass every three. I was thinking I could go up to London to see Tess but she always seems run off her feet. More fun to come here.'

'And be waited on by your mother.'

'And Hannah.'

'She's an absolute Godsend,' said Debbo. 'And of course you must come here. We demand it.'

Wilf laughed. 'So what about Grandpa and Maimes? How did you square it with them?'

Stork glanced at Debbo. 'Well,' he said, 'I was certainly braced for another battle but actually he rather rolled over. At any rate, your grandfather is still talking to me.'

'That's a relief. And, actually, I've got some news too.'

'Oh, yes?' said Stork.

'Yes, I'm officially an ace. Got an Me110 yesterday over Portland. So, that was my fifth.'

'Congratulations,' said Stork.

'Oh, darling, I can't bear the thought of you shooting down aircraft. You talk of it as though it's some kind of sport. Of course, I'm jolly proud, but it makes me feel quite ill to have to think about it.'

Wilf laughed. 'Well, bragging is deeply frowned upon, you know, but I've been bursting to tell someone, and I know you two won't mind me shooting a line. I'm only the second in the squadron after Bluey. Sim's only got two and a possible. But don't worry. I can assure you, Mum, I'm not remotely treating it as a sport.' He turned to Stork. 'And before you say anything, Dad, I shan't let it go to my head, and I'm not going to get complacent.'

Later, after it had cleared a little, Wilf and Stork took the dogs up onto the downs.

'I've become quite a methodical and calculating pilot,' Wilf told him. 'I learned a lot over Dunkirk.'

'Such as?'

'That I need to get in close, watch my back all the time and never stop moving my head. That a one-oh-nine can always out-dive my Spit. And that it's better not to take the risky option. There will always be another chance.'

'Good. Very glad to hear it.'

'And I've also discovered I've got really excellent eyesight. I probably have you and Mum to thank for that.'

'Must make you a very popular chap to fly with.'

Wilf laughed. 'Yes, it does rather.' They reached the top of Farrowcombe and found themselves wandering over to the Dutch barn where Dorothy was kept.

'Shall we have a look at her?' suggested Stork. 'Check she's in one piece?'

A path led through the barley, which was now almost golden. 'Funny to think this used to be the air strip,' said Stork. 'We'll have to start cutting next week.'

'You'll put it back to grass after the war, though?'

'I hope so.'

'And how is Brenda settling in?'

'All right, I think. It's terribly difficult for her, though. She feels something of a social outcast and to begin with she was understandably over-anxious not to put a foot wrong. But your mother has been wonderful and Brenda really is delightful. She's utterly charming.'

'And venturing into the village?'

'Yes, she is now, but no one could tell she's pregnant and we've not told anyone.'

'No one? Not even Maimes and Grandpa?'

Stork shook his head. 'We will, of course. But we've only just taken on Hannah. One hurdle at a time.'

'Careful, Dad,' said Wilf. 'You don't want another bomb to explode.'

'A point well made and duly noted.' They talked on, of the farm and Stork's concerns for the coming harvest: whether the weather would be kind and how they would physically manage. A much higher minimum wage had just been introduced for agricultural labour.

'That's a good thing, isn't it?' asked Wilf.

'Hopefully it will attract a few more to the land, but it's still us farmers who've got to find the manpower and pay the forty-eight shillings a week.'

'You'll find a way, Dad. Perhaps the Army can help now they're back from France.'

They returned to the current situation and the air battle that was gathering pace.

'I think Jerry's slowly but surely bringing units up to the French coast,' said Wilf. 'That seems to be what everyone thinks. Bluey gets notes from the station commanders, they get notes from Group and so on. We've been told not to fly over the sea and we've also been discouraged from operating as a whole squadron unless there's a raid over land.'

'They don't want you bailing out into the sea.'

'And I don't want to be bailing out into the sea. But sometimes it's not so easy. The Luftwaffe are attacking shipping in Portland, as they were yesterday, and we're told to go and intercept. What the hell are we supposed to do?'

'Keep in sight of land, I suppose.'

'That's what we've been doing.'

They reached the barn and Stork and Wilf opened the doors. There was the De Havilland, a drip-tray on the ground under the engine, the cockpit draped in canvas.

'She's getting dusty, Dad. Smudger still starting her up once in a while?'

'Every month or so.'

Nearby they heard the sound of aero engines and hurried out. Six Spitfires thundered over, heading north.

'From Middle Wallop, I expect,' said Wilf. 'How is Elsa?'

'Doing well on the farm. No *joie de vivre*, though. It's been a terrible shock to her, all that's happened. When you next get a pass, why don't you try to see her? Take her for a drink in the pub, perhaps.'

Wilf nodded. 'All right. I'd like that. Do you think Carin will be let home soon?'

'God knows. I've lost count of how many letters I've written. Tess said she'd asked her general about it. We can but hope.'

Monday, 29 July 1940

Harvest had begun. Elsa was in the garden at Rose Bower, reading the day's letters, from Ollie and her mother. She knew Ollie couldn't tell her too much about what he was doing at sea, so his letters were instead full of descriptions of the men on board, his fellow officers, and of the various customs, rules and rituals. And then, occasionally, there would be a throwaway line about a 'pretty heavy raid' or how 'we lost three ships on the last convoy'. Reminders of the danger he faced on every trip.

How she had pined for him when he'd first left Alvesdon. Now, though, she had become used to it, and, if she was honest with herself, missed him a little less. She was even used to her mother being away, although with Robbie and Maria now back from school for the holidays and her father out three nights a week with the LDV, she found she was increasingly playing the role of mother. Her father had brought in some help, and Mrs Cole was kind and a very good cook, but combined with working six days out of seven on the farm, it was exhausting. She was nineteen, but she felt much older.

Sitting out in the garden in the evening was a highlight of the day, especially if there were letters to read. The bench by the stream had been her mother's favourite spot and it had become hers too. She looked down at Carin's unmistakable handwriting. *She held this paper*, thought Elsa, *and put this ink on the page*. She read, imagining her mother's voice. She was, she wrote, a bit bored: *We've done the same walk every day. It's lovely but this really is a very small area and we are just starting to feel a little claustrophobic.* Anna had been trying to teach her to play the violin, but she was proving a terrible student. They were both determined to de-Nazify Leni, although so far, they had not been very successful. *Anna is trying to smother her with kindness*, her mother wrote, *and I am attempting to do the same*.

There was a third letter that day, and to her surprise – and delight – it was from Wilf and characteristically pithy: *Dear Elsa, Will be home on Tuesday 30th. Am bringing my friend, Sim. Let's have a night at the Three Horseshoes. Will come and pick you up. Love, Wilf.*

That might be fun, she thought. Perhaps she should mention it to the land girls too. She smiled to herself. Something to look forward to.

Wilf was as good as his word. Seven o'clock the following evening, there he was, still in his RAF uniform, grinning sheepishly.

'Ready?' he said. 'I take it you got my letter?'

'Yes and yes,' Elsa replied, shouted goodbye to the others and followed him down the path to where a dark blue Morris 8 was waiting, engine ticking over.

'This is my friend Sim,' said Wilf, as Elsa clambered into the back.

'Hello,' he said, leaning over and shaking her hand. 'Very jolly to meet you.'

'Thank you for picking me up.'

'Pleasure's all ours.'

Sim turned the car around and then they headed back down the valley to Alvesdon, taking the straight stretch at terrifying speed.

Elsa hardly dared look. She would have liked to remind them they were on a back road in Wiltshire not in a Spitfire but didn't want to sound prudish. Then Sim slowed dramatically as they approached a corner and Elsa felt herself lurch forward.

'You're such a show-off, Delaney!' said Wilf.

'Sorry, Elsa,' said Sim. 'Couldn't resist.'

'We've been tinkering with the engine,' grinned Wilf. 'It's quite a bit faster now.'

'I can feel that,' said Elsa.

In the pub, Wilf and Sim were bombarded by questions from the villagers. Were they giving the Luftwaffe a bloody nose? What were they flying?

'Er, Spitfires,' said Sim. He had wavy fair hair, was a little taller than Wilf, with full lips, dark eyebrows and a resolute chin. Elsa thought him terribly good-looking. The Spitfires had impressed Reg Mundy and Bill Sawcombe.

More questions, and a round of drinks 'on the house' from Fred Mullins, the landlord. Then the land girls joined them and they moved to a table in the corner. More drinks, pints for the boys, Elsa sticking with half-pints of cider along with the land girls but, later, at Hattie's urging, trying ginger wine. Sim told a story of Wilf flying

376

very low over a football match the previous winter and seeing all the players dive onto the ground and get themselves covered with mud. 'Very childish,' admitted Wilf, then told them of how Sim had been torn off a strip for performing a low pass at more than 360 miles per hour last week at the very moment the high sheriff of Wiltshire and his wife were getting out of their car for a visit. 'Blew her hat clean off her head,' said Wilf. 'Never seen again.'

They all laughed. 'Lucky to be allowed out today,' said Sim.

When Sim went to buy more drinks, Hattie nudged her and said, 'He's a bit sweet on you, isn't he?'

Elsa was starting to feel rather tight. 'What are you talking about, Hattie?' she said. 'Don't be ridiculous.'

And Hattie gave her a look. *I'm right.* And when he came back, he sat down next to Elsa and began talking to her about things they liked and disliked, and they discovered they had much in common. 'I'm going to come here again, if I may?' he said.

'Of course,' said Elsa. 'It's been fun.'

'Come on,' said Susie, eventually, after Fred had rung the bell, 'we should all go. Time for bed. Work tomorrow for some of us.'

'Yes, you're quite right,' said Sim, 'and apologies, ladies, for keeping you so long but it's been a most enjoyable evening.'

'Most enjoyable,' said Wilf.

'I feel a bit tight,' said Elsa, getting up.

'I feel very tight,' said Wilf.

They stumbled out of the pub, said goodnight to Susie, Hattie and Jill, then climbed into Sim's car.

'Strictly speaking,' said Sim, 'I probably shouldn't be in charge of this vehicle.'

'Drive slowly,' suggested Wilf. 'You'll be fine.'

Sim crawled down the back road to Middle Chalke. By the time they reached Rose Bower, Wilf was asleep, but Sim got out and held open the door for Elsa.

'I'll walk you to the door,' he said. 'Thank you, Elsa. It's been a lovely evening.'

At the door she turned and said, 'Well, goodnight. Thank you for the lift home.'

'May I kiss you?' he asked.

'Yes,' said Elsa.

He leaned forward and kissed her and then his arms were around her and she was kissing him back.

'I must go,' she said, pulling away. She turned and opened the door and saw Sim grin, then walk back down the path.

The next morning she woke at half past six, mouth dry, head pounding, and then, like a thunderbolt, remembered the kiss. She rolled onto her back and put her hands to her head. *Oh, no*, she thought. *What have I done?*

33

Crossroads

JULY GAVE WAY TO AUGUST. THE LUFTWAFFE KEPT UP ITS ATTACKS on Allied shipping in the Channel and tried to draw the RAF out over the sea, but of a German invasion there was still no sign. At 5 Shore Road in Port Erin, Leni Schiffler was undeterred. Hitler's forces were on their way, she assured them.

'It might be a few more weeks,' she told Anna and Carin, one morning, as they walked around the headland, 'but the invasion will happen. And then I'll be free, and you, Anna, will be forced to go wherever they decide to send the Jews.'

It had become something of a rather surreal sport, it occurred to Carin, this verbal sparring, in which neither side would back down. 'Hitler knows this is the great battle of our age,' Leni had told them one evening over their tea with Elsie. 'He knows that if we true Europeans, we Aryans, are to survive and regain our rightful place as the dominant race we have to defeat the Slavs and drive Jewry from Europe. It is a tragedy, I'll admit, but it has fallen to our generation to ensure future generations can live in peace and harmony. That is our burden. But we are blessed that our Führer has been sent to us to help us. I know you cannot understand that but in a hundred years from now, you British will be thanking Hitler and we Germans for what we have done.'

'Well, I don't know about that,' Elsie said. 'I can't say I have much time for Communists but I'm ever so fond of you, Anna, and while I can't say I've known many of the Jewish faith, the ones I have met have been very nice, respectable people.'

'Thank you, Elsie,' said Anna. 'And I am most fond of you too.' She then turned to Leni. 'Can you not see how absurd you sound, Leni? In what way am I different from you?'

'You're a Jew.'

'I'm not a practising Jew. I don't speak Yiddish. I don't go to a synagogue. If anything, I'm entirely agnostic, just like a proper Nazi.'

'So you keep telling me. And yet you were born a Jew. And I was born an Aryan.'

Anna sighed. 'A mere accident of birth. Racially, we're the same.'

Leni laughed. 'That we most certainly are not.'

'In what way are we different, then? We both have European eyes, we both have brown hair, we're even pretty much the same height.'

'Jews look different,' Leni retorted. 'Everyone knows that. Jews have bigger noses and darker brows. Physiologically, they're different.'

'I bet my nose is smaller than yours.'

'Of course it isn't.'

'Let's measure them.'

'Don't be ridiculous.'

'You're being ridiculous. You just said Jews have larger noses. Jews are not a race, Leni. Jews are like Christians, or Hindus, or Buddhists or Muslims. It's a different religion, not a different race. Honestly, I know you're a bright girl. How can you not understand that?'

'You're talking rubbish.'

'I am not. You are. And I'm going to prove it. Elsie, have you got a tape measure?'

'Somewhere.'

She disappeared and reappeared a minute later with one. And much to Leni's annoyance, it showed, beyond any doubt, that Anna's nose was shorter and narrower than Leni's.

'Leni, don't you ever worry you might have been sold a lie?' Carin asked her. 'My father and brother have become followers of Hitler too. It's so tragic because I know most Germans are kind, good and wonderful people. But you've been seduced by some very sinister men and their very sinister ideologies.'

Once, Carin had asked Elsie what she made of Leni, an avowed Nazi, living in her house. 'I think she's rather confused, poor lamb,' Elsie had replied. 'A bit brainwashed if you ask me.' Leni had been an au pair in London when war had been declared but had liked the family she was with. They hadn't seemed keen to throw her out, but she had kept her views to herself. 'I'm not a fool.' She had thought she might be able to send information home that would help the war effort and was confident that when the invasion occurred she would have a role to play.

And yet Leni was softening. That they were now, in the first week of August, walking together was a new development. Leni had even joined them swimming and last night had complimented Anna on her rendition of Brahms's violin concerto. She was so young, Carin thought. Her head had been turned. It could, she was sure, be turned back. Later, as they splashed in the sea together and she caught Leni laughing, it proved to Carin, as if it had ever needed proving, that the human capacity to empathize, to befriend and to love was fundamental and within everyone's grasp.

Whenever the sun shone, there were long days in the fields now that the harvest was under way. The Army had not yet been recruited to help although Stork had amassed an array of workers for the days when the sun beat down. While the regular farm workers manned the tractors and pulled the binders, women, young boys and older men from the village collected the sheaves left behind and put them into stooks.

A time for thinking, for musing on matters. As Elsa sat on Thor, pulling one of the reaper-binders, she decided she needed to give herself a bit of a talking-to. She'd been ashamed of herself for kissing Sim but it had forced her to take herself to task. She had been miserable for far too long. She missed her mother desperately, as she did Ollie, and that one kiss had made her realize how much. Forbidden fruit had been dangled in front of her and, while she had been far from sober, she had bitten from it. Now, though, she wanted it no more.

She had been surly with Ollie last time he'd been home. Precious time for him, for both of them, and she'd spoiled it by allowing self-pity to invade. So, there was a part of his life into which she could not venture. Why should that matter? She knew about as much of his life on board *Iceni* as she possibly could. His mother, Eleanor, had even acknowledged as much: 'Oh, I always come to you, Elsa,' she'd said, 'if I want to know how Ollie is getting on.' Elsa was, she thought, as Thor trundled up and down Cuckoo, very lucky to have Ollie in her life. To have his love for her. And now she worried afresh about his safety, about what might happen to him if Hitler really did try to invade and about what he would say when she told him about the kiss with Sim. Because she had to tell him. They'd always said no secrets. That they could always trust one another. She prayed he would forgive her.

She reached the end of the field, stopped the cutter on the binder, turned, then started it again and began another strip. Ahead stood the downs with their curves and soft immutability. In the field, workers were picking up the sheaves and making stooks, half of Cuckoo already lined with rows of them, bundles of corn stacked together. She breathed in deeply, smelt the dust and the freshly cut barley, and felt the sun beating down and the heat from the metal cover of the engine in front of her. The rumble of the Fordson, the clacking of the binder, the clunk and squeak, every twenty seconds or so, as another sheaf was bound and dropped from the side. A hare darted out and dashed across the field. She would make amends, she told herself. Plead Ollie's forgiveness. Perk up and be thankful that she didn't have to face Luftwaffe bombs and sea mines or fly Spitfires into the face of the enemy. And, unlike her mother, she was at least at home, doing her bit in her own way to help the war effort. She had friends and most of her family around her. She had, she told herself, so much to be thankful for.

Tom was also cutting the crop but in Kite Field, the other side of the downs, and with one of the farm's older binders, which was being drawn by two of the horses. His arm hurt a lot less but steering a tractor put a painful strain on it, whereas with the horses he could hold the reins lightly, even when turning, and felt no pain at all. In any case, he liked working with horses – they were nothing like as temperamental as tractors. He enjoyed the rhythmic pull and watching their heads and necks bow gently up and down. At midday, dinner time, he pulled them up, found a patch of shade for them to rest in, gave them each a bag of oats, then sat down and tucked into a hunk of bread and cheese.

He wanted to do what was for the best, but so much depended on his arm. His last medical had been a week earlier when he'd put on his uniform again and taken the train to Aldershot. The army doctor had looked at his original X-rays then cut off his cast, taken a new set of pictures and wrapped his arm in fresh plaster of Paris. It had been strange to see the bullet hole largely healed already, the skin pale and waxy, although he now had quite a crater in the upper side of his right forearm.

'How does it feel?' the doctor asked him.

'Bit sore, but all right,' he'd replied.

'Well, you're certainly not fit for active service yet. I'll see you again at the end of September. Perhaps we'll be in a better position to make a judgement then. How are you spending your time at the moment, Sergeant Timbrell?'

'Mostly working on the farm, sir. It's harvest time.'

The doctor nodded. 'All right, but don't overdo it.'

So, now he had to wait until September. He had been giving much thought to Mr Stork's proposition. The house would be wonderful; he'd also discussed it with his father, who agreed it was a rare and generous opportunity not to be passed up.

'You'd not mind, Father?' he'd asked.

'I'd miss you, but it's time you cut free. It's not like you'd be moving far after all.'

He'd also put things right with the master, who had summoned Tom to see him in his study, just as he'd used to when they still had the shoot. Mr Castell at his desk, Tom in front, standing with his hands behind his back. Formal, but that was the way the master liked to do things. Tom had worried about what the old man might say but he needn't have done. 'I'm sorry, Tom,' he'd said. 'I jumped to conclusions and it was wrong of me. I hope you'll forgive me.' Of course, Tom had told him. 'Denholm,' he had continued, 'should not – well . . .' He'd let the sentence trail. 'Well,' he'd said, after a moment's pause, 'let's never speak of it again. Draw a line, what?'

So, that was all right enough. *But I want to do the right thing,* he said to himself. Do the right thing by Hannah. He wanted to marry her and he wanted to share her bed, but Hannah wasn't Coco or

Edie Blythe or some of the other girls in the village he'd tussled with in the past. He was determined to do things properly but what if he took the house, got married, as he knew Mr Stork would expect him to, and then had to go off to war again? Hannah was only nineteen, same age as Miss Elsa. He couldn't leave her on her own in that house at the end of Windmill Lane. It wouldn't be fair. Wouldn't be right.

He sighed and lay back in the grass at the edge of the field. He could hear the horses crunching their oats. The sun shone down through the elms and the rays were warm on his face. He opened his eyes to see the leaves above dancing gently in the afternoon breeze.

Monday, 12 August 1940

The pilots of 599 Squadron were sitting around Dispersal – a small marquee at the southern edge of the airfield – most in an assortment of deckchairs, canvas stretchers used as day-beds, and even a couple of old armchairs. Not far away, their Spitfires were lined up, flying helmets and parachutes left on the wings. They heard an occasional clang from somewhere else around the field as an erk dropped a spanner, and skylarks singing their hearts out in the morning sun. Tony Madden and Brian Shepherd were playing chess, the board on an old box, cross-legged on the grass. Sim was reading a detective novel while Wilf, next to him, had his eyes closed listening to the birdsong.

An engine started on the far side of the airfield and Wilf opened his eyes.

Sim tapped him on the arm. 'Happy birthday again, Wilf.'

Wilf smiled. 'Thank you, Sim.' His friend had said it about a dozen times already. They all had. 'Happy birthday, Wilf. Happy birthday, Wilf.'

Sim had also given him a small aluminium model of a Spitfire, which he'd made for him and to which he'd attached to a keyring. Wilf had been rather touched.

As he'd been growing up, it had been wonderful to have a birthday in August, in the middle of the summer holidays, but today Wilf felt indifferent. So, now he was twenty. It would make no odds to the Luftwaffe. Perhaps they'd be kind enough to stay away and the squadron would not be scrambled but that was unlikely: it had been hazy earlier and Boscombe Down had been shrouded in mist at first light when the tumbrel had brought them down to Dispersal, but it had soon melted away and the morning had developed into a gorgeous August day. Conditions were far too good for the Luftwaffe to remain grounded on the far side of the Channel. Sim told him he had planned a bit of a knees-up in the mess later but, if he was honest, Wilf wasn't all that bothered.

Suddenly, the telephone rang, shrill and discordant in the still air, and Wilf opened his eyes. Everyone paused, waiting.

'Yes, all right, yes,' Wilf heard the orderly say. 'Right away, sir.' Then moments later the orderly was at the entrance to the tent shouting, 'Scramble!' and clanging his handbell. Novels dropped to the ground, the game of chess left unfinished.

Wilf pushed himself out of his deckchair and ran for his Spitfire. Grab the parachute, step into it, straps up under the legs and over the shoulders, brought together. *Click.* Helmet on, as Gregson fired up the machine, then leaped out and slid off the wing. Wilf hauled himself up, stepped into the cockpit, and dropped down, half-door up, clacking shut. The familiar smell: high-octane fuel, oil, rubber, metal. Chocks pulled clear, Davies signalling, open throttle, release the brakes and off, trundling over the grass to line up. Look each side. Clear. Open throttles wide, and off, speeding across the grass, 40, 50, 60 miles per hour on the clock, ease back on the stick, and Wilf saw the gap between his starboard wing and its shadow widen, and he was up, airborne once again. Switch hands, from right to left, so he could manually raise the undercarriage, and he was climbing, all twelve of them were, Wilf leading Green Section in B Flight and Bluey leading the squadron. A glance around. *Yes*, there was Art McAllister, the American behind him on his starboard side, and Archie Delafield on his port. *Good.*

The radio crackled in his headphones.

'Hello, Snapper Leader, Starlight calling. Head on bearing oh-seven-five. Bandits attacking Portsmouth and Ventnor.'

He heard Bluey acknowledge as they continued to climb, southern England spread before them, looking ever smaller, the higher they climbed. There, just over his starboard wing, were the valley and home, snaking between the two great ridges of Chalke, while to the south he could already see Southampton, Portsmouth and the Isle of Wight.

They flew on, and now, nearing Southampton, Wilf saw that Portsmouth was under attack. Smudges of anti-aircraft fire peppered the sky while suddenly there was a ripple of explosions and smoke. then more bombs still erupted over the city, smothering it in smoke.

Bloody hell, thought Wilf. *Portsmouth is really getting it.*

'Hello, Snapper Leader, this is Starlight. Patrol Ventnor angels twelve.'

'Hello, Starlight, Snapper answering.' Bluey. 'Repeat: angels twelve?'

'Hello, Snapper, yes, angels twelve.'

That was a bit low, thought Wilf. As they crossed the Solent, he could now see enemy fighters stacked up, Me110s and 109s. They would have to watch them very carefully, but it was the Stukas they were after, which he now saw were preparing to dive on Ventnor. Away to his left another Spitfire squadron was tearing into the bombers wheeling away from Portsmouth. A little too late but perhaps they'd make sure a few didn't return.

How many Stukas? Twenty? Two dozen? And above? *Christ*, forty or fifty, perhaps.

'Attack the Stukas,' called Bluey, over the R/T, 'but watch your backs.'

The sun high behind them. Below, Stukas starting their dives. He saw Red and Yellow Sections peel over and swoop down towards the enemy dive-bombers. A glance up, sun still behind him. *Here they come.* 110s and 109s starting to dive in turn, little dark crosses against the blue. Wilf's heart hammered and he felt the sweat under his flying helmet dripping down his temples. Mouth dry. Stomach lurching. Stick forward, engine screaming, and the altimeter dialling backwards. A Flight among them, Stukas scattering, but he fixed his bead on one, watching it carefully. *Don't overshoot.* Stick back. Starting to level out. The Stuka climbing up out of its dive, the machine still below his gunsight. Flip the switch on the gun button. Look behind. *Good, still clear.* And now the Stuka increasingly filled his gunsight. *Wait, wait . . . Now!* He pressed on the gun button, felt the judder from his wings and saw his bullets striking. A moment later the Stuka exploded, a ball of flame, and something whammed against the side of his cowling and he saw blood streak across the outside of his canopy, then vanish. Wilf gasped.

There was radio static in his ears. Jumbled voices. A bit of German, then one of theirs said, *'I've got one!'* He looked up frantically. A swirl of aircraft. Another Stuka diving, smoke trailing. Messerschmitts diving down. Wilf stayed low and banked north to be over land with the sun behind him, but heard Sim on the radio: 'I can't shake him! I can't shake him!'

Wilf scanned the sky and saw a Spitfire speed past over the Solent towards the New Forest, two Me109s on its tail. Was it Sim? He couldn't say but the Spitfire was now turning tightly, a 109 following, the other climbing.

Wilf saw what the German pilot was thinking: to climb, half roll, then dive down and open fire from height. Wilf opened the throttle and climbed so that as the Messerschmitt flick-rolled he opened fire and raked it from underneath then sped on past as another aircraft, this time a twin-engine 110, flew straight over him so close he saw the oil streaks and the black crosses on its underbelly and found himself ducking. *Good God, but that was close.*

The Messerschmitt he had raked was diving away, a thin trail of smoke in its wake but heading southwards over the sea. Where was the Spitfire? Suddenly he saw it, diving, catastrophically on fire, until it plunged into the sea but he also spotted a parachute fluttering down, thankfully over land. Was that Sim? He couldn't be sure. He looked around him, up, down, behind. Over the New Forest, the sky was suddenly and miraculously clear. He circled, watching the sky above but also checking the man at the end of the parachute safely touch down – *There, yes, safe*, the canopy collapsing. He looked around, then headed for home at tree-top height. Ten minutes later he was touching down at Boscombe Down.

Several Spitfires were already back as he slid off the wing and staggered to Dispersal. More landed as he collapsed into the deckchair he'd left just forty minutes earlier. He hoped Sim was all right, but his Spitfire had not returned.

Nor did it. By one o'clock, the eleven others were back but not Sim. Wilf recounted his own action to Paddy Lawson, the intelligence officer.

'I think that must have been Sim you saw,' said Paddy, 'because several others saw him heading in that direction and swear it was him.'

'Then he definitely got out,' said Wilf. 'I saw him. Waited for him to touch down.'

'All right,' said Paddy. 'We'll follow up. Try not to worry.'

Wilf helped himself to a mug of sugary tea, then sat down in his deckchair.

'Are you all right, Wilf?' Bluey asked him. 'I'm sorry about Sim, but I'm sure he'll be all right. Rotten birthday, though.'

Wilf closed his eyes. He was sure his friend would be safe. Picked up by some Home Guard men, probably.

But not until six that evening did any news come through, when the phone rang at Dispersal. As always, everyone stopped, listened, waiting to be scrambled. But the call was for Bluey. Wilf got up, walked over, and leaned against one of the poles at the entrance, listening.

'Yes, all right,' Bluey was saying. 'Yes . . . Please thank them very much . . . Yes, I'll let them know . . . Thank you. Goodbye.' He put the phone down and looked across at Wilf. 'Well, the good news is he's alive, but it seems he's been burned, Wilf. Quite badly. I'm so very sorry. He's being taken by ambulance to East Grinstead already.'

Later, after they'd been stood down and the tumbrel had dropped them back at the mess, Tony Madden said, 'Still have a few drinks after dinner, Wilf?'

'Yes, all right,' said Wilf. He knew Sim would want him to, although he felt even less like carousing than he had earlier that morning. Back in his room, Sim's bed was exactly as he'd left it: roughly made, pyjamas in a heap on his pillow. Photo of his family and the keys to his Morris on the small bedside cabinet. But so much had changed.

What a day, thought Wilf. He couldn't get the image of the blood streaking across his canopy out of his mind. What was it that had hit him? *Don't think about it*, he told himself. But it had been his bullets that had caused it. A wave of nausea rolled through his stomach. And then poor Sim. Wilf sat down on the edge of his bed. What a rotten birthday this was turning out to be.

Friday, 16 August 1940

It was cloudy as Tess walked to the office. She wondered what that meant for the air battle that was now raging in the skies over southern England. She hoped Wilf would be safe, but reading the daily situation reports made her shudder. He'd rung and told her what had happened to his friend Simon Delaney. She'd met Sim – a good-looking, cheery boy and an inseparable friend of Wilf's since they'd been at Cranwell together. It was too sad, but as she knew from reading the daily reports, all too many young pilots were losing their lives or suffering catastrophic injuries. The war was very real.

At her desk, she organized the overnight minutes, memos and reports. *Co-ordinated attacks on aerodromes,* she read, in the summary from RAF Fighter Command Headquarters. *Lympne, Hawkinge, Martlesham Heath, Driffield, Middle Wallop, West Malling and Croydon all badly damaged.* Luftwaffe losses estimated at seventy-six aircraft destroyed, RAF thirty-five. Clearly, the Luftwaffe was intensifying its attacks: a memo Tess had seen the day before assessed German tactics as having shifted from Channel shipping to a concentration on RAF airfields.

'This is it,' General Ismay had said, the day before. 'This is the Luftwaffe's all-out attack. They mean to destroy Fighter Command. All we have to do is hold on.'

There was a memo from the Prime Minister on the deal with the United States, signed the day before. The Americans would hand over 120 old destroyers in return for British bases in the Caribbean. It meant America was starting to side with Britain both materially and politically; that had to be a good thing. Certainly the general had been pleased. And then, among the other papers, she found a letter addressed to her, labelled 'Private' but still sent internally. She opened the envelope and pulled out the single sheet.

Dear Tess,

Thought you'd want to know the good news. Your aunt, Carin, and her friend Anna Hartman, are due to be released and allowed home. Ordeal almost over! Best not breathe a word until it happens, though, but imminent.

Your loving uncle,
Denholm Castell

Tess sat back and clapped her hands together. Thank goodness, she thought. *At last.*

She left the office that afternoon for a week's leave. She'd not warned her parents but intended to spend most of her time at Alvesdon. First, though, dinner with Alex. At Quaglino's, of all places. She'd never been before but Alex had insisted. He was spoiling her.

'Golly,' he said, when she opened the door a little before seven o'clock. 'You look ravishing, Tess.' She had made an effort: a full-length emerald-green sleeveless silk dress and a short jacket to cover her shoulders. Bright red lipstick, mascara, and earrings he'd given her last summer.

'You look very handsome yourself,' she said, kissing him. He was wearing his dress uniform, his arm finally no longer in a sling. He looked very dashing, she thought, and she felt a frisson of excitement to see him and at the prospect of the evening ahead.

Dinner was everything she'd hoped it would be. Alex charming, the food – and wine – delicious. He was still not fully fit but was back with the regiment on what he called 'light duties'. 'And I've had some rather pleasing news,' he told her. 'I hope you won't think me an awful show-off telling you this, but I've been awarded a Military Cross. An MC.'

'Oh, Alex, that's wonderful. Congratulations. Can you add the ribbon to your uniform?'

'Yes, I just haven't had the chance yet. The colonel told me this afternoon. In all honesty, I'm no more deserving than many others. They don't hand out too many but it reflects well on the battalion. And Tom Timbrell has been given a Military Medal, too. Isn't that marvellous? I made sure I put him in for one and it's gone through.

It'll be in the *London Gazette* next week so keep it under your hat until then.'

'Of course. I'm actually rather good at keeping secrets, you know.'

He laughed. 'Of course you are. The things you must see, Tess.'

She smiled. 'That's wonderful news for Tom.'

'How is he, by the way?'

'In love with our housekeeper at Farrowcombe. He's still got his arm in plaster.'

'I need him back.'

'I think he'd rather stay on the farm.'

'Hmm. He may not be able to.' He sat back. 'But let's not worry about such things now. I'm just very happy to be here with you. There have been many moments when I doubted I'd ever see you again. I'm a very lucky fellow.'

Tess felt a little bit in love with him again. She moved her hand across the table, felt his fingers entwine with hers, and said, 'What next, Alex?'

'Tonight?'

'Tonight, and beyond.'

'Well,' he said, 'I'm back in London now and hoping to see a lot more of you. Where I'll be in two months' time, let alone six, I simply don't know. It all rather depends on the war. But I'm very fortunate to be here now and I intend to live the rest of my life, however long it may be, without regret and as fully as possible. Let's worry about today, and tomorrow, and perhaps even next week. Beyond that, what will be will be.'

Diana was away for the weekend, so they had the house to themselves. A nightcap and then up the stairs to her room. He kissed her then began undressing and Tess felt a sense of excitement but also apprehension. It had been such a long time, and she felt rather shy again as he unclipped her dress and it fell to the floor. The room was lit dimly by just a small bedside lamp. She felt his smooth chest on her hands and then the livid scar of his wound, on both sides of his shoulder. A body defaced, she thought.

Later, after they had made love, she lay awake for a long time, uncertain of how she felt. The charm that had won her over last summer had not diminished; he was attentive, very good-looking and excellent company. Was that enough? She hardly knew him.

Not really. They'd had those wonderful weeks together last August and then he'd gone to war. Had it been love? She had thought so at the time. It was so hard to know what to think.

It was all very well wanting to live each day as it came, but where did that leave her? Would he propose? Would marriage come next? Because she wasn't at all sure she wanted to marry him, not yet at any rate. And when she thought of Edward and Brenda, theirs seemed a deeper love than anything she felt for Alex. That was the truth of the matter. *There*, she thought. *I've admitted it to myself now.*

Sometime later, she drifted off to sleep, but then a terrible sound entered her dreams: someone screaming. She awoke with a start. Beside her, Alex was shouting in pain and fear, his body contorting and writhing next to her. Like a man possessed.

Her heart hammering, she switched on the light and gently shook his shoulder, but he said, 'Get off me!' and lashed out with his arm. She cried out with pain as she fell off the bed and onto the floor.

My God, she thought, picking herself up. Her hip hurt and so did the top of her chest where he had hit her. She looked down at him, still writhing on the bed, and said, 'Alex! Alex, wake up!'

He turned and looked at her. 'Why are you standing there?'

'Are you all right, Alex?'

'A bad dream, that's all.' His brow glistened with sweat. 'Sorry if I woke you.' He turned over and, moments later, was asleep again. But for a long time Tess lay awake, staring out into the darkness and wishing her bed was once again her own.

34

Homecoming

THE POLICEMEN TURNED UP EARLY, JUST AS THEY HAD AT ROSE Bower when they'd taken Carin away.

'Carin, Anna!' Elsie called up the stairs. 'There are some men to see you.'

Carin hurried down, not daring to think what the meaning of their visit could be.

'Yes?' she said, with Anna right behind her. 'How can I help?'

'Mrs Carin Castell and Miss Anna Hartman?' said one of the men.

'Yes,' they said in unison.

'We're here to tell you that you are to be released.'

'Released?' Carin put her hands to her mouth. 'We're free?'

'Yes, madam.'

'When?' said Anna.

'Now. There's a little bit of paperwork but we've a car outside and we'll take you to Douglas, then put you on the ship to Liverpool.'

Carin's hands were shaking as she packed her clothes, folded away the photographs, the trinkets and pieces of jewellery she'd brought with her. She looked up and saw Leni leaning against the doorframe.

'You're going,' she said.

Carin nodded. 'Home.'

'I never thought I would say this, Carin, but I'll miss you. And Anna.'

'I will miss you too.'

Carin shut her case. 'Goodbye, Leni.' She paused, kissed her on both cheeks, then headed downstairs, where Anna was waiting. Both she and Anna promised to visit Elsie after the war.

'And do write, dears,' said Elsie. 'Let me know how you're getting on.'

Carin stepped into the car and glanced round, Anna beside her on the back seat. She saw Leni and Elsie standing in the doorway and waved. The car moved off and they drove away from Shore Road. Just like that. She had woken up an internee, but now she was free once more.

That day, the harvest was in at Alvesdon and Stork had asked the womenfolk of Farrowcombe to bring down some drink and cake to celebrate. Tess had not seen her father in such good spirits for a long time but the early finish to the cutting and the wonderful news about Carin had helped cast off a veil of despair that had lain over their family and the farm for too many months. The daily sound of aircraft overhead and the occasional glimpse of battle in the skies were reminders of the peril threatening the country, but any cause for cheer had to be enjoyed and celebrated. As she helped Hannah and Brenda make cakes in the kitchen that morning, her spirits rose.

'Do you realize,' said Stork, as he passed through on his way to the farm, 'this is the earliest we've ever finished the cut? And this year of all years!' He beamed then said, 'Your cakes smell absolutely delicious. I'll see you down there shortly.'

'Someone's in a good mood,' said Tess.

'It's nice to see him smilin',' said Hannah.

'It is,' agreed Tess.

'I'm ever so pleased to hear about Mrs John,' said Hannah. 'It'll be wonderful to have her back 'ere again.'

'I'm afraid Edward's not very happy, though,' said Brenda. 'At least, he wasn't when he wrote the letter that arrived this morning.'

'Why so, apart from the usual?' asked Tess.

'The regiment has lost their horses. They're being retrained as artillery. He says everyone feels it's frightfully infra dig.'

'That's so Edward to say that,' said Tess. 'What's happened to their horses?'

'Taken away and sold. Just like that. He wrote that he always knew it would happen at some point but they were all very upset about it. Wounded pride and sad to be parted from animals to which they were all most attached.'

'I can imagine. Although he'll be thrilled about Carin. I'll write and tell him later.' She looked wide-eyed at Hannah and Tess, then down at her stomach.

'What on earth is the matter?' asked Tess.

'I just felt movement. For the first time.' Another look of surprise. 'Goodness! There it goes again. Here.' She beckoned Hannah and Tess to her. 'Put your hands on my tummy.'

They did so, waiting, and suddenly there it was again. Movement.

They all laughed. 'It's quite the oddest sensation. I feel rather discombobulated,' said Brenda.

'A little life,' said Hannah. ''Tis amazing.'

'When did you last see Alwyn and Maimes, Brenda?' asked Tess.

'Not for a while. Debbo's been trying to ensure I avoid them. She's almost stopped inviting them to dinner and last time I had to have a "headache" and spent the evening in my room.'

'You are starting to show, you know.'

'I'm feeling it too. And I'm not sure I really want it to be a secret any more. I did to begin with, but I don't want to hide away or be made to feel ashamed for having our child.'

'Let me talk to my parents about this,' said Tess, 'because you can't miss out on Carin's homecoming. They all need to know and they all need to be happy for you.'

Brenda stayed at Farrowcombe while they headed down to the farm for the final cut of the harvest. It was in Cricket, a twelve-acre field next to the ground, backing on to the manor and lined by the track to Tippett's Wood on one side, the river on the other. It was Hattie who had the honour to cut the last strip, and when the binder spat out the last sheaf and it was placed in its stook, Stork gathered everyone around. There were a lot of people there, perhaps as many as sixty, Tess guessed, young, old, men, women, children, many of whom were the regular farm workers but several seasonal workers too.

'Well done, all of you,' said Stork. 'When it rained on the fifteenth of July, I feared the worst, because there's an old saying some of you will know that if it rains on St Swithin's Day, there's sure to be forty days of rain to follow. St Swithin has not lived up to his traditional reputation this year. Our farms are vital, and you, who work on the land, are very much our fourth arm, alongside the Navy, the Air Force and the Army. Without food we cannot win. But with it, we will win this war.'

High above him, some aircraft flew over, fighters heading south. Everyone looked up. When they'd gone, Stork said, 'Anyway, thank you all. It's a terrific achievement and I'm very proud of the lot of you.'

'Well done, Dad,' said Tess.

'I'm very relieved,' her father told her. 'We've already started threshing out in the fields and I can tell you the yields are wonderful, as much as fifty-two bushels an acre, compared with around forty on average last year. It's just what the doctor ordered.'

Tess ambled over to Elsa, who was with the land girls. 'I'm so thrilled about your news, Elsa. What a relief.'

Elsa grinned. 'I can hardly believe it. And a clean slate. She can do as she wants again.'

'Quite right. And she'll be back tomorrow?'

'Yes, Papa has gone to London to meet her and bring her home. I wonder whether she'll be any different. Whether it's changed her at all.'

'I suppose it might take a little while to settle back in properly. I don't know. It's such an unusual situation, isn't it?'

'The entire war is odd and unusual,' said Elsa. 'Everything has been thrown up in the air and is coming down again but not landing exactly as it was before.'

Tess thought that was quite a good way of putting things. As she sat with her parents in the drawing room, having drinks before dinner, and since Brenda had not yet appeared, she said, 'Don't you think it's time we were a little more open about matters? With Brenda, I mean?'

'I thought it was parents who were supposed to offer advice to their children,' said Debbo, 'not the other way around.'

'But Carin will be back tomorrow and we can't keep hiding poor Brenda away. You know, I felt the baby kicking this morning.'

Debbo looked up, her face radiant. 'Really? How wonderful!'

'It was rather. But Brenda does look pregnant now. It's not the sort of thing one can avoid and this isn't a Brontë novel where we hide her away in the attic.'

Debbo looked across at Stork. 'Tess does have a point, darling.'

'It'll mean lots of gossip and I'm afraid Maimes and Pa will find it very difficult.'

'But they've got to find out at some point, Dad,' said Tess.

Stork grimaced. 'True.'

'How about we let Carin get home,' suggested Tess, 'and we invite them all over here for a celebratory drink and supper on Monday. We can take a deep breath and tell everyone then. Hopefully, everyone will be in such a good mood about Carin that Brenda's baby might not cause a rumpus at all.'

'That, my darling,' said Stork, 'and knowing your grandparents, is a very risky strategy, as you well know. Let's mull it over.'

As Carin stepped off the train at Euston, she scanned the platform for John. A mass of people. Doors clacking shut and passengers surging forward, away, down the platform towards the terminus. She walked on, through the steam swirling from the locomotive, then there he was. He waved and grinned and she ran towards him.

'Darling Carin!' he said, kissing her and holding her. 'At last.' He stood back. 'Let me look at you. Yes, the same woman I married. You look well, darling. How are you feeling?'

'Happy, but a little odd. I'm not sure this is all real yet.'

He took her case and they eventually found a taxi, crossing London to Waterloo.

On the train, they talked until Basingstoke. Eventually Carin fell asleep, her head resting on John's shoulder. She awoke a little later with John nudging her. 'We're here, darling.'

Ten weeks she'd been away, the longest weeks of her life, Carin mused, in the car, driving down the familiar roads she knew so well. Here she was, as though she had never been away. She wondered how she would find life in the village now.

'The children are so excited to see you,' John told her.

'I can't wait. But I'm nervous, darling. Not about seeing them, of course, but about being back in the village.'

'Remember when you first came to Alvesdon?'

397

'Of course.'

'You soon won everyone over, didn't you? So you will again. And you don't have any silly category attached to your name any more. You're as you were, my beautiful wife and mother to three beautiful English-born children.' He smiled at her. 'We'll take it steady, Carin darling. There's no rush. Take some time to ease back into things, eh?'

And it was wonderful to be home, she thought, as the car pulled into the drive and John honked the horn. She got out, opened the gate, and the front door opened and Elsa, Robbie and Maria were running down the path towards her. All together again. *Home.*

Over dinner, she told them all about 5 Shore Road and the unlikely foursome they had made in the house.

'What do you think will happen to Leni?' Robbie asked.

'She remains convinced the invasion will come and that the Nazis will win. She's waiting for the day she's liberated. But I don't know. I suppose she'll stay there for the time being.'

'I'm much more worried about Anna,' said Elsa. 'She sounds lovely.'

Carin smiled. 'She is. Honestly, I don't know what I'd have done without her. She became a dear friend.'

'Invite her down, why don't you?' said John. 'We'd all love to meet her.'

'I will. I'm a little worried about her. She wasn't sure what she should do. She's a wonderful violinist but she's worried she'll struggle to find work. There are organizations in London to help people like her, though – refugees, I mean. She's clever, funny too. She ran rings round Leni. But in such a very gentle way. She's remarkable.'

Later, in bed with John, the window open and a gentle breeze ruffling over her. Somewhere nearby, owls hooting. She lay in his arms, head on his shoulder, arm across his chest. 'I've missed this.'

'Not as much as I have,' said John.

'This will sound odd, I know,' she said, 'but it hasn't been an entirely terrible experience. Oh, leaving you all was awful and something I never want to experience again, and the mill was truly terrible. But I've met some really rather wonderful people too. I honestly believe Anna will be a friend for life, and while I never, ever want to leave you again, my darling John, being away from you all has reminded me of how very lucky I am. How very fortunate we are.'

The family gathered in the drawing room at Farrowcombe, Stork opening champagne he'd been saving since the start of the war. On the news they'd heard of heavy air fighting over southern England that day. Wilf, though, was all right: he'd rung Carin earlier, she reported, to welcome her home.

Brenda and Tess had spent some time discussing what Brenda should wear and in the end she opted for a very long, light cardigan over her dress, which she hoped might hide her bump. All seemed to be going well enough until Alwyn suddenly exclaimed, 'My God, Brenda, are you with child?'

At that moment, everyone stopped and looked at her. She reddened and said, 'What a thing to ask, Alwyn!'

'Stork!' hissed Debbo, in his ear.

He stepped forward. 'Yes, this is, in many ways, a double celebration.' He saw the shock on his parents' faces. 'Carin, it's so wonderful to have you back among us where you rightfully belong. And . . .' he beamed at Brenda '. . . as Brenda is expecting Edward's child, Pa and Maimes, you'll soon be great-grandparents. Well, in January that is.'

'Well done, Brenda!' said Debbo. She and Tess started clapping.

Silence for a moment, expressions of disbelief, then Carin hurried to her and kissed her. 'Many congratulations,' she said. 'Isn't that wonderful, John?'

'Er, yes,' he said.

'Of course,' Stork continued, 'we know Edward and Brenda would have been married by now but unfortunately this wretched war has got in the way and he's been posted to Palestine. We wondered when we should tell you all and this happy occasion seemed as good as any.'

'But she's not married,' said Maud.

'Means the child's to be a bastard,' said Alwyn.

Brenda looked aghast, let out a muffled cry, then hurried from the room.

'Oh, for goodness' sake!' said Stork, as Debbo glared at Alwyn and then, with Tess, followed Brenda. 'What a bloody thing to say. Honestly, Pa, you really are the limit.'

'Haven't any of you got any decency?' said Alwyn. 'Sullying the Castell name like this. And how dare you keep it from us?'

'Father, please,' said John. 'We're here to welcome Carin back, not descend into acrimony.'

'Not my fault,' said Alwyn. 'Stork should have thought about that before bringing Brenda in. And what was she thinking, getting herself knocked up by Edward? The child won't be able to inherit. Sullied for life.'

'Don't talk such rot!' said Stork.

'Come on, Maud. We're leaving. I cannot believe how low this family has sunk.'

'Pa, please,' said John. 'Not tonight.'

Alwyn turned to Carin. 'Carin, my dear, it's wonderful to have you home, and I'm sorry to be making a scene. But really.'

Maud now eyed Stork. 'Honestly, Stork, how could you?'

'I was worried you'd react in this way. We all were.'

'So, you thought you'd hide it behind dear Carin's homecoming? Shame on you.'

When they'd gone, Stork realized John, Carin and their three children were all staring at him. Even Elsa looked a little shocked.

He sighed. 'I'm sorry you've all had to witness that. One of our perennial fireworks displays.'

'How long have you known?' John asked him.

'Six weeks or so. It's why Brenda's come down here. We couldn't have her fending on her own, unmarried and pregnant, in London.'

'I do wish you'd told us.'

'You had a lot of other things to worry about. And to begin with, she didn't look pregnant . . . and it's awkward, isn't it? For Brenda as much as for us. They are engaged. Were before she knew she was with child.'

'I think you've shown a lot of compassion, Stork,' said Carin. 'Imagine what Brenda must have been going through. It must have been a terrible shock.'

'I was a little, well, unsure to begin with, but Debbo talked me round. Made me see sense. That we've got to look after Brenda. Her parents are in Kenya, she's not much by way of family over here, and . . .', he looked up, '. . . what's a fellow to do, eh? It's Edward's child, damn it all.'

400

'Well, yes, it's just a rather . . . unusual situation,' said John. 'But I suppose she's hardly the first young woman to have become pregnant out of wedlock.'

'I think it would have been a terrible thing to get rid of it,' said Elsa. 'And it's illegal anyway. I don't care what anyone else thinks, but I'm glad for Brenda and Edward. A new life – it's wonderful.'

Stork smiled. 'And I rather agree with you, Elsa. These are extraordinary times we live in. And I know Edward would be married to Brenda now if he could have been.'

'Maybe better to tell Father and Maimes tête-à-tête first, though, don't you think?'

'Yes. In retrospect, you're probably right. But here we are, Carin just back from her ordeal, Ollie and Wilf in the thick of things, the country half expecting an invasion any moment. It seems so very silly to be getting het up over this.'

'They're a different generation, Stork.'

'Don't I know it,' said Stork. 'Now I feel we're back to square one.'

Edward had been sorry to lose the horses but not, he knew, as sorry as Dasher or some of his fellow officers, who viewed it not only as the end of an era but also of a way of life. He was altogether more sanguine. He'd been very surprised they'd gone to war with horses in the first place and, logically, saw little future in soldiering on horseback in a modern age. Dasher had promised them that, as a cavalry unit, they would soon be converting to armour but explained that at the moment the British Army simply did not have enough tanks to go round so instead, until the situation changed, they were to be retrained on artillery and would be manning coastal batteries in Palestine for the time being.

Edward had initially shared his fellows' disdain about such a move but discovered it was a lot more fun than he'd imagined. The regiment was now in Haifa, based in an old barracks, and Edward was sharing a really very decent billet with Peter. It was, they agreed, quite an improvement on tents, with proper beds, a writing desk, shared bathroom next door and even hot and cold water. The guns they were using were old 1902-model six-inch field guns, which had little place in the modern army, but Edward found the lectures quite interesting. He had the wit to grasp that when they were finally put into tanks their training on artillery would be very useful.

The regiment was split into batteries, with Edward, Peter and Mike all posted to X Battery, which was positioned on the coast just to the south of Haifa. A regular routine was soon established: PT first thing in the morning at 7.30 a.m., then a combination of manning the guns and training, officers and other ranks siphoned off in turn. In between, dinners in the mess, occasional forays into town and games of cricket. It was enjoyable enough, although Edward felt as though they were all treading water, filling time. Letters arrived in batches: three weeks with nothing, each passing day increasingly torturous, then a mass. Brenda wrote at least three times a week and already, by the end of August, he had had seventy-two from her alone, all neatly bundled together, every one read, re-read and read again.

Wider news they got from the wireless. Most of Edward's fellows thought they were incredibly lucky to have been given such a cushy posting. Others had already paid a terrible price. Peter had lost a school friend killed at Dunkirk, Mike a cousin put in the bag at Calais. Edward worried about Wilf, although he had received a letter from him in early August and a cable letting him know he'd become an ace. Proud though Edward was of his little brother, he'd far rather Wilf was out of the fray. Really, Edward wondered, what the devil were they doing out here in Palestine? He felt so impotent.

Italian bombers came over occasionally, a reminder that the Middle East was, in its way, in the war. The following morning, after regimental parade, Dasher called all the officers together. 'It looks like we're to be among the first out here to become an armoured regiment,' he told them all, over coffee in the mess. 'That means we'll be converting back to the old squadron system and I'm to send an officer from each prospective squadron back to England to go on a course at the Royal Armoured Corps Headquarters at Bovington in Dorset. I'm afraid I haven't dates yet or worked out who'll be going, but that will all become clear over the ensuing days. In the meantime, let's stick hard at these coastal guns, learn what we can and do the very best job. But, gentlemen,' he said, grinning at them all, 'we shall, before too long, be cavalry once more.

Our chargers will no longer be four-legged beasts but large, noisy and metal.'

Everyone cheered but Edward was wondering how on earth he could get himself onto that course. Afterwards he collared Monty, his old C Squadron commander. 'Look here, Monty,' he said, 'I'm not sure what the selection process is, but I'm terribly keen to be on that course.'

'You and everyone,' said Monty.

'Really? Surely not everyone wants to go back to bombs and the prospect of Germans invading any minute. I thought I was doing the decent thing in offering.'

Monty laughed. 'Very good, Edward. All right, duly noted. But I've got to talk to the Old Man. I've no idea what he's thinking.'

'What should I do?' Edward asked Peter that evening. 'If I tell Dasher that Brenda's pregnant, he might take a very dim view. Sullying the reputation of the regiment and so on.'

'I think you should tell Monty,' said Peter. 'Be honest with him. He's not a bad sort.'

'But what if it backfires?' He was sitting on the edge of his bed, his head in his hands. 'It's my one chance of securing a passage home.'

'Tell him the truth,' said Peter. 'There's far more chance of you not sullying the reputation of the regiment if you're back home and able to do the decent thing.'

A largely sleepless night followed, while the next day, Edward's anxiety only mounted. He felt crippled by indecision over whether to come clean to Dasher and Monty. Another day passed, during which snippets of detail about the course emerged: it would be six weeks long and they would be leaving at the end of September, by train to Alexandria, then flying to Malta, on to Gibraltar and then home. Six weeks! And in Dorset too. He could be with Brenda, get married and all would be well. Yet, somehow, he couldn't prostrate himself in front of either Monty or Dasher for fear of being rebuffed.

Then, on the last day of August, Dasher told them of his decision. It would be the squadron second-in-commands who would be heading back to England, not any of the troop leaders. For C Squadron, that meant Captain Dan Waverley.

Not Edward.

35

Crash

TESS HAD FELT SHE NEEDED TO MAKE AMENDS AND PUT A FEW things right. After the furore at Carin's homecoming, Brenda had been inconsolable and Tess could understand why. Suddenly the centre of attention amid a family not her own and humiliated cruelly.

Tess thought her grandparents had been needlessly callous that evening, yet she was also aware that it had been her idea to tell the rest of the family and that her father had, once again, taken the full weight of her grandfather's wrath. She had apologized profusely to him, but typically he'd brushed this aside. She'd also professed deep contrition to Brenda, but knew there was only one way to try to sort matters out and that was to speak with her grandparents. The following day, she'd walked down to the manor to see them both.

She had found Maimes in the drawing room.

'Good morning, Tess, dear,' she said, a little stiffly.

Tess sat down beside her. 'I'm sorry,' she said. 'It was my idea to tell everyone about Brenda last night, not Dad's.'

'I see.'

'Dad took a lot of persuading that Brenda should come and live with us and I'm afraid that was my idea too. Poor Brenda, she was so desperate. She didn't know what to do. She adores Edward and they were going to get married, but he didn't think it was fair on her to go overseas for however long while she was still so young, lovely and had her life to live. He was trying to do the decent thing.'

'I don't see how getting her pregnant was doing the decent thing.'

'I'm sure he didn't mean to.'

'Tess, dear, it's not the sort of thing one does by accident.'

'I know, but I don't really mean that. I mean, Edward and Brenda adore each other. They're meant to be together. Edward would marry Brenda like a shot if he could. It's not his fault he's been posted away. It's rotten luck – most of the Army is still here, in Britain. Just not him. Brenda was in a terrible state. She didn't want to get rid of the child – her child with the man she loves, Maimes – yet she knew that raising the baby on her own in London would be very difficult. Her parents are in distant lands and she was terrified her uncle would disown her. Bringing her down here seemed such an obvious solution. Mum agreed almost immediately but Dad was so worried about what you and Grandpa would think. He knows that society has difficulty with unmarried mothers, but it's 1940, Maimes, not 1904. Times are changing. And there's a war on. They would be married if it wasn't for the war, and it's much better that Brenda gets help, care, support and love, and that Edward's child is brought up properly cared for and surrounded by family. Surely you see that. And now Dad has been humiliated and is once again in bad odour with Grandpa and, even worse this time, with you as well. All he wants is for us to be happy and safe. He's working incredibly hard, has so many responsibilities heaped on his shoulders, he worries constantly about Wilf and Edward and all of us, and I feel it's me who should be in the doghouse over poor Brenda, not him. So, I've come here to apologize and to beg you to make amends with him.'

Maimes tapped her leg gently. 'It was good of you to come, Tess, and of course I forgive you. Because you're right on one thing and so was Carin last night: we all need to have compassion. One might not approve of certain things in life but one also has to weigh up what is right and what is wrong and what is also for the greater good. So, let me think about what you've said. Of course no one has any ill will towards Brenda, who, I agree, is delightful. Neither would I want to do anything to upset dear Edward.'

They talked some more; Maimes wanted to know how she was getting on in London and Tess was happy to oblige her.

'Is Grandpa here?' Tess asked at length.

'Leave him to me,' said Maimes.

'That bad, then?'

'He was very upset. Alwyn doesn't like surprises. Never has done, and both you and Stork should know that by now. One needs to plant a seed gently and nurture it.'

Tess walked back to Farrowcombe without having seen her grandfather but hopeful she might have started to build a few bridges. She found Brenda in the drawing room attempting to knit a scarf.

'I'm trying to be useful,' she told Tess. 'I've never learned before so it's taking a while to get the hang of it. Thought I'd start on something fairly simple.'

'How are you feeling today?' Tess asked, as she sat down beside her.

'Mortified, like an interloper. Embarrassed to have caused ructions in the family. Wondering whether I should head back to London.'

'Please don't,' said Tess. 'It was entirely my fault. I feel dreadful about it, Brenda.'

'Oh, it's all such a mess! Of course it's not your fault. I know you were trying to do the right thing and, if you remember, I told you I wanted to tell people. But what your parents must be thinking, God only knows.'

'They're on your side.' She told her about her visit to see Maimes, then added, 'I'm sure she'll come round and all will be well.'

Brenda put down her knitting with a sigh of exasperation. 'I don't want to be an unmarried mother with all the social stigma that goes with it. I want to be married to Edward. I want that more than anything in the world.'

'But how do you know? How do you really know that you want to be with him for the rest of your life?'

She smiled. 'Because he makes me laugh, because we share the same views on things, because I think he's ferociously handsome, because he's in my thoughts when I wake up and when I go to sleep. Because he swept into my life and now I cannot imagine him out of it. I curse this war, this stupid, pointless, awful, terrible war. I curse it for all the misery it's bringing but most of all – and I admit this is very selfish of me – I curse it because it's keeping me apart from Edward. I yearn for him, Tess. I really do.'

*

Back in London, her leave over, Tess arranged to meet Alex in St James's Park after she had left the office for the day. She'd not forgotten what Brenda had told her about Edward. Her words were still rolling around in Tess's mind now as she spotted Alex walking towards her, wearing his battledress and peaked cap. Really, he was quite a catch, and her heart sank at what she was going to say to him.

'How was Alvesdon?' he asked, kissing her. 'I've missed you.'

'It was lovely, thank you.' She told him about Carin's return, about the harvest being in, that they continued to worry about Wilf. And she let him know that Tom was on the mend too. But she knew she had to get to the point, so she said, 'Alex, there's something I have to say.'

'Uh-oh,' he said. 'Should I be worried?'

She smiled. 'I can't be with you any more. I'm sorry. You're a wonderful person. You're kind, caring, brave and very handsome. But I'm not in love with you. I'm so sorry. There, I've said it. I've seen what real love is, Alex – the love Brenda has for my brother and what he feels for her. What my parents and my aunt and uncle have. I don't feel like that.'

'Was it because of the other night?'

'No, truthfully it wasn't.'

'But we were so in love last summer. A year ago. What a magical time that was.'

'It was and I'm glad we had those times. But it's different now. I'm different. I suppose I've grown up. I can't give you what you want and you can't give me what I need.'

He looked down. 'All right. I won't pretend I'm not a little heartbroken, Tess, but . . .' He sighed. 'But thank you. It's been wonderful and I do wish you all the luck in the world, I really do.'

'And I do you, Alex.' She leaned up and kissed his cheek, then turned and walked away, her heart thumping, but with relief coursing through her.

Thursday, 5 September 1940

Shorter days now for the fighter pilots but no let-up in the air battle. Wilf was still in action most days. So far this week, though, the

Luftwaffe had focused its energies on the south-east, and the squadrons at Boscombe had been sent to cover the airfields south of London while the squadrons based there were airborne, tussling over London and the skies over Kent.

Mid-morning, however, they'd been scrambled again to intercept a low-flying raid heading in the direction of the Isle of Wight. They spotted them north of Southampton, a dozen Messerschmitt 110s, twin-engine fighters, flying at only two thousand feet in three formations of four each. As the Spitfires dived so the 110s began to scatter, one formation discarding the bombs Wilf now saw were slung beneath them while four more dived even lower and continued to speed north. Middle Wallop, Wilf wondered. Or even Boscombe.

In moments he was on the tail of one, the enemy rear-gunner spitting bullets and tracer towards him, but the German pilot was twisting and turning his machine, which made it hard for Wilf to get a decent shot.

'Come on, come on!' muttered Wilf, as they sped westwards, now suddenly alone, the pair of them, and then there was the spire of the cathedral and for a brief moment Wilf wondered whether the German pilot would head straight into it. *Ah*, he thought. *Clever. He knows I won't shoot.* On the other hand, it meant Wilf had barely fired any rounds and still had plenty left in his wings. And now there was the valley, the two ridges of chalk winding their way west and the Messerschmitt hurtling down it, ever lower, trying desperately to shake Wilf off his tail. The rear-gunner had stopped firing – *Out of bullets?* – and Wilf pulled up closer, so that he was only 150 yards away, maybe less. He could see the plane clearly, its mottled grey-green camouflage and the head of the rear-gunner at the back of the cockpit. Wilf grinned to himself, waited for the Messerschmitt to start crossing his gunsight. Just as the starboard wing appeared, he pressed down on the button and fired before the pilot could correct his movement. A long, four-second burst and Wilf saw the bullets strike the port engine and bits fly off the wing. And at that moment, he knew the Messerschmitt was finished. Thick smoke trailed from the wing and the plane began to glide ever lower.

Then a shock of realization. Wilf's stomach lurched with dread. *Oh, no. It's coming down over Alvesdon.* Anxious moments. The Messerschmitt getting ever lower. Wilf could see the pilot was hoping to belly-land in a field, but he was still travelling too fast. *No, he's going to overshoot.* Wilf glanced around him then hurtled over the top of the Messerschmitt and, climbing, banked and circled, watching it head straight down towards the water meadows and the manor beyond. Wilf barely dared breathe as he watched the stricken plane glide down.

Tom was in Tippett's Wood licking his new hut into shape when he heard the sound of aircraft and moments later machine-gun fire. Running to the track that led back towards the manor, he saw the German plane coming in low, smoke gushing from one engine, and wondered whether it was about to plough straight into the wood, then realized it was coming in to the south. Moments later it crossed over the hedgeline at the end of Manor Field and hit the ground with a grinding crash, the propellers bending and distorting, stooks flying into the air and the body of the Messerschmitt slewing, trailing dust and debris in its wake. And then, briefly, silence.

Without thinking, Tom jumped the hedge and ran towards it, his shotgun in his right hand. The aircraft finally halted about two-thirds of the way across. A plane thundered overhead and he looked up and saw a Spitfire circling above the field, the pilot clearly trying to look down at the crashed Messerschmitt.

As Tom neared it, he heard frantic shouting from the plane. Flames were spreading now from the port wing and he saw that the two crewmen were trying to get out of the cockpit but the canopy was jammed.

'Jesus,' he muttered, and as soon as he reached the aircraft, hurriedly climbed onto the nearer, starboard, wing. Using the butt of his shotgun, he smashed the canopy next to the airman at the rear, who quickly clambered out, and again above the pilot. Flames were now licking up the side of the fuselage towards the pilot and the German began to scream.

'I've got you,' said Tom, grabbing the man by his shoulders and hoisting him clear. He wanted to scream himself; the pain in his left arm was intense and the smell of burning flesh sickly sweet, but the pilot was out. Both staggered backwards and fell onto the wing. The flames were rising now, above the cockpit.

'Get clear! Quickly!' he shouted frantically, as he scrambled to his feet, and now all three men ran, away from the burning plane, Tom expecting it to blow at any moment. Only at the edge of the field did they stop to look back at the Messerschmitt. A moment later there was a loud explosion and Tom felt himself jolt with shock as the aircraft was engulfed in livid, swirling flames, thick black smoke writhing and mushrooming above it.

'*Danke*,' said the pilot. 'Thank you for saving us.'

'Don't mention it,' he said, then looked up to see the Spitfire speed away from them, climb and turn, and thunder low, right above them, over the field, waggling its wings from side to side as it headed off.

And only then did Tom look down and see the livid burns on the back of his hand. A stab of pain shot up his arm and he grimaced, then grinned to himself. Perhaps he'd done himself a favour, he thought, rescuing these Germans.

Elsa had watched it all from Blindwell, just to the north of Tippett's Wood, where they'd been threshing. They'd all dropped everything and run down the track. She and Hattie were the first to reach Tom, now marching the two Germans down the lane towards the yard, his shotgun still in his hand. In the field the plane burned.

'I don't think I've ever seen anything more thrilling,' she said to Hattie, as they walked behind Tom, a growing crowd of farmworkers following them.

'Where are you taking them, Tom?' asked Hattie.

'Not sure, really. To the village hall and to Donald Pierson. Someone needs to ring through to the Home Guard or to Jack Allbrook up at Middle Chalke.'

They paused in the yard where they saw Mr Castell. After he'd had a good look at the two German airmen standing in the yard and agreed to ring ahead, they continued the march. Word had quickly spread; most of the village, it seemed, had seen the plane come down, and those who had not now wanted to see the wreckage, still burning in Manor Field, and even better, the two downed airmen. As they walked through the village Elsa saw people emerging from every door, most to stand and gawp at the passing Germans.

'I still can't believe it, Hattie,' said Elsa, as they continued to walk behind Tom and his Germans. 'A real German plane shot down here on the farm!'

Donald Pierson emerged from the shop, buttoning his tunic, tin helmet already on his head.

'Well done, Tom, and, yes, please, let's have them in the village hall,' Reg said. 'PC Allbrook's on his way and they're sending the Army to pick them up. We're to hold on to them until then.'

Elsa now had a chance to look at the two men. They were both young – not much older than her and Wilf, she guessed. One had burn marks on his left cheek and his dark blue flying jacket was a little burned too, but otherwise they seemed unhurt.

'All right, you two,' said Pierson to the two men, 'inside the hall.' They looked at him quizzically so he repeated, slower and louder, and pointing. 'In the hall.' He looked around. 'No German speakers, I suppose?'

'I can speak German,' said Elsa, feeling a further frisson of excitement.

'Oh, Elsa, there you are. Of course, you can. Was forgettin'. I was goin' to call your mother, but if you're here there's no need to bother her. Can you tell them we're taking them into the hall and we'll wait for the Army to come and collect them?'

'*Sie möchten, dass Sie ins Gemeindehaus gehen,*' she told the two men. '*Einige Männer vom Militär werden kommen und Sie abholen.*'

The men nodded and allowed themselves to be taken inside. Dr Gready arrived and looked first at Tom's hand, then at the two airmen. Donald Pierson would not allow any more of the villagers into the hall, but Elsa insisted Hattie remain with her. 'I don't want you missing this, Hattie,' she said.

She asked them their names. The pilot told her he was Leutnant Alfred Schiffler and his fellow, Feldwebel Horst Liedmann. They were from a unit called Erpro 210. The pilot spoke again, 'That man,' he said in English, pointing at Tom, '*er hat uns das Leben gerettet.*'

She turned to Tom. 'He said you saved their lives, Tom.'

'It was nothin',' he said. 'They was stuck in their machine. No one wants to see two men burn to death. Anyways, they might have somethin' worth sayin', but they can't say nothing if they're dead.'

411

PC Jack Allbrook arrived next, then the fire engine from Wilton, bells clanging as it hurtled past. An hour later, though, and while they were still waiting for the Army to pick up the two men, Wilf appeared, wearing his uniform and leather flying boots, goggles pushed up onto his head.

'Wilf!' she exclaimed. 'What on earth are you doing here?'

'I wanted to see the crash and got permission from Bluey to motor over on the bike. We'd been stood down, you see. I was on my way to Manor Field when Claude Timbrell stopped me and told me the Germans were still here.'

'Yes, but how on earth did you know?'

Wilf laughed. 'Because I shot them down, of course!'

'You did?' Elsa was wide-eyed, incredulous.

'So, that was you circling overhead and wagglin' your wings?' said Tom.

The two airmen looked up at Wilf.

'*Das ist der Mann*,' Schiffler asked Elsa, '*der unser Flugzeug abgeschossen hat?*'

Elsa nodded. Wilf smiled genially and gave a mock salute.

'Well done,' said Schiffler in English and offered a hand. Wilf looked at Elsa uncertainly, took it, then shook Liedmann's hand as well.

'This is all rather odd,' Wilf said.

Soon after, the Army turned up in a lorry, and the two Germans were marched out, ordered into the back of the truck and driven away. Elsa and Tom watched them go.

'I'm sorry about Sim,' she said to him. 'Is he going to be all right?'

'I think so. I went to see him last week. It's the left side of his face that's badly burned, his left hand too. He did make a joke, though. Said you'd never want to kiss him now.'

Elsa reddened. 'Poor Sim.'

'At least he's out of it.' He glanced in the direction of Manor Field. 'That might be me any moment.'

'Don't say things like that. I don't want anything to happen to you, Wilf.'

'I don't want anything to happen to me, either.' He grinned. 'Anyway, don't worry, your secret's safe with me.'

'But I don't want you thinking that I—'

'Elsa, it's all right, truly.'

She bit her lip. 'Thank you, Wilf.'

He suggested she jump on the back of his motorbike and together they chugged through the village and turned down the lane past the manor. A number of people were in the field, including some men from the Home Guard and also Sid, Claude, and several others from the farm. Elsa also spotted her father. Wilf pulled up a little way short of the wreck and they climbed off and wandered over.

'Wilf!' exclaimed Stork. 'I hear this was your handiwork. Well done. I'm sorry I wasn't here when it happened.'

Wilf had a look at the wreckage, although there wasn't much left. Around it, the ground was blackened and scorched but thankfully most of the field was untouched.

'We've been lucky,' said Stork. 'Could easily have lost the entire field or worse. I wouldn't have been congratulating you then, Wilf.'

Wilf grinned. 'For a moment I thought it was going to crash on top of the manor. I can't tell you how relieved I was when it came down here.'

'Wilf?' Elsa asked, and he turned to her. 'Do you think we're winning?'

He shrugged. 'I think so. They've bashed our airfields about but we're still using them. And I can only tell you what I know, but every morning when I get to Dispersal there's always a full squadron of Spitfires waiting for us. Where they come from and how they get there, nobody knows. But we're not short of aircraft. We're definitely shooting down more of them than they are of us and, of course,' he said, 'we've got home advantage. Those two chaps today are out of the war, but if they'd been RAF, they'd be flying again tomorrow.'

'Well,' said Stork, 'Hitler's running out of time. Autumn's on its way. And then it will be too late in the year to cross the Channel.'

Stork told Elsa she could go home, so after saying goodbye to Wilf, she wandered up to the yard and cycled back through the village and out on the road to Middle Chalke. A jumble of thoughts tumbled through her mind. Feelings of exhilaration. It had been exciting to see the war so directly arrive in Alvesdon. Happiness that she'd seen Wilf. Her cousin, she reflected, was so straightforward, so practical. But kind too.

413

Then she thought of Ollie, as she so often did. It was hard, not seeing him. Not knowing when she might see him again. Yet she felt hopeful, she really did, for the first time in ages. With her mother home and the entire family together, the world was a better place and she felt all the happier for it. And perhaps they were winning after all. Wilf and Uncle Stork seemed to think so. It hadn't occurred to her before that invasions were seasonal and that Hitler was running out of time. What had seemed deeply shocking now seemed everyday. It was funny how one got used to things. The sun still rose, she still went to work six days out of seven, the harvest was in for another year and autumn was on its way. Just as it had always been, despite the war. They'd been waiting for the Germans all summer. But maybe, perhaps – *hopefully* – she thought, as she cycled down the familiar road, they'd been waiting for something that was never going to happen after all.

Yet two days later Elsa was at home when, at just a little after 8 p.m., the phone rang. She was writing to Ollie at the time but hurried down to the hallway.

'Hello, it's Brigadier Seagram here. Is Major Castell there?' said the voice at the end of the phone. 'It's rather urgent.'

Elsa found her father, then waited while he answered.

'Yes, hello, Brigadier . . . Yes . . . Good God . . . Right away . . . Yes, sir. Goodbye.'

He put down the receiver.

'What is it?' she asked.

'We've been put on alert. Immediate action.' He looked ashen.

'What does that mean?' And now Carin was there too, in the hallway, looking at him, with a worried expression.

'It means they're expecting the invasion.'

36

Alvesdon

COCO CASTELL WAS AT HER DESK AT 4 CARLTON GARDENS WHEN the siren started to wail over the city. She cursed. The sirens were sounded at the slightest incursion, and after looking around the office and seeing no one else hurrying to leave, she continued with what she was doing. Really, she thought, it was too annoying, especially as nothing ever seemed to happen.

Coco had been working at the Free French headquarters for over a month. Her father had got her the job, translating documents and other papers into English from French or vice versa. She found the work quite interesting, was enjoying being part of de Gaulle's movement, had made some friends and was beginning to think she might be falling in love with Lieutenant Félix Vasseur, a young officer in the 13 DBLE, the French Foreign Legion. She missed her home, she missed the sea, and she missed the carefree easy life she'd been living but she was enjoying London more than she had imagined. Even the weather had been markedly better than she had expected.

Now, with the siren still droning mournfully over London, she went back to her work. And an evening with Félix. He'd promised to take her to the Café de Paris and that meant she needed to leave soon so she would have time to go home and change first. She didn't want any air-raid sirens to get in the way of her evening.

She had nearly finished when sirens sounded anew. Soon after,

415

she heard distant bombs falling and the boom of anti-aircraft guns. She paused and looked up. A moment later Geoffroy Chordon de Courcel, de Gaulle's aide, came out of his office. 'That sounds a bit closer than normal.'

Élisabeth de Miribel now emerged from her office too. 'What do you think? Should we be heading to the shelter?'

'The roof, I think,' said de Courcel, with a grin. 'See what's happening.'

'Can I come with you?' asked Coco.

'By all means.'

They took the lift to the seventh floor, then the staircase that led up onto the flat roof.

'My God,' said de Courcel, his gaze turning east.

Coco watched, open-mouthed. Away, down the river, towards the docks in the East End of the city, they could see that the clear blue afternoon sky was smudged with flak bursts, and bombs exploding, slow, rolling clouds of smoke rising from the ground. High above, Coco spotted little dots of aircraft, and swirls of contrails. Fighter planes, glinting in the evening sun, like little darts, diving towards the bombs. A parachute was drifting down, then another. And all the while, a low, growling rumble of bombs and guns, sometimes in a ripple, sometimes more staccato. A diving streak of black smoke as a bomber plunged, and a pall of smoke rising over the docks so that Tower Bridge stood out against its backdrop. Huge mushrooms of smoke were rising into the sky, blotting out the barrage balloons sus-pended above the docks. She knew they were at five thousand feet above the city. It was mesmerizing, watching the first major attack on London unfolding.

Several others joined them in their grandstand on the roof. Every time the fighting and the bombs seemed to lessen, another wave of bombers appeared, so that it wasn't until after six that the all-clear finally sounded.

'Do you think that will be it?' she asked de Courcel. He shrugged.

She went back to her desk to get her jacket, then hurried home, back across St James's Park, determined not to miss her date with Félix.

He was punctual, arriving at the house in Maunsel Street at seven o'clock, wearing his uniform, his kepi under his arm. He was tall,

416

fresh-faced, boyish, even, yet had already seen action at Narvik, in Norway, and had told her very earnestly on one of their first dates that he had made a solemn vow to fight until the day that France was liberated. 'Quite simply,' he had told her, 'I shall not rest until then.'

Except, she thought, on evenings when he was taking her out for dinner. On such occasions he seemed only too happy to take a break from planning his vengeance on the Nazis.

'I was worried you wouldn't be able to come,' she said, kissing him on each cheek.

'A promise is a promise. I'm not going to let Nazi bombers spoil our evening.'

They went to the Café de Paris, had drunk a cocktail and were sitting at their table when the sirens droned again.

Félix cursed. 'Do you want to find a shelter? Or shall we brave it out?'

Coco looked around. Few others seemed to be leaving and the waiters continued bringing drinks and food. On the stage, the band played on.

'It does seem a shame to spoil the evening,' said Coco.

They heard the drone of aircraft and the first bombs at around half past eight, this time much closer. Coco couldn't tell from which direction they were coming but it went on for the best part of an hour. Occasionally, she found herself clutching her chest, or widening her eyes at a closer detonation, but then she would laugh and Félix would laugh too, and she thought that, assuming they survived, she would never forget that night: dinner with Félix in the Café de Paris with bombs falling on London while they ate, drank wine, and gazed into each other's eyes. Romance, excitement and danger all rolled into one. Quite intoxicating, Coco thought.

Tess and Diana spent that first night under their kitchen table, lying on cushions from the sofa and chairs, using rugs and their own pillows. During a lull, they went to the top of the house, looked out and saw the East End glowing red and fires flickering over Battersea and Clapham too, just a few miles to their south. The next day, Sunday, 8 September, Tess went to work as usual, while Diana promised to sort out the Anderson shelter at the end of their small garden: her parents had had it installed during the Munich crisis two years earlier. It had not been used once and, Diana reported, smelt damp and musty. 'Better musty than dead,' she said, cheerily enough. There were two beds in it, with roughly made wooden frames, but Diana had moved in two old mattresses and made them up nicely. The bombers were over the next night, and the next, and the one after that. All week, and in subsequent attacks, bombs dropped much closer, so much so that Tess and Diana even heard the whistle as they fell.

'Give me your hand,' Diana said to her and Tess had held out her arm and felt her friend's fingers wrap around hers. 'I don't mind admitting, Tess, I'm bloody terrified.'

Tess got through the week. Everyone looked exhausted, dark shadows beneath their eyes, and operated without the normal levels of brisk efficiency. On Sunday, she had a day off and was invited to lunch by Uncle Denholm. 'No point trying anything after dark,' he'd said, over the phone, 'but at least we might get a chance to wolf down some grub at lunchtime.'

Maunsel Street was not far from the house in Pimlico, but she was just about to head out when the sirens wailed again. More bombs falling to the south-east, the sound of guns and air fighting, but mercifully nothing close, and once the all-clear sounded she rang Denholm again.

'Yes, come on over,' he said. 'Hopefully that's it for the day.'

Smoke rose high over the city to the south of the river and she walked past the collapsed heap of two houses that had been hit on the far side of Vauxhall Bridge Road. One of the buildings had been almost sliced in half, a bath still fixed to the side of one wall on the second floor, a cupboard upright in another. Glass littered the street and crunched underfoot. Tess wondered why those houses had been hit. Fate? Chance? Or just bad luck? She glanced up again at the half-remains of a family home suspended in the air, then hurried on, feeling as though she were intruding on the privacy of others.

'I've realized,' said Denholm, over lunch, 'that while this lasts one cannot expect a good night's sleep. One can only expect bad nights, terrible nights or marginally better nights.'

'We're all in the same boat, I suppose,' said Tess.

'Lucie is most grumpy about it, aren't you, darling? Wishes she was back in France with all the Vichyites. Has no truck at all with battling it out alongside the brave Free French.'

Lucie scowled. 'You always make light of things, Denholm. I came with you, didn't I? You said we'd be safer over here.'

'I said we'd be free over here.'

'What use is freedom if you're hit by a bomb?'

Denholm laughed.

'I think Papa is right,' said Coco. 'We have to stand up to these people. I don't want to live under the swastika and the Gestapo and all those Germans with their jackboots and *Sieg-Heil*ing.'

'You wouldn't have to if we were at home,' said Lucie. 'We'd be in Vichy.'

'Pétain is a dictator and a Nazi puppet. Everyone knows that. We wouldn't be free.'

'She spends six weeks working for de Gaulle and look what happens,' said Denholm. 'Or is it the talk of the dashing Lieutenant Félix Vasseur we're hearing?'

Coco rolled her eyes. 'I am perfectly capable of forming my own opinions, Papa.'

'Of course you are, darling. I'm sorry to patronize.'

A quiche Lorraine, salad, crème caramel and cheese to follow. It was delicious, Tess thought, and realized she'd not eaten so well since she'd returned from her leave.

'Someone was hungry, I think,' Lucie said.

'I was,' Tess agreed.

'Well, make the most of it,' said Denholm. 'Rationing will get worse. There's still plenty about at the moment, but only those in the countryside will be eating half decently by next year.'

'You think we'll still be at war then?'

'Of course. Hitler's shot his bolt.'

'Oh, Denholm, what rubbish you talk!' said Lucie.

'Hear me out. He was attacking the airfields to try to knock out the RAF so that he could invade. Can't cross the Channel without control of the skies. That's obvious. But, clearly, that's failed. There are still plenty of Spitfires and Hurricanes buzzing around the sky every time I look up. So, now he's bombing London, trying to pound us into submission. That's not working either. Look at us, we're all right, having a convivial lunch on a Sunday. I don't see mass panic, do you?'

'No,' admitted Tess. 'Everyone seems to be taking it very well. General Ismay toured the East End the other day with the Prime Minister. He said the devastation was terrible but the people were defiant and cheering Churchill. He said Churchill was moved to tears by what he saw.'

Denholm laughed. 'He always was an emotional blighter. That's the Yank in him. But it rather proves my point. Britain can take it, we're not going to sue for peace, and Hitler's lost his chance to invade. It's a beautiful sunny day today, but it's mid-September. Days drawing in, weather worsening. Not a chance of an invasion. What was it Churchill said not so long ago? Something about Hitler knowing he must defeat Britain or lose the war. Well, I happen to think he was quite right.'

The sirens wailed again and they all stopped talking and looked at one another.

'I vote we stay where we are until we hear bombs falling,' said Denholm. 'Hands up?' They all raised them, but soon after, Denholm suggested they head up to the roof to see what was going on. There was a ladder into the loft and a skylight through which one could climb onto a ledge between the pitch of the roof. Lucie refused to go up there, but Tess and Coco followed Denholm. He'd brought a pair of binoculars and gave a running commentary.

'They've got one!' he said excitedly. 'A bomber, coming down!'

Tess watched the contrails making swirling patterns high over south-east London and saw small glints darting about as the sunlight hit a distant aircraft. The sound of bombs, a dull thud, close but strangely distant too. The clatter of machine-guns. Such events would have been terrifying, fantastical even, only a few months ago, yet here they were, watching with excitement as though they were spectators of a rather macabre sport.

The battle drew a little closer as a formation of bombers droned towards the centre of the capital.

'Dorniers,' said Denholm. 'Two dozen.'

'We should take shelter, Papa,' said Coco.

'Hold on,' said Denholm. 'It's not every day one gets to see a show like this.'

420

They stayed where they were, on the roof, watching the battle above them, Tess knowing it was madness, but strangely compelled to stay where she was. Hurricanes were attacking the Dorniers only a mile or two to the north of them. Hurtling in like little hornets. *Rat-a-tat-a-tat-a-tat.* Short bursts, like the rip of a zip. Some bombs fell, but the Dorniers were losing their formation. One dropped away, smoke trailing.

'Hurrah!' said Denholm. 'Another of the blighters gone.' Then he said, 'Hold on!' binoculars still glued to his eyes. 'Bloody hell – well, I never! He's sliced straight through him!'

And there was a bomber, shorn of its tail, plunging vertically to the ground. A pause, then an explosion and a cloud of smoke rising from somewhere near Victoria Station.

'Well, I'm jiggered,' said Denholm, as several parachutes drifted downwards.

'I've seen enough,' said Coco.

So too had Tess. 'I hope Wilf is all right,' she said. 'I wonder if he's up there?'

Wilf had been up there, although he had been patrolling Kenley to the south. He'd clobbered a lone Heinkel, taking his score to nine, then flown back to Boscombe Down. The next day the squadron was posted north to Acklington in Northumberland.

'I'm sorry, I won't be able to get home so often,' he told Stork, on the phone.

'I'd much rather you were out of the fray for a bit,' Stork said.

'We need it,' Wilf admitted. 'We've been in the thick of it since Dunkirk. We're all a bit fagged out.'

So, a relief that they could worry a little less about Wilf but now Stork fretted for Tess, living amid the blitz of bombs raining down on London. She, too, was exhausted, she told him, when she rang the following night. Everyone was, Stork thought, as he put down the phone. His brother and half his workers on the farm, up all night manning roadblocks with the Home Guard. Thank goodness that first Saturday in September had proved a false alarm. Apparently, the signal issued to the entire Home Guard that night had been to put them on high alert but had been interpreted as the invasion being already under way.

And there had been no invasion since then, for all the time John and the Home Guard had spent up on the downs. On Wednesday, 18 September, Stork drove over to the Deverills for a meeting with Richard Stratton. On every hill and at every crossroads, he was stopped by Home Guardsmen, all now wearing denim battledress and clutching rifles.

Each time he patiently drew to a halt, explained his business, handed over his papers and watched nervously as they eyed him suspiciously. Six times, he'd counted, in all. It made him late for his meeting. The war, he thought, was taking up precious time. Everything took longer: car journeys, train journeys, too, by all accounts. People were getting less sleep, productivity was falling. It had been an excellent harvest but they needed to make sure 1941 was even better. Now was not the time to slacken the pace, yet there was only so much that could be done.

As he drove home and was ushered through the last of the roadblocks on the top of the downs, he thought about other worries and concerns. There was Brenda and the baby that was on its way; there were his parents with whom he'd barely spoken in a month; there were the ongoing anxieties over the farm and the pressure to produce ever more food; and there was the constant, gnawing worry for his children and his family. As the car trundled down the hill towards the village, Stork realized he was utterly exhausted.

In the third week of September, there was a return to Aldershot for Tom and his latest medical. He'd been dreading it, but had once again dug out his uniform, now with the blue, white and red striped ribbon of his Military Medal stitched above his breast pocket. He supposed it was good of Alex Woodman to put him up for it, but he didn't feel he deserved it any more than a dozen others in the battalion. His father was proud, though, as was Hannah, and it had bought him a fair few pints in the pub. Even Mr Castell had congratulated him and pumped his hand. Since getting the news, he'd received a formal invitation to Buckingham Palace in November to be awarded his medal. Hannah was excited: he'd promised to take her and she'd never been to London before. 'You won't like it,' he'd told her. 'It's big and crowded. Too many people and nowadays too many smashed buildings.' She didn't care. She just wanted to say she'd been, and she also wanted to see the King.

The train stopped repeatedly and he worried he'd be late and miss the appointment altogether, despite having allowed himself a cushion of time. In the end, he arrived with fifteen minutes to spare. He'd made a promise to himself. If he had to go back into the Army, he'd not ask Hannah to marry him. He just didn't feel it would be right. On the other hand, if he was given another stay of execution or, even better, medically discharged, he would. He liked to picture them together in the cottage at Windmill Lane; it was a good thought, and as he sat in the waiting area, drumming his fingers on his legs and waiting for the summons, he prayed he would be spared, that he would be allowed to stay in Alvesdon, if not for ever, for a little longer at least. He couldn't bear the thought of leaving again. Of leaving Hannah.

'Your hand looks nasty,' the doctor told him after Tom had been called in to see him, 'and I fear the cast has chafed rather, preventing the burns from healing properly. How long ago did you say this had happened?'

'Coming up for three weeks ago now, sir.'

'Hmm. And the arm?'

'It's still quite painful. Didn't do it any favours hauling that Jerry out of his plane, to be honest.'

'So, it's still causing you a bit of gip to lift things?'

Tom nodded. 'Lifting and pulling.'

The doctor then cut off the cast, took another set of X-rays and told Tom that while the bone had healed it would be some time before he could use the arm properly. 'You need to exercise it, gradually build up the muscle. You've had a bad wound, Timbrell, and the burns you suffered have not helped. A brave but possibly foolish thing to have done.'

Tom said nothing. He could feel the verdict coming and his heart was quickening in his chest.

'Come and see me again in the spring. In six months' time. No soldiering for you until then. The regiment will have to do without you. I suspect they'll manage.'

Relief had coursed through him. He had wanted to shout and

cheer for joy, but instead had shaken the doctor's hand, thanked him, and left. At Salisbury, he had alighted from the train and visited a jeweller near the old Poultry Cross. He'd saved most of his army pay and had been putting a little aside for several years so he could afford something special for Hannah. Little had he known how much choice there was but despite the array of rings before him, he quite quickly chose a flower-shaped cluster of diamonds. It was simple, pretty, and quite the most expensive thing he'd ever bought, yet he'd handed over the money with gladness in his heart.

When he eventually got off the bus at Alvesdon, he walked home, changed, then strolled up the lane to Farrowcombe to wait for Hannah to finish for the day. At just a few minutes after eight thirty, the door at the back of the house opened and there she was.

'Hannah?'

'Tom! You're back! Well, what did 'e say?'

Tom grinned. 'Off for another six months at least.'

She kissed him. 'That's wonderful news. I've been het up all day for worryin'.'

They went back down the lane, the last of the day's light now gone, but behind Farrowcombe they were aware of a rising light creeping up from beyond the downs. They watched as, first, the very top of the orb and then, quite visibly, more of the moon crept up over the hill and spread its creamy light over them.

'Isn't that beautiful?' said Hannah, softly, and Tom knew he would never have a better, more perfect moment to ask her that most important of questions. From his pocket he pulled out the little box, opened it and, dropping to one knee, said, 'Hannah, would you make me the happiest man alive? Will you marry me?'

And Hannah gasped to see the ring, pulled him up from where he was kneeling, kissed him, and said, 'Yes, Tom Timbrell, I will.'

September had been a particularly torturous month for Edward. It was not that the imminent departure for England of the three seconds-in-command had been a constant topic of conversation, and he couldn't say anyone had been rubbing his nose in it, but to have this chance dangled in front of him and not be able to do anything about it had been a very bitter pill to swallow. His cause was a hopeless one and that was all there was to it.

The three lucky officers were due to depart on Saturday, 28 September, and as the day drew near, Edward felt only a mounting sense of doom and despair.

Then, on the Thursday, Dan Waverley fell ill. He was sick, then very sick and, by the following morning, in hospital in Haifa with severe dysentery. A glimmer of hope, after all. One man's misfortune was another man's gain.

At lunchtime Monty found Edward in the mess. 'I wish you'd been straight with me in the first place, Edward,' he said, whisking a fly away. 'Peter and Mike have been to see me. Tell me that Brenda's having your child and that you need to marry her to save her reputation and the regiment's.'

'I'm awfully keen to,' said Edward.

'Should have told me from the start. Means and ways of sorting that out.'

'I worried that if I made a fuss, I might make the matter worse.'

Monty tutted. 'No wonder you've had such a bloody long face. Been moping about the place for weeks.'

'Sorry. It's been much on my mind.'

'Wish you'd told me,' he said again. 'Look here, Dan can't go home now. Man's sick as a dog. I want you to go instead. Let me clear things up with Dasher, but as far as I'm concerned, I don't want to see you for six weeks from tomorrow, and when you come back, I'll want to know you've made an honest woman of her. All right?'

Hallelujah, thought Edward. He was tempted to kiss Monty and dance a jig around the mess, but instead shook his hand and said soberly, 'Thank you, Monty, thank you very, very much.'

'That's all right, but wipe that silly grin off your face.'

But Edward couldn't. He didn't stop smiling all day.

Saturday, 12 October 1940

A fine autumnal day, the leaves on the trees a patchwork of russet, yellow and green, and the sun shining down on the valley so that the chalk downs glowed with a vivid, fresh shade that Elsa thought highly fitting for such a special day. She stood at the end of the garden gazing at the downs, then at the stream until she heard her mother call.

'She's ready, Elsa!'

Elsa turned back to the house. It had been agreed that Brenda couldn't possibly stay in the same house as Edward so she had moved into Rose Bower for the week and now here she was, in the hallway, wearing a full-length cream dress.

'You look beautiful, Brenda,' said Elsa.

'She does,' said Carin.

'Oh, Brenda,' said Tess, who, as one of the bridesmaids, had joined them that morning and now came down the stairs, 'you look utterly radiant.'

'Thank you.' She smiled. 'Even with the bump?'

'The very neatest of bumps,' said Tess. 'And yes. Even more so.'

Outside a wagon awaited. It had been specially cleaned and decorated with late-blooming roses, and steps had been placed at the back to allow everyone to climb in. Brenda's Uncle Douglas had arrived too; they were all to travel together the short distance to Alvesdon church. Elsa knew that Brenda had been worried about her uncle and how he would react, but while he had apparently muttered a lot about reputation and what people might think, he had given his blessing. Edward was doing the decent thing, after all. How silly, Elsa had thought. It was hardly as though Edward was marrying her under duress! She'd never seen him look so happy.

Alf Ellerby shook the reins and off they went, trotting down the road. Elsa glanced at her mother, smiling at Brenda, then at Tess and Maria. What a happy occasion it was, she thought, and her beloved Ollie home too. She had told him about the kiss from Sim and was glad she had and that it was now a secret no more. Ollie had looked sad, but she had promised him it had meant nothing, that she loved him above all and always would, and he had seemed cheered by that.

'I worried about you,' he said. 'That last leave. You weren't my Elsa.'

But she was now, she thought. Well, perhaps not the same. A little older and maybe a little wiser too. She supposed she had grown up but she also knew now, with a deep certainty that she felt to her very core, that she never wanted anyone other than Ollie. Three weeks' leave. Three precious weeks! She was determined to make the most of them.

Edward was waiting at the front of the church, Wilf beside him.

'Stop fidgeting, Edward,' he said.

'I just want her to be here,' said Edward. He looked around at the flowers that bedecked the church and at the sea of faces. The whole family was there and half the village besides. He spotted Tom Timbrell, next to Hannah. He grinned and Tom winked back. *They'll be next*, he thought. He looked at his grandparents, relieved they'd come around at last. He'd not been sorry to miss that furore. And he glanced at Uncle Denholm, Lucie and Coco. How hard it must be for them, he thought. Then he turned to his parents and thought how lucky he was – how lucky he and Brenda were, that they had rescued her, helped her and been so incredibly wonderful.

'Got the ring?' he said, turning to Wilf.

'Yes,' said Wilf, patting his tunic pocket.

'My little brother, DFC winner, ace of the skies.' He looked down at the purple and white ribbon on Wilf's tunic.

'While you've been slacking in Palestine, playing cricket and drinking sundowners, some of us have been here at home defending the nation.'

Edward grinned. 'I'm so very glad you could make it, Wilf, and do me the honour of being my best man.'

Suddenly, a hush fell on the church. Then the organ began to play, and at the far end, the church door opened and there was Brenda. Edward wondered what he had done to deserve such good fortune. He wanted to weep with happiness.

'You look utterly beautiful,' he said, as she stood alongside him.

'Why, thank you, Mr Pooter,' she said.

Edward felt his eyes glisten, but he couldn't stop smiling. *At last*, he thought.

Stork felt Debbo take his hand as Edward and Brenda said their vows. He thought back to the last days of peace at the end of August 1939, about how worried he'd been and how threatened he had felt his world had become. They'd been at war for over a year now.

427

London was still being pounded, other British cities too, yet the country was not on its knees. Far from it.

Talk of an invasion seemed to have vanished on the breeze and all his family were alive, were safe and here together, in Alvesdon. He was even talking to his father again. 'It's different, now he's making an honest woman of her,' Alwyn had told him. There would be something else, another fuse blown and outrage felt, but not today. Stork smiled to himself.

And while he could not possibly know what lay around the corner, he was determined that for this one precious day at least, he would put aside his worries and relish it for the joyous occasion it most certainly was. He could, and would, allow himself that.

Acknowledgements

I would like to thank the following for their help, advice and invaluable contributions to the writing of this novel: Marcus Bailey, Nick Barton, Adam Batty, Stuart Bertie, Aedan Butler, Peter Caddick-Adams, Allen Chalk, Lucy Cowieflat, Trevor Dolby, Russell Emm, Philip Gready, Steven Hall, Alex Langlands, Alec Mackenzie, John Martin, Peta Nightingale, Richard Pocock, Steve Prince, Will Sherman, Richard Sparks, Ian Thackray, Tom Timbrell, John Tregoning, Patrick Walsh, Cora MacGregor and everyone at PEW Literary, Emily Hayward-Whitlock at the Artists Partnership, and Bill Scott-Kerr, Nicole Whitmer, Katrina Whone, Tom Hill, Phil Lord, Hazel Orme, and all the team at Bantam Press. Thanks too for the encouragement I have had for this book from my family Rachel, Ned, Daisy, my parents, Jan and Martin Holland, my brother Tom and his family, Sadie, Eliza and my eldest niece, Katy, to whom this book is dedicated. I would also like to doff my cap to Walter and Doris Gregory, my maternal grandparents, who I never knew, but who were known in the family as Stork and Maimes.

James Holland is an internationally acclaimed and award-winning historian, writer and broadcaster. The author of a number of best-selling histories, including, most recently, *The Savage Storm*, *Brothers in Arms* and *Normandy '44*, he has also written nine works of fiction and a dozen Ladybird Experts.

He is the co-founder of the annual Chalke Valley History Festival, which is now in its twelfth year, and he has presented – and written – many television programmes and series for the BBC, Channel 4, National Geographic and the History and Discovery channels.

With Al Murray, he has a successful Second World War podcast, *We Have Ways of Making You Talk*, which also has its own festival, and is a research fellow at St Andrew's University and a Fellow of the Royal Historical Society. He can be found on X as @James1940 and on Instagram as @jamesholland1940.